NOT
MINE
TO
KEEP

ALSO BY BRITTNEY SAHIN

Stand-Alones

Until You Can't

The Story of Us

Falcon Falls Security

The Hunted One

The Broken One

The Guarded One

The Taken One

The Lost Letters: A Novella

The Wanted One

The Fallen One

The Wrecked One

Dublin Nights Series

On the Edge

On the Line

The Real Deal

NOT MINE TO KEEP

BRITTNEY SAHIN

 Montlake

Published by Montlake, Seattle

www.apub.com

Amazon, the Amazon logo, and Montlake are trademarks of Amazon.com, Inc., or its affiliates.

ISBN-13: 9781662518645 (paperback)
ISBN-13: 9781662518652 (digital)

Cover design by Caroline Teagle Johnson
Cover photography © Daniele Fantoni

Printed in the United States of America

NOT
MINE
TO
KEEP

CHAPTER ONE

Alessandro

Nashville, Tennessee

"You know, you might be the only person in all of Tennessee that's ever had to look up this song." A sexy southern voice flew over my shoulder from where I stood by the cash bar at a fundraising event.

"You caught me." I smirked and swiped the music-identifier app closed to pocket my phone. Curious to see if this woman's face matched her sultry tone, I turned her way.

"Whiskey on the rocks, please," she ordered. "Make that *Tennessee* whiskey," she emphasized, busting my balls for not knowing this apparently famous song.

Eye contact now made, and well, damn. A quick, flirty wink from her did something unexpected to me. Something that never happened unless I was on a stair-climber or hunting a bad guy: my pulse kicked up.

I lost sight of those light-green eyes when the bartender slid over her drink. "It's on the house, Calliope."

The fucking flirt. Not that I wouldn't have done the same if I were a twentysomething bartender, but also, why'd he know her name?

She leaned my way to snatch a napkin from the stack near where my left hand sat on the bar, and I couldn't help but inhale her sexy scent.

"Pardon." Her pinkie brushed against mine, and she pulled away. A vision of those sparkly silver manicured nails biting into my back pounded into my head.

Yeah, I needed this woman. In my arms. Tonight. Well, once I dealt with the reason I'd been summoned there in the first place.

"And for you?" I assumed the bartender was talking to me, not that I'd yet ripped my focus from the woman.

"Clase Azul Ultra. Chilled," I ordered.

"But that's—"

"I know." I cut him off before he warned me of the high price. "It's fine."

"Good taste in tequila. But a work in progress in your music preferences," this beautiful woman surprised me by saying, one side of her lips hitching a touch as she swished the liquid around in her glass, our eyes locking once again.

I reached into my back pocket for my wallet, snatched four hundreds to cover the drink and a tip, then slid the bills onto the counter. "Work in progress, hmm?" I let the words pour out as slowly as the bartender was filling a glass with two ounces of tequila.

Her face was so breathtakingly beautiful that when she lifted her shoulder, it was the first time I allowed my eyes to travel south of her chin. It was normally a woman's body I paid attention to first.

Sex. No intimacy. No fucking strings. That was all I made time for in my life. I was bored. Bored to death, lately, when it came to dating.

But bored was the last thing in the world I was, standing before this woman wrapped in a dress straight from a fairy tale my late sister would've loved. It was a match in color to her shimmery nails and had a deep V that gave me the perfect hint of cleavage without the whole show.

At my height of six-one, even with her in heels, she was still a few inches shorter than me.

"Do you plan to answer what felt like a slight insult?" I finally broke the silence that was marinating between us like one of my chef brother's meals at his restaurant in Charlotte.

"When your eyes make it to my face, I'll give you my words."

Oh, this woman was smooth.

Music started playing from somewhere in the room. *I think.* And people were talking all around us. *Well, I'm pretty sure they are.* But the only sound, the only *voice*, I cared to focus on was Calliope's. Because Little Miss Tennessee Whiskey had my undivided attention right now.

I met her gaze while accepting the drink from the bartender, contemplating doing the classic charm shit I did back home in New York. Not that I ever really had to do much in the way of trying to win women over. They knew I was a Costa and dubbed one of New York City's top five wealthiest and most eligible bachelors. Of course, I had plans to be a bachelor until I met my expiration date.

"My apologies," I began. "It's not every day a woman tongue-ties me."

A soft laugh from her dusted all over me, giving me chills, forcing me to check my glass to ensure I hadn't been drugged given my odd reaction to her, but then I remembered I'd yet to take a drink.

"So you find me funny." Swirling the glass so the spirit coated it, I took a sniff from the bottom lip, then inhaled it again before taking a sip. The tequila sat on my tongue, then I swallowed hard.

"Only as humorous as not recognizing an iconic song by Chris Stapleton." Another wink from her, God help me. When had a wink from a woman ever made me feel, well, anything? "At least you had enough good sense to want to learn it."

Mmm. I had enough good sense to know this wasn't a woman I'd be walking away from tonight.

"Is it that obvious I'm not from around here?" I stepped away from the counter at the realization the bartender was too keenly tuned in to our conversation.

She followed me over to one of the high-top tables a decent distance away from the bartender's continued scrutiny. "You're not quite Mr. City Slicker. And I'm betting you go to these types of events all the time." That teasing, sexy tone, and the way her tongue skirted the line of her lips, had me forgetting I was a city boy. "But yes, you stand out." She indulged me with a smile. "In a sea of other rich people, I can still tell you're not from around here." She flipped her long, wavy blonde hair to her back as she gave me a slight nod.

I exhaled and counted back from three while reminding myself that although my little sister, Izzy, liked to joke my superpower was making women fall in love with me with just one look, I was never the one to become mesmerized.

And yet here I was, captivated by Little Miss Tennessee Whiskey. A.k.a. Calliope. A.k.a. *mine*.

"Maybe it's your eyes. Something about them makes me—"

"Never seen gray eyes, Calliope?" My turn to tease, to drop my tone a bit lower. Lay on my charm. Channel my superpower. Because for one night, yeah, I wanted this woman to love me. Well, in the bedroom.

"Callie," she rasped instead, her gaze flitting to the bartender as if putting two and two together on how I knew her name. "That's what everyone calls me."

"Except the bartender," I blurted.

Her green eyes, rimmed in dark liner, narrowed on me. "We're friends," she whispered without breaking eye contact. The woman could beat me in a staring contest, which was saying a lot. I'd won quite a few bucks in middle school from staring down assholes who challenged me.

"He wants to be more than friends," I said as casually as possible. "He used your given name like a term of endearment." A quick pause before I couldn't help but be blunt. "And men aren't friends with women like you without hoping for more one day."

A curious eyebrow lifted. "I think there was a compliment buried in there. But I guess you could say we're more like . . . work friends."

Her decision to clarify and ease any potential concerns I had about Wonder Boy over there as he did a trick with the shaker had me taking a step closer, and I discreetly inhaled her perfume.

"We play together," she murmured.

"Play?" The word rolled from my mouth almost in slow motion, and I eased back to afford us both more breathing room.

Red inched up her tan throat and moved into her cheeks, and she followed the hot path with her free hand. I didn't take her for a blusher, given how she'd initiated the conversation with me tonight. But there it was. "Sorry, I mean music. We jam together."

This had my attention. Not that she'd ever lost it. "You're a musician?"

"No," she said with a chuckle. "A teacher, actually."

"Music teacher, then?"

She closed her eyes and tipped her face as if feeling the sunlight wash over her instead of the chandelier lights overhead. "No, high school history. I wouldn't begin to know how to teach music. It's just . . . part of me, if that makes sense." She opened her eyes and added, "Music is my hobby. Side-gig thing."

The woman had such an innocent, ethereal look about her. Gorgeous eyes. A nose with the slightest lift that wasn't overpowering, and wrinkled in a cute way when she smiled or laughed. Soft cheekbones. Luscious lips that'd be even more sinful once swollen from kissing.

She was elegance and grace all packaged inside that sparkly dress, and I was more than likely the antithesis to her.

I also had no clue to her age. *Twenty-three? Twenty-eight?* I couldn't tell. But I had a hard limit of twenty-five as the youngest I'd sleep with, so I hoped she was closer to the latter. Thirty-five or older with no desire for kids or a husband was preferable when it came to the women I took to bed.

I probably should have walked away. But I didn't. In fact, I stayed glued in place when she tossed out, "Not that you'd know about side gigs."

Those light-colored eyes flew over my simple black suit as I continued to study her, and she went ahead and studied me right back.

No tie tonight. Not my style. Just a plain black shirt beneath the jacket. Custom-made in Italy. Brioni, one of my preferred designers.

"What you're wearing probably costs more than I make in a month. And my guess, your car back home is worth more than I'll ever save up in this lifetime and the next," she rambled, as if trying to explain why I wouldn't know a thing or two about side gigs.

When her eyes zeroed in on my crotch, my dick decided to twitch in greeting; those long lashes of hers flitted a few times before she lifted her almond-shaped eyes to mine.

But also, it sure felt like she was suggesting my fancy car and clothes (her judgments of me . . . all accurate) were an overcompensation for something (*not* accurate, because my dick was not in the lacking department).

I'd happily reassure her she was wrong if I opted to be an asshole and invited her to my hotel room later.

"I actually have a side gig." I sipped more of the tequila. "You could call it volunteer work, I suppose." *Since I work cases for free.* "And I sure as hell hope you make more in a month than my suit costs, because you're being grossly underpaid if that's not the case."

"How much is the suit?" She finished her drink and set it on the table already cluttered with abandoned champagne flutes.

I rid myself of my glass as well, deciding I wanted my hands available in case I needed to . . . what? Ask her to dance? Take her hand and lead her to the balcony I'd noticed earlier and tell her how I was a playboy prick (not my words, but you know, they'd been thrown my way a time or *fifty*) when it came to women?

"I don't know." I faked a light cough, suddenly feeling weird about being rich when it was normally one reason women flocked to me. "Maybe ten."

"Thousand?" She gave me an honest-to-God hearty laugh, then topped it off with a hand to her abdomen. "Yeah, that's three times what I clear in a month."

"Well, that's not funny at all. That's fucking awful."

"You're right, that's not funny. But the fact you thought I made over a hundred K a year is." She licked her lips.

Why? Why'd you do that? Fucking A. Those lips would look spectacular wrapped around my cock.

"Anyway, I'm performing a song with the cover band tonight. For free, but hey," she said while slapping a hand over my shoulder, "I'm accepting tips."

We stared at each other for a moment before she turned to the stage full of instruments. And fuck if I didn't want her hand back on me, but she rested her palm over her breastbone instead, and I couldn't help but wonder what she'd be playing.

"Well, I should probably go. I needed some liquid courage to play in front of a crowd like this."

I wasn't prepared for her to leave, even if I could feel my phone blowing up in my pocket. I knew it wasn't my burner, which meant it was one of my brothers or my sister calling, not the man who'd beckoned me to the event.

"I just realized . . . I didn't get your name."

"That's because I didn't give it." I frowned, not a fan of my own response. It felt like a dick thing I'd say back in New York. Correction: it *was* a dick thing I'd said in New York. I muttered a pathetic apology. "I'm sorry—it's Alessandro."

She gave me an uncertain look, deciding whether she wanted to place my name in her memory bank or forget the entire conversation, given my first response to her moments before. "Why are you here?"

The curveball of a question threw me off, and I pocketed my hands, sending the next call to voicemail with a quick touch of a button. "I was dragged here by an old acquaintance."

"Not a fan of charities where money is raised for our veterans?" Two quick, appalled steps back from me had me realizing my fatal error in speech yet again. Her gaze flicked to the sign that had a marine's name on it: Michael Maddox. It was his and his wife's event. They held fundraiser-type things all over the East Coast a few times a year. His way of paying it forward—a little different from mine.

"Not like that. In fact, I'm a veteran myself." That was probably a curveball right back at her. "It was a long time ago. Army." I felt the need to offer her a reason not to walk away from me. I never used my time in the military to try and bed a woman—it wouldn't work in the circles I ran in—but something told me she'd have more respect for that than the size of my bank account.

"Well, thank you for your service. Even though you don't want to be here, please consider writing a big check since you can clearly afford it. It's for a good cause, after all." She gave me a light, dismissive nod.

Shit. I'd failed to win her back over.

But then narrowed eyes greeted me as her arms folded over her chest, accentuating her breasts, and I did my best not to focus on the swell of her flesh. "Where are you from? Your accent . . . It's faint, but there."

Why'd it now feel like I was on the stand in a murder trial, and I was Suspect Number One in her eyes? I lifted my hands from my pockets as someone from the stage called out her name, but she didn't look his way as she waited for my answer.

"Sicily. Moved here when I was eight," I answered, my tone dropping lower as I finished my words, catching a slight wince of disapproval from her.

"You're Sicilian?" Her voice rose in surprise.

"I consider myself American after being here thirty-one years and serving in the military, but yes, technically speaking." Why was she so put off by that? The color that'd been in her cheeks was gone.

Her gaze flicked away from me, and I followed her eyes to a man in a dark suit fifty feet away who looked like a security guard trying to blend in.

When she opted to look at me again, that disapproval had morphed into fear. "He sent you, didn't he? You're another one of his . . . people, aren't you?"

"*Who* sent me?" What in the hell was she talking about?

"My father," was all she managed before a guitar player from the stage yelled at her, now on approach. He snatched her arm, and I sneered at his grasp, feeling the ridiculous urge to break every one of his fingers.

"Sorry," she said to him. "I'm coming."

I watched her walk away, and she shot me a quick backward glance before ascending the steps to the stage.

A guitar was handed to her, and she looped the strap over her shoulder before standing at a microphone next to the band's lead performer.

I looked around in search of the mystery man in the suit who'd been watching her before. He now had his back to one of the pillars with a plate of food in hand, casually observing the stage.

Who's your father? And why in hell would you think he sent me here?

I reached for my burner while waiting for the band to start, unsure what to think. Nothing from the man who'd summoned me yet. I swapped that phone for my personal one. I'd gone all day without being bothered by my family because it'd been off, but I'd forgotten I had powered it back on to identify the name of that song at the bar.

I opened the group text with my brothers and sister: Constantine, Enzo, and Izzy.

Izzy: Why are you in Nashville? And why aren't you answering our calls?

I groaned, casting a quick look at the stage, and when the band started to play, I realized if I wanted to preserve my hearing, I'd best back up from the nearby speakers.

Me: Did you track me?

Izzy: Wouldn't need to if you told us where you were or answered a call.

Me: I have a thing.

Enzo: In Nashville? What kind of thing? 💀

I couldn't answer that because they'd lose their minds if they found out who'd forced me to attend this event.

Me: I'm at a fundraiser for veterans. Owed someone here a favor. Plan to make a large donation.

I peered at the one wall of displayed items that were open for bids. I wasn't sure what I'd be buying, but I was a man of my word, so yeah, I'd be making a big-ass donation. At least it wasn't the kind of bidding that had landed Maddox married back in the day—winning a date or something like that. Or so the story went.

Me: I have to go. Stop tracking me.

Constantine: Stop ghosting us then.

Me: Clearly the intern you must be dating that's half your age is rubbing off on you . . . I mean . . . ghosting? Really? That or you've been watching a little too much of the clock app.

Constantine: I don't screw around with our interns, and you know that. And I don't do social media, so I have no clue what you're talking about. But given how often you wind up with your photo online, if I were you . . .

He left me to fill in the dots. Typical Constantine.

Me: Maybe you need to be screwing someone instead of worrying about where I'm at. 😏

I liked to ruffle my older brother's feathers. I couldn't help it. Even if I was nearly in the same age bracket of over-the-hill forty as him.

Me: I need to go. It's impolite to be texting while at a charity event.

Enzo: ☹ Fine. But I'll have the little jet on standby (since you took the bigger one) in case you need to be bailed out for doing God knows what while down there.

Izzy: Maybe he's there for a girl. 😳

Enzo: Alessandro wouldn't even travel to another borough in NY for a girl. You think he'd fly to TN for one?

And my younger brother loved to give me as much grief as I gave Constantine. It was the circle of life, I supposed.

Me: Goodbyeeee.

I turned off my phone so they couldn't bug me anymore and focused on the band. Well, on Callie softly singing behind the lead singer; her fingers moving perfectly over the strings of her guitar. A true pro, from the looks of it.

When our eyes met, she boldly stared back at me, and the playful, teasing looks she'd given me when I'd only been a stranger in a suit were gone. Unable to handle the sight, my attention settled on her hand as she flicked the strings. *No . . . fingered? Stroked?*

I needed my late sister, Bianca, who'd been a writer and basically a human thesaurus; she'd tell me the word I was trying to think of, as well as make fun of me for sounding like a sex-starved teenager hoping to get laid for the first time. *Fingering* the strings should not have popped into my mind while watching her strum the guitar. Fuck, even *strum* still sounded sexual to me right now. What was this woman doing to me?

Before I could contemplate writing a quick check, then ditching the plans to meet up with the man who'd sent me the invite—along with his demand to show up, or else—my burner rang. *About fucking time.*

I forced myself to walk away from Callie and took Gabriel's call outside on the balcony. "Where are you?" I nearly barked out.

"Not there."

"That's obvious. Why am *I* here, though?" *But really, why?* I massaged my temple with my free hand as I went over to the railing, taking in the view of the river.

"I need to hire your secret little security firm that you and your family run on the side."

At his words, my arm fell and I bowed my head. "You're out of your mind." And apparently, our firm's existence was no longer a secret to criminals. I wasn't sure whether that was good or bad.

"It's a long-term gig. Three months. Maybe six," he went on. His Italian accent would have stood out way more than mine had he been the one talking to Callie.

"Are you high? What's wrong with you?" Realizing the song was coming to an end, I faced the main room. "There's no way in hell my family would—"

"You're indebted to me, Alessandro. You owe me a favor." He repeated his words in Italian, as if trying to nail in his point.

A debt was a debt. Even when it came to a criminal. And this criminal was my former childhood best friend, so the lines were murky as fuck. The man had saved not only my life years ago but also Constantine's while he'd been on a mission for the US government (a story for another day). Two lives saved in my world really meant two favors, so I was lucky he'd only demanded one from me "when the time comes." And now was that time.

Ensuring no one was within earshot, I hissed, "No kidnapping. No killing *good* people. And anything else that'd send my soul to hell will be a hard *no* as well."

He laughed. "My friend, your soul is already heading there. But maybe this is your chance to redeem yourself."

"We haven't been friends in decades."

"Don't you wonder what would've happened had you stayed here instead of moving to America?"

Gabriel was one of those guys you wanted to hate, but he made it damn difficult, because he'd been the one to take the punches for me when I was bullied and Constantine wasn't around to do it. He was also the guy who'd give you the shirt off his own back so you didn't freeze.

But he was a bad guy now. He'd chosen the dark side. He'd made the choice, and I had to drill that into my damn head.

"What do you want?" I was done with the back-and-forth.

"I told you, I want to hire you. I need your help taking down Armani DiMaggio."

My stomach dropped, and a chill flew down my back despite the warm May air. "The head of the most powerful criminal organization in Italy?" I swallowed the knot in my throat and added, "And . . . your boss."

"*Sì,*" was all he gave me.

I closed my eyes and sighed. "And how do you propose I do that?"

"By marrying his daughter."

"Come again?" My eyes snapped open, and that chill turned into an ice storm in my veins.

"I've been watching you on the cameras, and I believe you've already made her acquaintance."

The band was now playing a new song, but she was no longer there. "Calliope," I said under my breath, putting it together.

"No man can resist a siren like her, and that woman drew you straight to her. And now, if you want to save her, you'll need to make her your wife."

CHAPTER TWO

Calliope

"Imani, do you mind if I look at the guest list? I met a potentially big donor, and he—"

"You forgot his name, and you don't want to ask for it?" Imani smiled and set aside whatever papers she'd been holding inside the staff room.

"Exactly. I think if I peek at the names, it'll come back to me." I shifted the skirt of my dress to the side, and her gaze swept over the gown as she handed me a clipboard with the guest names on it.

"I still can't get over that dress." She twirled her finger like the fairy godmother in *Cinderella* doing her thing, turning me into . . . "A fairy-tale princess," she finished my line of thought, then pointed to the mirror on the wall by the lockers as if I had no clue I'd made such a transformation from the typical khakis I wore at school to a ball gown. "It's an absolute showstopper."

I held the clipboard at my side and followed her request by facing the full-length mirror to take in the sight of the silver dress. The sparkle-dusted floral embroidered lace top had a plunging neckline and flared ball skirt with a sexy front slit. "Remember that designer I found on Instagram last month, Ella McAdams?"

"Oh, that's right. The one down near Birmingham?"

I nodded. "It's her design. So if you ever need anything, I highly recommend her."

"I'll double-check to see if I remembered to follow her on Insta." Imani didn't waste time and went for her phone from her locker, and I took the chance to peruse the guest list. "Was that big donor the same hot guy I saw you talking to at the bar—you know, while Braden was shooting daggers at him?"

A shiver rolled over my skin, because yeah, guilty as charged. But wait, Braden was giving him the evil eye? *Really?* "Braden and I are just friends." I deflected from conversation about Alessandro. I had to know whether he was another "suitor" my father was trying to plant in my life in the hope that I'd fall in love and get married to someone of his choosing. *The psychopath.* I nearly vomited at the fact it was now the second time tonight I'd referred to him as my *father.* Not the norm for me.

"There's no such thing as 'just friends' when you look like you . . . and Braden looks like he does."

Alessandro kind of said the same thing.

"You know . . . I heard rumors that Braden's you-know-what is pierced."

I nearly dropped the clipboard as she painted that image, though it wasn't because of Braden's rumored piercing—I'd spotted a last-minute name scribbled at the end of the list with a note next to it.

Alessandro Costa—no plus one.

"Jackpot. Found him."

"And I found Ella on Insta, and I'm now following her. Damn, the woman has style." Imani set her phone down when I offered her the clipboard back. "So are you going out there to talk to this handsome donor? Make Braden's head explode with jealousy?"

I went to my locker in search of my phone so I could google Alessandro. "First of all, Braden doesn't see me like that, and I don't want him to. And secondly . . ." No clue where I was going with that. Snatching my phone, I faced the small room, thankful we were still alone. "Anywayyyy." That was my master deflection strategy: drag out a word and hope she changed the subject. Just genius.

A subtle smirk flew across her lips before she nodded, letting me know she'd "let it go" and moved on. "Soooo," she teasingly mimicked my ridiculousness. "You must be ecstatic to be on summer break." She put her phone back in her purse, then closed her locker three doors down from mine.

"Technically, I have one more day. I need to proctor an exam on Monday for the kids who missed the test last week. But yeah, I could use a break."

She rested her back against her locker and peered my way, her big brown eyes still holding a touch of curiosity about Braden, or maybe Mr. Big Donor. And something told me he was big everywhere, based on those hands of his. I'd done my best not to stare at them while he'd sipped his $300 glass of tequila. Nice tipper, at least.

Still holding my phone like some sort of security blanket, anxious to look up Alessandro, I added, "I need to do my best to land as many gigs this summer as I can. And Broadway . . . Can you imagine if I could play there?" Broadway here in Nashville was as big of a deal as Broadway in New York. Heck, maybe bigger for us country singers looking for our big break.

"You'll get there. Don't worry." She tipped her head, signaling toward the door. "I should get back out there. I need to make sure these donors remember to empty their pockets before they drink too much and either bid more than they can afford or forget to bid at all."

I laughed. "I'll be right behind you."

"Sounds good." She pushed away from the locker, and the train of her black satin dress swished behind her as she made her exit.

Once I was alone, my fingers flew over my phone as I researched Alessandro. He was easy to find, given his family pretty much ran an empire and Alessandro had been dubbed one of New York's sexiest and wealthiest bachelors for the last five years in a row by multiple maga-zines and newspapers.

Five years and *still* eligible? *Talk about a red flag.* No mention of any girlfriends, but there were plenty of photos of him online with different gorgeous women. *Not* that I was interested in his love life; I just needed to know whether my father had sent him. Or had I simply made a fool of myself and accused him of such?

"Calliope, what are you doing back here?"

I looked up to see Braden in the doorway, and I fumbled my phone. It fell to the tiled floor, and cursing, I tried to bend to snatch it. But the dress fit a bit too well, and it made bending over without giving Braden an eyeful of my breasts a challenge.

"I've got it." He hurried through the room, dodging the obstacles of bins and random carts to get to me. He picked it up, and my eyes flew to his crotch. I slapped a hand over them at the realization I'd just wondered whether he was, in fact, pierced. I truly had no desire to find out, but the intrusive thought ran through my head on its own.

"Cracked," he said, handing it to me. "Sorry."

"Not your fault." I checked the corner edge of the phone, peeling the screen protector back a touch, confirming the good news. "Just damaged the screen protector. Phone is okay."

"Still, I startled you, and I feel bad. Let me make it up to you." He reached for my arm, and I forced my eyes back to his.

I had to admit, Braden was attractive, kind, and sweet. He'd make a great boyfriend for someone. He was only a few years older than me, but he said he felt a decade older. He'd seen a lot. Like war.

But I just . . . well, I didn't feel that way for him. I hoped both Alessandro and Imani were wrong about how Braden felt about me.

"You owe me nothing. Truly." I turned from his touch and locked my phone up. "Come on; we should get back out there."

Setting his hand on the small of my back, he guided me to the ballroom, where I spotted one of the Sperm Donor's three hired security guards. They rarely let me out of their sight. Thankfully, they never tried to follow me into the school building, because how would I ever explain to my administration that, to those three shadows, I was an Italian mafia "princess"?

The guards rarely referred to me by my name, which was annoying. Instead, they called me *La Principessa*. As Armani DiMaggio's daughter, I had the misfortune to be the only living heir to the throne of the DiMaggio dynasty. Once Armani croaked, I would be the last one alive connected to Italy's oldest mafia family. How lucky for me . . .

I rolled my eyes at Dickhead Number One (my names for the guards), then stumbled when I spied someone else's eyes on me. But Braden caught my arm, preventing me from tripping over the skirt of the gown.

"Thanks," I whispered, grateful for the save as Alessandro approached.

He cut straight through the crowd, and his presence commanded attention. Not just from me, but from everyone. Men peered his way as if recognizing an indomitable force to be reckoned with, and women gaped at him for probably the same reason, though they'd rather be wrecked via orgasm in the bedroom.

Not that I was thinking that about him and orgasms. *No.* I blinked. *God, no.*

I peeked at Braden, discovering his jaw was tight beneath his blond beard, his green eyes fixed on the man heading our way. And shit, was Imani right? Did Braden have a thing for me?

Feeling Alessandro closing in on us and realizing I was his target, doubts cut through me that he'd been sent by the Sperm Donor.

Braden's hand slipped to my waist in a slightly possessive grip as Alessandro, in his $10,000 suit that was probably as Italian as he was, stopped before us. His eyes briefly flicked to Braden's hand before he peered at me.

He pushed his double-breasted jacket back as he pocketed his hands. My eyes flew up the expensive fabric to the tan column of his throat, and boom—to those silvery-gray eyes.

"You performed beautifully. Nothing to worry about." Alessandro's words came out smooth and as sleek as that Lamborghini I'd seen him standing in front of in a picture online only minutes ago.

"She was never worried," Braden snapped, and although I adored him, I didn't love having someone speak for me. "Is there something we can do for you?"

"Hungry?" I wasn't sure how Alessandro packed so much intensity into such a simple word, but my stomach answered for me with a rumble, thankfully one that couldn't be heard over the band performing another song.

All I could do was nod. Maybe I did need someone to speak for me, after all.

Alessandro lifted one hand from his pocket and gestured toward the buffet area as his invitation to join him, seemingly forgetting Braden's presence.

"I'll be at the bar if you need me." Braden finally unhanded me, and I gave him a little okay nod. Then he left me alone with the man I'd embarrassingly googled a few minutes ago.

I told myself I was only escorting Alessandro over to the buffet because I'd been rude earlier and accused him of being sent by The Asshole. Yeah, that was a better name than Sperm Donor.

"I'm sorry about earlier." I finally spoke up as we started for the food stations. "My, um . . ." *Shit, I can't call him* asshole *right now, can I?* "My father"—*cue internal gagging*—"likes to set me up."

My words appeared to have derailed our current path to get to the food. He veered off to the side of Station One, where the chef's famous Nashville chicken sliders called my name.

Unfortunately, after stress-eating last week during my students' exams, I'd wound up battling the back zipper last night when trying the dress on again. So I hadn't eaten today in order to fit into it, and now I was famished.

"Your father wants an arranged marriage." Why'd that feel like a statement from him punctuating the air and not a question of shock?

I cleared my throat, grateful yet again for the soundproofing of my bodily noises by the band jamming to a Luke Combs song. "Something like that." And I had no plans to elaborate. Where would I even start?

The movie description of my life would be something along the lines of, *A mafia princess who wants nothing to do with the evil crown longs for the freedom she once had before learning the truth of her origins.*

Alessandro narrowed his bullet-colored eyes, quietly studying me like I was an enigma. Or the only unsolvable problem he'd ever encountered.

"So as I said, I'm sorry about the confusion." I crossed my arms, burying my fingertips into the soft flesh of my biceps.

"No apology needed." His words were clipped, like he was agitated. But I had no clue why, because it wasn't like I'd sought him out. If I'd pissed him off earlier, why come back for seconds?

"Food?" I reminded him, directing him toward the smells wafting our way.

He smiled, but it felt a bit forced, compared with the way he'd dazzled me back by the bar. Instead of heading to the food stations, he tore a hand through his hair, simply observing me.

The man had Henry Cavill's good looks and a thick head of hair, a slight wave to it. Not quite as dark as the actor's, but more of a sun-kissed brown, and I had to resist the impulse to reach for the lock of hair that caressed his forehead.

Also, without a beard, it was easy to see the chiseled definition of his chin and jawline. The man rocked clean-shaven as well as I'd rock a pair of Jimmy Choos if I could ever afford them. I mean, I did have great legs, or so I'd been told.

"You okay?" I finally unfolded my arms, unsure why he was still staring at me, unmoving.

He blinked, then looked over my shoulder toward the food, so I took that as my cue to walk again.

"What do you recommend we eat?" he asked, and his dark tone slid right under my dress.

"Aw, so you do remember how to speak. I was worried you were tongue-tied." I spun back around, but he was so close I bumped into him and my hands collided with his chest.

And oh, what a chest. I gulped, staring at my manicured nails where they rested over his suit jacket. *You really are the Man of Steel's Italian doppelganger, huh?* Ever so slowly, I dragged my eyes up to his face, and a pained expression greeted me.

"Sorry." I attempted a smile, certain it wasn't one of my best ones. Nerves and all. Not that I really got nervous. Hell, I dealt with teenagers daily who gave The Asshole and his men a run for their money from time to time. Handling some guy who had a *B* for the start of his net worth and devastating good looks shouldn't have had my heart skipping any beats whatsoever. "You asked for food recommendations, right?" *You did, didn't you?*

He nodded, eyes still pinned to mine, and I had to swallow again and physically force myself to back up and drop my hands from his chest.

Facing the line of food, I began walking by the stations, reading the little placards identifying the options as if he couldn't do it himself. "I'd suggest the smoked aged pork belly medallions with sweet barbecue glaze. But if you're into something a little healthier, and I think you are"—*judging by your superfit-looking body*—"the seared ahi tuna." I whipped around, and there he was, dangerously close.

"And what will you eat?" Somehow those five words and the sexy, deep tone of his voice curled in the air like ribbons and tied me all up.

"I can't eat, or this dress will have to come off." I closed my eyes, replaying my words and how they sounded. "This dress is too tight for me to dare eat in, I mean."

He leaned in to dip his mouth to my ear but didn't touch me, which both bummed me out and made me feel respected, all at the same time. "I think I'll skip eating then, too."

"You sure?" I whispered as he eased back, our faces so close it wouldn't take much for us to kiss.

"I'm absolutely certain." He stood tall, offering me space to breathe and to not sink into the feeling of desire that I hadn't realized I was so desperate to swim in until tonight. I hadn't exactly dated recently, ever since The Asshole had decided to have me watched while also sending potential suitors my way.

"Well then, maybe we should look at the items we can bid on?" I suggested, threading my fingers together, wishing I had a bracelet on to fiddle with instead.

"Sure." Another polite hand opened. Another offer to lead the way. So I did.

We quietly headed over to the items up for auction, and I zeroed in on what I wanted to win but knew I didn't have a shot in Hades of doing. "She's a beauty." I ran one of my freshly manicured nails over the glass case, admiring the multicolored, special-edition Martin 5-18. "This guitar was owned and signed by the legend herself." I sighed, reached for the pen, and scribbled down my information as well as the most I could afford to bid. I tucked the paper into the wooden box displayed by the glass case. "Do you know Doll—"

"Even I know her." A touch of humor caressed his tone, and it was even sexier than the dark rasp from earlier.

Mmm. Maybe you were sent by angels, not the devil incarnate? When I swiveled back his way, I remembered my research about him and the fact he'd always had a different woman on his arm in every photo I'd seen online. *Not an angel. An Italian Casanova.* Maybe one hot night was just what I needed, though? I nearly rolled my eyes at the ridiculous idea of having meaningless sex. It wasn't my thing. Never would be. I wanted intimacy in bed and breakfast the next day, not to wake up alone. *Now would be the time to abort, before he sucks me in with those eyes again and I find myself okay with living in the land of Delulu.*

"Maybe I should go mingle now? I'm here to get people to donate. I'm a volunteer, not a guest."

"So get *me* to donate. Then you're still doing your job." He motioned toward the painting encased in glass alongside the guitar. "What about this? You think it'd look good in my—"

"Penthouse in Manhattan?"

He casually looked at me over his shoulder, and I remembered Mr. City Slicker had never told me where he was from. That info was all from the crash course a friend gave me in how to "go FBI" on a guy.

"Just assuming." My turn to fake a smile. "You know, they never did identify the couple in that photo. Many people claimed to be them, but it's still a mystery." The watercolor painting was a recreation of the iconic sailor kissing a nurse, shot in 1945 in Times Square. "I do love a good mystery, though," I added when he wrote down an obscene amount along with his full name and phone number.

He folded the bid up and placed it inside the box while turning toward me, and I clapped my hands together.

"Mission success. I must be good at my job since you just bid half of what we're trying to raise in total tonight," I teased, but my heart was colliding with my rib cage at seeing that number written out, and so casually.

"I guess I need to find something else to bid on so you meet your goal, and so I can steal you away to talk for the rest of the night."

Steal me away? "You don't need to—"

"But I do." He frowned for some reason, then went over to the next item, barely taking notice of the sculpture, and wrote down a cool million again. "Now, can we talk?" He faced me with a hard look, his words coming out rough. No charm this time. Heck, no sugar of any kind.

"Two million just to spend the night with me?" That sounded horrible and suuuper *Indecent Proposal*–like.

"I'm not propositioning you," he scoffed, as if offended. But the line on his forehead relaxed as he added, "Well, not exactly."

"Care to elaborate?" I cut straight to it.

His gaze shot over my shoulder. "Not here, but we do need to talk."

I followed his line of sight to one of my shadows, Dickhead Number Two this time, and a bad feeling climbed up my body and settled in the pit of my stomach.

"The Maddox Group appreciates your bids, and I'm sure you'll win both," I rushed out, trying to keep my cool. "But neither my body nor my time is up for auction tonight. So if you'll excuse me." I turned, worried I'd misjudged this man; he was far more dangerous than simply giving me a great orgasm and leaving me alone in bed the next day.

When his hand went to my back, a plea to stop, I froze. It was his first time touching me, and it'd be his last if one of my shadows spotted him doing so. He brought his mouth down over my ear and rasped, "Please, Calliope." The word *please* sounded strained and hard for him to spit out. "We *must* talk."

"*Must* is an awfully strong word." I whirled around to face him, and his hand fell to his side. "Also, fun fact: no means no," I said, doubling down, worried he was about to insist upon having our fireside chat (minus the fire).

"In every language I speak, no does mean no. Even in the ones I don't. I agree," he said firmly, angling his head and shooting me daggers like I was a problem for him, not the other way around. "When it comes to *certain* things, no means no." His eyes dipped to my lips, and he blinked as if it'd been a mistake on his part to allow his attention to wander. Why'd I feel as if he was looking at me like I was the sin he craved, even if he didn't want to, judging by his angry glare? "But in this case, I—"

"No." I cut him off and backed up, realizing my shadow was now en route. "If you don't want to get hurt, I suggest you walk away."

"I want to walk away, I really do." He leaned in so close our mouths almost touched that time. "You have no idea just how much, in fact," he gritted out, then shook his head and straightened. "But I can't." He'd sighed his displeasure into those three words.

I opened my mouth, prepared to challenge him, but then he shocked me by doing the opposite of what he'd said: he left the ballroom without so much as a parting glance.

CHAPTER THREE

Alessandro

"Please tell me you have nothing better to do on a Saturday night than be at work," I said, wasting no time once the call connected with Hudson, both a friend and a colleague at my family's security firm—a.k.a. *my* volunteer work. Quite different from Calliope's.

"You know, I feel like I should be insulted you assume I have no life," Hudson drawled. "Oddly enough, I'm not. Of course I'm at work. What's up? And why the hell are you in Nashville?"

So they told you. "I'm taking a case." *Not that I have a choice.* "It's a 'need to know' situation right now."

"Need to know?" A deep, husky laugh cut over the line. "Are you shitting me? I've known you for twenty years, and we work together. I'm always in the know."

Sitting inside my rental Maserati, I leaned back and placed the call with him on speaker while I pulled up Calliope's address, which I'd far too easily found online.

She lived in Franklin, a small town about thirty minutes south of Nashville—where I was currently waiting for her. And thanks to a friendly chat with the valet, I was able to identify the Jeep Cherokee she drove as well. *Damn. She needs better protection; it was too easy to get her information.*

"Alessandro?" Hudson prompted, since I'd yet to reply.

"First, promise me you won't share what I'm about to tell you with my family. *Especially* Constantine."

Constantine had been Hudson's best friend since high school, when the Texan had moved to the Big Apple, where we lived. They'd also both served in the navy, and I had a feeling because of that, Constantine shared more with him than me. I wasn't jealous, but . . .

Hudson grunted his displeasure at my request, and from the sounds of it, plopped down into his desk chair and was drumming his fingers in a countdown, trying to make up his mind. "Why?" The word barreled out of his mouth like a gunshot.

"Because Constantine will do what he always does, and he'll try and sacrifice himself instead. And I don't need him doing that. This is my problem, and I'll handle it."

My problem, because Gabriel had made it my problem. My brother would offer to take over, and I knew he wouldn't want to marry Calliope and would exhaust every other possibility first before coming to that, just as I was about to try to do. But at the end of the day, my brother would do what was necessary to save a life, even if that meant tying the knot.

Temporarily tying the knot, I reminded myself.

"And what is this problem you speak of? I thought it was a case."

I pulled up the photo of Calliope I'd saved to my phone, one I'd found from the high school she worked at. She looked so sweet and innocent. How was she the daughter of Armani DiMaggio? *Must take after her mother.* It wasn't shocking that her father had had an affair, but it was a little bit of a surprise he'd done so with someone not of Sicilian blood. The man was old school about his bloodline. *Evidence of the fact I'm now in this mess.*

"As much as I enjoy sitting on the phone in silence, are you planning to answer me?" Hudson asked.

"I have no choice but to take this job. Or else . . ." I let my words trail off for dramatic emphasis. I needed him to buy what I was selling.

I also didn't like the idea of Constantine marrying Calliope. Or anyone, for that matter, which was crazy since I barely knew the woman.

"*You knew I'd meet her tonight. You were expecting that,*" I recalled from my earlier phone conversation with Gabriel.

"*She's a stunning woman. Born to stand out. Of course you'd wind up talking to her. You're you, after all.*"

"*You knew if I spoke with her, put a face to the name, it'd be harder for me to turn you down,*" I had hissed back.

"Just tell me what's going on. You have my word, even if I hate keeping secrets from the rest of the team."

"Thank you." I swallowed, taking a moment to prepare myself for the bomb I was about to drop on him. "I need you to find out everything you can on Calliope Dawn Anderson. She's based in Franklin, Tennessee. All I know right now is she's a high school history teacher, a musician on the side, and likes to volunteer for charities." I waited for him to take notes, and to buy myself even more time. "Also"—*Now would be a good time for an awkward throat-clear from me*—"she's the daughter of Armani DiMaggio."

An eerie quiet filled the air as he processed the news. "*The* DiMaggio? The head of the criminal group that has existed so long they predate the word *mafioso*? *That* Armani DiMaggio?"

Yeah, I thought he'd know of him, even if Hudson wasn't Sicilian like me.

"Yeah. Him." I rested my phone on my thigh to grip my temples, massaging a bit roughly, as if that'd do the trick and eradicate the tension throbbing there.

"You realize the DiMaggio organization is now the most powerful criminal group in all of Italy after The League took down The Alliance?"

"The League . . ." I muttered under my breath.

"Have you forgotten about them? The group of wealthy do-gooders your father was once part of in Italy? They make what we do look like we're just kids playing war games in the woods." He hit me with a sarcastic tone he wasn't all that well known for, but he'd managed it tonight.

"Yeah, yeah, yeah." My hands plummeted to my lap, nearly knocking my phone from my leg. "They're a hurdle I'll need to, uh, scale if this plan moves forward."

The League had cut off the head of an evil organization known as The Alliance, effectively wiping it from the map. But in its absence, evil had filled the power vacuum; it had been Calliope's father who took its place.

"Armani's brother and nephew died in a fight against The Alliance, just before it was eliminated by The League," I reminded him. "That's how Armani came to power, but it also left him as the last living member of the original DiMaggio bloodline."

"Humph. Or so they thought," Hudson remarked dryly.

"Right." I wanted to sigh, but this wasn't a sighing matter. My bachelorhood was at stake. My life. This was horrible on so many levels.

"So since when does he have a daughter, and why is she in Tennessee?"

I went back over my conversation with Gabriel, remembering what he'd told me. "All I know is that Calliope's mother, Christie Anderson, was a traveling musician in Europe and became one of Armani's mistresses. The man didn't believe in divorce, but he was fine with fucking around."

"Sounds about right." From his unusual tone, he'd been hanging with my sister too much, taking lessons from her.

"Christie never told him she was pregnant. Disappeared for a bit with plans to end the pregnancy, but her younger sister convinced her to have the baby and promised to take care of her. Calliope was raised by her aunt Tia here in Tennessee."

"How'd Armani find out he had a daughter, then?"

"Christie died last year, and Armani attended the funeral. He'd been seeing her on and off for the last three and a half decades. Both before and after his wife died. He never thought he could have kids, which is why even though he was the eldest, his brother was originally crowned king of their empire."

"So there he is, finding out his mistress had a daughter that's . . ." Hudson paused. "Well, Calliope's going on thirty," he picked up, researching while talking from the sounds of it. "So she would've been almost twenty-nine at the funeral. And well, look at that: you two share a birthday next month. When she turns thirty on June twenty-first—"

"I'll be forty," I cut him off. "Thanks for the reminder."

"What else do you know?"

I thought back to that damn conversation with my once-upon-a-time-ago best friend. "After Armani met Calliope at the funeral, he forced her to get bloodwork to verify whether he was her father. And he discovered he had an heir, after all," I finished the story for him.

"I assume he also attempted to fuck his way through Sicily after that to see if he could have more kids," Hudson said bluntly. "And no luck."

Not the mental image I wanted.

"Why didn't he force her to come back to Italy with him?"

"As much as I hate the DiMaggios, they have a few rules that they've maintained in their four-hundred-plus years of criminal enterprise that make them slightly less repulsive, one of which is no one in their organization can force themselves upon a woman in any way. No trading or trafficking of people. And nothing involving minors. Not even drug sales to anyone under eighteen." I revealed what my father had shared with me years ago when he'd given me the bad news my former best friend now worked for the DiMaggio crime family. "If anyone breaks the rules, there are consequences."

"So as the leader, Armani can't exactly force his daughter to try and give him a male heir without breaking a four-hundred-year-old tradition of not harming a woman. But now . . . something is clearly wrong, or you wouldn't be calling me."

"Armani's third-in-command is the reason why I'm here. We go way back. And clearly we're no longer friends, but I'm indebted to him. I don't want to get into why, but he doesn't support what Armani plans to do. He wants my help overthrowing him."

"And this involves Calliope somehow?"

"Since Armani couldn't kidnap his own daughter and force her to come to Italy, he's been trying to set her up in the last year with men he deems suitable: Sicilian, Catholic, and wealthy. She's rejected every one and quickly realized they were bait to try and entrap her. Give him the heir he wants."

"But?"

"Two weeks ago, Armani found out he's dying. A rare blood disease. He has a few years to live. So he's lost his patience. He's willing to bend the rules and family traditions to ensure Calliope is married and pregnant before he dies, and that her child will one day run the family dynasty."

"Get to the part where this involves you."

"If I want to save her life, I either need to force her to go on the run with a new identity and stay hidden forever or . . . well, marry her myself."

"Now you're just fucking with me, right?"

I wish. I gave him silence as an answer.

"So I assume you're going to push her to go into hiding until her old man dies instead of becoming your wife?"

"She'd need to hide a lot longer than that," I shared, my shoulders falling in frustration. "Armani's second-in-command, Marcello, will take over without an heir, and he's an asshole of the highest order. He'll hunt her down to ensure she's never a threat to his power. DiMaggio's people are loyal to the bloodline, and they'll choose Calliope over Marcello if it were to come down to it."

"So why not kill Armani and his second-in-command now," Hudson tossed out. "Problem solved." He went quiet for a moment, as if quickly realizing the issue with his solution. "Unless whoever takes over also has the same line of thought about her, and that's a lot of dead bodies we'd need to pile up. Shit . . ."

"I don't think she'll even run. Hell, she hasn't yet, and she's aware her father is a monster who has her under his protection even as we speak." I gripped the steering wheel and let go of a heavy breath.

"What does this old friend of yours that's third in charge get out of all of this if you marry her? What's his endgame?"

"When Armani dies and Calliope takes over, she'll then pass on the mantle to him. Give him her blessing publicly to run the family business. No one will hunt her after that. No one will come for her if he's the one in charge and it was a DiMaggio who put him there."

"Ah, so he wants to be crowned king. Of-fucking-course. So you're supposed to marry this woman until what, Armani dies? That's—"

"Insane, I know. And no, the marriage wouldn't last years." I sure as hell hoped not. "A few days ago, Armani went ahead and negotiated a deal with who he wants Calliope to marry. He's arranged for her to be taken on Monday and married by Wednesday."

"And if she chooses to marry instead of run, how will you convince her father to let you have her hand instead of his choice?"

Another problem to tackle, but Gabriel had thought out everything in advance before contacting me; he also knew he'd need someone he could trust who wouldn't ever want "the throne" once married to Calliope. "I meet his requirements, but I can also offer something that no one else in Sicily can, and that's—"

"A truce with The League, like The League once had with The Alliance," Hudson finished for me, connecting the dots.

"But if I marry into the DiMaggio family, that should alleviate their concerns The League would terminate the truce." Well, that was the idea Gabriel would help me sell to Armani.

"And do you think she'll choose you over this other guy?"

"I have until tomorrow night to convince her since Armani's men are taking her after she gets off work Monday." This was a damn tight timeline.

"Do you plan to live in Italy during all this?" A harsh breath cut over the line.

Just wait until I get to the real bombshell I haven't dropped on you yet. You'll breathe so hard you'll nearly pass out, like I almost did.

"No, I'll figure out something," I finally answered. "The thing is, as much as I'd prefer her to go into hiding forever so I don't need to get hitched, it'd be better if she doesn't choose that option."

"Why?"

I squeezed my eyes closed, memories from a past operation rushing to mind, and my stomach turned. "Because this might be our first shot to get the man we've wanted to take down for four years."

I let that sink in. Gave Hudson the gift of time to process it all.

"The savage who . . ." He cleared his throat, emotion cutting him up, and I felt it through the phone. "The man who tortured Constantine . . . is the man Armani wants to marry his daughter?"

"Yes," I hissed, my blood boiling at the very thought of Rocco Barone ever setting a hand on Calliope. The same man who'd nearly killed my brother had Gabriel not saved his life; hence the favor now. But this favor offered me a chance at revenge, so in a sense, I might owe him yet again.

"Rocco has been off the grid and is heavily protected. Plus, there's that truce your father made with his dad . . . But if this is our chance to finally take him out, count me the fuck in. I'll play the long game right along with you if I must. Just tell me what you need," Hudson said with conviction, "and you've got it."

"We protect Calliope from these assholes and get justice for what Rocco did to Constantine, one way or another." I opened my eyes. "But before we let everyone else know about this, let me first—"

"Convince Calliope to either go into hiding or agree to marry you. But if she chooses to run, that eliminates our shot at getting Rocco, right?"

Yeah. But I couldn't choose revenge over her life, even with how desperate I was to take out that animal, and Hudson knew that.

I thought back to the beautiful woman I'd met tonight, sensing the fire in her belly, right along with her stubbornness. She wasn't going to play ball so easily, and I'd have to find a way to make her see the light somehow. She wasn't from my world, and she was never meant to be. But now that she was being dragged into it because of the blood that ran through her veins, it was up to me to save her from the darkness before it swallowed her whole, like it had me.

"And you're right, Constantine can't know about this right away. He won't let you do this for him. And he'd never be able to share a room with Rocco, if it came down to that, without snapping," Hudson added when I'd yet to speak, because I was still trying to wrap my head around the possible idea of marriage, even if temporary. My mother would kill me for getting a divorce, but . . . "You sure you want to marry her, though? This is you we're talking about. What if you wind up falling in love with your wife?"

"Me? Fall in love?" I fake-laughed, but honestly, there were only three women I'd ever loved in my life: Izzy, Bianca (now from the beyond), and my mother. I had no plans to fall for Calliope, and I sure as hell wasn't giving Armani an heir. "I just have a feeling Little Miss Tennessee Whiskey is going to be a major pain in my ass, regardless of what choice she makes."

CHAPTER FOUR

Calliope

"Stupid garage door." I needed to figure out how to get some extra money to fix the darn thing. I attempted to punch in the code one more time since the opener in my Jeep didn't do the trick and sighed when it refused to budge. I was tired, hungry, and desperate to get free of my heels, but I almost laughed at the absurdity of my situation. With my luck, I'd also wake up my next-door neighbor, and Lord knew I didn't need a midnight lecture on getting home late or noise ordinances.

Giving up on the garage, I rounded my townhouse and went for the front door, doing my best not to catch my heels in the cracks of the sidewalk.

I waved my hand in front of the door, waiting for the motion lights to kick on so I could see. Of course they didn't work. *Another thing to be fixed.* Cursing, I finally managed to get the key in the lock.

Once inside, I kicked off my heels, knowing I had a good fifteen seconds to type in the security code before it went off and Mr. Crabby would be awakened by the blaring sound.

"Oof. Thank God." I moaned in relief, then searched for the lit-up keypad by the door. I was about to punch in the code when I realized . . . shit, it wasn't on. Did I forget to set the alarm before I left? *That's not like me.* A shiver rolled over my skin and spread into my arms at the realization that—

"Don't panic." A deep, gravelly voice had me tensing, and my fingers curled inward on instinct. "I'm not here to hurt you."

That voice . . . The lights flicked on, and I turned to see Alessandro Costa sitting in the armchair across the room, retracting his hand from the lamp at his side. He had one ankle casually crossed over his knee, and he was steadily eyeing me like *I* was the threat.

I looked to the left, calculating how long it'd take me to get to my handgun safe. He was taller. Probably faster. He'd get to me before I had a chance, but I had to try.

"Don't bother," he said, his tone so smooth it somehow rolled over my skin, heating me in places that it shouldn't have, because like hell was I allowed to have any type of positive reaction to an intruder in my home. "Your gun isn't there. Or the one up in your bedroom."

You went through my house? My back went to the wall by the door, my hands remaining in tight fists, wound and ready to go. "You couldn't possibly have opened the lockboxes."

"I didn't need to. Just moved them." He lowered his other foot to the floor, then gripped the chair's arms. "I also removed the bat by the door in your garage. Assuming that's a weapon since I didn't spot a baseball in there." He tipped his head a touch, gray eyes sharp on me. "And I hid all the knives in your kitchen. I don't want you accidentally hurting yourself if you attempt to try and hurt me."

Attempt, huh? I looked around the living room again, trying to figure out the best plan. Scream? Let one of my father's shadows come to my rescue? But also, why wasn't my heart thundering in my chest? My pulse in my ears? Goose bumps on my skin? Why wasn't I deathly afraid of this man inside my home? *What's wrong with me?*

"I honestly wasn't expecting you to have firearms. Your concealed carry permit was issued back when you used to need one here, which means you bought your Glocks before you learned you're the daughter of Armani DiMaggio. Why?"

Now that name set me off. Fire through my veins. Anger. Not fear. "Why are you here?" I bit out, not giving him the satisfaction of being terrified of him, if that was what he wanted.

"I told you we needed to talk," he shared, his tone almost businesslike.

"So that *man* did send you?" But it made no sense. "Based on what I know about you, you don't seem like the typical candidate he'd pick out, aside from being rich and Sicilian."

"You don't know me." A touch of a smile came and went from his lips. "Well, unless you researched me, too." His attention went to the bookshelf on the far side of the room where my safe had been hidden inside a cabinet. "So why the weapons?" he deflected.

"Oh, I don't know, maybe because I'm a single woman living alone and there are a lot of assholes in the world. Case in point." I lifted my chin, finding his eyes again, letting him know he was now said asshole.

"I'm not here to hurt you. In fact, quite the opposite." He frowned, his lips scowly-ish, as if he'd eaten something bitter or found my presence offensive.

Um, you're the offensive one. You're in my house. I should be annoyed. Angry. Probably screaming, too.

"Your father doesn't know I'm here. And he sure as hell didn't send me. The only time I talk to criminals is if I'm *questioning* them." Earlier, his accent had been more like a subtle, underlying note of seduction, but now, it was cutting through a touch thicker . . . sexier? I stifled a groan.

There's something seriously wrong with me. "I don't believe you."

"Ahh, but you do, or you wouldn't still be standing here. You'd run." He lifted his hand like a request to continue *not* running. "I'll get to the point."

"Please do, because I'm seconds away from screaming my head off. Mr. Crabby next door may be old and crotchety, but he's got a shotgun he's been waiting for a chance to use, and he won't hesitate to save me." *Even if I drive him nuts from time to time.*

"Glad to know he'd have your six. I'd trust him over your father's men parked down the street any day. Hell, they clearly have no clue I'm here." He kept his eyes on me as he continued, "I have inside information about your problem, and I've been tasked with helping you."

I pushed away from the wall at his words and relaxed my hands for only a moment, shaking them out at my sides. "What do you mean?"

"Remember I said I also have a side gig?" He started to stand, and I flinched and went back to the wall. Immediately clocking my reaction to his movement, he lowered himself back into his seat. "I help people out. People who are in trouble."

"You know, I've heard of that line of work before. What's it called again?" I briefly chewed on my thumbnail in mock thought before snapping out, "Oh, yeah. Billionaire comic book superhero. Totally fiction. They don't exist in real life." I turned to the side, unamused, and pointed to the door. "Now leave, or I scream and Mr. Crabby gets to use his shotgun."

"Calliope, please. I need you to listen to me."

"Don't say my name." Because I hated how beautiful it sounded rolling from his tongue.

"Your father's plans changed for you. You don't have until you're thirty-five to marry anymore. You have until this Wednesday. And the man he's chosen for you to marry is . . . well, he's a monster."

My heart stopped, and my entire body went cold as he rocked me to my very core. "W-who told you that if it wasn't Armani? How do you know . . . ?"

"An inside source who disagrees with Armani's plans to snatch you on Monday and force your hand. *And* to force you to give him an heir," he said, not holding back as he gripped the chair's arms.

"No. I'm not marrying or having a kid for him to steal away and turn into the king of his empire. Hell no. And he could never force me to do such a thing."

"He can. And he will," he rasped. "But that's what I'm trying to prevent from happening."

"Why? We don't know each other." I shook my head. "No way would you just help me. You're a stranger."

He pointed to the stairwell off to the side of the bookshelf. "I can take you somewhere he'll never find you. Anywhere you want to go. If that's what you want, I can protect you. You can pack your bags now, but you'll need to say goodbye to this life forever."

"First of all," I began, pushing away from the wall, "you think I'm going to take off with you? Maybe you watched a few too many serial killer documentaries and this is some new way to steal women and have your way with them."

"I'm not trying to have my way with . . ." He discarded his words, probably deciding they'd sounded sexual (or maybe that was just me), but with that intense, husky tone of his, sex seemed to ooze from every word he spoke whether he meant for it to or not. The fact that I let the thought even register meant I was clearly too hungry and vexed to think straight. "And secondly?" he prompted, waiting for me to carry on.

"Secondly, don't you think if I was the running type, I would have done it when I first learned who my biological father was and what he wanted from me?" The thought had crossed my mind a half dozen times in the last year. My aunt said she had a plan to deal with Armani when the time came, too. But I had a life here and didn't want to leave it behind.

"There are only two ways I can help you. If you won't take option one, which is a new identity and life in hiding, then—"

"Let's say I believe you." Searching for that spine of mine I'd lost for a moment, I tacked on, "I don't, just to be clear, but let's say I do." I kept my head high as I went on, "What's the second option that'll help fulfill your desire to imitate a comic book hero and save me?"

His forehead creased as he stared at me, his chest inflating with the mother of long breaths before letting it go. "That you marry me instead." His palm whipped up again like a plea not to run.

Was he kidding?

"Your father found out he only has a few years to live, and he's done waiting. He's going to force you to marry Wednesday." The dark words shredded me into practically nothing, because for some reason, I kind of did believe him, which explained why I hadn't bolted from the room or screamed yet.

I wanted Armani dead. He was evil as far as I was concerned, and I wouldn't mourn his loss. But if his death meant he'd force me to do the unthinkable, then maybe I had no choice but to give up my life in Tennessee and run. *Well, unless I ask my aunt for help. Pull her away from her hard-earned vacation and involve her in my mess.* God, that was the last thing I wanted to do.

"Good. I can tell by your face you're finally understanding the gravity of the situation." He slowly rose to his tall height, and I didn't cower this time. Not that I had anywhere to go; I was still only inches from the wall. As his hands slid into his pockets, he added, "Monday, Armani's second-in-command is coming for you. Those three assholes he's had babysitting you for a year will help him take you. You'll be forced to fly to Sicily. Forced to marry. And forced to fuc—" He let go of that horrible sentence, and I realized my hand was now over my mouth.

I was going to be sick. Because I knew, deep down I *knew*, that The Asshole would do exactly that.

Unable to stop myself, I blew past him and rushed for the bathroom in the hall and fell to my knees, hearing a rip somewhere in the back of the dress as I flipped up the toilet seat.

My stomach protested, but I hadn't eaten all day, so I was met with that horrible, gut-wrenching pain of my stomach convulsing and producing no result.

At the feel of my hair lifting and being twisted, I spotted the handsome billionaire on one knee alongside me, holding back my hair.

"Le-le-leave me alone," I cried, trembling as chills crisscrossed my skin. I gripped the sides of the toilet. Nothing came. Just pain.

"I'm here to help, however that may be," he said, his tone softer than it'd been before. I sure as hell didn't take the playboy (based on what I'd seen online) to be a hair-holder-for-a-girl-vomiting kind of guy. *No. He's just trying to gain my trust; he has to have ulterior motives.*

He must've realized all I was going to do was dry heave, because he let go of my hair and left me. I heard the water running before he offered me a small towel and his hand to stand. "You good?"

Hating that I allowed him to help me up, I covered my mouth with the hand towel and stared at this powerful man in a $10,000 suit, crowded inside the small half bath with faded wallpaper peeling at the edges. He didn't belong there. Or with me. "I'm just . . ." I closed my eyes, thinking back to the day Armani forced me to have my blood drawn, discovering I was his daughter. "I had the same reaction of wanting to puke when I found out Armani was . . ."

"Understandable." His firm tone had me opening my eyes.

"I need to change, and you need to go." I motioned with a little nod for him to move, and he didn't protest and let me exit the tight space.

"I can't go, though. We need to—"

"Talk." I flicked on the hall light and spun around to face him, lowering the towel to my side after determining my breath was probably fine. Not that I should've been thinking about that. The man had broken into my house and knew about my father and so many more *ands* I could write a book. At least I'd be writing again. I hadn't written a single song since Armani had come into my life. "So, you want me to run or to marry you?" If my stomach wasn't still nauseous and in knots, I'd fake a laugh at the ridiculous idea of marrying this man.

He set a hand on the hall wall as if needing it for support, which I highly doubted. "The marriage would be temporary." His brow tightened as if the idea sickened him more than it did me. "Trust me, the last thing in the world I want is to get married to you."

Yup, thought so. "Then why would you?"

His eyes lowered to the floor beneath us. "I owe someone a favor."

"I'm sorry . . . what?" I started to move around him, but his hand on the wall went straight to my wrist. It was a gentle touch, but I stopped nevertheless and peered at him.

"It's a long story."

"One that ends with us saying our vows? No thanks. I don't want to be part of that ending."

"Trust me, I know. But if you'd let me explain, we can formulate a plan." With a determined look, he pinned me in place, and that somehow made me want to bend to his will. That feeling alone was an immediate cause for concern. I shouldn't want to bend to him in any way.

"I can't do this right now. I need to get this damn dress off and breathe. Just please . . . go."

"Calliope." He closed his eyes and rasped, "Sorry. *Callie.* Can I call you that?"

I thought about it for a moment. "I don't want you to call me anything at all. I want to be alone," I pleaded, needing to wrap my head around everything.

"We're short on time. I had no clue I was . . ." He opened his eyes. "I didn't know who you were when we first met tonight. I didn't know I was there at that event because of you and for you until . . ."

"The call I saw you take while I was singing?" I whispered at the memory, hating I'd confessed to watching him while onstage earlier.

He lifted a brow, then nodded.

"I don't know if I can trust you."

"I'd say call your old man and verify, but I don't think he'll wait until Monday to come for you if he knows we're together. He'll send his men tonight."

"Why Monday afternoon?" And why was I continuing this conversation? This was utter madness.

"So no one will report you as having disappeared once school is out," he said rather bluntly, and knowing how calculating Armani was, *that* I believed.

"You broke into my house. Proceeded to hide my weapons. And are asking me to marry you because you owe someone a favor. You realize how this looks? Sounds?" I focused on where he held my wrist, and he cleared his throat and let go of me.

"I'm fully aware, but it doesn't change the fact it's the truth. I'm trying to help you. And to be honest, you don't know me. So you shouldn't just trust my word. I'd be worried if you did accept everything I was saying as the gospel truth, given I did break into your house tonight." His forehead did that frustrated-tight thing again. "But I need you to."

I studied him, taking a few breaths that were pathetically shallow and didn't relieve the tension in my chest. "Aside from this favor you say you owe, what else do you get from this deal? You don't need the money. I doubt you want to drag your family name down by marrying into the mafia. So why?"

There went his eyes again. Closed. What was he hiding? "Let's just say I have my reasons. This *temporary* deal will help us both, and after, we can go our separate ways. It'll be like it never happened."

Since he wasn't looking at me, I sidestepped him and went back into the living room. I tossed the hand towel onto the armchair he'd previously filled and looked up at the ceiling, trying to digest the indigestible.

"Get some sleep. Think about it. I'll be back in the morning."

At his words, I turned to see the gorgeous man in his expensive suit hanging back in the doorway of the hall. I had to assume he had no plans to go out the front door with Armani's shadows parked somewhere outside.

"I can't marry you," I cried out, hating the break in my voice. "When I walk down the aisle, I want it to be to the man I . . . love. My forever."

He casually leaned into the interior doorway, pocketing his hands. "Don't you want that, too?"

"I don't ever want to get married. Period. But I'll do what needs to be done."

"What needs to be done? Will that be in your vows?" I was tired. Shocked. And yet, there I was, throwing sarcasm at him. "How in the world will you even convince Armani you're the man for me instead of the one he chose?"

"I have a plan." He straightened in the doorway, as if sensing I was coming around.

I wasn't. But he didn't need to know that yet. I was close to getting him to leave me alone, and I didn't want to give him a reason to stick around. I just wanted to hide in a ball beneath my sheets and cry.

"If Armani is truly dying, does that mean we'd need to be married until he dies in a few *years*?"

He stepped back into the room, shaking his head. "No, he won't live that long."

"How do you know?"

"Because I'll kill him long before then," he announced as if sharing a stock tip. Just so matter of fact.

I stumbled back, tripping over the skirt of my dress, and there went another rip. At the feel of air hitting me from behind, I reached around and snatched the material, not needing this man to see me in only my panties. Gotta save something for the wedding night. *Ugh, no, not happening.* "What do you mean? You'll commit murder?"

"Is it really murder if he's a ruthless psychopath?" He peered at me like he was truly expecting me to answer that question with anything other than a yes.

Frazzled, among other things, I murmured, "Won't that put a target on your head?"

"No, because no one will know it was me." His lips curved at the edges, and I wasn't sure if he was on the verge of smiling or frowning. "Unless you want to stay married for years?"

"No!" I shot out, but wait . . . I wasn't considering this, was I? "I can't marry you. I'm not leaving my life here." I let go of the dress and waved my hands in the air. "And I'm not running, either."

"Then what will you do? Because they *are* taking you Monday, whether you want them to or not."

I whipped around, went to the fireplace, and set my hands on the mantel, trying to breathe, because it was becoming increasingly more difficult. My chest was tight, and the corset part of the dress was squeezing me to death.

"Eat. Get some sleep," he roughly commanded. "I'll be back in the morning. I'd suggest you not talk about this to anyone, because if word gets back to Armani, like I said, he won't wait until Monday."

I still didn't understand why in the world this billionaire playboy would help me. Side gig? Really? No, I didn't believe that.

"I won't be ready for you tomorrow." My shoulders fell, and the chill at my back reminded me he was potentially getting a hint of my ass right now, so I snatched the material together and faced him.

His eyes were pointed toward the hardwood as if he'd been respectful, not wanting to preview his bride before the wedding day.

Bride? No, no, no.

"You need to be ready, either to let me help you go into hiding or to become my wife." His gaze flicked up to meet mine as the words *my wife* fell from his mouth. "Good night, *Callie.* Sorry about breaking into your home. And, well, for everything else." He turned for the hallway. He must've planned on using the back door, which was most likely how he'd entered in the first place.

"Wait." My arm shot out at the same time the word did.

He slowly turned, remaining quiet as he waited for me to go on.

But I didn't know what I'd planned to say next. If he was being genuine, did I owe him a thank-you? I just . . . wasn't ready to trust him. "Where are my guns?" I blurted instead.

"Right where you left them." A soft touch of humor caressed his tone, then he nodded and disappeared into the hall.

I hastily removed my dress and let it pool at my feet, then dropped into the armchair and tossed my head back.

"Oh, and I—"

I snapped my head forward, realizing he'd come back. I was only in panties since the dress had a built-in bra, and my entire body became hot.

Alessandro remained fixed in the doorway of the hall, eyes flying over my body. I banded my arms across my chest, trying to hide my nipples as an Italian word—probably a curse—fell from his lips. He surprised me by peering at the ceiling to offer me as much privacy as he could. "I didn't think you'd get naked that quick."

Fighting off humiliation, I deflected. "What'd you come back to say? And please hurry." When he remained closemouthed, my sassy self had me asking, "Tongue-tied again?"

Eyes still hidden from view, a devilish smirk flitted across his lips. I hated the effect it had on me, because I had no clue whether I should believe him. What if this was all a grand plan from Armani? A way to trick me into marrying, letting me think it was my idea? It'd be ingenious.

"I actually don't remember what I planned to say." He shrugged, opened his eyes, then demanded, "Just go eat. Then get some rest. Be up by eight a.m. I'll be back to talk then."

Unable to stop myself, I asked, "If I actually believe anything you're saying, and that your motives aren't evil, and we do temporarily marry, do you plan to be so bossy?"

He responded in a low voice, "If it's for your benefit."

"And what makes you think you know what's good for me?" I blinked back more tears since I couldn't free my arms from my chest to discard them.

Instead of answering me, he roughly replied, "Eight a.m. Open your door for me. Or I'll find my way in, and you know I can."

"And if I call my father's men over to handle you?" I countered as he turned to the side, preparing to leave.

"Then I guess you'll have your proof that I sure as hell don't work for your father," he murmured darkly, "when I have to kill all three of them."

"Yeah, well, good men don't kill people." *Well, not unless . . .*

Before I could finish my internal string of reasons as to why killing might be justified, he cocked his head. "Who said anything about me being good?"

CHAPTER FIVE

Alessandro

Parked down the street from Calliope's house, I grabbed my phone to send Hudson a quick update. I hated keeping my brothers and sister in the dark, but it was for their own benefit right now.

Me: I think she believed me.

Hudson: And that means?

Me: That I'm probably getting hitched once we convince Armani.

Hudson: As long as Rocco doesn't kill you for stealing his shot at marrying into the DiMaggio family. That kind of alliance would make his family truly unstoppable.

Me: I know, I know.

I shook off the anger at that idea as best I could. I was still working to wrap my head around this fucked-up alternate reality I currently found myself living in.

Me: But we need Rocco to try and come after me. Remember? I'm the bait to draw that motherfucker out from the dark hole he's been hiding in and break the truce his father made with my family.

Before he could respond with any cautious warnings, I fired off another message.

Me: I received the file you sent me.

Hudson: You really plan to show her that? It's gory. I mean, it's the things nightmares are made of. Fuck, I didn't sleep at all last night after compiling it for you.

I peered over at the passenger seat, which had the documents Hudson had emailed me inside an envelope, sitting beneath my black ball cap. I'd printed all twenty-five pages and then erased any evidence I'd ever used the hotel's printer.

Me: If she doesn't either run or choose me, then she needs to know the truth about the man her father's going to force her to marry. This should convince her. Well, as long as she believes I didn't just print the script for a horror film. Going to see her now.

I checked the time. Two minutes to 0800 hours. When I'd driven by her house five minutes ago, I'd clocked her father's "guard" parked two houses down and fast asleep. *Some protection.*

Hudson: Keep me posted. I assume if she goes through with the "tying the knot" plan, you're flying commercial to Italy, so your family doesn't find out?

I groaned at the thought, but I had no choice.

Me: Unfortunately. And I'll need to make a stop first. Swing by The League leader's place in Sicily.

Hudson: Emilia Calibrisi's? Well, she's married to an Irishman now. Billionaire family. The McGregors. Guess she's not as crazy about keeping her bloodline pure Italian like Armani. But you think she'll just let you walk up to her door and ring the bell? You don't actually know her, and you can't ask your old man to call first since he's in the dark about your plan.

Me: I'll figure it out. I need her on board or this whole plan falls apart before it starts.

Hudson: Pretty sure you need your bride to accept your proposal first. 😉

Me: You're loving that part of this, aren't you?

Hudson: Better you than me. But none of us ever thought we'd see the day you'd be married, so yeah, it's . . . crazy, to say the least.

Me: And you're one to talk? You're as bad as me on the whole bachelorhood thing.

Hudson: No one is at your level when it comes to women, man. Give me a break.

Me: Yeah, yeah. Well, this whole thing is an assignment. Temporary. I'll be single again soon enough. I won't be treating her like she's actually mine.

Hudson: I need to make coffee before we start discussing your sex life with your future wife. Give me a minute.

Me: 😒 Fuck off, I'm going dark now. Be in touch.

I pocketed my phone, slid my hat on backward, then snatched the file and made my way down a side street to slip into her backyard unseen. Her guard may have been asleep, but I didn't need him waking at the wrong time and finding me on her doorstep. Or hell, finding myself on the other side of Mr. Crabby's shotgun.

I'd thought that was her nickname for him, but when I did a quick background check on her neighbors at 0400 hours, unable to sleep, I'd discovered that was his actual name. Just thought she was being cute.

She is cute. Shit. I could *not* think about this woman in any way other than as an assignment. Someone to save. And a way to get justice for Constantine and to prevent Rocco's family from being so powerful they could unleash hell on the world. Period.

Once at her back door, I knocked twice, and I was surprised she didn't waste time in opening up. Prompt. I liked it. What I didn't like was that when she swung open the door, she was in skintight black yoga pants and a white tank top, wearing an adorable scowl and a sexy-as-fuck messy bun.

"Hi." She folded her arms, using her hip to keep the door propped open, blocking my path with her gorgeous figure.

"Glad to see you're dressed this time." Not the morning greeting I'd planned to go with, but this woman had an uncanny ability to trip me up when talking.

You're off-limits. I can't have you. So of course, I want you. I was addicted to the chase, and it'd been forever and a day since the chase involved a woman and not a criminal. *That's all it is, though. My addiction to the hunt,* I rationalized. *Oh, how my therapist would be proud at my self-reflection.* She was going to have a field day with this whole situation in our next session. Well, I couldn't exactly tell her why or who I was marrying, but I'd learned to be creative in our conversations to hide the truth.

"How much of me did you see last night?" Calliope-Callie—I was still uncertain what to call her, even in my head—waited for my answer, scrutinizing me.

No puffy eyes from a night of crying that I could tell. In fact, she looked well rested. But her casual attitude concerned me. If she wasn't even remotely afraid of me, I'd need to keep a better eye on her.

I lifted a brow. "Truth?"

"That'd be ideal." Damn the sexy, just-woke-up, morning rasp that had my cock twitching beneath my jeans.

"Panties, which are basically like bikini bottoms, right?" I shrugged, then walked my focus down from her face to her tank top that accentuated the fullness of her breasts. "Maybe a hint of a bit more, too." *Way more than a hint.* I saw her tits. Those perky nipples. *And damn . . .*

"Well, you, uh . . . you certainly look different today." The stumbling of her words was unexpected, and I forced myself to meet her eyes again and push away thoughts of her nearly naked body from last night. "More military-like than billionaire vigilante in the jeans, black tee, sneakers, and backward hat."

I laughed. Actually fucking laughed. *What the hell?* "You ready to talk?" I had to cut to it before this woman cut through me. Shed a few layers of whatever armor I'd worn so damn well that I'd thought I was invincible for decades. Because somehow her slight tease coupled with that smile was more dangerous than the predator I'd hunted last week in Central Park. I'd scared the bastard enough that he'd turned himself in to the police, preferring to deal with them than the likes of me.

"Tongue-tied or lost in thought?" When I didn't respond, she let her arms drop and tossed out, "I'm going for a walk. We can talk when I get back. I need to clear my head."

"You seem shockingly *not* tense to me. Seems to me you're clear enough." I shoved the envelope her way, remembering it was in my hand, but she only examined it with mild disinterest.

"My aunt is always reciting the saying, 'Confidence in one hand and coffee in the other.' Well, I'm faking confidence right now because I already had my coffee. But in truth, I'm far from clear minded."

I nudged the envelope at her again, doing my best to stay focused on the mission. "This is information on the man your father plans to have you marry. I want you to look it over."

She took it, shifted to the side, and tossed it somewhere, then faced me.

"I'll walk with you," I said, making up my mind she shouldn't be alone since her guard was auditioning for the role of Sleeping Beauty outside.

"I don't walk with people I do like, let alone someone I don't." She shrugged. "Walking is my 'me' time. I'm not sharing that with you."

"You don't know me well enough not to like me. You just don't like what I told you last night, and with good reason," I countered, not ready to give up. I wasn't one to wave a white flag and surrender. Hell, rejection would only push me forward even more.

She stepped out onto the small porch, forcing me to back up so we didn't collide. After locking the door, she pocketed a single key on the side of her yoga pants before maneuvering around me to go down the three steps. "Fine, walk with me."

"Let me guess . . . but don't talk?"

"That'd be ideal." She motioned me along. "Come on, follow me. I know a way to give us a head start before my father's men catch up and wonder who you are."

"Your shadow is asleep right now. We're safe, but I'll let you lead the way." As long as she didn't put up a fight about my keeping her company, I was good.

A few minutes later, she was the one to break the silence she'd supposedly wanted. "Bicentennial Park is just ahead. There's a greenway there I like to walk. Has a nice view of Harpeth River. And I know a path no one ever takes. Always empty."

"You shouldn't be alone on pathways that are usually empty. It's not safe." I hated the idea of her traipsing through some wooded area alone. What was she thinking?

She abruptly stopped, and I nearly slammed into her since I'd been right on her ass, keeping up with her fast pace. "The place is safe, I promise. Been going there for years."

Facing me, Little Miss Tennessee Whiskey boldly flicked the brim of my hat to better see my eyes, since on our *speed*walk I'd swiveled the cap around to shield myself from the morning sun.

But whatever words she'd planned to hiss at me (and based on those narrowed eyes, they wouldn't be delivered with honey) didn't come.

"Tongue-tied, sweetheart?" The side of my lip hitched so I could flash her a hint of my signature cocky smile. Usually worked wonders. Not on her.

The woman sent me daggers and an adorable scowl back. But then her shoulders fell, defenses coming down a touch, and she let the slight breeze carry her soft tone my way as she shared, "Struggling to believe this is my life right now. Still feels like I'm dreaming."

I almost palmed her cheek when I lost sight of her eyes to the pavement. "Does this mean we're talking while walking now?"

"No," she said without peering at me, and she abruptly turned.

I mindlessly snatched her arm and brought my mouth down over her ear. "You're not dreaming. Dreams are nice." I let my breath hit the shell of her lobe as I added, "What you're experiencing is a nightmare." Maybe she needed a little fear to convince her to get on board?

She tugged her arm free from my grasp, shook her body as if a chill had rocked through her, then began walking.

It took her another fifteen minutes to speak, but she was the one to break first. "Do you do what you do because of what happened?"

She stopped walking, hanging back beneath a thick tree with sprawling branches. A few looked like they might snap and take her out, and I couldn't have that happening.

I grumbled under my breath, "What do you mean, 'because of what happened'?" I reached for her hand, laced our fingers together, and guided her away from the overhanging branches.

She looked down at our clasped hands, and I quickly pulled away. "Your sister. I may have done more research on you last night when I couldn't sleep. She was murdered about fourteen years ago, and you and your brothers were arrested for her killer's murder, but then you were all let go."

Yeah, we made a deal to trade in our souls for our freedom. I locked my arms across my chest, growing tense at the conversation. "In part, yes, I do what I do because of Bianca's death."

"And her killer? What happened to him?" She copied my move, folding her arms.

"What do you think happened?" The words sliced like a blade through the air, my anger toward the loss of Enzo's twin catching up with me whenever I thought about it.

I spied the movement in her throat as she swallowed. "So you did kill him?"

"I had a hand in her murderer's death, yes." *Story for another day. Or for never.* "What else did you discover in your Wikipedia search of me and my life?" I'd dug through the details of her life all night. Hacked. Poked. Prodded. Knew almost everything about her I could find online, right down to discovering the deleted photos of her old boyfriends from her Instagram profile, post breakups.

From what I could tell, she hadn't dated since she'd moved out of her ex-boyfriend's home last year, which was right before Armani had come into her life. I didn't blame her if he'd been secretly trying to set her up and she didn't want to risk accidentally falling for one of his plants.

Since the photos of her and that bartender—I'd identified him as Braden Davis—remained on her Insta and Facebook, I had to assume they were only friends like she'd said. Not that it mattered. He was a veteran, and I hadn't been able to find a reason to dislike him other than the way he'd looked longingly at my future wife last night.

Wife. Temporary. Not real. Well, just under the eyes of the law and God if the plan worked out. So it would technically be real.

My stomach banded tight, like I'd just done a thousand sit-ups. What was this feeling? Foreboding? Panic?

"You didn't lie about serving in the military. Army Ranger." She pulled me free from my thoughts. "Parents are from Sicily. You started school in New York when moving here at eight. And your family has a lucrative business. Nothing I could find on your supposed side gigs, though."

"We don't exactly take ads out in the newspaper for jobs," I shot out, forgetting I wouldn't win this woman over by being a dick. "Anything else interesting about me?"

"The fact you held my hair back last night doesn't seem to be a playboy-like thing to do. Probably should say thank you for that."

"Get the feeling one isn't coming."

"Not sure if I can trust you yet. Still on the fence."

"I need you to hurry up and get off that fence." I huffed out a semi-exasperated breath, the word she'd called me just now registering. "And playboy, huh?"

She stepped a touch closer to me, her eyes meeting mine like a dare. "You date a lot."

"I don't date," I grunted.

"Okay, sleep around."

I mulled over what to say to that. It was hard to defend the truth in who I was and how I lived my life if I said it aloud, which was why I rarely did when my shrink tried to push me to open up. It's not like I had a heart to give anyone anyway, so why waste a woman's time?

"Maybe I—" I let my words go when I spotted a flash of movement in the distance. Not just a flash . . . but two shadowy figures were watching us from behind a bank of trees. It wasn't the guard who'd been parked out by her place, that was for sure.

It'd been a relatively quiet morning while on our walk so far. Not many people out. Most probably on their way to church. So whoever was playing hide-and-seek behind the trees would soon make their move.

I focused back on her and gently snatched the sides of her arms. "Do you walk every Sunday morning around this time? Always in this park?" Why the hell had I left my sidearm locked in the rental?

"Yeah." Her eyes went wide. "Why?"

"Someone, other than your guards, knows of your routine. They're here for you."

"What do you mean?"

"Probably someone who doesn't want Armani to have an heir," I snapped out, gearing up for an impending fight. I pointed to the tree with those dangling arms for branches I hadn't been a fan of before, but now I needed her to . . . "Get behind the tree," I finished aloud. "And get down."

She blinked in shock, remaining frozen in place instead of moving like I needed her to do. I looked over her head, realizing the shadows had morphed into two hooded men who were coming in hot and fast.

"Go." I unhanded her, tossed my hat, and cracked my neck, spying knives in their hands instead of firearms. They wanted a quiet kill. *I can work with that.* When she'd yet to get her ass moving, I gritted out, "Just do what I say, and take cover. Now, dammit."

CHAPTER SIX

Calliope

Two hooded men, in their thirties from the looks of it, surrounded Alessandro with switchblades in hand, and he was all that stood in the way of them getting to me. Well, aside from the old tree I was hugging and peering around.

Alessandro's profile was to me as both men came straight at him, and without missing a step, he ducked the first assailant's attempt to cut him, then flipped the second man to his back, the muddy dirt trail padding the guy's fall.

There was a flash of quick movements, a UFC fight taking place before my eyes. I'd only ever witnessed such things on TV, but it'd never been two on one, like now.

It dawned on me I would've been here alone in the park with no way to defend myself had Alessandro not shown up at my doorstep, since I always did my best to ditch my shadows for as long as possible, assuming they were an annoying inconvenience.

I should've been terrified, knowing there was a chance I could die. *But* I wasn't trembling. Not scared. Something told me Alessandro wouldn't let these men get to me, no matter what. A gut instinct. That also meant I was starting to trust him, which was absurd. He was still a stranger, and his intentions were questionable at best.

Alessandro blocked another knifing attempt and sent the guy to the ground, trapping him between his powerful legs. He grabbed hold of his forearm and bent it back in a position that had the guy cursing. Hell, the man even let go of the knife to tap out as if he were inside an MMA cage instead.

As soon as the asshole was back on his feet, Alessandro laid him out with a wicked side kick.

"Alessandro," I warned, letting him know he had the other bad guy on his six. *On his six?* Okay, that was Braden and his military talk in my head right now.

Alessandro spun around to face the second man, only to take a hit to the jaw. It was the first time I'd witnessed him struck.

He shook it off, and I'd swear he was smiling at the prick. Then he made a come-hither motion, beckoning the attacker while swiping the blood free from his lip with the pad of his thumb.

Something about Alessandro fearlessly handling these men while sporting a cocky grin, blood on his lip, had me . . .

Oh my God. No, no. I'm not my father's daughter. I'm not his daughter. I'm not attracted to violence, and—

I squeezed my eyes closed, finding myself catapulted back to the past and a confrontation with Armani shortly after Mom's funeral. He'd forced me to his home in Sicily and stabbed one of his own men for looking at me the wrong way.

Right after that, he'd cleaned the blood from his blade with a dinner napkin and said to me, *"Nature versus nurture, Principessa. Your aunt may have raised you, but you're still my daughter. You have my blood. Your mother's. And she was no saint, either, trust me."* He'd stepped over the groaning man, and my back went flat to the dining room wall with every step closer he took. *"You have your mother's siren voice. And you have my strength."* He'd leaned in, drawing his face near mine, the smell of a vanilla cigar on his breath as he went on, *"One day, you'll experience a moment where it feels good to be bad. You'll be turned on by the darkness. You won't be able to help it. Because it's inside you, just waiting to be unleashed. It's part of you."* He'd grinned and held the blade between us. *"You'll become a DiMaggio in that moment, and you'll accept who you are."* He turned to the side, offering me his profile. *"Non c'è luce senza oscurità. There is no light without dark. Our family is a necessary force in the world to keep it balanced."*

"I'll never be a DiMaggio, and I'll never succumb to the dark," I'd snapped out, finding my backbone.

I opened my eyes, landing in the present. Also just in time to see a third man coming from down the hill. He must've been waiting for these assholes, and since they'd yet to return . . .

"Alessandro!" I cried out, alerting him again. "Gun," I added at the sight of the weapon in the hooded man's hand.

Alessandro swiveled at the sound of my voice, and dammit, I'd distracted him, and the guy who'd been on the ground by his feet drew his blade and slashed him near the ankle. He cursed, as if getting cut were only an inconvenience, and in one fast move, dropped to a knee and swiftly disarmed the man. Once the third guy was close enough, my unexpected hero flung the switchblade with eerie precision, and it landed right in the man's jugular.

I stepped back, sealing my eyes closed, only listening to the grunts and groans. Sounds of victory for one. Death for the others. And based on what I'd witnessed so far, I had to believe Alessandro was on the winning side.

When everything fell silent, I chanced a look, finding Alessandro holding the gun and three lifeless bodies on the trail by his feet.

I hesitantly stepped around the tree. "Are they . . . *dead?*"

Alessandro hid the gun beneath the back of his shirt. "I was trying to keep them alive for information, but they were stubborn, and I couldn't risk them getting to you." He knelt alongside one of the bodies and checked for a pulse, and I did my best not to look too closely to see exactly how he'd killed them. "All dead," he noted after checking the other two. "Are you okay?"

He came to me, and I had the urge to fling myself into his arms, but I held back, and instead nodded while clutching my arms, searching for goose bumps that should've been there. Blood. Violence. Death. And no reaction. *That* was what scared me. Where was my desire to go throw up, like last night?

"I'm not his daughter. No, no," I blurted, starting to panic. "This isn't the moment I become . . ." I shook my head with a little too much intensity. "That moment will never come."

He grabbed hold of my wrist, pulling my hand free from my other arm, and he was the one to snatch me against him, surprisingly holding me tight to his hard frame.

My cheek went to his chest, and the fierce beats of this stranger's heart managed to calm my racing thoughts. "You must be shaken up. In shock. You'll be okay, though."

"You just killed three men, and I'm . . ." I eased free from his embrace. He let go of me, wordlessly picked up his hat from the ground, and dusted it off before casually slipping it on backward, as if he hadn't unalived three people to save my life. "I'm okay. What is wrong with me that I'm okay?" I cried out, which probably sounded like the opposite of an "okay" thing to be doing.

"Like I said," he began while looking around the park, searching for anyone who might possibly stumble upon the three dead bodies, "it's just shock. You're feeling numb. That's normal." He reached into his pocket and produced his phone.

"Who are you calling?" I locked my arms across my chest again, unsure what to think or feel right now. Maybe Alessandro was right? I was numb. It wasn't because I was a DiMaggio and could handle what happened this morning. I was a schoolteacher. Musician on the side. Not *mafiosa*, not like Armani.

"I think one of your guards betrayed your father and gave up your routine and location to an enemy of his, or to someone hoping to take over when he dies instead of you," he shared, bringing the phone to his ear. "And I'm calling Armani's third-in-command to let him know what happened."

"Gabriel?" I almost tripped over the foot of one of the men at the mention of his name. "Is he the one you said you owe a favor to? The one feeding you your intel?"

He nodded. "We go way back. *Before* he became a criminal."

I lifted my eyes to the cloudless sky. The sunlight poured down over us, bathing us in the kind of light I didn't feel I deserved. *"Non c'è luce senza oscurità,"* I said under my breath.

"There is no light without dark," he translated, staring at me in surprise. "You speak Italian?"

"No." My posture relaxed, shoulders slumping. "It's just something Armani likes to say to me."

He frowned, then narrowed his eyes, and I assumed someone was now on the other line. "We have a problem," he said. "Three men just tried to kill her, and luckily, I was with her when they came. I tried to keep one alive for questioning, but I couldn't."

My attention skated to his leg, and I'd nearly forgotten he'd been cut. There was a subtle rip in the denim, and blood trickled down onto his white Adidas shoe. Not that he seemed to notice.

"I'm hiding the bodies before someone stumbles upon them, but I need a cleanup crew right now," Alessandro went on.

Cleanup crew? I looked up at him as he held the phone to his ear with his shoulder and began casually dragging a body toward shrubs on the other side of the trail.

"Yeah. Call Armani. Tell him someone's trying to murder his daughter, and I'll be the one to get her safely to Italy. That also means you need to clue him in on the fact you think I'm a better fit for his daughter." He came back for the second body, but at his words, I went before him and waved my arms in the air, letting him know I had no plans to go to Italy. "And tell him if any of his guards come for me or go near her, I'll lay them the fuck out as a precautionary measure in case one did help send these hit men after her today." He ended the call and shoved his phone in his pocket. "What's with the hand-waving? Decipher it for me." He gave me a genuinely puzzled look.

"I'm not going to Italy, is what," I bit out as he dragged Dead Guy Number Two into the shrubs.

"Do you want to go into hiding? Because it's not just your father who is after you now. What do you plan to do? Go to school tomorrow so another asshole can come into your classroom and attack you there?"

My stomach dropped. Fear. Yeah, that four-letter word snuck up on me this time, and fast, at the idea of any of my students being harmed because of me.

"That's what I thought." He busied himself with the task of hiding Bad Guy Number Three next, then snatched his phone, probably pin-dropping our location for Gabriel to send a "cleanup crew" our way.

What was this life I was in? Despite having shadows and Armani showing up from time to time, I'd been doing my best to live normally. To pretend I wasn't who Armani said I was. Land of Delulu and all. What had happened today, especially with three dead bodies in my hometown, made Armani's dark world impossible to ignore.

But there was still one other issue. One as pressing as the dead bodies ten feet away from me beneath the shrubs: Did I trust Alessandro was telling me the truth? Because what if this was all part of Armani's plans to get me to marry?

"The only way I can protect you, if you don't want to go on the run, is to marry you in Italy." He cocked his head, his brows slanting as if the idea were more painful to him than it'd be to me. "So what's it going to be? Running? Or are you becoming my wife?" His hands slammed to his hips when I remained quiet. "One way or another, you're leaving Nashville, whether it's voluntarily or over my shoulder."

CHAPTER SEVEN

Calliope

Not a surprise, but Alessandro let me stew in silence on our walk to my house after his ultimatum of physically taking me from my home whether I liked it or not.

After he'd grabbed his suitcase from his rental and we'd made it to my door, I couldn't help but break the quiet first. "I wouldn't put it past Armani to kill three men and have you look like my knight in shining armor to trick me into getting married. Maybe he's not even really dying."

"Yeah, well, I wouldn't be shocked, either," he snapped, irritation in his tone as I unzipped the key from my pocket.

Before I could open the door, he snatched my wrist. "Let me clear the house first. Make sure no one is waiting inside."

Clear the house? "Fine." I handed him the key, and I followed him inside.

"You didn't set the alarm when you left?"

"I never do for walks."

He grumbled something under his breath while setting aside his suitcase. "Turn the alarm on," he ordered roughly, removing the dead guy's gun from the back of his jeans.

I did as he asked and waited for him to check my home for threats.

When he returned and gave me the all clear, hiding the weapon at his back, I couldn't help but blurt, "Twelve men in the last nine months." I wasn't ready to drop my theory yet. "Are you lucky Number Thirteen he's sent?"

He removed his shoes, as if only now noticing there was blood on one. He'd probably left a trail on my hardwood during his check of the house. "More like the unlucky son of a bitch that—" He let go of his words, replacing them with a string of curses while throwing a hand in the air. "To be clear, I want to marry you even less than you want to marry me." He tossed his hat on my counter, where it landed on top of the envelope he'd given me.

"You keep saying that. Doesn't mean I believe you," I shot back, pushing away from the door but still very much in defense mode. Tense, reactive, ready to swing if necessary.

"It's the truth." He stepped closer, sending me back to the door, and his eyes briefly cut to my mouth. "And I don't need the money, so no, he didn't buy me off."

"But you have your reasons to be here, whether it's because Armani sent you or not." I lifted my chin in challenge. "It has to be more than a favor. If you're going behind Armani's back with Gabriel, what does Gabriel get out of this? What do you?"

His nostrils flared as he stared down at me, jaw locking tight, as if he were ready to go ahead and take me over his shoulder and end the conversation now.

"When your father's dead and you officially take over, you'll turn the organization over to Gabriel. With your blessing, no one will protest the transfer of power. And no one will view you as a threat since you willingly gave up the throne and the life. You'll be free of him. Of all of them." He took a step back, affording us both a chance to breathe. "I don't love the plan, but Gabriel's the lesser of the two evils, and you won't be wedded to a psychopath and will be safe. And I . . ."

"You what?"

"My debt will be paid back." His casual tone both reassured and frustrated me. He also didn't seem like the type to bend to another man's will, but he was still working with Gabriel.

Unsure how to respond, I pointed out, "You got blood on my floor." I studied his lethal and muscular frame, and he followed my eyes to his jeaned legs.

"Just a flesh wound."

Frowning at his dismissive attitude over his health, I knelt before him. Unsure what possessed me to feel the need to take care of a man who was still technically a question mark, I lifted the pant leg to see whether he was bullshitting me on the injury. "Doubtful you need stitches," I said decisively, "but let's get the wound cleaned up anyway."

He stared at me, as if equally surprised I was on my knees before him after accusing him of working for Armani.

I know, I know. I'm giving myself whiplash. But it'd been a wild twelve hours, so anything went at this point.

"You're taking all of this much better than I anticipated after—"

"Watching you kill three people?" I let go of the pant leg, and he offered me his palm to stand.

The gentleman killer? "If I believe everything you've said to me," I began, letting him know he wasn't off the hook yet, "I suppose there are some reasons that killing is justified." Once on my feet, I slipped my hand free from his big one, hating the little jolt of *something* I felt at him touching me. "But I guess I owe you for saving my life."

"If it wasn't some charade staged by Armani, you mean?"

"Right." I nodded, remembering I still owed him gratitude for something else. "And, um, thank you for the hair-holding last night *if* that wasn't part of the act to win me over." I turned to the side, setting my attention on the hallway. The only shower was in the primary bathroom upstairs.

At the feel of his hand wrapping around my forearm, I went still. "You're just full of surprises, aren't you, Callio—"

"Callie," I cut him off, facing him. "You can call me that, I suppose."

He kept his eyes on me for a bit before surrendering with a nod of agreement.

"Let's get you cleaned up. Come on."

"Not sure whether you're offering to wash the blood from my body and clean my wound, but I assure you, it's not my first rodeo. I can manage just fine."

I couldn't believe it, but my lips nearly betrayed me by smiling. "Now that's a word I never thought I'd hear a city boy say. *Rodeo.*"

He finally unhanded me and picked up his suitcase. No brand name in sight on it, and I'd expected something as expensive as yesterday's suit. "Where's the shower?"

"In my bedroom, where you clearly were last night since you went through my things to locate my firearms."

He ignored my words, and in a husky tone remarked, "You can't be alone while I'm showering. You'll stay in your bedroom and lock the door while I'm cleaning up. Understood?"

"Again with the bossiness." And yet, I was semiflustered at his commanding tone, those sharp eyes on me, not to mention the straight-up orders that kept falling from his lips. Frustrated by my odd reaction to him, I started down the hall to get to the stairs, but his hand on my hip stopped me in place. And what a place to stop—right next to the quote by Dolly Parton I'd had framed: "We cannot direct the wind, but we can adjust the sails."

"Do I need to remind you I'm wearing blood from the men who tried to kill you?" he murmured from behind, still holding my waist like I was already his wife. "Bossy is to keep you safe. You'll need to deal with it." His deep voice slid under my skin, and I wanted to rebel, but something told me I'd be wasting my breath.

Pulling my focus away from the framed quote, I then shifted free from his touch and fast-walked to the stairs and darted up them. Once in my bedroom, he set his suitcase by the door and looked around, acting as though it was his first time seeing my room.

It wasn't all that impressive. A queen-size bed with a fluffy white comforter I'd snagged from a Bed Bath & Beyond store-closing sale. Throw pillows from Hobby Lobby (my guilty pleasure store). One antique nightstand Imani had helped me fix up that now matched my dresser. Then there was the vintage floor lamp my best friend, Nala—a music teacher at my school—had gifted me. Aside from that, there was my favorite spot, a sitting nook by the window where I'd wasted a year trying to write songs with no luck. Armani had killed the creativity in me. I now had writer's block. Thankfully, he hadn't strangled the voice from me, and I could still sing.

"So, um, when will Gabriel call you back?" I did my best to come across as more sweet than sour that time. Sidestepping him, I was even a "good girl" and followed his orders, shutting and locking the door behind us.

"Gabriel's more than likely trying to talk Armani down from flying here himself. And since his plan was to send Marcello, his second-in-command, here to intercept you, Gabriel will need to also convince Armani not to do that."

"*Intercept* is a polite word for Marcello kidnapping me," I said as Alessandro removed the gun from the back of his jeans. "Those men, they—"

"They were hired hit men, more than likely. No one that would tie directly to who wants you dead," he finished, as if knowing where I'd planned to go with my line of thought even before I did.

"And how do you know they were hit men?" I set my back to the dresser, trying to get comfortable, but his overpowering presence in my room stamped out the possibility for that.

"Because it took me about four minutes to kill them, and if they hadn't been trained professionals, they'd have been dead in thirty seconds," he said flatly.

Before I could comprehend his words and ask how many dead bodies he'd racked up in his lifetime after the military, he started for the bathroom, gun still in hand.

I hesitantly followed him; he set the weapon on the vanity counter. You know, perfect place for that. Went great right alongside my pink hairbrush.

"You think Gabriel can convince Armani to trust you?" I asked while ducking down to grab a towel from the cabinet beneath the sink.

"Trust? No. But since I saved you, and someone on his team betrayed him, I bought us some time. Plus, my family name will give him . . . pause."

I was curious for him to elaborate, but when he didn't, I closed the cabinet and stood to face him, towel in hand that was as pink as my hairbrush. "And you also hope this saving-my-life thing will earn you a chance to marry me?"

The scowl cutting across his lips was probably from his disdain for marriage and not because he'd have to use a pink towel. But maybe I was coming around to the idea he was being honest, because his acting skills couldn't be that stellar.

"If you want to refer to the killing of three men who planned to play slice and dice with your body as a 'saving-your-life *thing*,' then yeah, that *incident* may help me get on Armani's better side. Not that he really has a good one."

"Nice image you painted." I raised my brows. "'Slice and dice'? Really?"

Angling his head, he leaned closer, the towel all that separated us. "What did you think those men planned to do with those knives? Show you their culinary skills?"

"You can be a real ass, huh?" *And there goes my attempt to be sweet instead of sour.*

"That 'ass' is trying to save your life, so maybe you could consider being less of a pain in mine." He righted his body, elongating his neck to show his six-plus-inch height advantage over me. But he also afforded me some much-needed breathing room. Because despite previously being outside, a little sweaty and now bloody, he still managed to come out smelling like masculinity and luxury bottled into the most intoxicating and expensive brand of cologne. And I kept wanting a dizzying whiff.

Alessandro reached around me, his arm brushing against my rigid body, then he forcefully shoved the shower curtain aside, clearly still irritated with my hot-and-cold attitude. But I was a vibe girl, and I tended to match the energy of those around me. And the man could go from asshole to hero and back again as fast as I could change things up.

"You know, for a charmer, like you were last night, you're—"

"I was only charming to try and get you in bed." He casually turned on the shower as if he hadn't just been incredibly blunt with me. "I'm leaving the door unlocked. If someone manages to get inside the house, come in and let me know. Got it?"

I nudged the towel against his chest. "Risk seeing you naked, or take my chances with an intruder? Those are my options?" Narrowing my eyes, I added, "Hmm. Tough choice." I could withhold the charm just as easily, dammit.

"Callie." His clipped tone had me flinching, but his baritone voice dropped into borderline silk as he followed up with, "You're not going to make this easy for me, are you?"

"What part?" I whispered as he finally accepted the towel.

"Being your husband." He shook his head and turned to the side. I went to the doorway only to stupidly turn around to see him discarding his phone and the towel to remove his shirt.

That was my cue to go. Not that I budged. He caught my eyes in the mirror, and I shamelessly moved my gaze to his rippling abs in the reflection. Arms made of steel. Strong shoulder blades and a touch of chest hair over those hard pecs.

He turned toward me, offering me an in-person view instead of just his reflection. I followed his hand, which was now at his belt buckle, finding the start of the happy trail above the leather belt. He popped the tail end out, slid his open hand across his waistline and grabbed the belt buckle, and swiftly pulled it free in one—*holy shit, that was hot*—move.

After the snap startled me, and he was looking at me like he wished he could take the belt to my ass, he casually tossed it to the floor. Without a hint of modesty or stain of red on his cheeks, he unbuttoned and unzipped his fly, allowing me to see his black briefs beneath. Well, something told me he was a briefs, not boxers, guy.

"Are you planning to watch me undress?" The dark finish in his voice jerked my attention away from his crotch.

"You did see me last night," I reminded him. "Well, *hints* of me." *Like my boobs.*

"You confuse the fuck out of me, you know that, right?" He called me out, and maybe I needed that.

Because who was this woman? "Makes two of us." At the feel of my lips crooking at the edges, I reached up to confirm the display of emotion there. "I'm smiling. Is there something wrong with me?" When his response was only a cocky grin, I added, "Heck, is something wrong with the both of us that we're bickering like an old married couple and now smiling after what went down?"

A dark brow shot up—you know, the sexy way Henry Cavill does it in movies? Yeah, like that. But somehow, it was even more just . . . well, *more*, in all caps.

"I know there's something wrong with me." One defined shoulder lifted with the perfect amount of casual effort. "But as for you? My guess is still shock."

I wish. "I, um, should be going now."

"Probably a good idea, Callie." The huskiness as he said my name managed to throttle my sense of awareness yet again.

I was standing in a bathroom with a shirtless and handsome guy, and no man had ever been in his spot before. I'd moved into the garden home only a month before finding out the dreaded news about Armani—two weeks after breaking up with my boyfriend.

"I'll be quick." That was his nudge for me to leave since I continued to stare at his bronzed chest, feeling like I could write a sonnet or two about his muscles.

"Okay," I mouthed, *finally* leaving. Once in the bedroom, I grabbed clean clothes from my dresser—cutoff jean shorts with my worn-out, favorite red tee that said NASH on it.

I caught sight of myself in the mirror atop the dresser and freed my hair from the bun. Using my fingers, I combed out the tangled locks since my brush was lucky to be sharing the same space with the naked stranger instead of me.

I bowed my head, hating the fact I still wasn't scared. Or nauseous. Or any of the things I should have been after the deadly encounter. Just oddly defiant, acting a little immature, and kind of turned on.

Thoughts of marriage to one of my father's men and being forced to produce a male heir had me sick last night. But death? Nope. *Not a DiMaggio. Not a . . .* My thoughts died at the sudden blare of my alarm.

My first instinct would have been to go to my lockbox, but with Alessandro there, I'd take my chances with him over a sidearm.

The bathroom door flung open before I had a chance to alert him. Gun in hand, towel around his waist, and eyes sharp on the door, he ordered, "Get in the bathroom and shut the door."

That was one directive I wouldn't argue with. Except, by the time I'd locked myself inside, the alarm went off as if someone knew the code. Only my shadow-guards had the passcode since Armani had forced me to provide it to them.

Not even a few seconds later, there was a loud thud inside the bedroom before Alessandro barked out, "Who hired you?"

A distinct back-and-forth began in Italian between the two men.

"Armani will kill me if he finds out about this," my *former* guard bellowed in English that time. *Pretty sure that's Dickhead Number Two.*

"What do you think I'll do to you if you don't talk?" Alessandro's threat sliced through the air. It was a low sound that curled around my limbs, giving me goose bumps. "I'll make you a deal. I'll give you a head start to run if you give me a name." He tacked on the offer, his tone menacing. "Who. Hired. You?"

"I don't know. That's the truth. You can torture me all you want. It won't do you any good. Whoever *forced* my hand in helping him has to be someone from the inside to know about Armani's daughter. Not many do."

Unable to stop myself, I opened the door, and Alessandro had the guard on the floor face down. The man's cheek was to the carpet, and with one knee on the floor alongside him, Alessandro's towel somehow remained snug in place.

"And so you came here to finish the job since those three hit men failed?" I joined in, doing my best to remain calm.

He tried to squirm, to shift on the floor to get a better look at me. "I didn't know you were with someone in the park. You're always alone." The balls on that man to talk about having me killed had me going for him, losing whatever chill I had in me.

Alessandro was on his feet in a second, winding an arm around my back to stop me from going after the traitor.

"I should've done the job myself. Snuck in at night and suffocated you with your pillow," he tossed out while going into a push-up position to rise, but Alessandro let me go to handle him.

"Suffocate her?" Alessandro smashed my guard's nose and mouth to the carpet with enough force that'd soon have him unable to breathe. "Oh, the things I want to do you." He switched to Italian as if not wanting me to hear whatever dark words he shared.

The guy was gasping for air, so I went over to Alessandro and tugged at his arm. "You'll kill him before he can answer you."

Alessandro turned his attention on me, then blinked as if freeing himself from some kind of drug-induced stupor, and he let go of the back of the guy's neck and stood. Without losing hold of his weapon, he secured his towel, hissing something again in Italian to the guard, but then let go of his words when a familiar voice began yelling from outside.

"It's my neighbor," I told him, unsure what to do.

Alessandro tipped his head toward the window. "Handle him from here."

I nodded and sidestepped the two men, still in disbelief at everything that'd happened that morning. Once I had the blinds and window up, and with the screen missing, I stuck my head out. "All good! False alarm." I waited for my neighbor to step off my porch to put eyes on me. "Sorry for the disturbance."

The old man craned his neck and shielded his eyes with his free hand. And yup, he had the shotgun in the other, in broad daylight. "You interrupted my morning shows," he grumbled, then waved me off in frustration.

Thankful that was over quickly, I returned the window and blinds back in place and faced the room.

"I need to gag and tie him up," Alessandro said, and I whirled around. He was looking at me as if asking where I kept the duct tape and rope. "I'd torture him myself, but I'll wind up killing him."

Yeah, that I believe.

"I'll leave it to Armani's people to do," he added before I answered his unspoken question.

"The garage should have what you need." *Thankfully, it's attached.*

Alessandro hooked his arm under the guard's and dragged him up to his feet. "Stay put," he warned me before leaving.

Noticing the floor lamp on its side, I fixed it upright, then looked around in search of my phone. I'd forgotten to take it on my walk with Alessandro showing up as scheduled earlier.

Finding it still attached to the charger but on the floor by the bed, I crouched and grabbed it. It was still on silent mode, so I flipped on the volume.

Five missed calls from The Asshole. Plus two texts from him as well.

THE ASSHOLE: I know what happened and that you're okay. Answer your fucking phone. You need to come home. Now.

Italy would never be my home, and I hated that man for ruining such a beautiful country for me.

Brittney Sahin

THE ASSHOLE: You're still in danger. I don't know who betrayed me yet. You can't stay there any longer. You have no choice but to become who you were meant to be. A DiMaggio.

I searched for the emotions I was *supposed* to have. Trying to locate the fear. Trying to remember the girl my aunt raised and not the DiMaggio trying to break free from the confines of this shell of a body.

I wasn't him. I wasn't evil.

At the realization I was no longer alone, with no clue how much time had passed, I looked over to see Alessandro filling the doorway, quietly observing me with folded arms and a sexy lean to complete the dominating look.

"That was fast."

Narrowed eyes skated over my body, and the heat in his gaze now matched whatever fire he'd just lit inside me with one simple look. "If I had stayed around him any longer, I'd remember what he wanted to do with your pillow."

Why'd I get the feeling he would've enjoyed killing the man? *Maybe you would.*

"I need to let Gabriel know the situation." He shoved away from the doorframe and headed for the bathroom, giving me a chance to check out his strong back and muscular calves.

"Armani called," I said once he returned to the bedroom, holding his phone. "I didn't answer. But looks like Gabriel already told him about the attack in the park."

"According to Gabriel's last text," he said while typing, "he's at least convinced Armani to allow me to escort you to Italy. And Armani doesn't have many options, considering one of his loyal men betrayed him." He stopped texting and looked up at me. "Plus, I'm a Costa, and even though my family doesn't exactly play well with the mafia, or any criminal for that matter, he knows I'd never hurt you."

I strode closer to him as he chucked his phone on my bed and started for his suitcase. "Except Gabriel?" I reminded him. "You're playing nice with him."

"That's different. A debt owed. And for a criminal, he's—"

"Hard to hate?"

He took one knee by his bag and unzipped it, tossing a look at me from over his shoulder. "So he has that effect on you, too?"

"Yeah," I admitted. "The only one of Armani's men who doesn't make my skin crawl. Kind eyes, and his wife has always been really nice to me." A few more chance steps his way as he rose to his full height. Quite the wardrobe change.

He threw the pants, shirt, and suit jacket onto the bed, and the pile landed atop his phone. "Some people are born bad." With his strong hands resting on his hips above that towel, eyes on the floor, he added, "Not Gabriel. He had a good heart. Was taken down the wrong path and got lost. It's my fault. We lost touch in high school, and he joined DiMaggio's organization shortly after that."

"You can't blame yourself. But maybe this is your chance to help him find his way back to the right side?"

He whipped his focus up, looking at me as if I'd asked him to bring back the dead instead.

When he remained quiet, I walked over to him, my eyes now glued south of his navel. I'd swear his dick was beginning to pitch the towel. Of course, I had to go and blurt, "Does fighting turn you on?" *Eyes back up,* I reminded myself, only to wish I hadn't looked up. The intensity greeting me in his gaze sent me back a step.

"I feel like if I answer that honestly I might scare you," he remarked darkly, "and I'd say you've been through enough today."

Pretty sure you just gave me your answer. "So of all the things to scare me today, you think admitting killing men and tying up a guy in my garage makes you hard is what will finally push me over the edge?"

"You're right, scared seems to be the last thing you are, even if it should be." He quietly studied me, allowing the moment to marinate to the point my knees were on the verge of buckling. "But now I'm curious . . . Does fighting turn *you* on?"

"Never before," I whispered before I could trap it between my lips, allowing him to read between the lines.

He cupped my chin, and I was at his mercy, unable to budge or look away. "If things were different, I'd . . ." His shoulders dipped a touch, as if weighed down by regret. "You're my assignment. And soon you'll be my wife, so we can't."

"I didn't recall asking." I swallowed. "But *if* I wind up marrying you temporarily, what will you do with me as your wife?"

"Not fuck this attitude out of you." That *fuck* hung in the air, heavy and strong, like I could reach out and grab it. Put my hands on it. Hell, taste it. "But I will protect you." His brows snapped together. "I should get dressed."

"Worried the towel will fall again, and I'll discover the rumor about big hands isn't true?"

A cocky grin tugged at his lips. "You can't help yourself, can you?" He let go of my chin only to swipe the pad of his thumb along the contour of my cheek while staring at me. "This mouth of yours worries me. The trouble it might bring."

"Well, you seem to be the only one who inspires these reactions from me."

His hand at my cheek slipped into my messy hair, and he cupped the back of my head, lowering his mouth to my ear. "Lucky for you I know just what to do with that mouth and how to keep it quiet when need be."

Oh, fuckity fuck fuck. The man lit a match with those words, and the intense heat went straight to my sex.

He brought his face back around, boldly staring at me. "Get your mind out of the gutter, sweetheart." A dark smile sat on his lips. "You're off-limits, remember?" He winked. The asshole. "But that doesn't mean you biting down on my belt wouldn't be a good look for you."

CHAPTER EIGHT

Alessandro

"I need to make a call before we leave." Standing inside the private hangar at the Nashville International Airport, I directed her to board without me, but she didn't follow orders. Not that I was surprised.

"To whom? Gabriel again?" The distrust in her tone had me taking a second to remind myself she barely knew me, or anything about my family. She'd witnessed me kill three people and tie up another, and then my control nearly snapped and I almost begged her to let me fuck that sassy little mouth of hers. So I supposed she should be on guard around me.

"Calling my family. I need to let them know about this, uh, new job sooner than anticipated."

She fidgeted with the buttons of her jean jacket, a sign her attitude was taking a back seat to her nerves. "And what will they say to all of this?"

I knew what Constantine would say, which was why he wouldn't be on the call. But Enzo? The second he learned I'd be tying the knot he'd bust my balls. And Izzy would lecture me. Lay into me hard. Harder than I had when my brothers and I scared off her last asshole boyfriend, who went by the name "just Pablo"—just a mistake on her part, in my opinion.

Callie's big eyes lifted my way as she waited for me to answer. She'd showered since the murder spree in the park. Then packed and unpacked her suitcase for Italy a half dozen times while we'd waited for the guard to be removed from her place by someone Gabriel trusted so we could leave.

In her leggings, tank top, and jean jacket, without any makeup and her hair still damp around her face, the woman looked way too fucking young for me. Hell, twenty-nine was still south of my preferred number.

Throw in the little music-note studs in her ears adding to her innocence, and I probably should've been considering tucking her in with a bedtime story on the jet instead of the spanking the dark part of my mind wanted to give her. Which was weird, because that was surprisingly not my thing. But something about this woman made my palm twitch.

She'd been right in her bedroom, though. I did usually have sex after fighting. But with this woman? Hell no. She gave new meaning to the term *off-limits*. I'd be keeping a safe distance from my wife once we were back in the US.

"Tongue-tied again," she said, shattering thoughts of my handprint on her ass. "Guess you're afraid to tell your family your assignment involves marrying the daughter of Armani DiMaggio."

"Something like that." I needed to cool off before I had to jerk off. "My mother's going to have my head when she finds out. Old school. Not a fan of divorce."

"Sounds like my aunt." Her eyes went wide a beat later. "Shit. My aunt. What will I tell her?" Her hands flew in the air, and she began waving them around while talking. *There's that Italian in you.* "She's going to freak out. She'll cancel her three-month see-the-world-on-a-cruise trip she's saved up her entire life for and try and come save me. And I don't want her going anywhere near that monster and—"

"She doesn't need to know. Maybe we can be done with this before she's even home. Okay?" I grabbed hold of her shoulder with my free hand.

So far, from what I could tell, there were two sides to this woman. Calm, collected, defiant, and unshakable at the sight of murder. And then there was this one—spiraling, panicked, wide-eyed, and rambling.

"Then we have until mid-August. That's when she'll be back in Nashville."

Her breathing slowed a bit to a normal pace at my words, and her light-green eyes found mine.

I had to resist the urge to murmur, *That's a good girl. Just breathe for me. Relax.* And there went my dick, ready to spring into action like a dog being offered a treat. What was wrong with me?

"August. Sounds like the perfect month for a divorce." I forced a smile, even gave a little tooth with it, which was rare, hoping to keep her on the calm train.

"This is all . . ."

"Madness, I know," I finished for her, thinking about what had gone down today. If I hadn't shown up at her house before her walk, the woman would be dead. And I couldn't allow myself to go to that dark place. The woman drove me nuts already, but the idea of anything happening to her was unacceptable.

Thankfully, she hadn't given me pushback on flying to Italy, and Gabriel had managed to get a cleanup crew to the park before the bodies had been discovered. Armani's people would work on interrogating the guard I'd tied up in her garage, to determine the truth.

In the meantime, I needed to convince my family to get on board with the plan, and then do something I sure as hell didn't want to do—ask my old man to make a call to The League in Italy for an alliance with one of their enemies.

I preferred to handle everything myself, but since Dad was former League, he was now our best shot at recruiting their help while I stuck by Callie's side to keep an eye on her.

"It'll be okay." I found myself attempting to reassure her when she went back to fidgeting with her buttons. I was two seconds away from helping her remove the jacket and shirt altogether if she didn't stop.

"Sure," she mumbled, then finally did as I'd asked and boarded the jet.

Once alone, I FaceTimed Enzo.

He picked up on the second ring, but when he answered, he had his daughter, Chiara, wrapped up in his arms. "What's up? You okay?"

"I'm about to invite Izzy and Hudson to join the call. I'll fill you in together," I quickly explained.

"Not Constantine, too?" Enzo asked as I dialed in the others.

"No, not yet." At the weird hitch in my voice, his wife must've clocked it, too, because she appeared on screen next to him.

Maria gave me a little nervous smile while taking Chiara, sensing the call wasn't meant for my niece.

"Hey, stranger," Izzy said, popping onto the call.

Hudson still hadn't answered, which was strange since he was the only one clued in on the situation. But not even a second later, he appeared on camera—well, in the same frame as my sister.

"Why are you two together? And at *her* condo?" *At least you're not wearing his shirt or something.* I'd probably blow a fucking gasket.

Hudson cursed under his breath while giving Izzy his signature scowl. When he returned his focus to the screen, he shared, "She stopped by my bar earlier, and I happened to be working on something for you in my office, and you know her, she's curious. Snatched my laptop from me, and—"

"I made him talk," Izzy cut him off. "Anyway, are you seriously getting married?"

"Wait, what?" Enzo had been chewing on something, and from the looks of it, he was now choking.

Maria appeared on camera, Chiara no longer in her arms, to slap his back.

"I'm fine, I'm fine," Enzo promised, clutching his throat for a second. "Just shocked."

"Marriage?" Maria asked, opting to stay on the call.

"He's marrying Armani DiMaggio's daughter this week." Izzy bit the bullet for me, and I was going to knock Hudson out for cracking so easily when she'd pressed him for intel. The man had been a Navy SEAL and had withstood interrogation by the worst of the worst and had never given up shit, but all it took was my little sister to get him to talk.

Hudson grimaced, shooting me an apologetic look, reading my thoughts.

"And who's Armani? And more importantly, who's his daughter?" Maria asked, pointing her curious brown eyes at my brother.

"Consider him mafia royalty," Enzo told her. "The king of the oldest criminal group still in existence in Sicily." He faced the screen again. "But I thought when he died, there'd be no more living DiMaggios. Since when does he have a daughter? And what do you mean you're marrying her?" Before he let me finish, he shook his head and cursed a few of the more colorful Italian words he reserved for situations such as these. Not that I'd ever thought this situation would happen to me.

Marriage. Fuck.

"Gabriel. This is Gabriel's doing," Enzo said, putting two and two together. "Why? How?" He turned to Maria, whispered something in her ear, and she left. He didn't want her hearing more, and I didn't blame him. He was always doing his best to keep his wife safely away from the darkness of our world.

"Armani found out last year that his lifelong mistress, Christie Anderson, has a daughter and that he's the father. She'll be thirty next month, and originally, he gave her until thirty-five to marry and produce an heir," I revealed. "But he found out his lifespan isn't what he hoped it'd be, and he's lost his patience. He's forcing her to marry *this* week."

"And this involves you how?" Enzo was still the only one not in the know. Well, aside from Constantine. And I had to assume Izzy hadn't told him anything, or he'd already have taken our other jet to fly straight to me.

"Because the man he's going to force her to marry is Rocco Barone."
I let the words sink in the way I had for Hudson yesterday. Gave Enzo
time to digest the news. "I'm going to convince Armani that I should
marry his daughter instead. Make it worth his while. That'll piss Rocco
off, put a target on my head, and he'll come for me. We'll save her and
get Rocco, and with any luck, his father. This is our chance to finish the
only job we've ever *not* completed."

Enzo closed his eyes, his breathing picking up, more curses falling
from his lips.

"We need the help of The League to make this work, though," I
shared. "Promise a truce between The League and Armani's organization
if he allows me to marry his daughter." I went over the rest of the plan
next. Explaining how Callie would hand over the reins to Gabriel once
her father died (prematurely at my hand while blaming some unlucky
bastard-criminal for his murder) and then . . . I'd be free of the marriage.

"Constantine should know," Enzo said in a determined tone, opening his eyes. "*But* once he does, he won't let you do this, will he?"

"Right." Guilt weighed me down about keeping secrets from
Constantine, but it was for his own good. "Which is why he can't
know until I'm already married. And I need you to convince Dad of
that. Can you do that for me?" I hated asking for Enzo's help when he'd
only found out last month his wife was pregnant with twins, but what
choice did I have?

"I'll fly to New York tonight. This conversation needs to happen in
person," Enzo agreed. "And then we should join you in Italy. We can't
let you go into Armani's home without backup."

"We have to make this work." *Failure's not an option.*

"For Constantine. To get Rocco." Enzo nodded.

"And to save this girl's life," Izzy added. "From what Hudson told
me, she's an innocent. Not like her dad. So protecting her is also part
of the job."

Izzy balanced out the darkness in us. When we'd created our
new security firm, we'd been reluctant for her to join. She went from

managing billion-dollar brands to managing us during covert missions. But she'd been right to join. Having her in our ears on comms, as well as being our voice of reason from time to time so we didn't go over the edge, was, well, nice.

I held the front of my throat, pinching at the skin there, thoughts drifting to Little Miss Tennessee Whiskey. "Keeping her safe is the main job, yes."

"You . . . like her, don't you?" Why was Izzy asking me that? Hell, *whispering* that in a state of shock.

"Don't be ridiculous. I barely know her, and this is me we're talking about."

"Mmm-hmm." Izzy lifted her brows a few times, clearly trying to fuck with me. "Wait until Mom finds out her forever bachelor son is getting married and plans to divorce by—"

"August," I blurted. "That's how long Callie will give me." Plus, she had to go back to teaching in the fall, so the timeline made the most sense. "I only need to survive three months of marriage. Hell, it's not even a full three months." I gulped a bit too hard. "I can do this. I can give up my freedom for the summer."

An unexpected soft chuckle left my sister's lips. "Or maybe, just maybe, you'll fall in love with your wife."

CHAPTER NINE

Alessandro

In the Air

"Will you tell me about your family?" Callie's southern voice was softer than normal, like she was asking for a truce between the little back-and-forth war.

I stared at her sitting across from me, knowing I needed to pour water, not gasoline, onto the fire between us to make the rest of the flight comfortable. But my damn mouth seemed to enjoy getting me in the same kind of trouble hers did, because I sarcastically remarked, "I thought you already did research on me."

Unbuckling and squirming a bit as if her ass hurt from the sting of my palm that'd only swatted her in my head, she brought her knee to her chest like a shield. *No, sweetheart, that won't save you from me.* Only *I* could save her from me, which was why I needed to keep my distance somehow.

"Can't really know a person, like *really* know them, from a simple online search." Since she'd come back at my vinegar with sugar, I opted to not be a dick in response.

"How about we trade biographies, then? I should know a little more about you if we're going to sell the marriage idea to your old man."

Her nose wrinkled in repugnance. "First, you should know I call him The Asshole." She used air quotes to describe dear old Dad, which was another cute thing for her to do that was fucking with me.

But I didn't fall for cute. Well, to be fair, I didn't fall at all.

"Noted." My attention guiltily fell to my palm, knowing I'd never set a hand on this woman, not even if she begged. Not even a slap on that ass of hers. Okay, fuck, *maybe* if she begged. "And secondly?" I cleared my throat, trying to pull my head from the gutter, where hers had been earlier in her bedroom. Well, I was enough of an arrogant asshole to assume she'd imagined my cock in her mouth as a way to shut her up when I'd nearly said as much. The blush on her cheeks had told me she'd wanted that to happen, too.

"Secondly, I don't think we have to play pretend that we had some love-at-first-sight thing." She ran her hands through her wild, messy hair. "We only need to ensure he believes you're the better choice than Rocco, right?"

Fair enough. Plus playing pretend will lead to sex. I could feel it in my bones, and I couldn't let that happen. *You're an assignment.* "So that means we don't need to swap details about ourselves, then."

She waved her finger like I was her student. Fuck if I'd ever had a teacher like her growing up. "I still want details."

"Fine," I relented. Giving in to a woman wasn't my normal go-to reaction. "What do you want to know about my family?" I didn't talk about myself, not unless I was paying my therapist $400 an hour to do it. Even then, she did most of the talking. I had issues. What could I say?

"Well." Dropping both feet to the floor, she gripped her thighs. "I'm worried I'll scare you off with any too-forward questions."

"Yeah, I might jump from the jet without a chute if you try and dig too deeply. I do frighten easily."

The smile she gave me was worth every second of my smartassery. *Fuck my life. I will not have sex with you.*

"Have you ever jumped from a plane?" No lip-chewing this time. Just a kill-me-now swipe of her tongue along the seam of her mouth. "Wait. Army Ranger. You probably did."

I nodded. "Back to my family." I'd rather talk about them than myself, including my time in the military.

"Okay." She unbuttoned her jean jacket and removed it.

Yes, great idea. Because so help me, this woman in a tank top with tits like hers would destroy my focus.

"You okay?" she whispered, reading me perfectly.

"Not even a little bit," I snapped out, which was not what I'd wanted to say, dammit. "I'm just not a fan of . . . sharing."

"Listen, if you don't want to—"

"It's fine." My shoulders drew together, my back muscles tense. "I have an older brother. Constantine. Well, not much older. I'll be forty next month, and he's just north of that number." I looked out the little window; we were well above the clouds now. "Even though our father is very much in our life, Constantine still takes on that role. He's a good man." I swallowed. "And my younger brother, Enzo, is a chef in Charlotte. He's married to the love of his life. Adopted his wife's daughter, Chiara. And they have twins on the way." My eyes fell closed when I thought about the fact I now only had one sister. "Isabella, although everyone but Hudson calls her Izzy, is the youngest. She's spunky, opinionated, has horrible taste in men, and now works with us at our side gig."

"And who's Hudson?"

I hadn't realized I'd even dropped his name. "Navy SEAL. Best friend to Constantine. Former FBI. Now owns a bar and also works with us." I went ahead and finished the painful part before she could ask. "And you already know about Bianca, Enzo's twin sister. She was murdered, and it was connected to my mother's side of the family." *And here's a little bit of news you won't like.* "My mother's family . . . they're mafia. But no connection to the DiMaggios." I'd made sure. Not that

I would have sex with Callie, but I had to ensure there was zero chance we were even remotely related before this plan went through.

"That's—"

"Why I don't like sharing." I filled my cheeks with air, giving her a clear sign I was frustrated and not able to hide it, then let the breath go. "Your turn. How'd you wind up growing up in Nashville?"

"Well." She squirmed in her seat again, when what she needed to do was squirm on my lap, get my cock hard again to distract me from my dark past with sex.

Maybe I'm the problem, not her. I was the one running hot and cold when it came to her, and she simply mirrored my behavior. And now my therapist had to be taking over my thoughts, because I couldn't possibly have psychoanalyzed myself like that, given my current state.

"My aunt was living in Nashville at the time I was born, so I grew up there," she finally went on, as if knowing my simmering thoughts needed a moment to settle first.

"You don't call your aunt Mom." I wasn't sure why I'd pointed that out, but . . .

"My mother told Tia she didn't want me to call Tia that. She said Tia could raise me, but she still saw herself as my mother, even though I never did."

"Did your mother visit?"

She held up her palm and wiggled her fingers. "Maybe five times since I was born. Never long enough for me to get to know her, which probably made it easier when she'd take off again."

"Oh." Yeah, that was my brilliant response. I was a work in progress on the showing-emotions thing when it came to anyone outside my family. Not that this woman ever needed a front-row seat to my emotions or the chaos in my mind. *Assignment. A job. The marriage would be a means to an end.* Why in the hell did I need to keep reminding myself of that?

Her hand went to her lap, and she fidgeted with the silver ring on her right hand, spinning it around. "When my mother died in an accident last year, my aunt took me to the funeral in Stockholm. It was my first time out of the country, but my grandparents were born and raised in Sweden, and Christie—my, uh, mother—had said when it was her time, she wanted to be buried in the same cemetery as her parents."

"I'm sorry for your loss."

She surrendered a little shrug. "Armani recognized my aunt, then he looked at me, and it was game over. He remembered when my mother left him as his mistress thirty years ago. She wasn't going to have me, but Aunt Tia couldn't have kids and begged her to let her raise me. And after I was born, she ran right back into that man's arms. Well, she was with him whenever her band wasn't traveling Europe. She was a singer."

"Is that why you never pursued music professionally? You didn't want to be like her?"

"A little bit, yeah. But in my twenties, it felt like there was a piece of me missing, and I finally gave in to my passion. I devoured anything and everything I could music-related and never looked back." She let go of her ring and gripped the chair's arms. "But yeah, Armani forced me to get bloodwork after the funeral, and that was when I discovered why she really abandoned me."

"And he's been the bane of your existence ever since."

"Yup, and this is the first time I've talked about this with anyone other than Aunt Tia."

"How'd your aunt handle the aftermath of Armani finding out?"

"I used to tease my aunt for being so paranoid my whole life. No listed number. No social media, either. Turns out, she was trying to protect us from Armani and not just worried Big Brother was listening in. Once the cat was out of the bag—God, I hate that saying—she blamed herself for taking me to the funeral and dug in her heels even deeper on the whole paranoid and overprotective thing."

"So what changed?" *Because something must've, or she wouldn't be on a cruise now.*

"She said she had a plan for before Armani tried to force my hand at marriage. Some former military guys she knew in Kentucky who'd help out, and she wouldn't tell me how." She shrugged. "Anyway, I forced her to take the dream trip she'd been planning for forever, reminding her I had time and protection—whether I wanted protection or not."

The more I heard, the more I liked her aunt.

"Just sounds so strange when I say everything aloud. Like how can this be my life?"

"I ask myself that almost every day about my own," I slipped and admitted.

"You do?" Her brows lifted in surprise.

I shifted in my seat, shocked at how candid I'd been with her. "Maybe we should talk about something else now instead?" My suggestion came out a bit rough, probably more like a demand. "I think you should know about Rocco Barone. Why he's so dangerous." I needed to focus on the mission. "In case you have any doubts about me as who you should marry, you should—"

"I don't want to get married, and I'll do my best not to let that happen."

"Ditto," I rasped, eyes meeting hers again. "But Rocco, you should know about him anyway." She nodded, and I took that as my cue to give her the CliffsNotes version that was inside the envelope I'd given her, which she'd yet to read. "Rocco's family is in the business of war. They're hired by everyone from corporations to terrorist groups to create conflicts in certain regions."

"I teach history, so I can guess why."

"War is a profitable business for some." And that was the messy truth. "It can also create instability and a power vacuum, and there's usually someone looking to fill that space, and they're willing to do what it takes to get that power. Rocco's father has been in this business since the 1980s. Rocco is being groomed to take over, but he's a sadistic son of a bitch and takes pleasure in being the one to help create conflict. There's no man, woman, or child that will stand in his way from completion of a job."

Her eyelashes fluttered closed at the truth, but she needed to hear it.

"His family is Italian, but no one knows where they currently live. Heavily protected. Always moving around. But an alliance through marriage with the oldest mafia group in Italy, and well, all of Europe, would make them truly unstoppable. So there are many reasons this man *cannot* become your husband. Not to mention the fact he'd take you off the grid."

"Well, you said you won't let that happen, so I guess it's time I start trusting you to keep your word."

CHAPTER TEN

Calliope

Catania, Sicily

"I thought Gabriel would be here. Where is he?" Alessandro blocked my path down the steps with his body, not ready to trust the men waiting for us.

The Monday morning sunlight fell overhead, and I had to shield my eyes when peeking around him to see if I recognized the goons Armani had sent. "Frankie," I said under my breath, not a fan of my father's guard who shared an uncanny resemblance to Sylvester Stallone circa the 1990s.

Frankie broke through a pack of five other guards and hung back at the bottom of the steps.

"Gabriel's back at the estate. He's in a meeting with Mr. DiMaggio about the information we learned." I was kind of surprised Frankie had bothered to speak English for me, considering from what I remembered he deplored anything and everything American.

"What new information?" I piped up before the six-one (maybe six-two?) blockade of muscle before me could. My knees were weaker than my stomach right now, so I snatched hold of the railing at my side.

It was three in the morning Nashville time, so my body was trying to remind me where I belonged, and it wasn't on a tarmac in Sicily.

Frankie answered, "Not for me to say." He beckoned us with a flick of his wrist, waving us over to three blacked-out SUVs. Tinted-to-the-max windows. Black rims. Not a lick of silver in sight on the Escalades. "We have a little over an hour drive. Let's not keep Mr. DiMaggio waiting."

Alessandro turned to the side, and I was still holding the railing with both hands like I was a mermaid with new legs, unsure how to use them. Okay, maybe it was more than fatigue hitting me. I was about to face Armani and potentially marry either Alessandro or a psychopath. Reality of my hell had caught up with me, and hard.

"You good?" That almost sounded like genuine concern from him. When he removed his Ray-Bans, there were no signs of exhaustion in his eyes. Of course, he'd dozed on and off on the plane, which had oddly frustrated me that he'd been able to sleep upright and so soundly. He'd offered me his bedroom, but the bed had only been good for tossing and turning.

My continued tight grip on the railing was all the answer he needed, and he surprised me by setting a hand over one of mine. I thought he'd planned to unglue my death hold, but he simply stood there, his touch like a quiet offer of support—a take-your-time gesture I hadn't expected.

"It's time," Frankie hollered, but Alessandro didn't move, continuing to protectively shield anyone from coming close to me.

I looked up at him, the light catching my eyes since I hadn't had the foresight to bring sunglasses. "We should go."

He dipped his mouth near my ear. "I won't let them hurt you."

I had a feeling the sweet side of this man could destroy my heart as fast as the dark side could destroy me in the bedroom. "Thank you."

He met my eyes again, a hint of a smile on his face at how easily I'd managed to get the gratitude out, since I'd been a bit more of a brat about it back in Tennessee.

"I'm ready. Let's go." *Hopefully, I can walk and not collapse.*

"Calliope," Frankie hollered.

"Don't use that name," Alessandro warned, his hand leaving mine as he slipped on his shades and faced Frankie. "She doesn't like it."

Frankie didn't challenge him, which was a surprise, and instead he asked, "Are you armed?"

Releasing the railing, I followed Alessandro down the steps, where he gave a handgun to Frankie. The man clearly didn't trust us, because he motioned to two men to pat us down up against an Escalade.

"You can check me." Alessandro blocked me yet again when the two guards came over to us. "But you touch her, and you lose the use of both your hands."

The men looked to Frankie for their cue.

"What do you think Armani will do to you if you feel up his daughter?" Alessandro drilled in another point to prevent the men from groping me in search of a weapon.

"Fine," Frankie bit out, then Alessandro willingly went up against the Escalade so the two men could check him.

"He's clear," one guy said, then opened the back door to the SUV.

"Get inside, *Principessa*." I wasn't a fan of that name from Frankie either, but I kept quiet, not wanting to start trouble at the airport.

Once our bags were in the trunk and Alessandro and I were in the back seats, Frankie joined our SUV, sitting in the passenger seat, then motioned to the driver to get going.

Alessandro gave me a little nod, letting me know he had my back, which he so clearly did, and then I peered out the window, quietly taking in the view as we drove, only the sounds of Italian music over the radio filling the space.

After about an hour of being chauffeured from the airport in Catania, driving past Mount Etna and the beautiful area of Taormina, then through Savoca, where *The Godfather* had been filmed, we finally made it to Messina. Messina was in northeast Sicily, only separated from mainland Italy by a strait.

A few months ago, when we made it to the Italian history section of the World History class I taught, I found myself doing a little extra digging about the land, specifically looking into Sicily, given my new connection to the place.

"You know, Messina's rumored to be the location where Odysseus barely escaped Scylla and Charybdis," I blurted, unsure why I'd chosen to break the comfortable quiet with a random fact about our current whereabouts.

"The story of Scylla and Charybdis," Alessandro began, meeting my eyes without giving me a WTF look for my out-of-the-blue remark, "is also about having to choose the lesser of two evils."

I hadn't expected him to know that story or to connect the dots as to what I was pretty sure I was suggesting without saying it—marriage to him being the lesser of the two evils in my case. "And it's also been said that the muse for *The Odyssey* was—"

"Calliope," he finished for me.

I fiddled with my silver ring, keeping my eyes on my lap. "A cruel joke on my mom's part to name me as such, given where Armani's from, right?"

"She chose the name hoping you'd have her voice." Frankie joined in on our private conversation, damn him. "Well, I've heard Armani assume Christie wanted you to have a siren's voice, like Calliope." He twisted on his seat and looked back at me. "Although Calliope was mythological . . . and you're very much real." His dark eyes cut over me, and I shifted uncomfortably beneath his gaze.

Alessandro took off his glasses, preparing to use those eyes as weapons to stare down Frankie. He set a hand on the back of Frankie's seat, demanding the man's attention. When they began speaking in Italian, it was clear the men were arguing, and it was growing intense and heated.

"How'd you know about the siren?" I reached for Alessandro's forearm, hoping to redirect his focus so he didn't find himself in trouble before we even arrived. "And Scylla and Charybdis?"

Alessandro abandoned whatever he'd been saying in Italian, and in a heartbreaking tone answered, "Bianca." Shades back on, he let go of the front seat and leaned back.

"I'm sorry." Fidgeting with my ring again, I thought back to my research on Bianca.

"She was a history buff like you. Well, only when it came to Greek and Roman mythology, at least," Alessandro revealed. "She used to talk about that stuff all the time. For some reason, I remember."

Of course you would. You loved her, and then lost her. I kept those thoughts to myself, worried Frankie would speak up and antagonize the man about the loss of his sister, and I was fairly certain that'd send Alessandro over the edge. "Armani's home is a castle. Well, a replica." Subject changes weren't my specialty, but I'd do my best if it meant keeping the peace in the SUV.

"Replica castle?" I could hear the *thank you* in Alessandro's tone for the new topic.

"It's a replica of *Castel dell'Ovo*, also known as the Castle of the Egg. For a family obsessed with being Sicilian, it's surprising they chose to imitate a castle from Naples with Norman origins." I shared what I knew. "Armani even buried an egg on the site of the place, just like at the real castle."

"Legend has it," Frankie said, not sounding as asshole-y as he'd been before, "that if the egg breaks, not just the castle but the city will fall."

"That was for the real one in Naples," I reminded Frankie, unsure why I'd bothered to reengage with the man.

Frankie twisted around. "You saved the egg from breaking in this case, *Principessa*. If not for your existence, the DiMaggios' bloodline would be over. The castle would fall."

"Almost there," the driver announced. I wasn't sure who he was, but he caught my eyes in the rearview mirror, and something told me he was less of a jerk than Frankie.

Thankfully, Frankie faced forward and didn't continue a history lesson I didn't want from him about the bloodline.

The SUV rolled up to a set of ornate black and gold gates, and once they parted and we were on the property, I unbuckled, my anticipation, or more like dread, growing for what was to come.

It was a long drive from the gate to the front of the property, but a frustratingly pretty one with all the flowers and trees cocooning us on the ride.

Once parked out front of the castle, the driver came around and opened the door for me. "Thanks," I tossed out awkwardly.

"I'm Leonardo, but you can call me Leo." He was probably fifty or so and looked nothing like the only two Leonardos I was familiar with, DaVinci and DiCaprio. But he was the second man at the estate who had kind eyes, and the first was en route to us now. Gabriel.

"Sure," I said to Leo as Alessandro came up alongside me, a hand moving to the small of my back, which managed to comfort me.

The men wordlessly followed Gabriel's order to head inside, and then Gabriel strode our way. He gave off Keanu Reeves vibes from the movie *The Matrix* with his slicked-back, black hair and dark clothes. I felt like I was stuck inside a matrix and ready to escape this nightmare. "Sorry I couldn't meet you."

He didn't reach for Alessandro's hand in greeting once it was just the three of us, but why would he? They weren't friends anymore, right? This was a debt owed for Alessandro.

"Not a fan of the assholes you sent to pick us up," Alessandro remarked, keeping his hand on my back, even though said assholes were gone from sight.

"You talk with The League? Your family? They on board with the plan?" Gabriel asked, not addressing Alessandro's comment.

"What, like the Justice League? I mean . . ." I turned toward Alessandro, and he lowered his hand. "Superman and Batman are in it, so . . ." At Alessandro removing his shades and shooting me a surprised look, I refocused and remembered where we were: not in a comic book but inside my own personal nightmare. "The League? Who are they?"

"My family leaves today for Sicily," Alessandro said instead, as if it'd be a waste of his breath to explain. "And my father spoke with Emilia Calibrisi, the head of The League in Italy, two hours ago."

When Alessandro hadn't been staring at me with frustration on the plane, and I hadn't been tossing and turning while he snoozed, he'd been glued to his phone. So it wasn't a shocking revelation to discover this news. It would've been more surprising had Alessandro shared it with me before.

"I need to speak to Emilia myself, but my dad believes The League will have our backs," Alessandro went on when I didn't interject and demand more information, and I was pretty sure he'd been half expecting me to. "So what news did you find out that kept you from coming to the airport yourself?"

"The men who interrogated the guard back in Tennessee were able to get him to talk." Gabriel folded his arms, studying me. The man really did just need that full-length leather coat to complete the whole Neo persona from *The Matrix* look. "When the guard learned Armani's plan to force Calliope to marry this week, he reached out to Armani's rival in Rome—let him know about an heir to the throne and for the right price, he'd give her up. Give you up, I mean."

Right. I'm standing here. This is my life we're talking about. "You're saying Armani's rivals tried to have me killed?"

"Yeah, and that gives Alessandro a better shot at your hand in marriage now," Gabriel said, eyes back on Alessandro.

"How? I don't follow." I asked him, turning his way to demand his attention and answers, "What is it?"

"I need to kill the man responsible for your attempted murder—I have to take down the head of the Esposito mafia family in Rome," Alessandro said, his tone almost too casual for me to handle.

"Premeditated murder is different from saving my life in the park yesterday." I grabbed hold of his arm, refusing to let him kill for me, even if the man was the head of a crime family.

Ignoring me, he asked Gabriel, "How long do I have?"

Gabriel began, "Armani will go over the details, and you'll still need to try and win him over in other ways, but Joseph Esposito's wife turns forty tomorrow night, and they're having a party in her honor. He wants Joseph and his right-hand man killed there."

Keeping hold of his arm, I rasped, "You can't be considering this. I won't let you do it." My body, mind, and my everything was wide awake now. The foggy haze of shock had also been lifted.

Alessandro looked me dead in the eye, and in a deep voice, he hit me with, "Scylla and Charybdis."

I hung my head, letting go of my grip on his arm. *The lesser of two evils.*

CHAPTER ELEVEN

Calliope

"I don't need an outfit change. I don't care if you think I'm a hot mess."
I waved off Frankie's attempt to direct me up the stairs to change into
something "more suitable"—his words—to meet with Armani.

A protective arm swooped behind my back as Alessandro stood on
defense in the fancy foyer that could pass for the location of the stairway
scene from *Titanic*. "I'm not letting her out of my sight. She remains
in what she's wearing."

"She's safe here, I can assure you." Gabriel jerked a thumb toward
Leo. "He'll escort her."

"One of the guards back in Nashville betrayed Armani." Alessandro's
hand curved around my side beneath the jean jacket. "I'm sure there're
more traitors beneath his own roof."

"I'd give my life for Mr. DiMaggio," Frankie hissed, and maybe I
believed that. But would he for me? Doubtful.

When more men joined us in the foyer, the message was clear. If I
didn't willingly go, Alessandro would wind up playing bowling with the
men in his attempt to knock them all down. And then Armani would
kick him out, and I'd be on my own.

"I'll go," I said, turning to face him, but his hand stayed on my
body, tracing the line of my waist with my movement. "It's fine."

"My wife's upstairs in your room. She'll help you out. Rosa went shopping for you," Gabriel shared.

"I've got this," I reassured Alessandro. Beneath the beyond-five-o'clock shadow of facial hair the man was now sexily sporting, his jaw visibly locked at the idea I'd be out of his sight.

"We'll wait in my office for her to change before we meet Armani." Gabriel cut over to our side, waiting for Alessandro to back down.

Judging by the hard look in his eyes, he wasn't ready to budge.

"I'll be okay." I gave him a determined nod, hoping he'd believe me—and that it'd also be true.

"Fine." He pulled his hand back, and I stepped away in search of Leo to lead the way. I forced myself not to glance back at Alessandro, afraid any more eye contact between us would have him chasing up the stairs after me.

Once in the bedroom Armani had designated as mine nearly a year ago, Leo closed the door, thankfully not joining me, and my attention went straight to the crescent-shaped window over the bed that had a view of the sea in the distance.

"Callie." Rosa entered the room from the closet, carrying a black dress draped over her arm. "I'd say it's good to see you, but . . ."

I nodded in agreement, unsure if we were supposed to hug. She was close in age to me and had always been kind in the past, but she was married to Armani's consigliere, and I couldn't understand why a woman like her, a former teacher herself, would marry into the mafia. "Hi." I finally managed to speak.

She set the dress on the red velvet sofa by the closet and crossed the room but didn't attempt to gather me in her arms.

"This is crazy," I whispered. "Marriage."

Rosa swept a hand through her black hair. "*Finché c'è vita c'è speranza.*" She translated her words a moment later. "As long as there is life, there is hope."

"Hope," I said under my breath, feeling the need to cling to that word as much as possible, given my situation.

"Alessandro will keep you safe. Gabriel trusts him." She toyed with the gold bracelets on her wrists, waiting for me to respond.

Was I supposed to say I trusted her husband? Finding Gabriel hard to hate was one thing, but trusting him just because of that was a stretch.

"You can't marry Rocco." She let go of her bracelets.

"And if I just say no to marriage?"

She snatched the sequined black dress again. "You don't have a choice."

I knew an American saying or two as well. "There's always a choice."

"*Sì*, but Armani will ensure you make the choice he wants. You know him. He will find a way to make marriage *your* idea."

She handed me the dress as I blurted on instinct, "Not possible."

Rosa's red nails walked down her throat to her collarbone, as if trying to suppress a secret that wanted to escape, but then she blinked and said, "Let's get you dressed. A little makeup, too. You'll be good to go."

I didn't push her to talk about whatever she was keeping from me, because the last thing I wanted was to get her in trouble.

Within ten minutes I was ready, and we followed Leo downstairs to Gabriel's office.

Alessandro was at the bar, head slightly bowed, a tumbler next to his left hand.

"A little early for drinking, isn't it?" I said, letting him know I was back.

"Morning here. Late-night drinking hours back home," Alessandro remarked, his tone raspy. He lifted his hands and slowly turned. I hadn't expected a pissed-off look from him as he took in my transformation from "a quick errand run to the store" to "princess going to the ball." Well, to a mafia ball.

The dress was a showstopper, though. A sweetheart neckline that reminded me I had damn good breasts. And I didn't totally hate that I was rocking Jimmy Choos for the first time in my life. Plus, Rosa was a queen at doing makeup, and my green eyes popped from the smoky eye shadow. So what was the deal with his angry face?

"Why in God's name . . . ?" Alessandro dragged a hand through his hair, mussing up those wavy locks. "Why?"

"Why what?" Rosa asked, stepping alongside me. "Armani wanted her in something fancy."

He tossed a hand in the air my way and began speaking Italian. Just great. Way to leave me out of the conversation focused on me.

"Relax," Rosa said as Gabriel came up next to the angry beast still snarling at me.

With Alessandro quietly stroking his jawline, continuing to stare at me like I offended him, I faced Rosa for answers instead. "What am I missing?"

She smirked. "You look hot, Callie. Smoking hot. Gorgeous. Stunning. And he doesn't like it because your father's men will see you." She made a *tsk* sound probably directed toward Alessandro. "Your future husband is a jealous man, it would seem."

"I'm not jealous," Alessandro snapped, then returned to the bar and tossed back whatever was left in the glass.

Gabriel crossed the room, took his wife's elbow, and kissed her cheek. "Maybe you should wait for me upstairs, *amore mio*."

"Good luck," she said to me, and why'd that feel like she was talking about my "marriage" to Alessandro and not facing Armani?

Once it was only the three of us—well, plus there was Leo hanging outside the office doors, waiting—I snatched the skirt of the dress so I didn't trip as I made my way to Alessandro. "Are you okay?"

He didn't have his suit jacket on, so when his back muscles snapped together at my question, it was hard to miss. "No," he hissed, then faced me. "How am I supposed to go to Rome and handle the Esposito family and leave you here?" His silver-gray eyes went to my cleavage, shamelessly parking there for several long beats.

"Ahem." I nearly crossed my arms to help with my scolding look, but that'd only have my boobs on display more, and probably inspire those veins at the side of his neck to pop as well.

"What?" Alessandro snapped out.

"You're snarling at her, is what," Gabriel commented, saving me from having to say it. "Calm down. I'll be here when you leave. She'll be fine."

I'd been so taken aback by Alessandro's reaction to me in the dress, I'd nearly forgotten the whole him-leaving-me-to-commit-murder thing. *Kind of a big thing, too.*

"Let's get this over with, shall we?" Gabriel gestured toward the double doors of his office. Alessandro gave me one last angry look, then stepped to my side, a hand moving to my back again, and I took that as a cue to walk. So help the man who did try and steal a quick view of my cleavage, because I was pretty sure the growly grump at my side would knock them out.

Alessandro abruptly stopped walking, made eye contact with Leo in the hall, then removed his hand from my back to shut the doors. "She needs to know what's going on before we face Armani."

"Wait, what?" I spun around, nearly falling in the heels, but Alessandro was quick and caught my arm, keeping me upright.

"We agreed not to tell her," Gabriel remarked, gaze pointed his way.

"No, you said that. I only listened." Alessandro focused back on me. "Armani figured out a way to force you to marry no matter what. We just need to ensure it's to me."

I thought back to Rosa's ominous words upstairs, and then it made sense. The truth had been in plain sight from the beginning. The loophole to how Armani would get me to bend to his will in marriage without him breaking his family's ancient rules.

"Aunt Tia," I whispered, as chills coated every inch of bare skin. "If I don't do what he says . . ."

Rosa was right. I didn't have a choice. Whether Armani chose Alessandro or Rocco for me to marry, it no longer mattered. I'd do what I had to do to keep my aunt safe.

CHAPTER TWELVE

Calliope

The bastard was at the head of his twenty-person table when we entered the dining room. Alessandro and Gabriel had me wedged protectively between them, and we hung back at the other side of the table. I assumed Gabriel was waiting for some cue from Armani to speak.

Armani set aside the book he'd been reading, and for some reason it irritated me he was a reader, because I didn't want to like anything about him. He removed his dark-rimmed glasses and looked up at us.

How had my mother fallen for that man? Not that he was unattractive. More like a sixty-five-year-old Joe Mantegna from the movie *The Godfather III* and that *Criminal Minds* show. But he was evil, and she'd been a young musician, living her dream before he'd entrapped her in his world for decades.

Armani adjusted the knot of his red tie as his dark eyes swept over my dress, and I'd swear he had a similar reaction as Alessandro had minutes ago. There was a definite *what-the-fuck* look in his eyes.

Armani snapped his fingers and flicked his wrist. "Someone get my daughter something to cover up with before I have to cut your eyes out for staring at her."

"One thing we agree on," Alessandro said, ice in his tone as he broke his silence for the first time. At the offering of a throw blanket from Leo, Alessandro visibly relaxed once my upper half was covered.

Now I understood Rosa's reasoning for choosing such a sexy dress, knowing it'd make both Alessandro and Armani snap. Show Armani that Alessandro was as protective of me as the bastard felt he had a right to be.

Well played, Rosa. Well played.

"Costa," Armani bit out, hands on the table while standing to his height of six-three. "Gabriel tells me you wish to marry my daughter?"

Hardly. But what choice do we have, you prick? Not that I could voice my thoughts. I also had to remember to check my sass. I couldn't let Aunt Tia die because of my runaway tongue.

Alessandro kept quiet, and I realized why. Marcello, Armani's second-in-command, had appeared in the doorway behind where Armani stood. He casually thumbed down the black collar of his starched shirt as he looked at me wrapped up in a blanket like a child. There was a darkness about him that managed to give Armani a run for his money.

He peered at Alessandro. "You shouldn't be here." Cold eyes cut to Gabriel as his next target. "And your throat should be slit for going behind our backs to seek the help of a Costa."

"He's my consigliere for a reason," Armani said, defending Gabriel. "He always has the organization's best interest at heart." Lifting his hands from the table, he pushed them into his pockets and faced Marcello.

"I'm not the one who was being groomed to take over before Mr. DiMaggio found out about his daughter, and now you've lost your shot at running the empire," Gabriel said, his tone much lower than I'd ever heard before. "Of course he'd come to me for advice instead of you."

Marcello's dark eyes snapped Gabriel's way like he'd been challenged to something. Pistols at dawn. I'd swear I'd fallen down the rabbit hole and wound up in Hades instead of Wonderland.

"Calliope would be dead if not for Gabriel's decision to send Costa to Nashville, and you'd be back in line to take over the business." Armani quietly studied his second-in-command.

"Maybe you were part of the plan to have Calliope killed?" Gabriel suggested.

At the sight of Gabriel drawing a weapon, Alessandro pulled me farther away from the scene, drawing me tighter against him.

"Don't be ridiculous." Marcello kept his hands in view, not going for a gun like Gabriel had. "I'm loyal to you, Armani. To the bloodline."

Gabriel rested his gun against his thigh. "You're loyal to power and money."

"This is madness." Marcello focused on Armani. "You can't seriously think I'd sell you out to the Espositos and betray you." He fixed the cuffs of his jacket, seemingly not worried about being shot. "Gabriel wants your daughter to marry a Costa. Alessandro's father was League. The Costas helped take down the Sicilian mafia division in New York just last year. Are you—?" He cut himself off before insulting his boss.

Too bad. Marcello was one man I wouldn't mind watching Armani kill. Thank God the man was married and Armani didn't believe in divorce, or I was pretty sure he would've forced me to marry his second-in-command.

"The Costas' relationship with The League will play into our favor," Gabriel said with the kind of conviction even I could feel. "An enemy of our enemy is our friend."

I still needed to get the bullet points on The League and who the hell they were, but now I knew Alessandro's father had a connection to them.

"The League broke their truce with The Alliance, or have you forgotten?" Marcello scowled.

Alessandro seemed content to let the three of them go back and forth without getting involved yet, and considering he had Gabriel fighting his war for him right now, it was probably the smart play.

"The Alliance killed my brother. My nephew." Armani's words had Marcello's attention. "Or have you forgotten?" He paused for a moment. "And it was The Alliance that first violated the pact with The League, prompting war between the two."

"I'm prepared to speak on The League's behalf today and offer your organization the same deal they had with The Alliance," Alessandro finally said, catching me off guard. "If you don't break the deal, there will be peace. Your people can stop looking over your shoulder and worrying about them coming after you."

"Why you?" Armani slapped his hands to the table. "Why would you want this?"

"*Non c'è luce senza oscurità.*" My knees about buckled at Alessandro throwing Armani's words to me back at him. "There will always be evil in this world. Corruption and crime. With The Alliance gone, someone will attempt to fill their spot. You're the lesser of two evils."

Damn that phrase.

"We'd rather it be someone we know at the least has a moral code." Alessandro let go of me to lift his palms in the air as if offering a truce. "If you force your daughter to marry a monster, then you're turning your back on your family's legacy."

"But why *you*, in particular? I did my research. You're not the marrying type." Yeah, it wouldn't have taken Armani much googling to draw the same conclusion I had Saturday night, based on there always being a different woman on Alessandro's arm in photos. "Gabriel tells me you owe him your life, but I find it hard to believe a man like you would marry into the mafia to cancel out a debt."

I peeked at Alessandro, and his jaw was locked tight as he stared back from across the room.

"As for me marrying your daughter"—he turned to find my eyes—"it'd be a business deal, and we all benefit from the arrangement." His tanned throat moved with a deep swallow before he focused back on Armani. "I don't need your money or your power. Consider me the sacrificial lamb. I'm being offered as a gesture of good faith. The League will only make this deal if someone they trust is within your organization, and you'll know that they'd never break their side of the pact if I'm here as well."

Sacrificial lamb? My stomach turned, hating I had to be quiet about my own life. But I had to keep my aunt safe.

"But do you want to marry her?" Why did Armani care? It wasn't like he was asking me the same freaking question. The asshole.

"Yes," Alessandro bit out, his arm going behind my back again, and it was the first time Armani left the head of the table to approach us. He walked by Gabriel, who still had his gun in his hand as if itching to take out Marcello.

Standing face-to-face with Alessandro, Armani narrowed his eyes. "Then take out the head of the Esposito family, as well as his right-hand man, and I will *consider* you as an option."

"Consider it done," Alessandro responded without hesitating.

"Tomorrow night, Esposito's wife turns forty. He's throwing her a surprise party. Do it there. Be sure his wife is the one to find her husband's dead body, too." Armani took a step back, his gaze sliding over me. "After that, we shall talk. And I'll need reassurances from Emilia Calibrisi of the Italian League that she's on board with the deal."

"What about me? Do I get a say in any of this?" Shit, I'd been doing so good at keeping quiet.

"My guess is Gabriel, who clearly has a soft spot for you, especially since he went to his old friend to marry you instead of the suitor Marcello recommended . . . has already told you that your options are limited." He reached for me as if about to cup my cheek, and I flinched and startled back.

"My aunt Tia, is she okay?"

Armani lowered his hand. "From what my man says who followed her, she's having the time of her life on her cruise. She'll stay unaware of your situation if you do as I ask."

"Wouldn't hurting her break your moral code?" I doubted I could reason with him, but I had to try.

"In life, there are unfortunate accidents. She just might fall off the ship. Or the brakes might stop working in her car." He kept his dark eyes locked on me. "Do you understand?"

I forcibly nodded, doing my best not to snap and hit the bastard. But knowing him, he'd like it. He'd say that was the darkness inside me trying to break free.

"You have a plane to catch, Alessandro. A plan to put together," Armani said casually.

"I'm not leaving her here alone." Alessandro's hand left my waist so he could link our palms together. I gulped and looked down at him holding my hand, feeling something akin to comfort from his touch despite where we were.

The hand-holding even caught Armani's eyes. "She's safe here. And not safe anywhere near the Espositos in Rome."

Alessandro kept hold of me, peering at Marcello as he stated, "I won't leave as long as he shares a roof with her. He has the most to gain from her death, more so than Esposito."

"I'll cut your tongue out for that," Marcello warned.

"I'd like to see you try," Alessandro snapped out. When Marcello started our way, Gabriel blocked his path.

"Marcello will leave when you do," Armani announced, and when Marcello began hissing something in Italian, Armani turned his attention toward him, motioning to the other guards, who'd previously been shadowy protectors hanging back quietly in the room.

"You can't be serious." Marcello looked around Gabriel, meeting my eyes. "They're the ones trying to deceive you. You shouldn't trust them. Any of them." He switched to Italian, then turned and left, taking most of the negative, bad energy with him.

Once Marcello was gone from sight, two guards following him out at Armani's directive, Alessandro remarked, "You're making the right decision."

"I guess we'll soon find out." Armani gave me one quick look, then gestured for Alessandro to get going.

Alessandro kept hold of my hand, and we walked through the maze of halls to get outside. Gabriel hung back behind us like a safety net, and only once we were by one of the parked Escalades did Alessandro let go of my hand. "I hate to leave you."

"You don't have a choice. My aunt's life is on the line now."

"I programmed my number in your phone." Alessandro frowned. "Check in with me, okay?"

"When did you do that?" I arched a brow, trying to remember a point where he'd had access to my phone.

"On the plane when you were in the bedroom, tossing and turning."

I thought about asking him how he also knew I hadn't slept a wink but instead went with, "And how'd you know my password?"

"Your birthday." He shook his head. "You should change it. Too obvious." He looked over at Gabriel, who was near the front of the house, then faced me again.

"This isn't how I thought things would go in there, but it, um, went okay, right? He's giving you a chance. Trusting Gabriel over that asshole Marcello," I admitted, trying to refocus. "But you still have to kill for me, and I feel sick about that."

"Lesser of two evils," he reminded me. "No choice. Let's just hope he continues to believe a deal with The League is better than one with the Barone family."

Clutching the blanket to my chest, grateful for it given the chills whipping up my spine, I murmured, "I guess I'll be asking Gabriel to clue me in on this mystery group while you're gone."

"Maybe stay in your bedroom as much as possible? I'll be back tomorrow night after it's done."

After it's done? How was he talking about killing a man at his wife's birthday party so casually? But it was to save me. Save Tia. *So yeah, lesser of two evils.* "I should be the one telling you to be safe."

"You don't need to worry about me." He reached out as if to run his fingers through my hair and offer me reassurances, but then hesitated and lowered his arm to his side. "If for some reason something happens to me, my family will come for you. They'll protect you if I can't."

I lost hold of the blanket at his words, and he snatched it as fast as he'd done with the towel yesterday in my bedroom. "Wait, what?"

He wrapped it back around my body, drawing himself close in the process. "Don't worry; if you have to marry Hudson or Constantine instead of me, they'll take good care of you."

But the way his brows slanted and his eyes narrowed told me that idea pained him to even say.

"Don't," I cried out.

With the blanket covering me again, he asked with a confused look, "Don't what?"

I squeezed my eyes closed. "Die on me."

CHAPTER THIRTEEN

Alessandro

Rome, Italy

"Why the hell haven't you messaged yet?" Irritated, I about launched my phone out the open balcony door inside my hotel room. It was the tenth time I'd felt some strange and uncomfortable pit of disappointment in my stomach when looking at my phone and seeing no text from her.

Had I not been clear enough that I wanted to hear from her? Like every hour on the fucking hour?

Could I call her? Text her? Sure. But I'd never had to follow up with a woman before and wasn't in the mood to start. Hell, the only women I checked in on happened to share my blood.

I reread the last few messages I'd exchanged with Gabriel, reminding myself he had her six. He'd told me she was safe in her bedroom and just fine—fine enough not to feel the need to check in with me, dammit.

I went outside to the balcony, catching sight of the afternoon sun unobscured by clouds, pouring light down over *Fontana dell'Acqua Felice*, also known as the Fountain of Moses. *Felice. Luck. I could use some of that today.*

Enzo, Izzy, and Hudson were caught in traffic and running late, so I was on edge for that reason, too. Well, that was what I was trying to tell myself as to why I was so anxious.

I looked at my phone again, feeling like it was a ticking time bomb and maybe I had to bite the bullet and message first. To not take a criminal's word she was fine.

Me: Are you okay?

The relief I felt at her instant response, and the fact I knew it was her and not someone else pretending to be her just by how she'd answered, had me hanging my head for a second.

Little Miss Tennessee Whiskey: Define "okay."

Not sure why I'd gone with that contact name, but it bothered me to type in Callie when that was what everyone called her. Everyone except Braden.

Me: Alive. Untouched. Hydrated.

Little Miss Tennessee Whiskey: Hydrated? (that's cute). Well, I'm hiding in my room currently, so I'm safe. But now that you mention it, a little thirsty. No appetite, though.

Me: Yeah, I'm not exactly hungry, either. But you should eat. (And hydrate.)

No clue why I decided to copy her and throw in some parentheses in my text back, but I wasn't exactly acting like myself. Hence the borderline panic attack at waiting on someone to text me.

Also, that was probably the first time the word *cute* had been tossed my way for any reason.

Little Miss Tennessee Whiskey: Why aren't you hungry? You need your strength to do . . . "the thing" tomorrow.

"On to quotation marks now, huh?" And now I was talking to myself. Enzo and Izzy would have a field day with this. My balls would be on the chopping block.

Me: I'll be sure to load up on food tomorrow before "the thing."

And now I was smiling while discussing murdering the head of a crime family.

Little Miss Tennessee Whiskey: For a songwriter, I have a way with words, don't I? "The thing" sounds like the perfect song title.

Damn, my smile stretched to the point my cheeks fucking hurt. *I need help.*

Me: You write, too? I didn't realize.

I went back inside the room and dropped down on the bed, the agonizing pain that'd planted roots in my chest dissipating now that I was in touch with her.

Little Miss Tennessee Whiskey: I did before I found out I was the spawn of Satan. Writer's block now.

Me: Sorry on both accounts. Being Satan's daughter and the writing issue.

Little Miss Tennessee Whiskey: There's that sweet side of you again.

Before I could figure out what to say to that, she sent me a few more messages.

Little Miss Tennessee Whiskey: Gabriel showed me a live video of Aunt Tia to let me know she's living her best life and okay. But the fact Armani has eyes (and a camera) on her has me in knots. (But oddly, somehow more at ease knowing I can see her at any time for proof of life, too.)

Little Miss Tennessee Whiskey: Gabriel is too nice to be bad.

Little Miss Tennessee Whiskey: Does that make sense?

Me: Total sense.

I considered whether to keep the conversation going or to stop it now. I knew she was safe, so mission accomplished. No sense in talking. *But maybe I should reassure her everything would be fine?*

Me: Your aunt will be okay. My family will make sure of that.

Little Miss Tennessee Whiskey: That bit of knowledge is what's keeping me from losing my mind with worry. I just hate that you have to do what you're going to do tomorrow because of my mess.

Me: A mess would imply you got yourself into something and need a bailout. You were born into this. Not your fault. And helping people and taking down assholes is what I do. What my family does. It's no problem.

Well, that wasn't the total truth. There were quite a few fucking problems happening. Marriage as part of my mission was up there as one of them. High-high up there.

Little Miss Tennessee Whiskey: And if Armani's lying about the Esposito family working with my guard to try and kill me? Do you think maybe he's just trying to . . . find an excuse for you to take out his competition?

The thought had crossed my mind, but if Armani wanted war with the Espositos, he could have attacked them long ago. Plus, I knew Gabriel wouldn't send me on a kill mission if he didn't believe the Espositos were responsible. (Even if he was a criminal.)

Fuck, now I'm thinking with parentheses.

Little Miss Tennessee Whiskey: Sorry, I'm sure you would've brought that up if you'd thought it was possible.

Me: I do think the head of the Esposito crime family's responsible for the attack in the park. But it wouldn't matter either way. Armani wants him dead, and I have to do it. Part of the job.

Little Miss Tennessee Whiskey: Job? Right. I'm a job for you.

Maybe our new "security company" needed some sensitivity training, because I'd fumbled the ball there. Forgot to be sweet or cute. Then again, being nice might . . . *complicate* things.

Little Miss Tennessee Whiskey: And these Espositos really deserve to die?

Me: Your father may be more powerful than them, but the Espositos make Armani look like a gentleman in terms of their tactics to achieve their goals. They have no moral code whatsoever.

Little Miss Tennessee Whiskey: I guess that should make me feel better about you doing "the thing" tomorrow.

Me: Try not to think about it.

She'd already seen me kill three people; no sense in her having nightmares about me killing more.

Little Miss Tennessee Whiskey: Okay . . .

Me: Not very convincing that you're "okay."

Little Miss Tennessee Whiskey: I can sing. Not act.

Little Miss Tennessee Whiskey: Oh, and shit, I forgot to tell you.

I'd swear it was as if we were talking over the phone instead of texting right now. I could hear her sexy accent, and every little inflection came through her tone with each word sent.

Me: Forgot to tell me what?

Little Miss Tennessee Whiskey: A friend found out I called in sick today at work. Dropped by with soup. Mr. Crabby (did I ever tell you that's his real name?) told him I left with some guy that "looks too good for his own good."

All I could focus on was the word *him*. Who was the "him" who had "dropped by" to see her when he found out she wasn't in school?

Little Miss Tennessee Whiskey: I'm telling you this because now he's worried, and he keeps calling and texting. He's concerned I was kidnapped. What do I do? Do I answer? Text him back?

What was this ridiculous need to want to tell her that the "him" in question didn't need to worry about her, because she wasn't his to worry about? *You're* . . . I let that unfinished thought go. Because she wasn't mine. Not in the real sense. Never would be.

Me: Who?

Little Miss Tennessee Whiskey: Remember the guy you met at the bar at the event? Bartender I jam with from time to time.

Of-fucking-course.

Me: How could I forget . . . ?

Me: Told you he wants to be more than friends.

Little Miss Tennessee Whiskey: Why do you sound jealous?

Me: I can't sound anything. We're texting.

Apparently, she could hear my voice through text, too. But jealous?

Me: And I don't "do" jealous. Not even sure how that feels.

Little Miss Tennessee Whiskey: I guess I believe you considering your reputation.

My reputation was what it was for a reason. I didn't want anyone getting the idea I'd fall in love. No heart to give. No fucks, either.

And there I was, feeling like I was giving one. Well, a fuck, at least. But it was to keep her safe, because she was clearly a decent human being.

Little Miss Tennessee Whiskey: So what do I do?

Me: Text him back so he doesn't report you as missing. Send him a happy photo with the backdrop in Italy, letting him know you're playing hooky because you decided to make an impromptu trip to visit family. If he pushes for a call, make it quick.

Little Miss Tennessee Whiskey: He'll never believe that.

Me: Fine, tell him the partial truth. I swept you off your feet after the fundraiser and took you to Italy for a trip.

Little Miss Tennessee Whiskey: . . . You can't be serious. Braden will lose his mind.

Me: Yeah, Braden's going to lose something if he doesn't back off.

"Fuck." I backspaced each word before sending the text and typed something more appropriate.

Me: Just figure out something to tell him so he doesn't call the cops.

Little Miss Tennessee Whiskey: Roger that.

Little Miss Tennessee Whiskey: Sorry, I think Braden's military talk has rubbed off on me. What I meant is, I'll think of something to say and handle it.

I closed my eyes and took a calming breath or two before I barked out some crazy commands about not wanting Braden's "anything" to "rub" anywhere on my future wife.

Before I could come up with something less psychopathic to say, or God help me, *jealous*, my phone rang.

It was an unfamiliar number coming from Sicily.

Me: I have to go. Be in touch. And don't forget to hydrate.

And to tell the marine to fuck off.

Little Miss Tennessee Whiskey: Be safe.

Me: Always.

"This is Alessandro Costa," I answered the call, assuming it was Emilia Calibrisi and not Marcello or one of Armani's men. "Emilia, that you?"

"*Sì*, and I had an interesting meeting with your father." She cut right to it. Good. I preferred that over small talk. "He let me know about your precarious situation."

Precarious is one way of putting it. According to the conversation with my father when I'd arrived in Rome, he'd told me she was on board with the plan. "I appreciate your help with what we're asking you to do. It's a big ask, but it's to save a life and—"

"And a chance to get Rocco Barone," she finished for me. "Only I have a condition. One of Claudio Barone's rockets took out a village in Egypt three months ago, and a lot of innocent people were killed. We've been searching for him ever since. Claudio Barone is our mark."

"Just Rocco's father?" I tensed as I waited for her to answer because Rocco was mine. His head. On a motherfucking platter.

"You can accompany my team on the mission to intercept the Barone family, and we'll give you first rights to kill Rocco. But Claudio . . . We'll handle him. This is non-negotiable."

Technically, Claudio Barone had been our target four years ago. Sent after him by the US government. And we'd failed when Rocco got his hands on Constantine instead. I hated leaving a mission incomplete, even if we no longer answered to the government, but I supposed a win was a win. If The League killed him, it'd still be mission success.

"Deal," I rasped. "I assume you're already aware of the fact I'm in Rome and what Armani DiMaggio wants me to do in order to have a shot at marrying his daughter?"

"*Sì.* And my husband, Sean, and my most trusted friend in The League, Sebastian Renaud, will have your back tomorrow to assist. I'd come myself, but I'm six months pregnant."

"I didn't know. Congratulations."

"*Grazie.*" She didn't waste time getting back to business. The woman was harder than I was. Damn. "You obviously can't get an invite to Esposito's party tomorrow as a Costa, so Sebastian is working on ways to get everyone in. New identities for you and your siblings. My husband has your number. He'll be in touch later."

"Thank you. I'm forever indebted to you."

"Consider your debt paid when Claudio Barone is dead." The woman of few words hung up without any pleasantries, which was fine by me. As long as we had the support of The League, that was all that mattered.

I set aside my phone when I heard a knock coming from the living room of the suite. By the time I reached the door, my sister had already yelled out, "It's us."

I swung it open and immediately bowed my head at the sight of Constantine in the hall, too.

"It wasn't me. Blame Dad. He told him." Izzy was quick to defend herself.

Constantine quietly barreled around me. A man on a mission.

"You could've given me a warning," I mumbled while stepping back to allow more space for Enzo and Hudson, carrying the bags, to come in.

"He was adamant about us keeping our mouths shut," Enzo said as I closed the door.

"Like Dad was supposed to do." I faced the room and folded my arms, waiting for Constantine to start his lecture.

"You invited Izzy but not me. I can't believe you tried to keep this a secret," Constantine began, earning him the side-eye from Izzy.

"What does that mean?" Izzy aligned herself beside me at his borderline insult. "Just because I've never killed anyone doesn't mean—"

"And you never will," Constantine barked out, stabbing a finger her way.

I was on the same page there as he. The last thing I wanted was my little sister to know what it felt like to take a life. My brothers and I were numb to death now, and it was a fucked-up feeling that no amount of therapy could help me push through. Not that I could tell my therapist about the lives I'd taken outside the army.

"You're too overprotective for your own good." Izzy went over to the bar, snatched a bottle of wine, and began to uncork it.

"No, I'm the exact right amount of overprotective," Constantine fired back as Hudson quietly moved the bags over by the couch.

Enzo dropped down on the lounge chair and gripped the back of his neck, his eyes red with exhaustion. "Dad wanted us all here for you."

And now I was feeling guilty that Enzo had come. He should've been back home with his pregnant wife and daughter.

Constantine tossed his suit jacket on the couch and began working his sleeves to the elbows, taking out more of his anger on his custom-fitted shirt. "It should be me. You should've told me. I should be the one—"

"Marrying Calliope?" *Calliope.* Yup, out came that name. Smooth, like fucking butter.

"You shouldn't be the one sacrificing yourself to get to Rocco." Constantine slammed a palm over his heart. "It should be me."

"Are you sure we can even trust Gabriel?" Enzo spoke up before I could shut down the ridiculousness of my older brother's words. "He's *mafioso.*"

Like I needed the reminder. "And if it wasn't for him, I'd be dead. Constantine, too," I snapped out, forgetting this information hadn't been common knowledge. I hadn't wanted my brothers knowing I was indebted to a criminal and why. I didn't need Constantine shouldering more guilt. He already did his best to carry the weight of our problems like he was our father.

Hudson was the only one I'd shared bits and pieces to about Gabriel, and he'd given me his word he wouldn't repeat what I'd said. So based on Constantine's and Enzo's shocked looks, I had a feeling Hudson hadn't opened his mouth.

"I'm sorry, what?" It was Izzy to pipe up first, a glass of red in hand.

I shoved my hands into my pockets, trying to remain grounded. Calm. "After Gabriel took out a sniper seconds away from killing me on our mission to get the Barones four years ago, he helped find out where Rocco was keeping Constantine. If it wasn't for him, Dad never would've been able to negotiate your release with Claudio Barone." *Rocco would've finished you. And I'd be without two siblings.*

"Why'd he do that?" Izzy whispered. "Gabriel chose the dark side. How'd he get involved in your mission for Uncle Sam? Why help?"

"I'm sure he had his own motives, as he does now." Not that he'd revealed them back then when I'd pressed. Enzo steadied his eyes on me, as if worried I was misplacing my trust and faith in a criminal. *Maybe I am?* "Lesser of two evils in this case after Armani dies." *The theme of this fucking mission.* And it was starting to feel like the theme of my life.

"If we're going through with the plan tomorrow, and this insanity that you plotted behind my back to marry Armani's daughter," Constantine began, heading for the bar, "then no more secrets. Are we clear?" He filled three glasses with Macallan and turned toward us.

"Crystal," I remarked in a low tone while accepting what felt like a peace offering from him, and I tossed back the whisky like it was a shot.

"You're sure Rocco Barone is really in the mix?" Enzo stood, took the tumbler, and swirled the liquid around. "What if Gabriel's using him as bait to draw you into his plan, knowing you couldn't resist the chance to get to Rocco?"

"I guess we'll soon find out if I'm a horrible judge of character or not," I said under my breath, then refilled my glass. Two fingers of whisky instead of the one Constantine had poured.

"Yeah, well, I'd like to work on more than just gut instinct and the 'we'll find out' approach." Constantine set his eyes on Hudson. "After this op ends tomorrow, do a deep dive into Gabriel's background. I want to know everything he's been up to in the last four years since he supposedly saved our lives."

Hudson nodded, then focused my way with an apologetic shrug. Maybe Constantine was right, though. I'd been worried my brother wouldn't be able to think clearly with Rocco in the mix, and I was the one thrown off instead.

"You're seriously going to marry this woman?" Constantine asked me.

The idea of marriage had my throat constricting. Body growing tense. "I don't have a choice."

"There's always a choice," Constantine said, his tone less vinegar this time. "Say the word, and we find another way to protect her. And if Rocco's really in the picture, we'll get to him, too." My confident and rock-steady big brother was showing his true self right now. There was a reason he was often in charge of our ops: aside from being the eldest—along with having the most experience in war, apart from Hudson—it was his ability to remain objective.

I should've trusted him from the beginning with the truth about the call from Gabriel. Maybe it was me who'd lose my cool if in the same room with Rocco.

"No." My shoulders collapsed. "Calliope's mine." I blinked at the realization of what I'd said instead of what I'd *meant* to say. "My responsibility." I cleared my throat and faced the room. "That's what I meant."

Izzy exchanged a look with the ever-quiet Hudson for whatever reason before finding my eyes, a slight smirk touching her lips. "Sure you did." Then, damn her, she winked.

CHAPTER FOURTEEN

Alessandro

"I'm not a fan of bringing my brother in on this, but I'd like to have someone else on the inside before the party starts." Sean McGregor looked up from the laptop where the architectural blueprints for tonight's venue were displayed. We'd be going into an underground club with too many tunnels for our liking. "You won't have a chance to meet Ethan before we head out, though."

"Do you not trust me?" Enzo rounded the table in the living room to face off with the Irishman.

The blond stared right back at my brother without batting a fucking eyelash. Guess he could hold his own or else Emilia Calibrisi wouldn't have married him.

"I'll be there as part of the catering staff," Enzo added, as if Sean had forgotten the alias he'd provided my chef brother.

Sean smirked, letting my brother know he didn't intimidate him with those dark eyes and the marks of death tattooed all over his arms. "If we didn't trust you, we wouldn't be in this bloody room with you now." He angled his head to his "teammate," if that's what they called each other. He was probably the only man who could ever give Enzo pause.

There were "dark vibes," and then there was Sebastian Renaud. The man was the walking epitome of "don't fuck with me, or else." I couldn't help but admire that, though.

Sebastian looked around the living room at all of us and casually scratched his bearded jawline. "Sean's brother's not League, but Ethan's agreed to help, and you should be thankful for any help we're offering." His tone was void of emotion. Just laying out the facts.

"And what's his cover story? Why him?" Of course Izzy wasn't intimidated by the man. That worried me, actually. It may have also explained her poor choice in men.

"Musician on the side," Sean said. "Ethan's already rehearsing with the band playing in the main room of the club tonight."

Sebastian peered at my sister and explained, "We arranged for one of their band members, along with their backup, to fall ill."

"I don't even want to know how you did that." Izzy waved her hand his way. She really was like my brothers and me—the backbone, right along with being too brave for her own good. (It had gotten us into trouble here and there over the years, like with Rocco Barone.)

"I'm still not a fan of Izzy's alias." Especially the fact she had one at all. Normally, she sat a safe distance away from our missions. She was never directly involved.

"You mean her being Hudson's girlfriend tonight?" Enzo asked. "Or her going into the club at all?"

"Both," Constantine and I said at the same time.

"Bella will be at my side the whole night. I won't let anything happen to her," Hudson said, his tone deep and meant to reassure us, but there was something in his eyes when he looked at her—worry?—that did nothing to dispel my unease.

"She's your tech person on the security cams. Our eyes and ears tonight," Sebastian pointed out, his Irish brogue cutting through more than Sean's had. "With the club being underground beneath archeological ruins, it's too great of a risk we'll lose her on comms, and then we'll be moving around in the dark."

"As much as I don't want to agree with the decision to have her undercover at Esposito's party, Renaud is right," Constantine said, the concern etched into his voice not doing wonders for that backbone of mine right now.

"I'll be fine. Relax." Izzy unfolded her arms and went over to Hudson, nudging him in the side. "This guy won't let anything happen to me."

"Not if he wants to live to see another day." Doubtful Enzo was joking, either, with that comment.

Before I could interject my two cents, my phone vibrated in my pocket, alerting me to a text. After I read it, I rushed out, "Excuse me for a moment," already on my way to the bedroom.

Little Miss Tennessee Whiskey: The son of a bitch had me tested.

I closed the bedroom door and dropped down on the bed. We hadn't talked much since our last exchange yesterday. I'd done my best to keep my distance and only sent quick messages to ensure she was okay, so I didn't blow a gasket while worrying. This was her first time initiating contact.

Me: What do you mean?

I leaned forward, resting my elbows on my legs as I waited for her to respond, anger barreling through me with worry about what the "son of a bitch" had done. *What kind of test?* I tried to calm myself down by the fact a call would've signaled a more urgent and pressing matter than a text. So she had to be okay.

Also, maybe now was the time to change her name in my phone to Callie? While waiting, I went ahead and did it—not exactly loving doing it, but I needed to place some distance between us somehow. This felt like a small step.

Callie: He had a gynecologist come and take blood and do a pelvic exam to make sure I'm not on birth control and I am fertile. (I had to take an hour-long bath after that to ... not feel so ... invaded. I know that's the doctor's job, but the fact I was ordered by Armani just ...)

I reread her message, feeling my control seconds away from snapping.

Pelvic exam?

The fucker had forced her to spread open her legs and . . .

"I'm going to kill him and the doctor," I hissed under my breath while standing, and I went out to the balcony, needing air. There didn't seem to be any in the bedroom.

I set aside my phone, slammed my hands on the balustrade, and looked up at the sky, stars blinking overhead without a cloud in sight. *Breathe, dammit. Fucking breathe.*

After corralling my thoughts, only seeing carnage in my mind of all the men I was ready to destroy, I grabbed my phone to answer her, but another text came in from her first.

Callie: I'm sorry, I shouldn't have bothered you with this right now. It happened earlier, and I told myself I would keep my mouth shut until you got back. But my anger is only getting worse the more time passes. The more I think about it I just want to . . . kill someone.

Me: How can I help?

Callie: Listening is all I needed. (Or in your case, reading my words.)

Callie: Everything set for tonight? Gabriel mentioned you have to go to some underground dance club. He said the Espositos rented the whole place out since it's normally closed on a Tuesday.

If she needed a distraction, I supposed I'd give it to her, even though I wasn't quite ready to drop the subject of killing Armani for this sooner rather than later.

Me: We'll be leaving in about two hours, but my sister has to come inside with a fake identity now instead of staying outside like normal, and it's got me nervous.

Callie: I take it you don't normally "do" nervous.

Only since I met her.

Me: We won't let anything happen to her. I'm just a little bit more on edge now than I was before.

Callie: Just a little bit? Well, I'm officially over that edge after today. I was managing to keep it together (kind of) until now.

Callie: These comments from me aren't helping you. I'm sorry.

Me: You need to stop apologizing. And you're helping me just fine.

Callie: How?

Me: Because now I'm in the mood to commit murder.

◆ ◆ ◆

Three Hours Later

Standing by the bar, the drinks courtesy of my new enemy, the Esposito family, I waited for the bartender to pour the whiskey, catching sight of Hudson and Izzy at a booth at my three o'clock. They were focused on the band doing a cover of a U2 song, and Sean's brother was on the keyboard behind a mic.

Ethan had come through for us, providing a heads-up on how many security guards we'd be up against.

As for Enzo, he'd discreetly smuggled me a knife ten minutes ago while refreshing the food on Level Two of the club. I'd soon be using the blade tucked at my back beneath the suit jacket to cut Esposito's throat.

Izzy had already hacked into the security system, and she had the cameras available on her smartphone; she'd been relaying information to us over comms since we'd arrived. Everything was going as planned. Zero hiccups. And there was always at least one, and that had me nervous for when it would happen.

I brought my wrist near my mouth to talk over my comm. "This is Four. One, how are we on time?" I wasn't accustomed to just a number as my call sign, but that'd been the agreed-upon way of referring to ourselves. Constantine also wasn't used to being second-in-command, but we had to play nice with The League, and Sebastian was "One" tonight.

"This is One. Almost ready for the distraction to take place."

"Roger that," I replied before accepting the drink from the bartender. "And Six"—my sister's number tonight—"you have eyes on you. At your six o'clock. Put down your phone for a second and look like a couple."

There weren't many people on the dance floor blocking my path to them, so it was easy to make out Hudson peering my way as if unsure he wanted to follow my directive.

When he didn't make a move, my sister did it for him. She set a hand to his cheek, then decided to drive me nuts by slanting her lips over his, and the poor guy didn't have much of a choice now. Thank God it was me in the room with them and not Constantine.

"Not what I meant," I grumbled over comms at the sight of my baby sister making out with a guy a decade older than her. When Hudson slipped a hand into her hair, further selling a kiss that no longer needed to be sold, I rasped, "Heat is gone. You're good." When neither backed off, and I was worried my sister was seconds away from climbing onto his lap, forgetting this was an act, I snapped out, "Six, back off."

"Fuck," Hudson said loud enough to be heard over comms after detaching himself from my sister.

"This is Two. Everything okay there?" Constantine cut over the line.

"Everything's fine," Izzy remarked, scooting back in the booth, placing a little distance between herself and Hudson now, while snatching her phone from the table.

"Status check." I nearly forgot my alias that time, still shaken up by that fake kiss that didn't look all that fake. Nor the near heart attack it almost gave me.

"This is Three," Sean said. "Distraction is now in effect. We're clearing a path for you. You can move into position now."

"Roger that." I set aside the drink and did my best to casually walk by my sister and Hudson's table for the spiral staircase off to the side of the stage. Two guards rushed to the fight breaking out in one of the other rooms that Sean and Sebastian had arranged to happen.

"There are a lot of hallway-like tunnels between you and your target location. I'll guide you to the HVT." Izzy's voice popped into my ear as I climbed the steps, and I had to suppress a smile at hearing my sister use military jargon. I wasn't sure if Esposito qualified as a "high-value target," like the kind I'd hunted for the government both during and after the army, but I supposed tonight he was our HVT if I wanted to marry Callie.

Want? More like have *to marry her.*

"Take a left when you're at the top of the stairs," Izzy directed me. "Then hang a right down the next hall."

So far, the Espositos hadn't shown their faces at their own party and had remained in a private room on Level Two that apparently would take me walking through a maze to locate. Thank God for something. Who the hell had designed a club like this, anyway?

"This is One. We've got the left side of Level Two clear for your passage."

"Five, time to make your bathroom trip," Constantine told Hudson.

I hated leaving Izzy alone, but we needed to quietly take down as many guards as possible before word got to Esposito that he was in danger, and we'd need Hudson's help to do that.

"This is Five. On the move now," Hudson confirmed.

I followed Izzy's first set of directions, keeping myself out of sight from the cameras, then she rattled off the next set of directions.

So far, no sounds of gunfire competing with the band, which I'd take as good news in trying to keep our presence unknown until the very last minute.

I turned the next corner that led me down another barely lit hallway, and my world flipped upside down at the man standing on the other side, staring back at me. I didn't need it to be lit up to identify him, to know who else was there with me.

"This is Four. We're not the only ones here for the target," I alerted the team as Rocco Barone made the first move, coming for me.

I snatched the blade from beneath my suit jacket and dropped to a knee as tonight's "hiccup" came at me. I managed to duck and slide beneath his outstretched arm, then swivel around, getting back to my feet before he could stab me. Both of us were working with kitchen cutlery tonight. Of all the ways I'd imagined killing him over the years, and now . . .

"Been a long time, Costa." The motherfucker smiled and beckoned me with a flick of his wrist. "What are the chances we both crashed the same party?" When I didn't follow his request, he charged my way. The guy was bigger, but I was quicker. "Guess we're both here for the same reason. Not sure why you want to marry into the DiMaggios," he went on, missing each time he tried to strike.

Unlike his wasted attempts to hit me, I managed to land a gut punch and an elbow to the face. After spitting blood, he grinned, enjoying this too much, and came at me.

My teammates were in my ear, trying to figure out what was going on, but I was too wrapped up in defending myself from a psychopath to share.

At some point in the chaos, we both lost our weapons, and Rocco managed to put me up against the wall, smashing one of the few lights there. Him getting the drop on me—not one of my finer moments in life.

I felt his breath in my ear as he leaned in and hissed loud enough to ensure my team could hear his voice. "Is Constantine here? He is, isn't he? How's he doing? Can he hear me now?"

"He's mine," Constantine ordered, and yup, he'd heard the fucker, loud and clear. "I'm on my way."

I couldn't let that showdown happen. Not tonight, anyway. I also couldn't end his life now without jeopardizing the plan to use him to get to his father.

Anger and adrenaline allowed me to break free, and I managed to take a knee to secure my knife from the floor. Back on my feet in one fast movement, I set the blade against his throat. "Neither of us will get to Esposito if we exchange blows all night." I hated myself for that, and for what I did next. Let him go and backed up.

Breathing hard, Rocco stared at me as if worried I was setting him up for a trap.

"What's it going to be?" I lowered the knife to my side, needing to end this confrontation before Constantine arrived and killed him.

"I guess . . . may the best man, or in our case, *groom* win." Rocco grabbed his knife and rolled back his shoulders, as if ready to throw down again with me anyway. But then he turned and went the way he'd come, which meant he had another route to get to the mark.

"I can see you on camera," Izzy alerted over my earpiece. "Which means so can security. Get out of there."

Shit. "I need a new way to him. A quicker route before Rocco gets to him first."

"I'll handle Rocco. Go after the target," Constantine snapped out.

"This is One. Do not fucking pursue. This is not time for your revenge." Sebastian paused before ordering, "Five, can you slow down Rocco instead?"

"This is Five. I'm on it," Hudson said, and from the sound of it, he was on the move. Now Izzy had to direct the two of us to our marks before it was too late.

"This is Six," Izzy said a few seconds later. "The HVT is barricaded in a room with two armed guards, his wife, and Target Two. There are two more armed guards in front of the door now as well."

So much for the knife.

"You need to stand down," Izzy *suggested*, and that's all it was, because like hell would I back off.

"I can't." *Or Armani picks Rocco, and I may not be allowed back at his house to get to Callie without fast-roping in from a helo while being shot at.* I also had no clue whether Constantine was obeying Sebastian's orders, because he'd been eerily quiet.

"Fine," Izzy whispered. "But you can't avoid the cameras with the only other route I can find to get you to the HVT."

"It's safe to say that no longer matters," I answered as a guard rounded the next hall.

Sean appeared behind the guard, swiftly wrapping an arm around his neck. He slowly dropped him to the ground, then motioned for me to advance.

I nodded my thanks, then followed Izzy's new instructions, taking off down another tunnel-like hallway, stacked rocks for the walls and concrete beneath my shoes.

"Stop," Izzy abruptly shouted into my ear just before I went down the next hall. "You're there. The target room is around that corner."

I set my back to the wall, trying to come up with a plan armed with only a knife to go up against—*how many men again?*

My free hand curled into a fist as I tried to steady my breathing. At least I'd made it there before Rocco, which meant Hudson, instead of Constantine, was hopefully stalling him.

At the sound of someone at my six o'clock, I turned and nearly flung my knife. I'd never been so happy to see Constantine, especially carrying two 9mms.

"Revenge can wait," he said, once closer. "You need me."

I tucked the knife at my back and accepted the 9mm, then spied Enzo coming from the same direction. Clearly, he'd been following Izzy's directions as well.

"Can't let you do this without us," Enzo said, holding two huge-ass kitchen knives.

I looked back and forth between my brothers, and Hudson popped over comms, letting us know he was doing his best to distract Rocco without killing him.

Constantine closed his eyes for a moment, and I knew it killed him not to be the one fighting Rocco, but he chose me. Family over revenge. The man was the best of all of us.

"Let's do this," Constantine said while opening his eyes, and without hesitating, he stepped around the hall and took the first shot.

CHAPTER FIFTEEN

Calliope

"Checking on you. You good?"

At the sound of Gabriel's voice on the other side of the door, I hopped off the bed and hurried over to let him in. "I'll be better if you have news." My heart was going to break a rib with how hard it'd been pounding as I'd stared at my phone for the last few hours, waiting for confirmation Alessandro was alive.

Once in the room, Gabriel flipped open his laptop, hit a few buttons, then spun it around to show me the screen.

"What am I looking at?" I leaned in closer, taking in the sight of people running every which way in chaos. Not the most comforting view.

"I hacked into the cameras outside the nightclub on the street level to see what's going on," Gabriel shared, then with his free hand, he pointed at someone on camera getting onto a motorcycle. A few seconds later, police cars were following him.

"Who's that?" It didn't look like Alessandro, but the angle wasn't great. "Do you have good news or not?" My patience had left my body about three days ago, so . . .

"That's Constantine Costa. My guess is he used himself as bait so the others could escape the club unnoticed. You know, so Alessandro can make it back to you. Typical Constantine. Sacrificing himself." He looked at the screen, then caught my eye as I digested the news. "We haven't confirmed yet if the target is down, but I have to assume everything went as planned. Well, mostly everything. Winding up in a police chase means something went sideways."

Sideways? "So you haven't heard from Alessandro?"

"Not yet. They're probably still trying to put some distance between themselves and the crime scene. But I did get word League members were spotted at the club."

"Is that good or bad?" Shit, I needed to sit.

"If Alessandro completed Armani's task, it was most likely purposeful The League opted to be seen on camera. Helps cement the idea the DiMaggios are in league with, well, The League."

"Oh, uh, yeah, that makes sense," I murmured, my head spinning as I finally sat.

Gabriel followed me over, but before he could sit, an uninvited visitor joined us.

"I thought he kicked you out," I said at the sight of Marcello barging in.

"He came to his senses, realizing I'm like a son and he can trust me," Marcello said, eyes snapping to Gabriel. "What are you doing alone with her?" He snatched the laptop from Gabriel.

"She wanted to see her aunt," Gabriel gritted out, and it was obvious he was doing his best not to take the laptop back and hit Marcello over the head with it.

If only you could.

Marcello checked the screen before chucking the computer onto the bed, and I stole a look at it to see Gabriel had changed the view to the cruise ship, where my aunt was enjoying a midnight party on the top deck.

Fast fingers. Thank God. "What are you doing in my room?" I stood, forcing my legs to behave and be steady so I could face off with a man who, in truth, scared the hell out of me. Maybe even more than Armani did, because at least I knew Armani wanted me alive.

Marcello grunted, displeased with my very existence, then jerked a thumb over his shoulder as Armani joined us. "Costa pulled it off," Marcello added under his breath. "Esposito and his second-in-command are dead."

"And is Alessandro okay?" I asked Armani as he worked the knot of his tie loose.

"Haven't heard from him yet. But looks like Costa beat the suitor I'd hoped you'd marry to the punch in killing the targets," Armani shared, and I faltered at the second part of what he'd said.

"Wait, you sent Rocco Barone there, too?" Gabriel pushed his hands into his pockets, his forehead creasing as he stared at his boss, mirroring my own shock. "Rocco is in Rome?"

"You don't need to know everything I plan." Armani wrapped a hand over Gabriel's shoulder. "But of course, I had to give him a chance as well."

"Looks like the best man won, then," I couldn't help but remark, hating the idea Rocco was currently in the same city as Alessandro. What if that monster was why I'd yet to hear back from Alessandro?

"You should've told me." Gabriel backed away from Armani's touch, eyes on Marcello now. "And the fact you let him back in your home when he has the most to gain from her death . . ."

"Watch yourself." Marcello stretched his neck, tugging on the lapels of his suit jacket as if itching to strangle the life from Gabriel. Or more like me.

"You two were like brothers before—"

"She came into your life," Marcello cut Armani off, earning him a sharp look from his boss. "Rocco is the better choice. I stand by that."

"And he lost. If he can't kill the man who tried to murder my daughter, then he can't protect her when one day I'm not around to do so." The idea of needing Armani's protection was insane; I wanted nothing to do with him or his empire. If only he didn't care so much about his bloodline, I could make him see that, make him understand I could never be like him or replace him. "I'll be notifying the Barones the deal with their family is off. Calliope will marry Alessandro." He slipped his hand into his pocket and produced his phone. "An unknown number calling. Answer it." His attention volleyed between Gabriel and Marcello as if unsure who he wanted on the call, then he tossed the phone to Gabriel.

Gabriel brought the phone to his ear and quickly shared, "It's Emilia Calibrisi on the line, and she wants a word."

Armani looked at me instead of taking the phone from him. "Tomorrow morning, you get fitted for your wedding dress. You're to be married in the church where I wed my wife. No formal reception. Just dinner. Then straight to consummating your marriage."

"Wait, what?" *Consummate?* "You can't be serious."

Armani snatched the phone from Gabriel but didn't bring it to his ear. "I need you to take this seriously. Tomorrow night, you'll start the process of providing me with a grandson."

The process? "Sex," I cried under my breath. "You can't even say it yourself. You don't want your own men checking me out in a dress, but you think you can force me to—"

"There are more efficient ways the doctors can ensure you wind up pregnant. The choice is yours." Armani then brought the phone to his ear, talking in Italian on his way out.

"Artificial insemination or your future husband," Marcello, the prick, remarked, as if I couldn't read between the disgusting lines. "Your choice." He looked to Gabriel and hissed, "Stop treating her like glass. If she's going to become the head of this organization, she needs to toughen up. And if you ever come after me again or try to get Armani to turn on me, I'll slit your fucking throat."

Chills racked my spine as I watched Marcello leaving. "He can't force me to get pregnant."

Gabriel reached for my arm, urging me to sit, but I could barely budge, too repulsed and shocked. "At least Alessandro is the one marrying you tomorrow and not that psychopath. Well, as long as he—"

"Makes it out of Rome alive?"

CHAPTER SIXTEEN

Calliope

Me: Tell me you're okay.

After ten minutes and still no response from my text to Alessandro, I went into the en suite bathroom and started the tub, prepared to take my second bath that day in the hope that it'd somehow calm my nerves. Drown out my wild, panicked thoughts. Well, technically it was after midnight, so it was a new day. *My wedding day, dammit.*

I double-checked the door to ensure it was locked, then texted him again. Of course, I'd called, too, but the line kept going to voicemail.

Me: I'm worried. I know Esposito is dead. But I also heard Rocco's in Rome. Please, please tell me you're okay.

Nothing.

If he was fine, why wouldn't he message me? Call me?

I removed my cotton pajamas that had cute little bananas with sunglasses on them (a gag gift from a coworker) and tossed them and my plain cotton underwear on the counter. I'd packed the least sexy nightwear I had, preferring no one in Armani's home ever see me in anything I'd normally wear to bed—an oversize sports tee and panties.

One more check of my phone before I went into the clawfoot tub, goose bumps forming all over my skin. With my foot, I stretched my leg, turning the water on at full blast to help fill it quicker, then startled at the knock on the door.

Another loud knock, followed by, "It's me," had me bolting from the bath.

There was only one "it's me" I had been waiting for, and I'd never expected him to show up outside my door. "Coming," I called out, getting my voice to work as I snatched a towel.

Quickly wrapping myself up, I unlocked the door and flung it open with a little too much excitement.

Alessandro's head was bowed, eyes closed, and he had his hands set on the exterior doorframe, leaning forward a bit like he might collapse right into the bathroom.

"You okay?" Clutching the towel to my chest with one hand, I took the chance and reached for his arm, but he groaned and immediately dropped to one knee as if I'd accidentally touched the one Jenga piece that'd caused the whole structure to collapse.

"I'm fine," he sputtered as I went down with him. He fell back onto his heels and slammed his hand to the wall by the bathroom door, placing me nearly in his lap now. His hand rested on the crotch of his suit pants, mere inches from my towel.

"You don't look fine. How'd you even get here?"

"I had to see you. They said not to come, but I'm . . . stubborn." He sounded drunk, which didn't make sense. I didn't smell booze on him, and I didn't take him for the kind of guy to need to get hammered after killing people. "I had to see you for myself. Make sure you're . . . you're all right."

"I'm good. But are you? I've been trying to get ahold of you." I walked my hand up his arm, finding something soft beneath the fabric of his shirt. *Bandage?*

He looked up at me for a moment before his head fell forward like it was deadweight. "The doctor stuck me with a needle, even though I didn't want it. I'm just . . . drugged." He slowly worked to lift his chin again, just enough to find my eyes, then eased his face close to mine.

"Mmm." He closed his eyes, and I was pretty sure he inhaled my scent. "You smell good."

A little lightheaded myself from the proximity of his mouth to mine and his husky words, I had to force myself to refocus. "Why are you drugged? Did you get hurt?"

"Yeah, but I don't even take cold meds. I'm not good with any kind of drugs." A slight lift of his lips gave a hint of a smile as he appeared to fight to get his eyes open but was failing. He really was out of it. "Call medicine my kryptonite. Funny, right? I can kill a guy, but a little fentanyl will take me out."

Hoping the towel would remain snug in place, I freed both my hands to hold his cheeks, attempting to angle his face so I could get a better look at him. "What happened?" This couldn't only be a reaction to pain meds.

"I got distracted by Esposito's wife," he murmured. "I couldn't kill her husband in front of her. I hesitated and . . . Well, the woman shot me, and Enzo disarmed her while Constantine finished the job of killing her husband."

"What?" I gasped. "You were shot? Where?"

"Just nicked my arm. No big deal. It's the broken glass the doctor had to remove from my back and hitting my head pretty hard on the table that stings a bit."

"You also might have a concussion?" This was getting worse and worse. "How'd you get glass in your back?" I let go of his face and began working at the buttons of his shirt. Someone must've changed his clothes because the material looked intact.

"Armani's people won't let me stay here," he said instead of answering me, then snatched my hand, stopping me from finishing the job of removing his shirt. He peered at me, eyes open again, but I doubted for long. "I only have a few minutes with you. My brothers are outside waiting. But everyone's okay. Constantine had a close call with the police, and Rocco was there, but we're okay. And Gabriel gave me the happy fucking news we're getting married."

Happy? Sure you are. "Did Rocco see you there?"

"We fought, yeah. And as much as I wanted him dead, we need him alive so he can lead us to his father." He pushed away from the wall and brought his hand to my face, smoothing the pad of his thumb along the contour of my cheek. "You see, Rocco and my family have a history, and this is our chance to finally get to him and his old man."

I went still at his confession, and it was an admission, wasn't it? He'd never have shared that if not for the so-called kryptonite and possible concussion. "What are you saying? You're only helping me to get to him? Is this a revenge thing for you?" And why'd my voice break?

"It's complicated. But your safety is my priority. Getting revenge for what Rocco did to my brother four years ago is a by-product of your situation."

Only a man like Alessandro could be off his game and use words like *by-product of your situation. Not that I know you well enough to make that observation.*

He hung his head again, and when his arm fell, so did the towel.

I was so stunned by the revelation about Rocco, it took me time to grab it myself. Not that him seeing me naked was my biggest problem.

"You have beautiful breasts," he said groggily, eyes falling closed— probably not on purpose—as I resecured the towel back in place. "And a beautiful smile. And eyes. And that voice—not just when I heard you sing, but when your sweet southern mouth opens at all, it's perfect. Fuck, it's so perfect," he semi-slurred, but his words still came out sexy and raspy.

Also, he was showering me in unnecessary, drug-induced compliments, so it was hard not to feel something in response.

He opened his eyes again, blinking a few times to get the lids to stay parted. "Well, you're just beautiful all around, aren't you?"

Unsure how to react to this tough guy acting like he'd been shot by Cupid's arrow, I forced myself to focus. Well, to try and get him to focus. "I want to know more about this thing with Rocco, but right now doesn't seem to be the time." I set my back to the wall by the bathroom door, not sure what to do next. Telling him about Armani's consummation demands didn't sound like the best plan now, either.

"I have to go." He attempted to stand, but nope, that wasn't happening. How'd he even get up the stairs on his own? For that matter, hadn't I locked the bedroom door?

"Easy there, big guy. You need help." I set my hands on his chest in the hope that would stop him from trying to get up. "Gabriel?" I called out, assuming he had to be waiting outside in the hall.

The door opened a moment later, and Gabriel grimaced at the sight of Alessandro on the floor and started our way. "Never seen him like this before." He knelt alongside him, and I did the same on the other side, and we both helped Alessandro to his feet, but the muscular man was heavy.

"You shouldn't be in here," Alessandro grumbled in a drunken-like tone, peering at Gabriel. "She's in a towel. It could fall off again."

"Yeah, well, I need to get you to your brothers before they storm the place, looking for you," Gabriel said, eyes on me with a light shake of the head. "I need someone else to help get him down the stairs. He's worse now than when he came up." He pointed to the bed with his chin. "Let's have him sit for a second. I'll be right back with help."

"Okay," I said in agreement, and it was a miracle we got him to the bed.

After Gabriel left, I focused on my future husband, a hundred questions cutting through my mind, but I needed to wait for answers.

"I'd pick you, you know." Alessandro set his hand on my bare thigh and lightly squeezed. "Just like Constantine did for me tonight." He hadn't exactly slurred that time, but what was he trying to say?

I looked up at him, shocked he was still sitting upright.

"I'd choose you over revenge." His head bobbed a bit, as if it were too heavy for his neck and he'd soon nod off. "I'll protect your life with my own. Always." He eased his hand free from my thigh, turned in toward me, and cupped my chin, and in a low, almost sad tone, he said, "But don't trust me when it comes to your heart, okay?"

CHAPTER SEVENTEEN

Alessandro

"Fucking hell." *Where am I?*

"You really are allergic to drugs, aren't you?" Was that Hudson? "I'll get your brothers. Be right back."

I tried to look around to get my bearings, but the pain behind my eyes had my skull feeling like it was going to crack open, so my eyelids slammed shut.

"You're awake. Finally." That was definitely Enzo.

I think. "Why does it feel like someone roofied me?" Lifting my arm to hold my head, I groaned at the pain there, and my hand plopped down onto my chest, about the only part of my body that didn't feel like it'd been used like a punching bag.

"Have you ever been roofied to know what that feels like?" My sister's words had me forcing my eyes open, and I looked over to see her and Enzo hanging by my side.

Fuck. My wedding day. That's today, right? It's happening. Gabriel said it was, didn't he? Or was that a lucid and twisted dream? "Someone talk."

Enzo helped me sit, and Izzy offered me a bottle of water.

"Esposito's wife shot you. Then one of his guards tossed you onto a glass table, and it shattered when you landed on it." Izzy rattled off the details of last night, speaking too damn fast. "Unfortunately, they were using that table to do lines of . . . something illegal, so you may have inhaled some of that, too. But on top of hitting your head, then the doc jabbing you with fentanyl—safe to say you needed the beauty sleep."

"I heard about every third word you said." I sucked down the water, then crumpled the plastic between my palms, wishing the jackhammer in my head would call it a day.

"You were distracted last night." Enzo sat next to me. "That's not like you."

"You know he's a big softy when it comes to certain things." I wasn't sure if that was a compliment or an insult from Izzy. "I think this woman has him a little shaken up, though."

"Probably the loss of his bachelorhood's more like it." I was too out of it to detect whether Enzo was being sarcastic with that comment.

"Rocco was there. Seeing him was what shook me up." It had nothing to do with Callie, dammit. "Where's Constantine?"

"On a call. He'll be in here in a second." Enzo nudged my side, and it was thankfully my good arm.

"The doctor we dragged from his home last night. Is he going to be a problem?" I slid my legs around to the side of the bed and tossed the crumpled bottle toward the wastebasket but missed. "Also, you should've clocked him so he couldn't drug me."

"This is Enzo we're talking about." Izzy grabbed the bottle and threw it away. "He nearly did, but I held him back. We don't punch doctors. Not a good-guy-gal thing to do."

I rolled my eyes, not the norm for me. "There can be exceptions."

"The sizeable donation we made to his bank account for his help should buy his silence," Enzo answered my other concerns.

"You sure you're up to getting married today?" I looked over to the doorway to Constantine there, concern in his eyes.

"Not exactly, but I don't have a choice." I checked my wrist, but my watch wasn't there. "What time is it?"

"Three," Izzy said, and based on the light streaming through the windows, she didn't mean 0300 hours.

"We've held Gabriel off as long as we can." Enzo stood, lining himself up by Izzy. "Well, I should say, he's held Armani off as long as he could. But you're getting hitched in about two hours."

Two hours?

"Time to shower and get over to the DiMaggios'. Armani wants to speak with you before you walk down the aisle," Enzo said, infiltrating my thoughts before I could panic about having two hours left to be single.

"You should've woken me sooner." I tried to stand but lost my balance, landing back on my ass on the bed—one other part of me that didn't hurt. Thank God.

"We tried. Just like we tried to keep you away from Callie last night, and you wouldn't listen. You're one stubborn prick when you're drugged." Enzo showed his left cheek, and there was a faint mark there. He wasn't suggesting I . . .

"Like hell I hit you." My gaze snapped guiltily to my palms.

"Kidding, this was courtesy of Esposito's wife if you can believe it." Relieved, I looked back up at Enzo's words. "And no, I didn't hit her back."

"But I would've liked to," Izzy shot out. "Your tux is being delivered any minute. I can't believe we're going to be watching you get married today. It's surreal." She folded her arms, staring at me with a wistful look that shouldn't have been on her face. Because this was a tragedy, not a fairy tale.

"*You're* coming to the ceremony?" My second attempt to stand had me back on my ass again.

"Of course. Not every day our forever bachelor brother ties the knot." Izzy smiled, and considering her cheerful mood, that had to mean—

"Tell me Sebastian and Sean still have eyes on Rocco," I said at the memory of that important detail.

"Rocco's in Romania. And we learned that Armani gave word to Claudio Barone that the wedding with his son is off, and the Barones are obviously not happy," Izzy answered while I cataloged my brother's reaction to the mention of Rocco. I doubted I'd have a chance to do a mental health check on Constantine before the ceremony, but he couldn't be doing well after last night.

"Which is what we want." Enzo seemed far less worried than Izzy. Not a total surprise. "Because with any luck, they'll break the deal they made with Dad and finally come for us, and we can get Rocco. And The League can have Claudio."

Dad and his deals. Just like the one he made for us years ago, turning us into mercenaries for the government.

"It was Dad's arrangement with Claudio that kept his psychopathic son from ever coming after you again," Izzy said to Constantine, and her words earned her a disapproving look from him; he'd wanted the son of a bitch to climb out of whatever hole he'd been hiding in long ago and come for him. But Rocco hadn't, much to Constantine's frustration and, well, to all of ours.

"Consider the cease-fire between our families null and void." I stated the obvious, wondering if I'd be walking down the aisle with the pain in my head, or if my sister had called Mom for her magic remedy to save my ass.

Hudson joined our group chat in the bedroom on my third and finally successful attempt to stand. At the sight of him, the memory of my sister kissing him last night resurfaced. Before I could make everyone uncomfortable and ask about it, another oh-shit memory decided to make its debut in my mind.

I told Callie about Rocco's connection to our family, didn't I? Knowing her, she was pissed. Probably thought I was using her as bait to get to the fucker. "I need to get over to the DiMaggios'. I have to make sure we're on the same page about what happens after the wedding."

"And what page would that be?" Constantine asked me.

Considering the measures Armani had already taken to ensure Callie wasn't on birth control and also was fertile . . . "The page we want him to be on," I grumbled in a half-assed answer.

"You need to negotiate that Callie comes back to New York with you." Constantine shot me a sharp look. Did he actually think I planned to live in Italy? "You can't live under the same roof as that man."

"Clearly," I snapped, holding my head, trying to stifle a groan.

"Tell him there're too many cooks in the kitchen," Enzo remarked. "You know," he added with a shrug, "too many people in his organization who have a reason for Callie not to be the one to take over."

"Keep sowing doubt that someone in his house is a threat to his bloodline," Constantine tacked on to Enzo's advice. "More than just one someone."

I reached around for my back at the achy pain there, a reminder of what had happened last night. My brothers saving my ass when I nearly fucked up the whole op because I couldn't kill a man in front of his wife. "Shouldn't be tough to do . . . There are plenty of people in that house that more than likely want her dead."

CHAPTER EIGHTEEN

Alessandro

Standing in the tux my brothers had delivered from my favorite designer in Italy like a damn miracle—or in my case, this felt like a curse—I waited inside Armani's office for him to join me.

Callie was somewhere upstairs getting dressed, and we were due at the church in thirty minutes, but it was only a five-minute drive from the egg castle, or whatever it was called.

From a quick online search performed by Izzy on our ride to the castle, she'd discovered the cathedral where we were to be wed had been built in 1197. It'd been destroyed by an earthquake in 1908 and rebuilt. Not that it mattered, but it was one of Sicily's most famous churches. With any luck, when Armani stepped inside, someone would stab his vampire ass in the heart, and he'd turn to dust.

I grabbed my phone from my inside jacket pocket, anxious to get the terms and conditions about the wedding over with. Whatever magical concoction Mom had provided Izzy, along with a cold shower, had me feeling at 90 percent now, which was far better than I'd been earlier.

I opened up my last message to Callie and reread her texts, followed by my unanswered ones.

Callie: Tell me you're okay.

Callie: I'm worried. I know Esposito is dead. But I also heard Rocco's in Rome. Please, please tell me you're okay.

I'd been unable to answer her last night, but I'd still felt like a dick for making her worry, and after my shower, I'd sent her an apology.

Me: I'm sorry about last night. (This morning?) I just woke up if you can believe that.

After no response, I'd texted again.

Me: Of course, why would you believe me? You don't really know me.

Me: I'll be over soon.

Ten minutes later and two calls straight to voicemail, my nerves had gotten the best of me.

Me: Still no answer from you. I'm concerned. I'm reaching out to Gabriel to see if you're pissed and ignoring me or something else is up.

I'd phoned Gabriel for answers after that. Apparently, Marcello the dick had made a comeback, and he'd taken her phone in the morning, despite Gabriel's insistence it wasn't necessary.

"I was beginning to think you might stand up my daughter today." At Armani's words, I switched my phone to silent, pocketed it, then faced my future father-in-law. "Too bad your parents can't make it to the ceremony." The asshole actually sounded genuine. "I assume your brothers and sister will be at the church?"

Unfortunately. Of course, it was probably a good idea to have them there in case Rocco managed to slip The League's overwatch and make a surprise debut to object to our nuptials. "We need to iron out a few details before we leave."

Armani went over to his bar, which took up the entire length of one wall, and poured two drinks. "Grappa. My mother's homemade recipe."

Drinking was the last thing I wanted to do after my fucked-up night, but I accepted the glass and swished the liquid around, buying myself time to feel the familiar burn of grappa warming my chest post-drink.

A few of Armani's guards hung back by the doorway, but far enough away they'd need to strain their ears to hear our conversation. So he clearly wanted our talk to be mano a mano.

"There are many details we need to discuss." He sipped his drink, appearing satisfied with the taste. "I spoke with Emilia Calibrisi last night and your father today. We're in agreement this union will work favorably for us all."

I'd only found out about the recent conversation with my dad on the ride over to the estate. I wasn't thrilled they'd spoken, but Dad was playing ball to help us succeed with the op, so I supposed I ought to be grateful. He could've stopped the whole mission in its tracks had he not garnered Emilia's support.

"I suppose you have terms you'd like to present?" Armani looked my way, keeping his distance from me to just beyond a choke hold reach.

Smart bastard. "I need six months in New York with Callie before we move to Sicily." I lowered the glass to my side. "I have business there. Deals I need to wrap up. A life. But more importantly, you need to clean house before I allow my wife near your associates. I'm not happy you let Marcello back under your roof, either."

He quietly studied me, only a subtle change in his expression to indicate my words made it to his damn ears.

"I don't believe Esposito is the only one who wants Callie gone. And if one of your trusted guards could be turned, I have concerns you have more traitors"—I pointed to the ceiling—"here as well."

"You think you can protect my daughter in New York?"

"My family is off-limits in that city. Untouchable. And after the wedding tonight, we'll have the backing of The League. She'll be safe as long as she's with me." I lowered my hand and shoved it into my pocket. "But here, I won't be able to sleep with both eyes closed, worried someone will *try* and sneak in at night and slit our throats."

He tossed back the rest of his grappa and headed to the bar to add more to his glass.

When he began speaking in Italian, I demanded, "English," not in the mood to cater to him or his preferences.

"Let's say I may agree on the fact that some may want Calliope dead," he said, switching to English without pushback. "Power does mess with a man's head. But I can't give you six months. I want my daughter back home before summer's end. And, preferably, pregnant by then, one way or another."

He took the bait. Gave me the three months I'd actually hoped for. I still wanted to chuck my glass at him for the pregnancy comment. It wasn't time to lose control when I was managing to get him to agree without much fight, though. I had to assume my father and Emilia had already planted the New York idea in his head and given him the nudge, warming him up before this conversation.

"Define 'one way or another,'" I remarked, unable to stop my tone from dropping low, all the way to the depths of hell, where this man would soon forever live.

"If you can't get her pregnant naturally, then we'll have the doctor artificially inseminate."

Now I needed a drink.

"I had my people look into your medical records back in New York. Seems you get regularly checked, given your active sex life. And based on what I read, you're clean and fertile. We wouldn't be having this conversation otherwise."

I swallowed, trying to control myself. To not go for him now. I'd managed to hold myself back from killing Rocco last night, but this fucker was testing my patience.

"If I find out you lie with another woman and cheat on your wife, my men will cut off your testicles, understood?"

"You're the cheat, not me," I reminded him.

"Have you ever been in a relationship to test your fidelity?"

I wasn't about to satisfy him with an answer or think about my ex. So I took another sip, and the grappa warmed my chest.

"Tonight, my men will be in the bedroom while you consummate the marriage to ensure there's no use of protection."

At that, I snapped. The glass slipped from my hand, and I started for him. When his guards hurried in, barking out orders in Italian to step back, I hesitantly surrendered. I was still close enough to squeeze the life from him as I warned, "You put your men in the room with us, and it'll be them who lose their balls, I can assure you of that. No one sees my wife but me. Non-fucking-negotiable." My body locked tight as I stared him down, and the prick smiled.

He was testing me. My limits. Control. My *feelings* for her. And I was pretty sure I'd shown my cards. I *would* protect his daughter no matter what.

"Fine, fine. Just outside the room, then. And they'll come in after consummation to make sure it's been done."

The way he could so easily talk about his daughter being fucked . . . Well, I'd really, really enjoy taking my time to make his death painful. "I won't force myself on her. If she doesn't want to 'consummate'"—I tossed his ridiculous word back at him—"then it won't be happening." Not that I had plans to have sex with Callie. Period. I only needed his people to think we were actively trying to provide him an heir.

"I see the way you two look at each other. You can't fake that."

I ignored his words. Well, did my best not to think about what he'd said. Did I want Callie? Yeah, the woman was gorgeous. But would I ever have sex with her, even if she wanted it? Hell no.

"I have more conditions." Armani set aside his glass, went over to a leather chair, and snatched his suit jacket.

Realizing my hands were in fists, I unfurled them and faced Armani as he buttoned up.

"The wedding night happens here. Tomorrow, you can leave. But two of my trusted men will fly on your jet with you back to New York. They'll be staying in your home for protection." He lifted his hand as if worried I'd protest. And yeah, I planned to.

I not only didn't trust his men, but also, having his people in my house meant I'd be forced to share a bedroom with my wife to keep up appearances.

"You want her in New York this summer? This is the only way." He made a dismissive hand gesture. "Have your people check into their backgrounds if that makes you feel better. But they're coming, or she's not going."

"Fine," I gritted out, hating myself for giving in, but I was too close to getting what I wanted to start shit now.

"I need your word you plan to do everything in your power to protect the DiMaggio organization, too." He walked my way and had the fucking nerve to offer his hand, as if my word were as good as my bond.

"Your daughter, you mean?" I stared at his palm, not ready to give him mine.

"I already know you will keep her safe. Die for her. Your eyes don't lie." He angled his head, waiting for my hand—my *submission*. "But my family name, the bloodline, and my people in the organization must also be protected with your last breath. Especially the grandson you'll give me."

This favor to Gabriel was turning into quite the mindfuck, but I accepted the man's hand and shook on it. And damn it to all hell, my word was something I'd never broken before, and now I'd have to.

"One more thing," he said, once our palms departed from the handshake. "I need you to work on teaching my daughter to be more like you. Help her see the way."

"What do you mean, more like me?"

He smiled. "You may be a Costa, but you're no saint. You've racked up quite the number of bodies since you met my daughter last weekend, just to protect her. But that doesn't change what you are. A killer. She needs to see the light. Understand it's okay to let that part of her out, too."

My insides turned at what he was proposing. God help me if he demanded she murder someone over the summer before I could take him out. I'd never let that woman know what it was like to take a life. I had no choice but to snap out, "Understood."

"Good." He narrowed his eyes, and what else was coming? "Is Rocco Barone going to be a problem for you? I learned this morning you two have a history together."

I should've been expecting this, but I didn't have the mental bandwidth left for the conversation. "Not unless he comes after Calliope as retribution. You do realize he's one sick fuck, don't you?" I pointed out, unable to dull the blade of my bluntness. "The vile things he would've done to your daughter . . . No father should've ever let that man within a hundred feet of his child."

"He won't come after my daughter. He knows there'd be hell to pay." He flicked his hand toward the guards, who were hanging back in the doorway again, and Gabriel was there waiting for us, too. "Time to go."

I'd never been so grateful to see a criminal. But after the last few days, I was beginning to think Callie was wrong about him needing my help to see the light.

Either I was becoming a horrible judge of character, or Gabriel had already seen it, and this was his chance to become a better man. Change the DiMaggio organization into a legitimate one after Armani died.

Gabriel met my eyes and gave me a little nod, and I hated the nagging gut feeling that told me I was too off my game to truly know anything.

For now, I needed to focus on one step at a time.

Marriage.

A fake honeymoon.

Then devise a plan to take out Marcello, Armani, and any other threats to Callie's safety.

And also, somehow survive three months without actually impregnating my wife.

CHAPTER NINETEEN

Calliope

"You make one beautiful bride."

At Rosa's wispy, almost sentimental tone, I faced the full-length mirror inside the back room of the church. "Thank you, I think? Not sure I want to be a beautiful anything today."

"Can I come in?" someone called out while knocking. "It's Isabella Costa."

Izzy? "Can you give us a minute alone?" I asked Rosa, my heart going into overdrive at the idea of meeting Alessandro's sister for some reason.

Rosa patted my shoulder, then went to the door and swapped places with Isabella.

Once the door was closed and we were alone, Isabella hung back, wearing a soft yellow dress that'd make a perfect bridesmaid dress.

She was gorgeous. Not a shocker given Alessandro's looks.

"Hi," I whispered, my nerves catching as I waited for her to talk.

"Well, you're absolutely stunning. Not my brother's normal type." She raised her hand, eyes narrowing as if an apology was on the way. "I mean that in the best possible way." A little laugh left her mouth. "You're who I would wish . . . if this were real, you know?"

I processed her words.

Then took time to process a bit more as she kept studying me. She and her brother had the whole staring-at-me-like-I-was-a-mystery-to-be-solved thing down pat.

She drummed her fingers on her collarbone as I continued to remain quiet. "I ramble sometimes. Lack a filter, too. Apologies in advance."

"I can relate to that," I admitted. "Your brother isn't always a fan of my mouth." *Well, that didn't sound right.*

She chuckled. "Oh, I'm betting he's secretly your biggest fan." When she ate up the space between us and pulled me in for an unexpected hug, I went still.

My arms became awkward dangling limbs at my sides, and it took me a moment to remember what to do in a scenario like this. Hug back.

"It's nice to meet you," I finally said when she let me go. "How's Alessandro feeling? Gabriel said he slept most of the day." I wasn't about to admit how worried about him I'd been after our encounter last night, but yeah, the knots in my stomach had knots.

"Rough night. He'll be fine. No worries." She played everything off with a shrug while standing alongside me, catching my eyes in the mirror now instead. "He's a tough guy, but he's a teddy bear underneath. Just don't tell him it was me who shared that."

Teddy bear? More like sweet and then sour (but on steroids).

"This dress, though. Just . . . wow," she murmured, fingering her wavy brown hair that had some blonde sun-kissed highlights in it.

I focused on the mirror, studying my "costume," which was all it needed to be to me. The base of the dress was a mermaid gown dripping in sparkles, but I currently had the gorgeous detachable skirt covering it with a long train of tulle and lace.

The bodice of the gown cinched in my waist and featured a plunging neckline, and the back had sheer tulle with gorgeous pearl-like buttons.

"This is probably going to be the only time I ever witness my brother get married since he hates the concept of relationships ever since, um . . . so, yeah."

My ears perked up at that. "Ever since what?"

"And I know the marriage won't last, but you're just . . . well, perfect," she went on, sidestepping my question, and I had a feeling I wouldn't be getting an answer.

"That's sweet of you to say." I faced her, not in the mood to look at myself anymore. "I owe your family my life. I'm a stranger, and you're helping me."

"We're not strangers anymore, and you can call me Izzy."

"But Hudson calls you something else?" Embarrassment heated my cheeks. "No filter. See. Case in point."

"I'm just trying to wrap my head around the fact my big brother told you that. He's not all that forthcoming about details." She tapped a black-painted fingernail against her lips as her eyes went wide. "Don't tell me he told you about the kiss while he was acting drunk last night?" She spun away from me, setting her sights on the room, where the church's history bled into every square inch of the space.

"The kiss," was all I managed out, wondering whether she'd go on if I left the words hanging in the air. I could use a distraction from the fact I'd soon be kissing her brother before strangers and God.

An exaggerated sigh fell from her lips as she gathered the skirt of her dress and plopped down on a chair. "I was undercover as Hudson's girlfriend, and Alessandro said we needed to look more couple-y. Hudson hesitated, so I leaned in and kissed him." Her hand went to her mouth as if remembering the moment. "Only, he kissed me back. Like tongue and all." She let go of the skirt and uncovered her mouth to point to her bare arms. "See? Chills. I have chills, thinking about it." Her eyes swept up to mine. "I have no one to talk to about this, because my brothers would lose their minds if they knew Hudson tongued me. And I think we both enjoyed it." She laughed.

"So maybe one day you and—"

"No," she cut me off. "There can't be an us. Hudson would never. He's too loyal to Constantine, and he'd never cross that line with me." She bunched her skirt and stood. "I need to forget it happened. I have bad taste in men, and although Hudson is a great guy, he's like Alessandro. No plans to marry and have kids."

"I barely know your brother, but I'm guessing there's a reason Alessandro's the way he is. Same for Hudson."

She waved her hand. "I can't believe I'm being all sulky and making things about me right now. I'm so sorry."

"The distraction from this madness is welcome, trust me. Plus, I've never had a sister. Any sibling. So even if this is all fake . . . you seem like a nice one to have."

"Well, damn. Now I'm going to get attached to you, aren't I?" She stared at me, blinking a few times as if unsure how to feel about that. "And it's going to suck when you guys go your separate ways." Her shoulders fell, and she shook her head. "So, do you have the something-borrowed-and-blue thing already? Or maybe you don't want to do that because this isn't a marriage of your choosing. I mean, way better choice to pick Alessandro over the other guy. And no worries, my brother won't get close enough to a woman to ever break her heart, so you should be fine there, too."

Don't trust me with your heart. He'd warned me last night. For a playboy, he didn't seem to fit the stereotypical model. He didn't want to hurt anyone, and a playboy would think with his dick and not care, wouldn't he?

When I'd yet to speak, she went on, "As for something blue, you'll be giving my brother blue balls in that dress. So you've got that part covered."

I snort-laughed, shocked I'd done that on a day like this, but she chuckled right along with me. "You and I make quite the pair, huh?" I tossed out, and there went my stomach again. Knotting up. Because yup, I'd be losing her from my life, too, when I walked away from Alessandro.

"Probably good we get along since we'll most likely spend a lot of time together in New York this summer."

"Wait, what?" I blurted in shock.

"Shit." She winced. "I forgot you haven't seen my brother since he negotiated the terms of the marriage with your dad."

I gulped, feeling a little lightheaded now. "What were the terms?"

"That you get to live with him in New York instead of here for the next three months. Armani's sending two of his men to bunk at your future husband's penthouse to keep an eye on you, which means you'll really have to sell the whole husband-and-wife thing."

I didn't want to spend my summer in Italy under the same roof as Armani. But the idea of living in New York instead of Franklin was just . . .

There was also something I'd yet to tell Alessandro. Another message had come in from Braden before Marcello took my phone.

Braden had landed us my dream gig of playing on Broadway.

Wagner's "Bridal Chorus," "Here Comes the Bride," started playing, and the devil offered me his arm to walk me down the aisle. I stared at Armani, unsure what to do, but for the sake of appearances, allowed him to link our arms.

Peering through the veil, I took in the sight of the guests. On Armani's side, it was a sea of mostly unrecognizable faces. In the groom's section, it was practically empty. Izzy and three men were there, and I had to assume the guys were Constantine, Enzo, and Hudson.

Can I do this? Get married? My shoulders fell at the memory of Aunt Tia being watched. Her life was on the line. Of course I had to go through with this.

Izzy caught my eyes, gave me a light nod of "you've got this"—well, that's how I translated it—then I looked beyond her to put eyes on the groom for the first time.

Each nervous step down the aisle matched three quick beats of my heart.

Alessandro was too far away to make out his expression, but the man truly looked handsome in his tuxedo. He was also standing on his own two feet without support, confirming what Izzy said, that he was now "okay" despite a rough night.

No maid of honor or best man stood up there with him, only a man decked out in a fancy outfit—someone on Armani's payroll to officiate the wedding.

When Alessandro's palm went to his heart over his tux jacket and he tipped his head a touch, I was pretty sure he was signaling something to me as well. His way of letting me know everything would be okay. To keep walking to him. Or maybe he was on the verge of a heart attack about losing his bachelorhood?

I swallowed, surrendered a nod, and kept on moving, stepping on rose petals. However, there was no sign of a flower girl or cute kid as a ring bearer. Honestly, I was grateful everyone in this nightmare inside the church appeared to be over eighteen.

As we closed in on the platform, Alessandro's eyes on me gave me comfort. His stoic look, hands now clasped in front of him, and a warm, gentle expression that kind of surprised me, given our situation, managed to help slow my pulse a bit.

The facial hair he'd started to sport was now gone. Clean-shaven. His wavy hair was tamed and pushed to the side of his forehead with gel. And the man wore the tux. It didn't wear him.

It took me a moment to realize I'd made it to the top, and Armani was now turning toward me to lift the veil. I resisted the impulse to throw up when he leaned in and kissed my cheek. He murmured something in Italian, and this was one time I was grateful to be clueless at what he'd said.

The priest—I assume that's who he was—motioned for me to step alongside Alessandro, and when I looked at the groom without my veil, my legs became wobbly. Because up close with an unobstructed view, I could see "calm and collected" had only been an act. He was as nervous as I was. There was a visible vein at the side of his neck, as if he were clamping down too hard on his back teeth. Dots of sweat at his hairline. And as the priest began speaking in Italian, I realized Alessandro was wringing his hands together, not calmly clasping them.

When the next part of the wedding took place, we quietly studied each other like we were at a funeral instead. I barely heard the Liturgy of the Word spoken. Not that I would've understood it since everything was in Italian.

"The vows are next," Alessandro mouthed to me a moment later, and I had to assume he was politely translating whatever the priest had said, clueing me in on what was going on at my own wedding. He fingered the collar of his shirt just above the black bow tie and stretched his neck around a bit.

Was he going to be a runaway groom? I wouldn't blame him; *I* was on the verge of bolting. But Aunt Tia's life kept my uncomfortable heels rooted in place.

"I don't have vows prepared," I whispered, hoping I didn't need to make any up on the fly.

"Same." Alessandro frowned, then turned his attention to the priest and said something in Italian. "Can you repeat what he says in Italian instead?" he asked, eyes meeting mine again, and all I could do was nod for my answer.

Sweat trickled between my breasts and down my back as I echoed the Italian words to the priest to the best of my ability.

It was Alessandro's turn to recite the vows next, and listening to him speak Italian was almost too much for me, because he could quickly reignite my love for the language after Armani's very existence had ruined it. Every word from him was so smooth and silky, I had to look away for a moment to collect myself. To remember this was fake.

I stole my focus toward the assembly to see them standing during the Rite of Marriage. Rings I'd forgotten we'd need were brought out. Two yellow-gold bands were removed from a little see-through, netted bag—symbols of the eternal love for your partner.

The priest spoke again in Italian while offering a band to Alessandro, and he came over to me, noticeably swallowing. I forced up my left hand so he could slide the lie onto my finger.

When it was my turn, he held my eyes instead of looking at the eternal symbol on his hand, and told me, "We have to kiss now."

"Calliope?" the priest prompted.

Wait, does the kiss mean we're married now? Is it over? Trembling, I started to feel dizzy. *Shit, don't faint.*

As if sensing I was losing control, Alessandro pulled his hand away from mine only to snatch both my forearms, helping keep me steady and grounded.

"We can do this," he promised, but could we? Really?

It's just a kiss.

His brow tightened as he continued to study me, slowly dipping in closer for the inevitable moment my heart would probably burst from my chest. I copied his move when he shut his eyes, and my heart galloped double time as I waited for his lips to meet mine.

And God help me, help us all, when they did. I hadn't anticipated a groan from him, or for my lips to naturally part, offering him an invitation to deepen the kiss.

My lips softened and relaxed, and his tongue dove into my mouth and dueled with mine. He expertly guided the kiss to the point I was pretty sure we both forgot where we were and why we were there.

I returned my *husband's* moan, and he swallowed it and gave it right back to me. His hand slid around to my back, and I arched into him.

Someone was talking now in Italian, but neither of us stopped. Cloud nine was a real thing, and I was there. Blissfully ignorant to anything and everything aside from this unexplainable connection with this man.

At the sound of cheers and more Italian, the spell broke, reminding me we were in a church because of Armani, and I pulled back and blinked in confusion as to what in the world had just happened between us.

Alessandro opened his eyes. Nostrils flaring. An almost panicked but definitely confused look pointed right back at me.

Yeah, same. Because what was that kiss? And why'd I suddenly feel inspired to write again? Chills wrapped around my limbs, and I stepped back, needing space. Needing to breathe. Needing to remember that, *You're not mine to keep.*

CHAPTER TWENTY

Calliope

Inside my bedroom, I kicked off my heels and faced my *husband*. He'd lost his bow tie and tux jacket before our forced dinner with Armani and his favorite assembly of bad guys—Alessandro's family hadn't been invited—but now the man was distracting me by working free a few buttons of his starched white shirt.

Thankfully, he stopped at only three, because if he kept going, I'd need a cold glass of something. I didn't want to feel heat of any kind right now. I couldn't give in to what Armani wanted, especially with Frankie and Leo parked in the hallway listening for us to "consummate."

And if that kiss had proved anything, it was how hot things truly could be between us, especially in the privacy of a bedroom without eyes on us. *Just ears.*

When he produced what looked like a lighter from his pocket and began walking around the room like a man on a mission, I blurted, "What are you doing?"

When he crossed the bedroom and dropped his mouth over my ear, it was to whisper, not to give me goose bumps. Of course, my skin pebbled at his breath and proximity anyway. "Checking for cameras and listening devices. We can't talk until I know it's safe."

So that little thing does all that, huh? "You talked last night without checking first." I reminded him of his drug-induced state, and he eased back to find my face.

"Right." He bowed his head, almost as if in shame, then went back to his *Mission: Impossible*–looking device.

While waiting for him, I removed the detachable skirt. I was only in the mermaid gown now, but I'd be needing help to get completely undressed.

I should've had more than two glasses of champagne at dinner. But I clearly hadn't been in a celebratory mood while Armani had feasted and toasted. Now I wished I'd had the entire bottle to get through the night—well, to help me fall asleep without much effort, at least.

Alessandro disappeared into the bathroom, then returned a few moments later and wordlessly snatched my wrist, tipping his head in a request to follow. "We're good," he said once in the en suite bathroom. "But the *idioti* in the hall might hear us, so we should talk in here."

"Armani expects us to have sex tonight," I blurted. "But you know that, don't you?"

He set the lighter-looking device on the vanity and reached for my forearm. "I told him I wouldn't force you to do anything."

"How'd he take that?" My gaze fell to his grip, and although he followed my line of sight, he didn't unhand me.

"I think it's in our best interest to just fake it tonight."

"Fake it until you make it, huh?" I smiled at my dumb joke. *Okay, maybe two glasses of champagne were enough.* Eyes back on him, I resigned myself to my fate and asked, "How are we faking it?"

"I just don't want Armani changing his mind about letting you come home with me, which is why I think we need to sell the sex thing," he explained instead of answering my question of how.

"You didn't discuss the plan to move with me first."

"I didn't have a chance." He frowned and let me go, pocketing his hands. "You don't want to stay here, do you?"

"No, but I want to go home."

"I can better protect you in New York. I'd never convince him to let you go back to your old life. He wants you to become more like him," he said in such a matter-of-fact tone it was like he was negotiating a business deal, and it made my stomach hurt.

I knew he was right, but it didn't mean I had to like it. "Are you feeling better?" I deflected, not wanting to ask a man for permission to live my life—a.k.a. perform on Broadway with Braden on June 6. Maybe I'd wait for that conversation to happen. I supposed the conversation about what he'd accidentally admitted about Rocco last night could be tabled for now, too.

"I'm fine. Sorry about last night. I shouldn't have come over." His brow tightened, and there was clearly more he wanted to say, but I doubted he'd open up more.

"And I'm sorry you had to kill people for me." My shoulders fell, and I faced the mirror as he came up behind me. Since he was a head taller than me, he didn't need to sidestep me to catch my reflection.

"Maybe we should get you out of this dress?"

I arched a brow, and he closed one eye, as if regretting his choice of words.

"You know what I mean."

"Not sure if I do. You've yet to tell me how we're faking it, so the men outside believe we're doing as Armani asked," I reminded him, growing even more tense. I was a married woman now, and that was just . . . When his hand went to my shoulder, I spied the wedding ring there, and whispered, "That band must feel like handcuffs to you."

"It's . . . fine." The grit to his tone suggested otherwise, but we were in this together whether we wanted to be or not.

If he could suck it up, I could, too. He was saving my life and my aunt's, after all. Tonight, of all nights, he didn't deserve my sassy mouth, even if Izzy thought he was a "fan" of it. *Not a chance.* "Should we get this over with, then?" I hiked a thumb over my shoulder. "Unbutton me, please?"

One palm skated over the pearl buttons that were in line with my spine, and he began undoing them with only one hand, the other resting on my shoulder.

Impressive. "So how are we convincing the men in the hall we're doing it?"

His hand went still as he met my eyes in the mirror. "Given the fact he had you checked the other day, I have concerns he's sick enough to—"

"Same," I cut him off, the idea terrifying.

"I won't let that happen. I promise." Without answering my "how" to the faking-it question, he finished the job of unbuttoning me. I let the bodice fall forward and collapse at the waist, showing him what I had on beneath it, which wasn't much.

A fairly see-through lace teddy. I studied myself in the mirror. Nipples hard and visible through the transparent fabric. He'd already seen my breasts twice now, and we were technically married, so what was the point in hiding?

But when I looked up at him in the reflection, he had a hand stroking his chiseled jawline, and his attention was sharp and focused on my tits.

"What's the plan?" I whispered, hating the heat in my belly traveling south between my thighs with his eyes on me. "How are we faking it?"

"I'm going to ask you to do something that's going to have you wanting to smack me."

"Didn't expect your wanting *me* to dominate *you* to be a kink of yours." There went my mouth. I couldn't seem to help it sometimes. I told myself it had nothing to do with the fact I was half DiMaggio.

His dark brows rose, and he spun me around to face him, then set his hands on the counter, trapping me against him. My body responded as if it were a place I needed to be—at his mercy. "I have no kinks of any kind, especially involving violence. Not in the bedroom, at least."

So you get off on hurting people outside the bedroom, huh? I should be scared. Yet, I'm not budging. Something is wrong with me, too. "So you haven't thought about taking a belt to my ass for my runaway mouth?" I asked, testing the waters. Seeing if he was bullshitting me about his no-kinks thing. Also, proving my point about my mouth.

"I would never hurt a woman." Gray eyes journeyed to my breasts again before landing on my lips, and I couldn't help but remember that kiss. It'd been more than an expert tongue schooling me on how a real man kissed a woman. "*But* maybe I wouldn't be opposed to swatting a woman's ass if she really needed it. *If* she'd been bad enough to deserve it."

Oh, fuck me. Why was that so hot? And how wet could this man possibly make me? "You're not seriously telling me you've never spanked a woman before?"

He cocked his head, a flicker of surprise in his eyes, and maybe he was mirroring my own look. "I can take a man's life, yes. But I've never set a hand on a woman in or out of the bedroom, no."

Why was that such an oddly sweet thing for him to say? *Sure, I'm a killer, but I draw the line at spanking.* "And yet you wouldn't mind making an exception for me, would you? Swatting your *wife's* ass?" I couldn't bite my tongue, not right now. Not with how he was peering at me like he wanted to bend me over and—

"You may be bad enough to need my handprint on your ass cheek," he said huskily, his tone a match to the bold, dark look in his eyes. Before I could summon any type of response as I contemplated if I wanted to be his bad girl, he continued, "But Callie, I need you to remember I don't feel anything. Ever." Lines cut across his forehead as he studied me, as if worried we were on different pages in totally different genres of books. "Sex is just tension relief for me. It will never be more."

"And why does it seem like you're warning me, like you did about my heart last night? Warning me not to tempt you because I'll get hurt?" Our faking-it conversation had been derailed, and we were going in quite a different direction. Murky waters and dangerous territory. "You keep trying to save me from you, and maybe it's *you* who will need saving from me."

A cocky grin slipped across his lips, and I hated how much I wanted to kiss the edges of his mouth and taste him. Hated how much he was right—that my temptation was real, as was the fact he'd break my heart if I actually did give in to the desire I couldn't pretend not to feel for this man.

"Tell me why I'd want to smack you." I had to get back on track. Remind myself there were two men in the hall waiting for us to have sex, and it had to be fake, and I was pretty sure we were on the verge of it being real if we kept this hot back-and-forth going.

"I need you to get yourself off. I need you to come for me, Callie." At his erotic words, he pushed away from the counter, allowing me the space I needed to set my hand on my breastbone without hitting him with my elbow in the process.

"Why?" I closed my eyes, drawing up an answer on my own. "Because my father's men are pigs, and the smell of sex will help sell the idea." And it wasn't like semen really had a smell, so it'd be up to my body to do it. "I don't want to smack you." Opening my eyes, I shared, "Just everyone forcing us to do this."

His fingers went to his shirt, and he pulled it free from his pants, then in one fast move, snapped his belt free like he'd done in my bathroom the other day. "They'll be expecting noise, too."

My eyes cut to the leather hanging from his hand, and maybe he didn't have kinks, but seeing him with that belt certainly had me wondering if I did.

He looked at me, then at the belt, then dropped it as if the thing were on fire in his hand. "We can say fuck it and not do this."

"The alternative is possibly staying here longer," I said as he finished the job of unbuttoning his shirt. "Or worse, him holding my aunt's life over my head."

"It's up to you. Tell me what you want." He kept his shirt on, but with it open, I had a view of the hard ridges of his abdominal muscles.

"Are you staying in the bathroom while I get myself off in the bed?" Why'd I sound so breathless? "How is this going to work?" When he continued to simply fix his attention on me—that unraveling-the-mysteries-of-the-universe look—I rambled, "Do you need to be in the room making noise? Headboard banging, maybe? Should I be under the covers?"

"Under the covers would be . . . a better idea to the alternative." The heavy lift of his chest pulled me back to the exposed wall of muscles I wanted to run my palms over.

"And the alternative?" I nearly panted out the ridiculous question. I knew the answer, but I wanted to hear him say the words.

Instead, he hissed, "You're on very thin fucking ice." He brought his face near mine.

Eyes up, I did my best to come across as tough and told him what he had to know already. "I don't frighten easily."

His smile nearly touched my mouth. We were *that* close. "Clearly, or you would've run a year ago. And surely Saturday night." His hand went to my waist, and his other palm made its way to the nape of my neck as he made me his prisoner. "And definitely right now."

"Yet I'm still here. But I shouldn't be, though, right?" I whispered, eyes falling shut with his mouth there, unsure whether he might give in and kiss me.

His grip tightened at my waist as he drew me firm to his body, letting me feel how hard he was. "No," he snapped out. "Now, finish getting undressed and get under the covers. Or I'll carry you there myself." He let go of me, and when I opened my eyes, he'd already left the bathroom. Probably removing himself from temptation that we were both struggling to navigate. How would we survive a whole summer with Armani's men forcing us to shack up together?

I splashed some water on my face, hoping my waterproof eyeliner and mascara would hold up so I didn't look like I'd been crying, then quickly freed myself from the dress. Only in the white teddy and white thigh-high stockings—probably not what he wanted to see me in—I went into the bedroom.

He was on the edge of the bed, wearing only black briefs and a thin white bandage around one arm, with his forehead resting in his palm. He walked his focus up the length of my body as I checked out his nearly naked one myself.

"Calliope." My name was more like an exhausted breath from his mouth. "What do you want from me?"

"To say my name again." I confessed all that was in my head while lowering my arms to my side, wanting him to look at me. To see me.

He came over, snatched my wrist, and spun me around so my back was to his chest. His hot breath at my ear sent a shiver through me. "Calliope *Costa*." His hand climbed up my torso, and he palmed my breasts beneath the lingerie, the decision to refrain now a distant memory. "What else do you want?" he asked, rolling my nipple between his fingers.

"What I want or what I need?" Maybe they were one and the same?

Mouth back to my ear, clearly not wanting the guards to hear anything real between us, he said in a gravelly tone, "What you need is to be properly fucked." His other hand went to my abdomen, and he held me tight to his hard frame. I was desperate for his palm to go between my thighs. "But you don't want to need it. You also don't want to get hurt."

"Sure you aren't speaking for yourself?" I set my hand over his and threaded our fingers together.

When he pulled his palm free from mine and let go of my breast, I knew it was less about rejection and more about not letting Armani win. And maybe not wanting anyone to get hurt. The teddy bear, as Izzy had called him, was fighting to break through.

Without looking at him, I went to the bed, peeled back the covers, then took a knee on it and arched my back. I startled at the feel of him caging me against him, his arm flying across my midsection to hold me tight. "What are you doing?"

"Losing my fucking mind, is what." He swept my hair over one shoulder with his free hand and brought his mouth to the side of my neck. "Tell me to fuck your cunt with my hand. To help get you off. That's all I can give you. I won't let those men outside win by giving in to what we both need."

Curving into his frame, I nodded, anxious to feel him.

"Say it, Calliope. Be very clear what you want me to do."

"Please." I wasn't above begging. "Touch me. *Everywhere.*"

He groaned against my neck, and at the feel of his tongue sliding up near my ear before he lightly nibbled my lobe, I about came undone. But the moment his hand feathered over the lacy material hiding my clit, I bent forward, both hands to the bed now, pretty much ready for him to have his hand on my ass cheek.

He followed the curve of my spine and rested his free hand next to my left one, then he located the slit in the lingerie—an opening for easy access. He pushed two fingers inside me, and I cried out his name as he coated them in my arousal.

"Why are you so wet for me?"

"I think you know," I confessed as he moved his fingers in and out, then added his thumb to my sensitive spot like he already knew how and where to find it. "And I hate you for making me feel this way."

"Sure you do," he remarked in a dark tone, continuing to push me just near the edge.

I rotated my hips, shimmying my ass against his hard cock, and his fingers stilled. "Stop moving like that, or I'm going to flip you over and fuck you instead." His warning only fueled me to move more, but when he added, "And then Armani wins," I hit the brakes.

What am I thinking? You're right. That asshole couldn't ever get what he wanted.

"Good girl." He resumed strumming my clit. "Fuck, you're tight." I wasn't sure if he was back to playing a role for the men in the hall or was only helping further me along, but I was too close to coming to care.

"That's it," he said when I began rubbing against the heel of his hand, moving in time with his fingers inside me. "Come for me, Calliope."

And that'll do it. My moans and cries had to have been heard outside the room. No way they'd think they were fake, considering I'd lost control and cried out Alessandro's name again. Breathing hard, every nerve ending electric, the most amazing feeling spread throughout my limbs as I fell apart on his hand. My *husband's* hand.

I was mush, and I collapsed onto the bed and stared at the man in his briefs as he covered me with the comforter.

"Time for part two," he mouthed, reminding me we would have to fake something—*him* getting off now. He grabbed hold of the headboard and began rhythmically beating it against the wall, never losing hold of my eyes in the process as he fake-pounded into me.

If only it were real . . .

After he completed the act with a long, fake groan and grunt, he tipped his head toward the bathroom and whispered, "Be right back."

So he didn't want to get off in front of me, huh? Not quite fair, but smart. If I had to watch him stroke his cock, I'd sink to my knees before him and use my mouth in a way he'd probably be much more a fan of than my sass.

At the bathroom door, he turned around and peered at me, and I could read the look in his eyes—*this can never happen again.*

CHAPTER TWENTY-ONE

Alessandro

Naked, I stepped into the shower without turning on the water. I'd never been so close to losing control in all my life. And hell, I kind of did—I got her off.

I brought my hand beneath my nose, inhaling her scent, then fisted my cock.

Angry at the desire pushing through me for a woman I couldn't ever have, I slammed my left hand to the wall, catching sight of the wedding band.

I'm married. And I nearly fucked my wife.

I slid my hand up and down my length, hating how much I wished it were her hand. Or God help me, her mouth wrapped around my dick instead. On her knees. Eyes meeting mine as she took me.

Her tits were spectacular, but when she showed me her ass in that lingerie as she'd turned and taken a knee on the bed . . . Well, I'd never thought I was an ass man, but after tonight, consider me a convert.

And also weak, because I couldn't fight temptation. But hell, those pricks in the hall had heard her come. The only restraint I'd shown tonight was not going out there and killing them for now knowing how my wife sounded when coming.

I let go of that insane thought, remembering the marriage was for the sake of a job. *You're not mine to get jealous over.*

But for now, thoughts of her would be what got me off. My taut muscles flexed, and every part of me locked tight as I climbed the much-needed edge of release that normally took me forever to get to. I was about to become a sixty-second man for the first time since I'd lost my virginity in high school.

I cursed and curled my fingers into a fist against the wall as I came hard all over the shower inside Armani Fucking DiMaggio's house of all places.

Energy spent and breathing hard, I did my best to pull myself together and finally turned on the water, careful not to let the hot water hit my back, which still burned and ached.

After rinsing off, I grabbed a towel, then went out to face the music. In this case, the *musician.*

The second she saw me, she drew the covers tighter to her body while her eyes wandered down my wet chest to where the towel sat on my hips.

This woman was going to be the death of me. Frustrated for reasons I wasn't sure I quite understood, I went for the door, needing to get the conversation with the guards over with.

I gripped the brass handle and flung open the door, catching sight of Frankie and Leo in the hall. "You can go to bed now."

Frankie attempted to walk in, but I remained a blockade to his entry. Callie was barely wearing anything in that bed, and God help the man—or in his case, the devil—if he tried to peel back the covers. "We need to come in. Make sure you consummated the marriage. DiMaggio's orders." He attempted to stare me down, and it wasn't going to work.

"We'll make it quick," Leo said, and since he appeared to be the less offensive of the two, I debated possibly allowing only him to enter.

"Orders are orders, Costa. You don't run the business yet," Frankie remarked, drawing my eyes again. "So I'll be coming in, or we'll send the good doctor over to do a more thorough check."

"Just let them in," Callie called out, trying to be the voice of reason when all I wanted to do was kill a motherfucker. Correction: *this* particular one.

"Do what the lady says. Move," Frankie said, and it sure as hell felt like he was trying to antagonize me to the point he got off on it.

"Please." Callie's soft tone allowed my walls to drop, and I begrudgingly surrendered room for the guys to enter, but Leo hung back in the hall. Smart man.

Frankie walked around the room, having the indecency to sniff the air like a hound, which I'd called happening.

I wasn't sure why I'd expected Calliope to be nervous, given how she'd been holding up. But when she said in a low, cutting tone, "Don't forget, you'll be answering to me one day. This is not the best way to woo me," I about fell the fuck over.

"They're good," Leo said, filling the doorframe. "Let's go."

Frankie sneered at him, as if unhappy with the good-cop-bad-cop thing they were probably doing, then he brushed past me, shouldering my bad arm like an asshole on the way out. But he was going in the direction I wanted, so I didn't stop him.

Once Frankie was gone, I nodded my thanks, if that's what I wanted to call it, to Leo, then closed and locked the door.

Callie's gasp had me whirling around in worry. *What happened?* Her hand was over her mouth, and she'd let the cover drop, giving me a view of that sexy lingerie again. "Your back. It's—"

"I'm fine." I went over to my suitcase, which someone must've brought up earlier, unsure what the hell I would wear to bed. Sleeping in the nude was standard for me, but that wouldn't work alongside her. "You should sleep." I snatched a pair of briefs, and keeping my back to her, let the towel fall.

"You don't miss glutes day at the gym, huh?"

"Neither do you, sweetheart," I tossed out while putting on the briefs.

"Tell me you're wearing more than that to bed?"

I faced her. "This *is* more for me. I'm usually naked," I said, letting her in on my secret, and it really was since I didn't sleep next to anyone. Not in a long time, at least.

"Oh." She chewed on her lip, and my hands slammed to my hips as I fought the urge to think about that sexy mouth of hers wrapping around my cock.

"How about you? You plan on changing?"

She twirled her finger, signaling for me to turn so she could walk to the bathroom, and I almost laughed. "Shy now?"

"I have my moments." She waited for me to be good and look away, and I obliged her request as she went to her suitcase.

"I'm rinsing off, too, like you did." I took that as my cue to look her way again. "I feel . . . dirty after letting those bastards hear me. You know, since I wasn't acting."

"I'm sorry," was all I managed before she retreated to the bathroom and shut the door.

The second I was alone, I grabbed my phone, in need of someone to talk me off the ledge I was climbing before I jumped without a chute.

Me: You awake?

I dropped onto the bed, planting my feet on the floor while bowing my head, waiting for my brother to respond so someone could talk some sense into me.

Enzo: Yeah, I'm up. I was talking to Maria. I'll call her back. You okay?

Me: No.

Enzo: ???

Me: Physically okay. Mentally . . . not so much.

Enzo: Are you texting me because you need advice on how to resist your wife? Because you do remember I tried to keep away from Maria and wound up married, and we're having twins. I'm not the best one to ask.

I almost laughed. Because hell, he was right. But this didn't feel like a conversation I could have with Constantine. And definitely not Izzy.

I couldn't believe I had told my *wife* I wouldn't mind slapping her ass. What the hell had come over me?

Me: How am I going to share a bed with her all summer? This is me we're talking about.

I left out the fact I'd already screwed up tonight and fingered her.

Enzo: Do you think you should get it out of your systems so you can move on?

Me: And risk her falling for me? Breaking her heart? Getting her pregnant?

Enzo: Easy with the ego, bro. Maybe it's you who falls for her. It's her that breaks your heart. And use a condom.

Shit, he threw her words from the bathroom right back at me.

Enzo: Before you say you don't have a heart, don't f'ing lie to me.

Me: Why are you writing f'ing like that?

Enzo: Don't change the subject. (Maria says I need to work on my language.)

Enzo: But back to you. The fact you go out of your way to protect women from falling for you, worried you'll hurt them, suggests you DO have a heart, bro. Otherwise, you wouldn't give a F about the consequences of your actions.

Me: Am I paying $400/hour for this session? Because when did you become my doc?

Enzo: You did message me on your wedding night for advice to refrain from touching your wife, did you not?

Enzo: Calliope Costa. Does have a nice ring to it.

I couldn't believe how easily her name had rolled from my tongue tonight when she'd asked me to say it again.

Enzo: Not as nice of a ring as Maria Costa, but . . .

Me: You married for love. I married to save a life. Different stories. There will be different endings.

Enzo: If you say so.

Enzo: Important side note: does she want you back? Or is this just a "you" problem.

I thought back to our kiss at the ceremony. The little whimper from her just before she'd invited my tongue into her mouth. Why was it the kiss I thought of first when he asked me that? Not getting her off with my hand?

Me: Yeah, pretty sure she wants me back . . . But she's a client. I need to protect her, not F her.

Enzo: Maria is now rubbing off on you, too. "F her?"

Enzo: Scratch that. I don't want my wife rubbing off on anyone but me. 🙄

Me: I hate you.

Enzo: I love you back.

Me: Fuck you.

Enzo: Fuck does feel much better to write/say. And . . . do. 😉 (Just go for it. You're married. Maybe no one gets hurt and you live happily ever after. Because you CAN'T last three months sharing a bed with this woman and not . . . do it. That's why you're messaging me.)

Enzo: Also, when was the last time you shared a bed with someone? 1989?

Me: You know who it was with, and it's been a long time.

Enzo: Right, sorry to remind you of her.

He didn't need to apologize, because I hadn't thought about "her" or her house in Westchester with her husband, three kids, and two dogs. Not lately, at least.

Enzo: How about a pillow wall between you at night? Maria said that's a thing that happens in books.

His wife was an avid reader, and I could already see the stories she'd be writing in her head about what would happen with my situation. I was getting enough shit from Izzy, and I didn't need more.

Me: Thanks for the "advice."

Enzo: Anytime. Also, Constantine wants to take the big jet home. We need to strategize and coordinate plans moving forward, and you can't fly with us since you'll have babysitters tagging along. You can have the little jet. Plus, we'll be in talks with Sebastian and the others while flying. Don't need Armani's men knowing about our plans for Rocco.

Rocco. How'd I let the memory of his involvement in all this slip free from my head?

Me: Any updates from The League? They still have eyes on Rocco?

Enzo: You might be focused on your wife right now, but don't you think if I had news on Rocco, I would've brought it up sooner??

Enzo: He's still at the compound.

Me: Right. Okay then.

Me: Any potential fallout from what we did in Rome?

Enzo: No, I don't think anyone who takes over for the Esposito family will come after us now that we're (you're) in bed with Armani's family, and they're now "in bed" with The League. But we should still add some extra security back in NY.

Me: I was planning on it. I don't trust these two idioti coming back with us to be my wife's only protection.

Enzo: "Your wife"?

Shit. I rested my phone on my thigh and felt the need to remove the wedding band. Maybe it was screwing with my thoughts in some weird way. I set it on the nightstand by the bed and texted him.

Me: Just trying to get used to playing the role. I'm going to need to sell this marriage idea to the board when I get home. When they find out who I married . . .

Enzo: Pops already has a meeting set up with them tomorrow when we land.

Me: Of course he does. See you in the morning. Meet you at the airport at 0800 before Armani can change his mind.

Enzo: Roger that. Later. Get some sleep . . . or not 😏

I ignored his parting jab, then pulled up my favorited contacts to message one of my assistants. I had quite a few tasks I'd need handled before returning to New York tomorrow. I'd let my main admin know I was in Italy the other day, but he had no clue I was now married. Of course, word was bound to get out soon. My dad was probably trying to get ahead of the story by having a meeting after we landed tomorrow, and with the time difference, it was doable.

Before I could text my assistant, Callie opened the door. She was in cotton pajamas that had funny little dancing bananas on them, and my shoulders collapsed. I nearly dropped the phone, because how'd she still take my breath away with her hair in a messy bun and wearing pajamas like that? Barely an inch of visible skin in sight, too.

She pouted. I hated when she did that since it was cute. And I kept finding myself now "falling" for cute. "Don't laugh. I tried to choose the least sexy thing to pack for this trip since I was coming here."

"Not a bad idea. But . . ." *You're still sexy.* I set the phone on the nightstand, opting to wait to text a hundred last-minute requests to my assistant until after she fell asleep. I shifted my legs on the bed and slipped beneath the covers, doing my best not to put too much pressure on my achy back.

She joined me in the bed, surprising me by turning toward me instead of away.

"The lights are still on," I pointed out.

"Maybe they should stay on?"

"Afraid something will bite you in the dark?"

"Something? No." She lifted a brow. "Someone, you mean?"

"I don't bite." *Unless you ask me to. And dammit, please don't. I just might do it.* "We'll, uh, get through this." Those words were for me, not her.

"Which part?" The little break in her voice before she wet her lips had me sliding my hand beneath the pillow so I could curl my fingers into a fist and find my control—to remind myself she needed to go back to being off-limits.

I frowned, fear cutting through my body about the unknown. I wasn't accustomed to that emotion, but then I relented and shared, "All the parts."

CHAPTER TWENTY-TWO

Alessandro

"Did you sleep there all night? Or are you just an early riser?" Callie covered her mouth, hiding a yawn, then peeked at the alarm clock. "Wait, you're dressed. So you—"

"Yeah, I slept on the couch." I rose from the uncomfortable piece of furniture meant for looks and not for thirty-nine-year-old backs. "I think I'll have a couch with a pull-out bed added to my bedroom before we get to New York today. I can't sleep next to you."

After she'd tossed and turned for an hour, she'd finally passed out, but it hadn't taken her long to plant her body right up against me. And the woman was a damn furnace.

Like a cat, arching and curling tight to my side, she'd hooked one leg over mine. I'd remained still, doing my best not to further entangle our limbs. But since I'd been on my side facing her when she'd decided to do gymnastics and a one-eighty, she'd positioned her ass against my dick, and how the hell was I supposed to sleep like that?

I'd gone into the bathroom, rubbed one out again, then shut off the lights and slept on the couch.

Callie sat all the way up, resting against the headboard I'd had to bang against the wall last night. She unleashed her hair from the bun, and the messy locks framed her angelic face. "Why not?"

You know damn well why. "Because maybe I do bite." I was pissed for reasons she didn't know yet. *Un*reasonable reasons, sure. "You move around a lot in your sleep. It was annoying," I grumbled as she swung her long, sexy legs around and stood. "I'm not used to sharing a bed."

"Right, I forgot. A regular Casanova. Wine, dine, bang, and move on," she sassed me right back.

"Looks like you woke up on the wrong side of the bed," I grumbled, in the mood to spar after the messages from Braden I'd shamelessly read on her phone after taking it back from Marcello ten minutes ago.

On her knees by her suitcase, she looked up and snapped, "At least I woke up in a bed, Mr. Attitude." She focused back on digging through her bag, and yeah, hello, itchy palm. I did, in fact, want to smack that ass of hers. "Also, for your information, no one's ever complained about me being annoying while sleeping next to me."

The mental gymnastics it took me doing to forget the image she'd painted of sharing a bed with other men was too much.

"That didn't sound right." She cut off my thoughts, which were about to edge into the realm of murdering a half dozen people, and at the top of the list was Braden. "I've only lived with one guy. I didn't mean to make it sound like, um . . ."

And now the one guy she'd lived with was on that list, too. My death count was going to grow, the longer this woman was in my life.

Fully facing me, her shoulders slumped as if she were ready to give up the fight inside her already, which was a little shocking. She'd just put on her gloves. "Are you mad at me?" She blew away a hair in her face, making a dramatic *humph* sound. "For what happened last night, I mean? Is that why you're all snarly and grumpy?" Her beautiful eyes cut to my bad arm. Although it really was just a flesh wound. I could lose the bandage. "Or is pain catching up with you?"

I locked my arms across my chest, and my back muscles yelled at me from the movement. "I think it's best if we keep some distance is all, don't you?"

"How do you propose we do that?" She angled her head, catching my eyes. "Ohhh." A little nod from her in understanding before she added, "My heartbreaker husband is worried about my fragile little heart, so you plan to be a dick to me?"

"You're clearly not made of glass." I actually wasn't trying to be a dick that time. I was just still pissed at the secret she was keeping from me. "I don't plan to be an ass," I conceded while she stared me down, gloves back on. Not that it'd be a fair fight. Because I'd never raise a hand to her, and I'd let her whack me all she wanted. Although Little Miss Tennessee would only throw verbal jabs at me, I had a feeling those would be more painful coming from her.

"If not an ass, then what?"

"Cordial."

Another eye roll from her. "Riiiight." She went back to the business of trying to find something to wear. "Have you talked to Armani this morning?"

Yeah, about that. I slipped my hand into my pocket and grabbed hold of her phone. "I did. We're good to go." I thought back to my conversation with Gabriel after my coffee chat with Armani. Gabriel had asked me to trust him to handle shit on this side of the world while I dealt with the rest of our plan to bring down DiMaggio back in New York. "But I do have to tell you something. We'll have ears on the ride to the airport and on the flight back, so we need to get this conversation over with now."

She slowly stood, dropping the clothes back into her suitcase, as if recognizing she wouldn't like what I had to say.

I finally removed her phone from my pocket and tossed it to her. She caught it, never losing hold of my eyes.

"I woke up to several messages this morning, and so did you," I shared. "Armani leaked the story of our marriage to the press last night. It went viral."

Wide, panicky eyes. Check.

I gave her a few more seconds to absorb the news and to do a quick search on her phone. Or maybe she planned to check her texts and voicemails.

One particular story kept buzzing through my thoughts from a tabloid I'd had a beef with since they'd botched the story of my sister's murder years ago, and of course that was the one she found and started to read aloud.

"Does love at first sight exist?" she said under her breath. "Just ask billionaire playboy Alessandro Costa, who was swept away by school-teacher Calliope Anderson, also rumored to be the daughter of Armani DiMaggio. Not familiar with that name? Well, get familiar. He allegedly runs the longest-lasting mafia group in Italian history."

"People were bound to find out," I said before she continued. I didn't want to hear more, and neither would she. "But I didn't expect Armani to have it leaked like this." I should've expected it, though. He wanted to ensure the world knew my family was in an alliance with him. He'd even shared the photo of our one and only kiss from inside the church.

Without acknowledging she'd heard me, she continued swiping at the screen, probably flipping from one "breaking story" to the next.

"You have almost as many texts and missed calls as I do." I spoke up after giving her what I'd felt was an adequate amount of time to spiral. "But none from your aunt. I did a quick check."

She finally gave me her attention. "My aunt can't find out. She'll freak. Fly to Armani and threaten him. Possibly get herself killed."

"We'll get ahead of this. For her, at least, we will," I reassured while trying to be cordial. Also, fuck that word. "Don't worry."

"I guess this is the one time I'm glad my aunt hates social media, is unlisted, distrusts all news sources, and didn't sign up for the international phone plan while traveling. But . . . what about my friends? Principal? They must've heard about this. With the time difference, we—"

"I noticed a voicemail from your boss. Well, I saw a voicemail notification from Principal Edwards on your phone when I got it back from Marcello." I cleared my throat, uncomfortable to share more. "Among other messages."

"Did you listen to any? Read them?" she asked, and I was seconds away from losing what little trust of hers I may have had.

"I might have looked at a few." I had on jeans, so I couldn't hide my hands in my pockets all that easily like when wearing a suit, so I crossed my arms at the increasingly awkward conversation. "I also listened to one message."

"Broadway," she whispered, as if now understanding my temper this morning. "You know."

"I do, and you're not going to Nashville." The quicker I laid that out, the better. "And Braden needs to watch his tongue, before I cut it out. I don't care if he's a friend or a vet. You're my wife, and the bullshit he said to you on the phone when he found out is—" I cut myself off, realizing I was the one who sounded off his rocker with jealousy right now, even worse than how Braden had come across in his voicemail.

"I'm sorry, but what?" She tossed the phone on the bed and mimicked my move, crossing her arms. It was hard to take her seriously in the dancing-bananas pajamas, but if I smiled, she might try and throw me out the window next. "You had no business looking through my messages."

I stepped before her, needing to dip my chin to find her eyes. "No, maybe not. But you're my *job*. I'll do what I have to in order to keep you safe and to complete the mission. So, no Nashville. No Braden." I may have hit a new, all-time low in my voice that time, but I really hated that guy.

Her gaze moved to my hand, and I followed her eyes, realizing I'd never put my ring back on. I cursed and went to the nightstand and grabbed it. The thing felt like it weighed fifty pounds in my palm.

"I'm going to lose my teaching job. My life is in shambles because of this. I know it's not your fault, and maybe you have a point about Broadway if it's to keep me safe, but—"

"You don't need the money." I slipped on the ring and shook out my hand at my side.

"You think I teach for money? Thought we established my salary sucks last weekend." She went back to her suitcase and grabbed something to wear, as if needing a distraction. "And no, I won't take his blood money."

"Then take mine. It's clean," I said, hating her defeated tone, preferring sassy over sad, because her being sad gutted me. When she shot me a look that said, *Hell no*, I added, "Does your school need a new library? Gym? I'll build them a wing. Don't worry, if you want to keep your job when this is over, I'll make sure you do."

"You can't buy your way out of every problem."

"Clearly, or we wouldn't be married right now." Another low blow from me. I was on a roll this morning. But we were about to head home. We'd be in my city, and I'd need to be this woman's husband for three months. I had no clue how to navigate the situation. So I was on edge. "We need to go. Flight leaves soon."

"Maybe I'm glad we can't talk in the car or on the flight." She strode by me with her clothes and started for the bathroom. "But I'm not letting Armani ruin my dreams when he's already forcing me to live in this nightmare of a situation." She stopped by the door to face me. "Since you think you can buy your way out of most problems, surely you can come up with a creative way to keep me safe when I go down there to perform."

"Calliope," I hissed.

"Callie," she said softly. "It's Callie again. You're the one who doesn't want to be friendly."

Unable to stop myself, this foreign feeling of jealousy propelled me her way. "So just Braden gets to call my wife her given name? We're back to that?"

Her nostrils flared as she met me halfway, ready to face off with me. "I'm not your wife. Not really."

"Says God. Says the law you are." I stabbed in the direction of the ground instead of the sky, which would've made more sense. But I was lacking the whole rational-thinking thing at the moment.

"Braden cares about me. You don't. He's a real friend, and you don't want to be anything other than cordial with me. So yeah, he can call me Calliope, and you sure as hell can't call me your anything." The dig cut. Right below the skin. I was pretty sure she'd opened a not-so-old wound, and I was bleeding. "Well," she said while letting go of a deep breath, "I suppose I'm one thing to you—your mission."

"Right," I gritted out.

"I need to get ready." She gave me her back while sputtering, "I'm mad at you."

"Noted."

But the fall of her shoulders as she stood by the bathroom door had my chest aching more than my damn back.

"I'm still grateful to you for helping me, even if it doesn't seem like it, though," she whispered, making me feel like a shitty human being. "Maybe your reasons aren't *just* for me, but I'm still indebted to you for what you're doing." With that, she slipped into the bathroom and closed the door.

Indebted to me? No. No more favors. She owed me nothing.

I just needed this mission to be over with. The sooner the better.

With any luck, I'd kill her father before the Fourth of July, we could annul the marriage, and I'd be free again.

And she could go be with the one man who so clearly loved her— Braden. Well, as long as I didn't kill him first for wanting my wife.

CHAPTER TWENTY-THREE

Calliope

New York City

"Please, call me—"

Alessandro cut off his mother before she could say her name, and they began rapidly speaking in Italian. I looked back and forth, following the Ping-Pong match between them, unsure what to say or do.

I hadn't known his parents would be meeting us at the airport. From the look of Alessandro's shocked face when the jet door had opened, he'd been equally clueless of their plans.

Alessandro's brothers, father, and Hudson were now outside the hangar, talking away from Frankie's and Leo's ears—and yeah, they'd been the ones Armani had chosen to send with us.

I turned to see Izzy beckoning me off to the side of what was becoming a heated conversation between Alessandro and his mother.

"They could go at it all day," Izzy said as she guided me away from them.

"What are they talking about?" I asked her.

"I can't hear them now, but he's worried she's going to get attached to you. And then it'll be too hard for her to lose you when the inevitable divorce happens."

"It's sweet of him to protect her," I said as Alessandro peered at me. Twenty feet apart didn't erase my ability to see his pained irritation.

The man had spoken all of a handful of words on the jet—none of which had been to me. *"Don't talk to my wife. Look at her. Or even think about her. And I won't throw you from the plane,"* he'd ordered Frankie and Leo before taking a seat and keeping his mouth shut the rest of the way.

"He wants to protect you, too, you know," Izzy said, her tone light. "You'll get attached to Mom as well. It'll just hurt all around when the time comes for you to leave us." There was a sad edge to her tone now that was like a knife to the heart. "Alessandro is uber protective. He tries to act like a tough guy, but he's a—"

"Teddy bear." I repeated what she'd said to me yesterday. Maybe she'd forgotten she'd given me the heads-up, pre-wedding. I surely hadn't.

"And he hides that inner teddy bear beneath a few layers of asshole," she said with a light laugh. "But, um, how's the fallout going from the story breaking about the marriage? Your phone must be blowing up from your friends."

"I don't have a ton of friends. My close circle is like a dot. People tend to break my trust, so I don't give it out so much these days." I hadn't meant to overshare, but her little nod was as if she was on the same page and understood me. "I did speak with my principal over email on the plane. She said there are parents asking me to resign. She's giving me time to consider what feels more like an ultimatum."

"Damn." Izzy squeezed my arm. "I'm so sorry."

"I could be dead from being attacked in the park or married to Rocco, so I guess I should focus on the positives for now." I had to convince myself of that, at least, so I didn't spiral about my potential forced resignation. "As long as my aunt doesn't learn about this disaster of a situation, I can handle almost anyone else."

"We sent one of our guys from the security office to keep an eye on her as well. Try not to worry." Izzy had my heart climbing into my throat.

"You did? Why didn't Alessandro tell me?" I focused back on the man full of surprises as he threw a hand in the air, and from the looks of it, he was being lectured hard.

"It was his idea. He has a lot on his mind, though. Probably forgot to mention it." Izzy unhanded me and reached into her purse and offered me an iPhone. "He asked me to get you a new one. New number as well. You know, to avoid reporters. I, uh, programmed all his numbers in there. Mine, too."

I clasped it between my palms and gave her a nod of thanks.

"Well, he's on his way." She pointed as Alessandro strode over. "Good luck with him. If you need me, call, okay?"

"Thank you." I hugged her. "I really appreciate that."

"We should get going," Alessandro remarked, his first words to me since we'd left Italy. "I have to drop you off at my place, make sure security is set up, then head to the office for a board meeting."

"Yeah, okay." I twisted toward the exit, but he snatched my wrist.

"My stubborn mother wants to have a dinner party tomorrow night. I told her that wouldn't be happening. If she calls you on that new phone of yours, because I'm sure she had Izzy add her number, please ignore her. Do not give in." His eyes fell to the iPhone I'd forgotten was in my hand. "Okay?"

"You want me to send your mother's calls to voicemail?" Was he kidding?

"Please do." He let go of me and reached into the inner pocket of his suit jacket; he'd changed into a gray three-piece suit aboard the flight, making me feel seriously underdressed in my jeans and tee. Retrieving his sunglasses, he pointed with them toward the Range Rover parked outside. "That will be your ride this summer. If you go anywhere without me, someone from my team will accompany you along with those two *idioti* of your father's."

"You're going to let me go out without you? I'm shocked." I'd envisioned him holding me captive for "my own good" all summer.

"You're not my prisoner," was all he said before walking ahead of me. He didn't go too far, just to the passenger door of the black Range Rover, and he opened it and waited for me.

"What, no Lamborghini?" I jested, unable to help myself.

"Only two seats. Need security," he said, as if not recognizing I was being a smartass.

"You seem to be all I've needed so far." That part wasn't a joke. The man could handle me in more ways than one.

He lowered his sunglasses to meet my eyes, shook his head, then motioned for me to get a move on.

I managed a thank-you for the door holding, then slid inside. Leo was in the passenger seat up front, so we were saved from Frankie's presence for now.

Alessandro palmed my door shut with a loud thud, then went over to his brother Enzo and hugged him before Enzo started back inside the hangar. Was he heading back to his wife? I was pretty sure he'd said Enzo lived in Charlotte.

Alessandro exchanged a few words with his family and Hudson, then joined me in the SUV and told our driver to get a move on. He kept his eyes on his phone, rapidly firing messages.

He didn't speak to me until he had me alone in the fancy closet of *our* bedroom at his penthouse.

"How'd you do this?" My fingers flew across my clothes all neatly hung up inside the luxurious walk-in. My wardrobe only took up one sad side of the massive space that was larger than my bedroom back home. "How'd you—?"

He leaned inside the doorframe of the closet, casually observing me. "I had my assistant send a team to pack up your stuff and get it here ASAP."

"When? How?" *Also, your people went through my personal things? Underwear? How lovely.*

He sighed as if annoyed by my questions, then peeked at his fancy watch. "I don't know. With the time difference, it was still early yesterday before we went to bed, and my people work fast when I ask them to do something."

I did another double take of the massive closet. "Where are your things?"

"In the other closet."

"Another closet?" I blinked. "Of course a billionaire would have two closets like this."

"Mine's smaller. Thought you'd need the bigger one. Clearly, I was wrong." He pushed away from the doorframe, reaching into his back pocket for his wallet, then offered me a credit card. "For shopping."

I waved his hand away. "I don't need anything. I'm good."

"You might." He nudged it my way, but I refused to take it. I was his job, not his mistress. I wouldn't act like my mother once had with Armani—shopping on his dime.

"Fine." He put away the card and quietly left the closet. I followed him like a lost sheep unsure where to go, and I hated myself for that. But this was new territory.

I was in a penthouse in the sky—literally, we were in the sky, because clouds loomed just outside the bedroom window—and this was all madness.

Frankie and Leo were currently with Alessandro's security team going over things, and Alessandro's meeting was in an hour, so we didn't have much more time alone. So if I had questions for him, now was the time to ask them.

I spied a couch that looked out of place alongside one wall, wondering if that was the pull-out bed he'd said he wanted to buy before we arrived. His people really did work fast.

"I should take the couch," I said at the sight of his king-size bed, which had a gunmetal-gray comforter, a perfect match to his steely eyes.

Facing me, he adjusted the knot of his red tie. It was the first time I'd seen the man wear color. "No. You'll take the bed."

"Maybe I don't want to, considering how many miles it must have on it." Welp, if Alessandro hid his inner teddy bear beneath layers of "asshole," then I hid my sweet side with sarcasm and sass.

"Zero miles." He emphasized his comment by making an *O* with his hand. "I had my assistant buy a new mattress in case you had such ideas. Not that I've ever slept overnight with anyone in my room."

"I didn't mean sleep-sleep." Trying to push away the unwanted feelings of jealousy that other women had been in this room, moaning out his name, I rasped, "You probably have a sex room, anyway. Or a separate apartment for hookups?"

"Gee, tell me what you really think of me," he ground out, then began muttering in Italian.

"I just want to make sure I never accidentally walk in on you doing it somewhere in this maze of a penthouse. Is there a certain room I should avoid?"

He stalked across the hardwood and came before me, that angry look he sported so well on display—tense jaw, flared nostrils, and disdain in his eyes.

"I know you can't let the guards see you with someone else, but I'm not naive enough to think you're going to go all summer without sex." I slapped my arms across my chest, feeling the need to put up a guard with him so close and staring at me like I was next on his kill list.

"There's one thing you need to know about me." He pointed at his chest. "I may have a certain reputation when it comes to women, but I'm not a cheat. And before you say I don't do relationships to have ever had a chance to cheat, so I don't know if I can be faithful—I do, in fact, know," he gritted out. "And there are no sex rooms here, dammit." I opened my mouth to say something, but then he leaned in and added, "So let me be crystal clear. I will not touch or so much as look at another woman while we're married. End of story."

"But what about your needs? You're giving up sex for me? For a job? I don't think I can ask you to do that." Although, the idea of him being with another woman made me sick, not that I had a right to feel that way.

"Do you plan to have sex with anyone else while you're my wife?" His bladed jawline became an edge you could sharpen a dull knife on as he stared at me.

"Of course not."

The slight droop of his shoulders let me know he was relieved to hear that. "As for my needs, I can go three months without sex. It's not your problem to worry about."

So our hands will be busy all summer? Thankfully, I kept that comment trapped in my head.

"I have to make a few calls before I leave," he said after a deep exhalation.

"And I'm safe here?"

"Do you think I'd go if I thought otherwise?"

Fair enough.

"No one would dare mess with my family in this city. My security is also keeping tabs on your father's men. If they touch you, my men have my permission to kill them," he quickly shared, no change in his tone of voice. Well, not until he added, "And we have eyes on your aunt." He cleared his throat, and before I could thank him about protecting my aunt, he threw me off by adding, "Rocco, too, in case he gets any revenge ideas."

Revenge ideas?

"We'll talk about him later," he said, reading my thoughts, then he turned and went for the door, only to abruptly stop and position his hand on the wall instead of leaving. "There's a gym downstairs if you need to unwind. Release some . . . tension."

Sounds like you do.

"Also, third door down on your left, there's a music room. I had the team bring your equipment here. And the chef will be here at six to cook for you. You have my number if there's a problem. But don't wait up for me."

He left before I could summon a response. *Music room?* He sure as hell was making this an attractive prison, even if he didn't want to refer to it as one.

I didn't waste time and followed his directions to get to the music room.

Talk about living inside a fantasy. Not the land of Delulu, either. This room, this *life*, was real. Well, temporarily real.

The clouds must've only been hanging out on the other side of the penthouse—and he occupied the entire floor—because light streamed in through the ceiling-to-floor glass windows, casting a glow over the instruments.

I slowly walked in, finding a sleek black modern desk in front of one window, my notebook and pen from my bedroom back home sitting on top of it. The pages were blank. Writer's block and all, but maybe I'd write again?

My keyboard and guitar were there as promised. But there was another guitar case I didn't recognize, leaning against the wall by the door.

I set it down and knelt alongside it, and I was pretty sure the blood drained from my face at what was inside.

After a few deep breaths that did nothing to appease my nerves, I rushed out to find Alessandro before he left.

Breezing past various rooms, I ran to a spiral staircase at the back end of the hall, remembering he'd said he had to make a few calls, and I was pretty sure we'd passed an office on our way up to the primary bedroom.

The office door was cracked open, and I could hear him talking. I wasn't a fan of eavesdropping, so I went inside, where he was sitting behind a modern desk much bigger than the one in the music room with his cell to his ear. His eyes now locked with mine.

"I'm going to have to call you back." He frowned, ended the call, and sat back in his leather chair while waiting for me to explain my interruption.

I fiddled with the wedding band as I slowly approached the desk, feeling like I was about to face off with a stranger, not a man who'd had me moaning his name while climaxing last night. "How'd you get that guitar? Someone else won it at the auction. Definitely not you. I remember. And for that matter, what'd you do with the two things you did win?"

"I made a call. Found out who won it and asked them for it," he said casually, steepling his fingers against his lips. "Donated the items I won to charity."

Of course you did. It's so hard to hate you. "So you just asked for The Legend's guitar, and they gave it to you?" I tried to chase away the chills on my arms with my palms, but touching my skin only seemed to provoke more goose bumps, especially beneath his gaze. "And what, they hand-delivered it while we were on our flight back here?"

"Your sarcasm doesn't change facts. It is what it is. Money. It buys things. In this case, the thing you wanted," he said bluntly. "It's a wedding gift. I thought you'd like it, and since you have to live here when you don't want to, I—"

"Damn you, Alessandro Costa." Were there tears in my eyes? At the sight, he lowered his arms and stood, setting his hands on his desk as I cried out, "I hate you." I hastily swiped at the traitorous drop of liquid that'd escaped. "I hate that you'd do something so freaking crazy for me, because it makes it hard to actually hate you."

His eyes narrowed, jaw locking tight. "You're confusing."

Ditto. So much ditto it hurts.

"I can't accept it." I brushed away another stray tear. "Donate it, too. Please, have it taken away."

"I don't understand. It's just a guitar." He lifted his hands from the desk, tearing one through his hair, which fell perfectly back into place.

"You don't understand what that woman's music means to me. Her songs got me through so much in my life. And to have her guitar is everything to me." I was going to ugly-cry. Break down.

Armani hadn't broken me, but Alessandro buying a guitar seemed to be the straw that broke the camel's back.

"Then you should have it. I truly don't understand." He started for me, and I shot my palms up as a plea to keep his distance.

"Maybe money can buy happiness, after all, since you could buy the guitar. But money can't buy me," I cried, cupping my mouth before I sobbed. That was the last thing I wanted to do in front of him. "Please, take it back." I turned, knowing I was on the brink of losing it.

"Calliope!" he called out, and I froze in front of the doorway and slammed both hands on the frame, preparing to bolt so I could cry in private.

"What?" I whispered.

"I'm sorry. I was just trying to do something nice." The teddy bear. There he was. That side of him would destroy my heart. Pulverize it into nothing.

"It *was* nice." My shoulders broke forward. "Too nice. Not even remotely *cordial*. And that's the problem," I murmured before taking off, not wanting to give him a chance to stop me.

Once back upstairs and in our room, I went over to the bed and snatched my new phone from where I'd left it, wishing I could talk to my aunt. To cry on her shoulder about the mess I was in, but I had no one to talk to about this. Not in my very small circle of friends, either.

I blinked back tears, then startled at the message that popped up from Alessandro.

Alessandro: I'm really fucking sorry. I didn't realize . . .

Alessandro: I'll get rid of it.

Alessandro: I don't know how to do this. It's been a long time since I've done this.

I reread his last message a few times, trying to understand it.

Me: Done what?

I caught a few salty tears with my tongue as I watched the bubbles as he typed.

Alessandro: A relationship. I know ours is temporary, and we didn't choose to be in this situation, but we're here. So if I fuck up again, like with the guitar, please be patient with me, I'm a work in progress—remember?

Oh jeez. I thought back to our first conversation at the fundraiser, which was a million years ago now.

Me: You didn't mess up 😣 It was sweet. Expensively sweet. And sweet will hurt me in the end. You're in no danger of falling, but I think I am.

I couldn't believe I'd admitted that to him, but he needed to know the truth. He had to know the power he already had over me. Not just my body, but my mind. And if he wasn't careful, my heart, too.

He didn't respond right away. No bubbles from typing. It took another solid minute before a text finally appeared.

Alessandro: I'm just not capable of falling. You get that, right? Consider me damaged goods. Defective. It's not you, okay?

Me: Did you really just give me the 'it's not you, it's me' speech on Day Two of our marriage?

Me: Sorry, I know this isn't a "real" marriage. Just no more sweet gestures.

It took him another minute or so to respond. Way to ramp up my nerves.

Alessandro: Roger that. Asshole it is 😉

The wink from him.

Damn the wink.

Me: I hate you.

Me: Well, I'm sure as hell going to try.

CHAPTER TWENTY-FOUR

Alessandro

The woman was going to kill me, and I wasn't even home. I needed to stop checking the security cameras. Right now, Callie was using my home gym and wearing yoga pants and a pink sports bra. Luckily for Frankie, Leo, and my guards, I'd revoked their access to the interior cameras, aside from the kitchen and living room. I didn't need them seeing my wife doing a Downward-Facing Dog. Hell, I didn't need to see it, either, but I couldn't seem to look away. I also had no idea how she had the energy to work out when today felt like we'd crammed two into one.

"You okay? You appear starstruck. What's on your phone?"

I closed out the security camera app, finding Izzy in the doorway to my office. Well, our *other* office—the one for our "volunteer" work, which was technically Enzo's old home before we'd converted it into our new headquarters a few months ago.

"So?" Of course Izzy wouldn't let it go. "What was on your phone?" She came into the room and plopped down on the leather chair before the desk, giving me a knowing smile. "Ahhh. You were creeping on her, weren't you?"

"I wasn't creeping." I dropped back into my seat, feeling very much like a psycho stalker. "I was making sure she's okay."

"Don't trust your security? You did hire half the city to stand guard in your building. It's probably more secure than the White House. Pretty sure your neighbors will believe the rumors you're married to a mafia princess."

"Ugh, don't remind me." They did, in fact, think that. Mrs. Newman had given me major side-eye in the lobby this afternoon, clutching her little poodle to her chest like I might kill the mutt. Her ridiculous reaction had been about the same as the board members', though. That uncomfortable meeting at our family business had lasted three hours too long, but we managed to set aside their concerns about my wife's father for now.

"So if you weren't worried about her physical safety, why were you creeping?"

"Because I messed up earlier," I confessed, knowing she'd get it out of me one way or another. We ought to consider bringing her in the field for interrogation purposes. "I was making sure she wasn't crying or something."

"Don't take her for a crier."

"She has her moments." *Why'd I admit I know that?*

"And what'd you do?" She sat taller, staring at me as if she very much enjoyed this show that was now my life. Still paying me back for running off her boyfriends over the years.

Reluctantly, I went ahead and told my sister about buying the guitar, which had been a lot more challenging than I'd let on—the man had practically wanted my kidney in return.

"What were you thinking, getting her that guitar?" Izzy stared at me with wide eyes. "Do you want her to fall in love with you?"

"Of course not!"

"Well then, next time you think about some grand gesture, run it by me first."

"And next time you're undercover," I countered, tossing her own words at her, "maybe run the whole making-out-with-our-friend thing by us first."

"Made out with who?" Constantine rasped, and Izzy startled and looked over to see him filling the doorway.

"No one." She swung her attention back around, a plea in her big brown eyes to keep my mouth shut. I gave her a quick nod, and she stood.

"Hudson will be here soon," Constantine said, "and then we can go over the plan we discussed on the flight that you missed out on."

Right. I'd been on the other jet and hadn't yet heard their thoughts on how we'd take out both Rocco and Armani before summer's end. I had my ideas, but I was curious to hear theirs.

"Can we have a second alone?" I asked Izzy, tipping my chin toward Constantine.

She gave me her signature don't-screw-me-over eyes, not wanting me to mention the kiss, then left the office.

"What was that all about?" Constantine went to the bar cart and poured his preferred brand of Kentucky bourbon.

"Nothing." I stood and rounded the desk to accept the glass he'd extended. "We haven't had a minute alone since the club in Rome, and it couldn't have been easy on you to walk away from Rocco. How are you doing?"

"I'm great." He perched his hip on the side of my desk and kept his eyes on the bar cart. "You all care more about what he did to me four years ago than I do." I highly doubted that, but I wasn't going to argue. "Your restraint in not killing him when you had the chance shows how much you care about Callie."

"I barely know her." I finished the drink a little too quickly and grabbed the bottle and added more to my glass. "She's my assignment, and our opportunity to take out Rocco and his father."

"You're married," he said in disbelief, and yeah, you and me both. "I still can't believe it. But with any luck, you won't need to stay married all summer. We have a plan to help get that ring off your finger much sooner."

That had my attention.

"If that's what you want?"

I laughed, and oddly, it felt forced. "Of course that's what I want."

He casually sipped his drink, then pushed away from the desk, his gaze shooting to the door. Hudson was in the hall now and talking with Izzy. "Something I should know about them?"

"No. Izzy was just being Izzy." I'd take a bullet for my sister both literally and metaphorically, so it would seem. "All good." I caught her eyes and waved them in, giving them the okay it was safe to join us. Not that I really accepted Constantine's answer about being "great," given the Rocco situation, but I knew not to press. "So what's this plan that'll get me out of the marriage faster?"

Instead of answering, Izzy went to my bar and poured herself wine and Hudson whiskey. Did this plan require liquid courage to be shared? Why were they stalling? *And* all looking at me like I was the subject of an investigation. I reached for the knot of my tie, forgetting I'd already removed it on the drive over from the other office an hour ago.

"Do I need to sit for this or something?" I asked, uneasiness burrowing into my stomach.

"How do you feel about using Callie's thirtieth birthday as the bait to draw Rocco to us?" Izzy pitched the idea. "A joint birthday party for the two of you since you're forty on the twenty-first, too. Invite Armani and Marcello as a little peace offering to the party as well."

"And at the party, we frame Rocco for Armani's death," Hudson tacked on casually, eyes meeting mine as he spoke. "And *attempted* murder of Callie."

Use my wife as bait for a psychopath? I was okay with being bait, but I wanted her to be far away from me when that time came. With The League now watching Rocco's every movement, I'd fortunately be able to anticipate his arrival and hide her away for safekeeping from the sick bastard.

Constantine joined in on the conversation and said, "The plan was always to kill Armani and Marcello to set Callie free by turning the reins over to Gabriel, correct?"

"This idea kills two birds with one stone," Izzy said before I could answer. "We make it look like Rocco was pissed Armani betrayed the deal to unite the families and wanted revenge by going after the DiMaggio organization."

"Then we'll get retribution for Armani and Marcello's murders by killing the Barones," Hudson said casually. "There shouldn't be any concerns you or Callie were tied to their deaths. Then she'll pass the power over to Gabriel, you'll get a divorce, and she can live her life as she did before."

I went around to my desk, needing to sit. It was a good plan. The idea of blaming Rocco had crossed my mind, especially when Armani had asked whether Rocco would be a problem for me before the wedding. But the time frame . . . and placing her in potential danger threw me off. I didn't want that sick fuck breathing the same air as her.

"And if Rocco doesn't take the bait? If his father convinces him to stick to the cease-fire arranged between our parents and not come after me? Us?" I finally spoke, my head still spinning.

"Whether he comes or not, we still pin the blame on him," Constantine said. "The League's eyes in the sky confirmed Claudio's also at the compound in Romania. I've convinced them not to storm the place to take him out for now—to wait so we can use Rocco for Armani's murder."

"Think about it," Izzy began on approach. "You stole Rocco's chance to marry Callie by killing Esposito at his wife's fortieth birthday. So what better revenge plan for him than to learn you're having a party for your wife, and for him to want to take action there? It's believable, and I have a feeling he won't be able to resist coming, regardless of whether his father chooses not to start shit with us and The League."

"You're getting scary good at this job," I muttered, taking a sip of my drink, buying myself more time to think. "We'd need to have the party off the island. No hotel or anyplace that can chance the risk of civilian casualties." I thought through the idea a bit more. "A mansion we can secure that has a safe room I can hide Callie in if Rocco or his men do show up."

"And a way to kill Armani and Marcello privately to pin their deaths on the Barones," Izzy said with a nod. "We can do this. And hey, this gives Mom a party to plan, and she'll get off your back about having a family dinner."

I shook my head. "Real funny."

"Not a bad idea, actually," Constantine chimed in. "Better to keep Mom away from your wife as much as possible. She'll get attached, and her heart will get broken when you two split."

Mom's heart? Yeah, another heart I needed to worry about breaking alongside Callie's, which was why I'd been so adamant earlier at the airport that Mom keep her distance from my wife. "I might need to talk this over with Gabriel first."

"No, he stays out of it." Constantine set down his glass, and I looked Hudson's way, waiting to see if he'd share whether he'd had any luck digging into Gabriel's background like my brother had asked him to do in Rome.

"Still looking," Hudson said, reading my thoughts. "He's been with the DiMaggios since he was a teenager. I'd question his motives for working with you, but—"

"Taking over the DiMaggio organization seems like a legitimate one," I finished for him.

Hudson discarded his unfinished glass on the bar cart. "But I'll keep checking."

"So?" Izzy circled the desk, waiting for my okay on the plan.

"I think it can work." I lifted my hand to tell her to pause her excitement for a beat. "*But* I need daily reports about Rocco's whereabouts from The League. If the man takes a piss outside that compound in Romania, I want to know about it." I turned toward Constantine next. "You sure you're good with this plan? You talked to Dad about it? We held off on hunting Rocco down all these years, not because Dad arranged a deal with Claudio, but because *you* asked us to follow Dad's orders."

"Dad was trying to keep us from having to look over our shoulders every five minutes." Of course Constantine would defend Dad. "But it's time Rocco gets to look over his shoulder. And when he does"—and there was that anger that'd been missing from him before—"I'll slit his throat."

"Lovely image," Izzy whispered. "Well, I have to get going. I'm going to let Mom know about the party and hope that distracts her from her efforts to cozy up to your wife."

"Mom can't lose another daughter," Constantine said somberly, and fuck, that comment hurt. "We'll talk later. It's been a long day. Everyone should get home," Constantine deflected, then motioned to clear out, but I hung back and once alone, rested my elbows on the desk, placing my head in my hands.

I'd be single again soon enough. *I can do this.*

I finally had the energy to look up before I fell asleep right there, my eyes catching sight of my wedding ring in the process. *Shit.* I grabbed my phone and called up my assistant, not caring it was after 2100 hours. "I need a favor."

"Another one?" I heard the smirk in his tone.

"I forgot to get her an engagement ring. She's a Costa now. She needs a diamond on her finger, or people might—"

"I'll pick one up tomorrow."

"No, now. I need to go *now.*"

"Sir, it's late. The stores will be closed."

"Get a manager on the phone," I directed, not prepared to back down on this. "Something on Fifth Avenue. The best jewelry store there is. They'll open up for me. Text me the location. I'll be there in thirty."

"Yeah, um, okay. I'll do my best, but you owe me a nice vacation when this is all over."

"All expenses paid on me. Got it," I said before hanging up, then went and refilled my glass, my nerves shot to hell as I thought about buying a diamond—something I hadn't done since I was twenty-two. Of course, I'd gotten down on one knee then, and I had no plans to ever do that again.

CHAPTER TWENTY-FIVE

Alessandro

"About time you showed up. You don't plan on letting your wife sleep alone, do you?" Frankie had the nerve to stop me in the hall of my own damn home on the way to my bedroom, and it took all my restraint not to shove him against the wall. His attention dipped to the bag in my hand. "Ah, got the princess a diamond, did you?"

I was too tired and had had too much to drink to deal with him right now. No response was the best way to handle the prick. So being the bigger person, I ignored him and hurried up the stairs, exhaustion setting in hard and fast with every step closer to my bedroom—a room I'd never shared overnight with a woman until now.

Testing the handle and finding it locked, I reached into my pocket for my keys. I'd had a deadbolt installed today, not a fan of Armani's men having access to my wife. At least she had the good sense to lock the door.

Once inside the room, I kicked off my shoes and gave myself a few seconds to adjust to the darkness so I didn't trip over anything and wake her.

I had every intention of setting the little blue bag on the nightstand without a word, but she caught me mid-act placing it there. She turned on the lamp, and I let go of the ring bag and took a few uncomfortable steps back.

"What's this?" She sat upright, wearing a pink nightshirt from the looks of it, and I had no clue whether she had on bottoms, too.

"It'd be strange if my wife didn't have a diamond. I thought of everything but that before we arrived." I'd spent almost two hours in that store tonight, wavering on which ring to buy, now knowing way more about diamonds than I ever wanted or needed to.

"Oh." She removed the box from the bag, and I swallowed, oddly nervous whether she'd like it. I'd wanted to buy her the biggest rock there, but her "you can't buy everything" comment earlier had me going with a simple solitaire with small diamonds on each side instead.

The smile from her as she slipped on the too-big-for-her-finger ring did something funny to my chest. "This is . . . well, perfect."

"Don't worry, my assistant picked it out," I said as fast as possible before she got angry at me again, like she had with the guitar. "Nothing sentimental about the ring."

"Good. Um, great."

Such a little liar. *Just like me.*

"Tell your assistant they have great taste."

"Sure." I was ready to get this conversation over with and sleep before I lost my head and asked her to scoot over, to let me sleep on my side of the bed she was currently occupying.

"Well, thank you. I'll need it sized." And yet, she didn't take it off, just fiddled with it on her finger.

I pushed out in a nonchalant tone, "You're welcome. It, uh, was nothing."

Still fidgeting with the diamond ring, she asked, "How'd the board meeting go? Your family business okay? Will you survive the fallout?"

"Fine." Not really. But we'd done our best to keep people's heads from exploding. "Are things okay on your end with damage control?" *Did you talk to Braden?*

"I need another day or two before I make any calls. Just sent a few texts. Tested the waters with my aunt via email. She only gave me an update on her location along with a few photos, seemingly oblivious to this hell, which is good news."

Speaking of . . . "I have more good news."

She let her hand fall to her lap atop the gray duvet, attention shooting to me.

I had to pocket my hands so I wouldn't reach for her. Or ask her to let me finger fuck her again. "We're getting divorced much sooner than expected. Right after our birthday."

The little *oh* sound she made that could've been confused for disappointment wasn't lost on me. "I forgot your birthday is on the twenty-first, too. I saw that in my search, but I got distracted by photos of you and . . ."

Other women. I never gave a damn about my reputation. Until now. Until Little Miss Tennessee Whiskey blew into my life like a storm, setting everything off course in my perfect world that was probably far from ever being perfect.

"Wait, that's soon. Today's May twenty-ninth, right?" Her being twenty-nine and counting on her fingers fucking killed me. Too cute. Too innocent. Too *everything* for me. "That's in twenty-three days." The bedding went to the wayside as she stood, revealing she had nothing on under that pink nightshirt that went to midthigh.

"Told you, good news." Mindlessly, I began unbuttoning my dress shirt and went over to the couch, discovering she'd already turned it down into a bed and had the sheets and blanket prepped for me.

"How? I mean, um, does that mean you're killing my father in three and a half weeks?"

My fingers went still on the buttons at her words, and I slowly faced her, my arms falling to my sides. "You called him your father. You—"

"Shit." She blinked as if surprised herself. "It's just a lot to take in. Helping murder someone. A man who gave me life. Even if I hate him for his very existence."

I went back over to her, worried there was about to be a major disconnect and problem with the plan. Searching for her gaze, I waited until she gave me her eyes. Instead, she chewed on her already short thumbnail—not one of her nervous habits I'd yet to witness. No, this was doubt infiltrating her mind.

She freed her thumbnail from between her teeth to ask, "How will you kill him?"

When she'd yet to give me her eyes, I reached for her elbow. "At our birthday party that we invite him and Marcello to. We'll frame Rocco and his father—revenge for choosing me over him to wed."

Refusing to meet my eyes while taking shallow breaths weren't the best signs. "How will you kill him, though?" The break in her tone had me letting go of her elbow, and I stepped back.

"Look at me," I demanded roughly, but if this plan was about to go to hell in a handbasket, as my mother liked to say, I needed to do damage control, and fast.

Marriage. Murder. Revenge. Divorce. That'd been the plan. Was she changing it on me?

"The man had a doctor check your fertility. He's trying to force you to fuck me so you can give him a kid, a child he wants to raise to become a killer." She had to remember the details, to commit the gritty, dark truth about the bastard to memory before she changed her mind. "Where's this coming from? Why do you care how he dies as long as he ends up six feet under?"

She sidestepped me and sat on the pull-out bed. "I'm sorry, you're right. I just . . ." Those light-green eyes finally landed on me, and I nearly regretted demanding her attention, because that sad expression was a painful sight. "Talking about it happening at the end of the summer felt like forever away, and this feels real now." She tugged her lip between her teeth, appearing contemplative when there shouldn't have been anything to think about. "What if having a hand in his murder makes me as bad as him? What if he wins anyway because I let the darkness out he wants unleashed?" Tears pricked her eyes, and they poked a hole in my chest.

Unable to stop myself, I sat by her and held her hand. The diamond had spun around and dug into my palm. "Don't do this. You're not him, and you never will be." Feeling a bit panicked myself, because if she changed her mind I had no damn idea what to do, I brought our linked palms between us and turned toward her. "We're in this together. Okay?"

She stared at our united hands, blinking a few times. Uncertainty still clung to her soft gaze when it returned to my face. "*Non c'è luce senza oscurità.*"

Squeezing her hand a bit harder at the sight of tears now slipping down her cheeks, I leaned closer and set my forehead to hers. "You're the light in this scenario, okay?" I murmured. "And you need to let me be the dark. I can handle it, I promise." *I already am it.* "You're just tired. I should've waited to tell you this until after you slept," I added when she'd yet to speak, and her silence was brutal.

"Maybe you're right." Her determined voice was what I needed to hear, and I pulled away to check her face, see if some color had returned.

Realizing I was still holding her hand to the point her ring was now leaving an imprint inside my palm, I let her go, and she swiped at her cheeks with the backs of her hands.

"Tell me the truth about Rocco."

Since I'd already opened my mouth tonight, it was time to go ahead and rip the Band-Aid off, I supposed. Maybe this would help ease her concerns about the plan, too? But I'd need to stand for this and keep my back to her. "After my brothers and I were arrested for killing our sister's killer—which we got wrong back then but didn't know it . . . and don't worry, the person responsible is now dead—well, my dad negotiated a get-out-of-jail-free card for us."

Her hand was at my back, which meant she'd joined me on her feet. She was careful with how she touched me. Gentle. Comforting. As if letting me know she had my back. That wasn't something I'd allowed a woman outside my family to have before.

"Go on," she prompted when I'd become tripped up.

"The deal was charges would be dropped and no prison time if my brothers and I worked for the government. Three veterans killing a killer—the Feds didn't really want us in jail, either. So they arranged to have us do off-the-books, clandestine stuff. Not exactly reporting to the CIA, but kind of . . . But four years ago, we were sent after a high-value target, Claudio Barone. The intel must've been bad because the plan went sideways, and Rocco captured Constantine. He had him for ten days. Slowly tortured him. The kind of torture you need trigger warnings for before watching a movie. Only this was . . . real." Fuck, now I was going to be sick. I still had no clue how I'd faced off with that animal in Rome and hadn't killed him.

Who was I kidding? When she urged me to face her, I knew why: taking out Rocco would've jeopardized the woman before me.

Her palms landed on my cheeks, and I quickly held her wrists but didn't shove her hands away. "I was working on a rescue, but a sniper had me in his sights on overwatch, and apparently, Gabriel also had me in his sights, because he took out Rocco's man on the long gun, saving my life."

"Gabriel saved you," she whispered, surprise in her eyes. "Why? How'd he know? Armani wasn't working with Rocco then, was he?"

I slowly lowered her hands from my face, finding myself a little short of breath, walking down memory lane. Holding her wrists still, but down at our sides, I shared, "Gabriel heard my brother had been taken by the Barones. He didn't have Armani's blessing, nor did Armani know his plan, but according to Gabriel, he went there to help save Constantine."

"This is why you owe him a favor. The reason you're helping me is all because of what happened four years ago." She studied me for a long moment, and I wasn't sure where her head was at right now, but she didn't make me wait long to find out. "Does everything really happen for a reason? If Armani hadn't chosen Rocco to marry me, would you not have helped? Maybe Gabriel would never have gone to you in the first place."

I let go of her wrists and slid my hand into her hair, cupping the back of her head. "I don't know if Gabriel would've come to me if Rocco wasn't involved, but regardless of the man your father chose, I would've said yes to helping you."

Her eyes locked with mine. "Why?"

"Because I met you," I admitted hoarsely. "And Gabriel knew I'd never be able to walk away from you after that."

"But you will be walking away," she reminded me, a single tear breaking free as she pulled away her hand. "Right after our birthday party, you'll walk away." She removed the diamond, which had me oddly feeling as if I'd been punched, then she gave me her back. "Do you still work for the government?"

"No. We were given our freedom. Everything we do now is because we want to. No red tape, either." Doing my best to shake off the fact I felt like I'd been through the emotional wringer my therapist had tried to put me through in the past without much luck—and this woman in the space of a heartbeat had managed to do it—I finished the job of unbuttoning my shirt and tossed it on the pull-out bed.

"You help people because you can, not because you have to." She faced me again, eyes landing on my naked chest. "You're not the dark in this scenario, Alessandro." Slowly, she worked her attention to my face. "You're the light."

I closed the space between us. Hands tight at my sides so I didn't touch her, I rasped, "No, I am. You need to remember that, too. And remember I will walk away from you when this is over, because I am *that* guy. I can't be anyone else." It took all my strength, all my energy, to spew those words—words that didn't want to come out, but I had to hammer in the point. "I'm not the hero in the story." My palm went flat over my heart. "I'm the man who'd go scorched-earth on the world to save his family. A hero would put their country first."

What in the hell was on her mind? Why wasn't she backing away? Running?

"At the end of the day, I'm a killer," I said, reiterating my point, worried she'd yet to receive it with her peering at me as if she'd be okay if I sacrificed the world for her. "You're a schoolteacher. A musician. A woman with a good heart." I stabbed the air. "You're not a DiMaggio. You're not like us. Like me." Breathing hard, worried I was on the verge of snapping and gathering her in my arms to feel her light wash over me, to experience what it felt like just to have a taste of her sweetness, I sidestepped her to get to the bathroom, needing the conversation over with.

"I get it. You're trying to push me away. I all but begged you to do that earlier after you gave me the guitar." Her soft tone stopped me in my tracks, preventing me from slamming the bathroom door shut. "But you are a hero, Alessandro. What you're doing for me, for Constantine . . . We have different definitions of that word. The only villains are the ones you plan to kill."

I slowly faced her from where I stood inside the doorway of the bathroom. I set my hands to the frame, trying to stop myself from going into the room and fucking her so hard I'd destroy us both, just to prove she was wrong about me.

She slipped the ring back on her finger while approaching me, eyes steady on mine as she took small but confident steps.

"Calliope," I hissed as she stopped before me, and I couldn't help but take notice of her nipples piercing the fabric. "Thin ice." I reminded her about my control and its limits when it came to her. "You told me earlier you want to hate me, or have you forgotten?"

"I said I'd try." Her palm went over my heart, and on instinct, I flinched. "Feel that?" She arched a brow and peered up at me. "It beats."

For you.

Fuck, it seems to beat again for you.

211

Chills like I'd never known scattered across my skin, and I was pretty sure she was aware of her effect on me. This woman, and my reaction to her, scared the ever-loving hell out of me. "Callie," I forced out this time. "This is just . . . desire. That's all it is. That's what you're feeling." I swallowed, hating myself enough for the both of us. "We need to stay away from each other. I can't be near you without . . ." *Wanting you.* "And you're confused. It's the adrenaline and shock of your situation. You don't want *this.*" I pushed away from the doorframe and removed her hand from my chest, unable to handle it parked there any longer.

"Based on how wet I am, I'm pretty sure I do." And there it was. My good girl's naughty side. But that side would get her in trouble. Especially with me. Her attention wandered to my dress pants, and I knew she was able to see I was as hard as steel. "What if we get it out of our systems? Maybe that'll help? Maybe that's what I should have said earlier in your office."

I closed my eyes, unable to stand looking at her any more without showing my cards. The fact I *may* have had an emotion or two still left in me after the life I'd lived.

"You'd get bored of me after the one time, right? So no concerns we'd do it again after that."

Bored was the last thing I'd ever be with this woman. "How would that make you feel if I fucked you and moved on?" I did my best to be an asshole, even though I didn't want to be one right now.

"Sad," she confessed without making me wait, and I opened my eyes at that bit of truth. "Because you're not mine to keep, and I'm afraid I'll want to." She blinked back tears.

"Maybe you're right. I'm not a villain, because a villain would take you now and not care," I ground out. "And I can't do that." I leaned in close, but not so close I'd slip and kiss her. "I don't want to hurt you." My voice broke that time. "Please, for the love of God, stay away from me for the next three weeks so I don't do that. So I don't become the villain of your story."

CHAPTER TWENTY-SIX

Alessandro

"What are you listening to?" Hudson was in the doorway of my office at the security firm, staring at me with a puzzled expression.

I turned off the music app on my phone and leaned back in my desk chair. "You're telling me you're from Texas and don't know Chris Stapleton?"

He laughed. "Of course I do. I just didn't think you would." He pushed away from the door and came inside. "Your wife's influence, huh? Thought you were avoiding her, though?"

I'd done my best to steer clear of Calliope after I almost lost my control Thursday night. It was also why I was at the office on a Sunday night—officially June and the month I'd divorce—listening to country music. *What's happening to me?*

I was stalling going home, worried about having another late-night encounter with her. The last few mornings, I'd disappeared before the sun rose and hadn't gotten in until at least zero dark thirty.

Hudson didn't press me to answer him, and I was grateful for that. He snatched my black bottle of Clase Azul Ultra and filled two tumblers with a single shot.

"Why are *you* here?" I asked, instead of admitting to him my wife was rubbing off on me in ways I wished she wouldn't, even if I'd barely seen her in person. "Shouldn't you be running your bar? You do have another job."

He handed me the glass and took a seat in front of the desk. "Bar's closed on Sundays, remember?"

"Right." I looked to the open doorway, half expecting my sister to pop in, too. She'd been a constant pain in my ass since we'd arrived in New York by checking on me, or having Enzo text me, to ensure I hadn't *snapped, crackled, or popped*—her words. I was pretty sure she'd meant them exactly as they sounded. I was a ball of tension without doing the two things I was good at—hunting criminals and having casual sex.

"I'm worried about you." He crossed his ankle over his knee, setting his glass on his thigh.

"Izzy sent you, didn't she? She saw on the cameras I'm here late again." I should've known. She was creeping on me, just like I'd been *checking* on my wife over the security system at our house the last few days.

He frowned. "No."

"Liar." I sipped the tequila, waiting for him to fess up.

"I had some time to kill, didn't feel like being home myself, and thought I'd come here and do a little more digging into Gabriel."

I sat taller at his words. "Why didn't you want to be home?" I had my own reasons; what were his? "And what'd you find out? Or did you find anything?"

"First, tell me, are you good? Do I need to worry?"

I laughed. "Is this an intervention?" Snatching my phone, I looked up toward the camera, wondering if my sister was watching now. "I haven't checked on her all day." I wasn't the best liar.

Three hours ago, I'd flicked on the camera in the music room, even though I'd vowed not to stalk-view her again. In my defense, I hadn't been able to spot her anywhere else in the house, so I'd been worried.

She'd been playing her guitar while singing, and I'd been glued to my seat.

Yeah, maybe I am a creeper. At least I hadn't whacked off at my desk at the sight of her in those sexy cut-off jean shorts and cowboy boots during my private performance.

Of course, tonight while she slept, it'd happen in my shower, just as it had Friday and Saturday nights. I could barely breathe in that room, knowing she was half-naked in my bed, remembering how her pussy had responded to me on our "honeymoon" night. And that mouth of hers when we'd kissed . . . What a mouth, dammit.

Realizing I was waving my phone at the camera in the corner of my office and the light wasn't on, so no one had eyes on me, I let it fall to the desk and finished the tequila. And right, I *did* have eyes on me. Hudson's shocked brown ones, to be exact.

"You haven't answered my questions yet, and you clearly have the answer to yours, that I'm not okay. You should worry. A lot," I found myself admitting on my way to get another drink. "I can't be saved or helped, though, so what's going on with you? With Gabriel?"

"No red flags I can find on Gabriel yet, which feels like one itself. I get you two have a history, but he risked a lot four years ago, saving you and Constantine. Doesn't add up."

After refilling my drink, I went over to his and added more, even though he'd yet to touch it. "He's not a bad guy for being a bad guy." Shit, now I was talking like Calliope. And also, I was back to calling her by her full name (at least in my head). I couldn't help it. Fuck Braden and his use of it, though, and the fact I had a feeling my wife had talked to him since arriving in New York. The only shocker was she'd yet to bring up the gig on Broadway again, not that I'd given her a chance.

"But you believe he saved you and Constantine just because?"

I returned the bottle to the cart. "He knew I'd owe him for it, and he has enough patience to wait to collect on a favor one day. That much I believe." I faced him again. "But keep looking. My judgment isn't so great." After another sip, I asked, "Why don't you want to be at home?"

Hudson set the glass on the desk, grabbed hold of the back of his neck, and squeezed. "Because your sister's there."

I about dropped the glass. "Say that again."

He held up a hand and shook his head. "It's not like that. There was a gas leak at her place, and she didn't want to stay in Long Island at your parents' other place, and she said your mom would bug her about visiting Calliope if she went to their place by Central Park. So she asked to spend the weekend at my place."

"She has other friends. *Female* ones. Ones she didn't kiss—well, that I know of, at least," I snapped, way too tense to be thinking about my sister shacking up with my good friend. "Also, what am I, chopped liver? Or there's Constantine?" She'd been blowing up my phone all weekend, checking on me, and yet had failed to mention where she was while harassing me.

"Bella doesn't take no for an answer, you know that. She showed up at my door yesterday with a bag and determination. I suggested your place. She said you have concerns about her getting attached to your wife since this is a short-term assignment." He paused to let that ugly truth sink in. "And she did try Constantine first, but he had . . . company."

"What kind?"

"The kind you normally have." He shrugged. "A no-strings-attached friend for the weekend. Someone he knew once upon a time ago and bumped into her."

Great, now Constantine was getting laid while I resorted to jerking off in my shower. The fact Constantine hadn't mentioned this old friend visiting pissed me off. Everyone was walking on eggshells around me ever since we'd gotten back to New York, like I might blow a fuse.

I glared at my phone on my desk, remembering my fuse was pretty short, so maybe they weren't wrong. "And what about her friends?"

"She said they're all married and I'm her only single friend, yada yada yada." He snatched his glass again and took a sip. "I tried."

"You can't 'yada yada yada' your way out of my sister spending the weekend at your place, and the fact you don't trust yourself to be alone with her means . . . what, exactly?"

The calm and normally quiet man probably wanted to chuck his glass at me, but I knew he wouldn't. "She drives me nuts, that's all. Don't be ridiculous." He polished off his drink. "That kiss in Rome was your sister being a pain in all of our asses, too, and you know it."

"About that."

"There's nothing else to say." And yet, he was refilling his glass.

"You sure?" I waited for him to face me so I could stare him down. "Bella's like a—"

"Don't say *sister*. You'll throw up in your mouth if you do." Because fuck, I knew that look. Recognized desire when I saw it, because I was right there with him when it came to Calliope. I wasn't sure how I felt about him feeling that way toward my sister, but with her track record, Hudson was quite the improvement. The only problem? He was like me and would break her heart one day.

Hudson glanced up at the ceiling for a breath, then asked, "You feel like going hunting?"

Find an asshole or two that needed to be taught a lesson? We wouldn't have to go far in the city to stumble upon one lately. "Best idea I've heard all day."

CHAPTER TWENTY-SEVEN

Calliope

"Friday's tomorrow, and you're still not here," were Braden's first words when I finally answered his call instead of only swapping texts like we'd been doing. "Also, about damn time you picked up," he laid into me before I could speak. "I assume it's your husband's doing as to why we haven't talked on the phone before now."

My husband? The words came out bitter from him. Resentful and maybe jealous, too. He had as much right to be jealous of Alessandro as Alessandro did him.

"Can't believe you married a stranger. And the fact you haven't told your aunt is suspect. If I had her number, I'd call her. And believe me, I tried looking her up."

Thank God she was paranoid enough to keep her digits safely hidden from the world.

"This isn't like you." He wasn't going to let up, was he?

"If you wanted to have a one-way conversation we could've stuck to text." I dropped down at my desk in the music room and flicked one of the balled-up pieces of paper there. *Writer's block be damned.* If a view of the Manhattan skyline couldn't cure me, nothing would.

Well, maybe not until I was freed from the shackles of a marriage my husband didn't want, and I shouldn't have wanted. *And I don't. Not now.* Maybe one day with a man who didn't marry me because of a favor and revenge. Also, with someone who saw more than a body to bang and a woman with the potential to be loved.

"Calliope." His tone softened this time, but my name from his lips felt traitorous. Like I was cheating even talking to him, especially at ten o'clock on a Thursday night while my husband had been mostly MIA every day the past week.

He'd done his best to keep away, aside from two run-ins the last week. Once on Monday while reading the newspaper at the ass crack of dawn and sipping his coffee, dressed like a million bucks (well, billion) in his suit at the kitchen table.

He'd spilled his coffee on the paper. I'd teased him about reading the actual paper like an old man, instead of the news online, then he'd lectured me on walking around in my pajamas with so many other men in the house—including him.

I'd upgraded from the dancing PJs to singing cherries that'd been an impulse buy on Amazon over the weekend. He hadn't been a fan of those, either, so it seemed. Or my eye roll from his reaction.

"Calliope." There was my name again, a reminder I was now letting Braden have that one-way conversation because I was jogging through the two encounters with the only man I wanted to actually call me by that.

Yesterday had nearly done me in when seeing him. *Also* at the ass crack of dawn, but in the gym. I'd been unable to sleep, so I thought I'd run on the treadmill to stop the thoughts running on repeat through my mind. Worries about what to do about my job since I'd yet to resign. Then there were my friends badgering me for answers. Stress about my aunt and what if she found out.

So walking into the gym to see Alessandro sweaty and shirtless and jumping rope had only added to my plate of why I needed to run after that.

Of course, he'd stopped jumping the second he set eyes on me and nodded a curt hello as he studied my gym clothes, as if finding them more problematic than my singing-cherries PJs, then he wordlessly tossed the rope and left. Talk about a cold shoulder.

"Don't call me that anymore," I finally said, remembering Braden was waiting for me to participate in the call and I'd let my mind wander too long into dangerous territory by thinking about my husband, a man I couldn't help but think about nearly every hour of every day since he'd come into my life.

The fact I'd gotten myself off in the shower, feeling too dirty to do it in his bed, even if it was a new mattress, had me all kinds of messed up. I'd had the weird sensation of being watched all week, and even that and knowing there were cameras in the penthouse didn't prevent me from touching myself. Not that I'd seen any in the bathroom or bedroom, but still.

What made it worse was *who* I'd thought about while touching myself. Not a celebrity or favorite fictional character. Nope, a real man. *My husband.*

I'd been unable to write music, but my creativity had shifted to conjuring up the kind of fantasies that even made me blush. The idea of him spanking me had sent me over the orgasm cliff twice in the last twenty hours alone. (I'd taken more than one shower a day.)

"What do you mean?" Either he'd had a delayed reaction, or I was still stuck on thoughts of the sexy man who'd shared a bedroom with me for the last seven-plus days but hadn't touched me and just now heard Braden talk. "I always call you Calliope."

"Callie. I prefer that now."

"This is his doing, isn't it? He's controlling you. You're letting a man you don't know tell you what to do, and that's not even remotely like you."

He wasn't telling me what to do. Not really. Just to keep his distance so he didn't bang me and break my heart. I'd yet to broach the subject of Broadway again, even though we needed to leave in the morning, and I had every intention of having a *third* ass-crack-of-dawn moment with him to let him know I'd be flying there to perform.

"You're coming, right? Just tell me you're coming. This is your dream. Do you know how hard it was for me to land this gig for *us?*"

"Pretty sure you told me a half dozen times over text in the last week. The guilt you laid on was thicker than molasses."

"You roll your eyes any harder they'll get stuck."

"You can't see me." But I did roll them. Again for good measure.

"But I know you, *Callie.* Unlike the playboy you married."

He probably thought that playboy was having his way with me every day, and yet, nope—zero way to be had. I still couldn't believe I'd gone from upset about his sweet guitar gesture, insisting it was best to hate him, to nearly falling to my knees before him that very night, asking him to ravage me and screw the consequences.

He'd even had a messenger drop off the official legal marriage documents to sign to avoid any unnecessary contact with me on Tuesday.

So yeah, his willpower was much better than mine. I was all over the place when it came to that man. He was probably right to keep away.

"The silence you're blessing me with is also a curse. It's fucking with my head while I try to figure out what's going on in yours," Braden told me, and damn, he wasn't holding back now that he had me on the phone.

At least Imani, and my best friend, Nala, had used kid gloves when they tried to talk sense into me about my "strange behavior" of allowing a man to whisk me away like I was in some Hallmark movie. I was pretty sure Hallmark wasn't in the business of making movies about the mafia or murder. But I left those comments to myself while denying the rumors about Armani.

"I'll be there. Tomorrow afternoon," I finally said, hoping my husband would let that happen when I confronted him.

"Good. We need to rehearse beforehand. We're on at nine p.m. I'm sure you've been too busy to do it up in your mansion."

"Not in a mansion." *Well, not quite.* "And I have had time, actually." No plan to explain to him why.

"If you don't come, there's something you should know," he said a beat later, his voice inching into you're-about-to-hate-me territory. "Britt will be standing in for you if you're a no-show. I need a backup in case you blow me off."

I stood and pushed the chair back. "Of all the singers we know. Britt, really?"

"Britt's the only one who knows our stuff and who can pull off a last-minute gig."

"Of course she knows our stuff. She was part of the band before she slept with my boyfriend." The year between then and now hadn't seemed to dull the betrayal from one of my best friends. She'd hurt me far more than my boyfriend had, because she'd been my person. My go-to for everything. And she'd taken our friendship and stomped all over it, breaking my heart.

"I'm sorry." His apology was flat and only further pissed me off, because was he going to be another friend who hurt me? "This is important, though. And it's her or no one if you don't show. Lesser of two evils."

Oh, for the love of . . . I fell back into my chair at his words, hating them so, so much. "You're doing this just to make sure I come down there. You're playing dirty, damn you."

"This is our dream. We've talked about this for so long. Hell, the three of us used to, before she fucked up," he said, instead of rejecting the notion. "I won't let some billionaire asshole take this from you. From us."

"I hate you." Not the way I hated Alessandro, though. No, that man inspired a sonnet of emotions and a whole notebook of feelings. If only I could turn those feelings into words on paper to sing. "But I'll be there, and so help Britt if she shows up, too." I ended the call without a proper goodbye, unable to talk to him any longer after the fresh hell someone I thought I could trust was now putting me through. I could only handle so much before breaking.

"You okay?" At Leo's voice, I swiveled in the desk chair to see him in the doorway.

I peered at the camera on the ceiling, then pointed to it. "Red light means it's not active, right? You weren't watching me, were you?" How'd he know I was the opposite of okay to come in and check?

He looked at the camera, then back at me. "It's off, and only your husband's security team here has access to the exterior camera feeds."

"So no one's been watching me?"

His lips twitched into a smile. "There's only one person who can view the interior cameras, and he hasn't been around so much, so you'll have to ask him when you see him next."

I wasn't sure what to make of that, or the fact I *had* felt like I'd been watched from time to time in the last week, which meant I was either losing it, or my husband had his eye on me more than I realized.

"Are you okay, Mrs. Costa?" he asked again, still hanging back in the doorway.

"Armani send you here to ask?" I didn't yell or shout on the phone, did I?

Another quick smile came and went. "He's not a fan of the game of dodgeball you've been playing when it comes to his calls. But no, I was walking by, and from the sounds of it, you were upset."

"I'm . . . fine." *Hardly.*

His brows scrunched, then he straightened his posture and caught me off guard by sharing, "You look like her; you know that, right?"

There was only one "her" he had to have been talking about, and the only motherly figure in my life I cared to think about right now was on a cruise ship and still blissfully ignorant of my situation.

"I worked your mother's security detail for ten years. Whenever she was in Sicily, he had me keep an eye on her."

"So she didn't cheat on him while he cheated on his wife?" I couldn't help but blurt.

"I know you must think she chose him over you, but she was clearly trying to save you from being raised as a DiMaggio."

"You say that like it's a bad thing. Aren't you supposed to be on his side, not mine?" Of course, Leo had been nothing but nice to me since day one, but like Gabriel, he worked for Armani, so I couldn't fully give him my trust.

"I can see why Gabriel chose Alessandro for you." That wasn't an answer to my question. Well, not exactly. It did feel like a cryptic message, though.

"What do you mean?"

"You think I'm an *idiota?*" The third smile was the charm. The most genuine from him that time. "I know a sexually frustrated man when I see one. You two haven't consummated the marriage." Before I could protest and lie, he lifted a hand. "I won't tell anyone. I'm loyal to the code of the DiMaggio family, and that means not hurting a woman. It's obvious Gabriel chose Alessandro because he knew he'd never touch you against your wishes. And you must not want him to, because he's walking around like a ticking time bomb."

I stared at him, tongue-tied and shocked. "What are you . . . What do you want?" Everyone wanted something in this game we were playing, which was starting to feel more like Russian roulette with every day that passed.

"I think we want the same thing," is all he said before winking, then he left me alone, and I had to assume—to *hope*—that meant he was somehow on my side in all this. An unlikely ally when the time came.

I grabbed my phone from the desk at the memory I promised Braden I was coming to Nashville, and maybe waiting until tomorrow to confront Alessandro was a bad idea. I needed to do it now while I had the nerve.

No clue where he was so late at night, I called him up to track him down, but I didn't expect a breathless, "Are you okay?" from him when he picked up.

"What are you doing?" *Oh God . . . or who are you doing?*

"I'm in the middle of something," he said in a clipped tone. "What do you need?"

"To talk," I rushed out, hating the snap of jealousy popping through me, visions of some woman naked beneath him in my mind now.

"I can't. Not now. I'm busy."

Oh, I bet. "Where are you?"

"At work."

Liar.

"I'm going to ask again, are you okay?" he asked steadily.

"Yes."

"Then I have to go." The call ended, and I lowered the phone, anger lighting a hot path through my body, feeling like I was being cheated on all over again, which was absurd. The marriage was . . . still technically real, dammit. And so was the pain in my stomach at thinking about him with another woman.

"Leo," I called out, already on my way to the door. "I need you to take me to my husband. Now."

CHAPTER
TWENTY-EIGHT

Calliope

"What are you doing here?" Hudson asked, eyes scanning the three men behind me on the stoop of the gorgeous home. According to Alessandro's head of security, the home was now the location for the Costa's security firm, though.

"I need to talk to Alessandro. Are you going to let me in or have me freeze out here?" Okay, it may have been June, but it was only fifty out, and I'd been in such a rush I'd forgotten a jacket and was only in a T-shirt and leggings. My anger should've been heating me up just fine, though. I'd been delusional to think the playboy could go a whole month without sex. Hell, we'd been married a little over a week, and he'd already given in to temptation.

Breathless, tense, and refusing to talk to me on the phone . . . What else could he have been doing other than having sex?

"This is a bad time." Hudson frowned, shooting me what appeared to be an apologetic look, because he was about to send me away, wasn't he? "You need to take her back home." He angled his head as a directive to Alessandro's head security detail, now at my left.

But my absurd jealousy kept me from budging, even at the feel of a hand on my arm, urging me to back away. "I need to see my husband." Tell him I finally did hate him, especially for making me feel something for him even when he'd kept his distance all week to try and prevent that.

"Not right now." Hudson remained in the doorway, keeping the door propped open with his shoulder, blocking my path. "I'm sorry. But no."

Damn the sting of tears. I wanted to be tough, not a hot mess. "Please," I begged. "I'm going to Nashville tomorrow, so if you don't think he'd like to know I'm leaving, then you—"

"What?" Hudson and Leo asked at the same time.

Right, I'd left that part out to the men on my protection detail.

"He's going to be pissed you're here." Hudson stepped back, catching the door with his palm. "Angrier if I tell him you're out here on the verge of tears and planning to run away and I didn't tell him, though.

"Stay in the foyer," he said once we were inside. "I'll go get him."

"No, I want to see what has my husband so preoccupied he couldn't talk to me. I'm going with you." No way was I letting Alessandro off the hook, even if he had every right to have sex with someone since this marriage would be over soon, and we'd been forced to walk down the aisle in the first place.

"Callie." My name sat on Hudson's lips for a beat as indecision warred in his dark eyes. "Fine," he relented. "But you're not going to like what you see. And he's going to kill me."

"I think you can hold your own," I said at the memory of Hudson's former employment as a Navy SEAL. "Wait here," I told the others, then followed Hudson down a set of steps and walked by an indoor pool before he stopped outside a door.

"Are you sure?" Resting his hand on the knob, he looked at me from over his shoulder.

Not even a little bit, because was he about to take me into some sex room I'd only been half-teasing about last week? "Yes," I lied.

He cursed while opening the door before taking me down another set of stairs that fed into a dark hallway. Hudson punched in a four-digit code on the wall by a door, then swore one more time, and opened it.

"Where are we?" Inside the dark space, I grabbed hold of the sides of my arms to chase away chills.

He flicked on the light, and I walked backward as shock had me in a choke hold. Hudson hooked my arm and revealed, "They can't see us in here."

Eyes on the glass window that showcased another room, I swallowed at the sight of a guy tied up, hands shackled to a pipe. His head was bowed. Chest naked and bloody.

But it was the man crouched before him, holding what appeared to be a chef's knife, who had me feeling the need to gasp for air. A skull-like ghost mask covered his face and hair, only leaving his eyes exposed.

I'd be able to recognize his body anywhere. "Alessandro."

He stood to his full height and faced the glass, as if sensing he was being watched. He cocked his head and came closer, lowering the knife to his side. The back of his knuckles hit the glass, and the masked man—my *husband*—tipped his head like a directive.

"I thought they can't see us," I said as Hudson went to a different door in the room.

"He can't, but . . ." Hudson let Alessandro into the tight little space, and I backed up against the other door.

I'd been expecting sex, not a masked man torturing a guy. God help me, why was I so relieved?

Without removing the mask, Alessandro ground out, "What in the hell is she doing down here?"

"Stubborn," was all Hudson said, and he was probably peering at me, but I couldn't rip my eyes away from my husband, draped in darkness, still holding a bloody knife at his side.

"Bring her to my office. I'll deal with her there." Alessandro barked out the command.

Only when Hudson reached for my arm, a gentle urge to move, did I finally look away from the shadowy masked figure that was my husband.

My heart was flying as Hudson guided me through the hall and up the stairs.

"He's pissed," I murmured after we'd gone up a second staircase.

"You think?" Hudson grumbled, opening a door a moment later. He turned on the light, and I was relieved to see what appeared to be an office and not another torture chamber.

Spotting a bar cart alongside one wall, I went over to it, in need of a drink. I filled a glass to the brim with whiskey. My hand was shaking as I lifted it to my mouth, spilling a few drops in the process.

"You okay?" Hudson asked, his tone softer this time.

At my first sip, I winced, then took another, much-needed one. "I thought he was having sex, not killing someone." Working up the courage to face him, I slowly turned around.

"Sex? Are you serious?" Hudson swiveled his black ball cap backward and pushed up the sleeves of his black shirt. "He'd never cheat on you, even if marrying you is part of his assignment."

"So he said himself, but that was not what I'd been expecting, and I . . ." I blinked, still reeling from shock. "Who's the guy down there?"

"A sinner, not a saint, I can promise you that," was all he gave me, and that wasn't good enough.

Swallowing down a bit more liquor for the sake of courage I now needed, I demanded, "Do better than that. More details."

Hudson folded his arms, hanging back in the doorway. "Side-gig thing."

I set aside the glass, needing to pull myself together and not get drunk. "What does that mean?"

"Consider that man a predator, someone who goes after those weaker than him."

Maybe I didn't want to know. Jesus.

"We hunt the hunter before he can catch his prey, if you get what I'm saying. And Alessandro's been in the hunting mood."

My hand slapped to my abdomen, and my stomach roiled. "I think I get it. Will you, um, kill him?"

"No. Just making sure he understands there are things much worse that can happen—aside from prison time—after he gets out of jail, so he doesn't fuck up again." His casual tone about the "side gig" of torturing people should've had my stomach turning more. Strangely, it didn't.

I swiveled around and dropped my hands to the desk, but chills flew up my spine when I realized we were no longer alone.

"Handle him for me," was all Alessandro said, and at the sound of the door shutting, I forced myself to face the music—my angry husband, who'd been playing some type of punisher role.

His back was to the door. Mask gone. In black dress pants and a dark button-up shirt, sleeves cuffed at the elbows, he was back to looking like the billionaire businessman, but the dark, stormy look still clung to his eyes, giving away the fact he was much more than that.

"You shouldn't be here," he said in a low but steady tone.

"I, um." My back went to the desk, and I set my hands down for support. "You hung up on me, and we needed to talk."

He angled his head, brows slanting as he casually said, "So talk," as if I hadn't caught him torturing a guy in his basement.

"I wouldn't have come if I'd known what you were doing. You shouldn't have answered the phone."

He gave me a funny look I couldn't read before saying, "You've never called me before, since being in New York; of course I'm going to answer."

"Well, I um, thought you were doing something much different," I confessed, fiddling with my diamond ring, even though it now fit perfectly since I'd had it sized a few days ago.

Alessandro's eyes cut to my ring for a moment before moving back to my face, and there was a flicker of anger there. "I wasn't fucking someone."

"Clearly." I gulped.

He pushed away from the door and stalked across the room. "You were jealous." Statement, not a question, and it had me lowering my hand to my side before I struck the words free from where they hung heavy in the air.

Because I hated the truth of them. Also despised the burn of jealousy in my stomach and chest still there, even knowing he hadn't been with another woman tonight.

"What were you planning to do? Come here and catch me in the act? And then what?" Was he seriously wanting me to answer that? And why'd his voice sound so flat and void of emotion when my insides were flooded with an entire dictionary full of feelings?

My fingers curled into my palms, still in need of the support of the desk to keep me from slipping into a puddle before this man. "I'm going to Nashville tomorrow. I'm set to perform at nine," I said at the memory of the other reason I was there, opting not to give in to his inquisition.

He closed the last bit of space between us and cupped my chin, a gentle touch despite the angry flare of his nostrils and the look of darkness still flashing in his eyes. "You think this is the best time to fuck around with my emotions?"

"And the idea of me going to Nashville does that? Fucks with your emotions?" I tried to stand my ground, even though I was seconds away from my knees buckling.

His hand slid to the side of my neck before going back to my ponytail, and he fisted my hair and tugged. Still a light touch despite the harsh words, he brought his mouth over my ear. "You pissing me off, in the mood I'm in, is a very bad idea, sweetheart." His rough voice had goose bumps flying over every inch of my skin.

"Why?" I challenged, unable to stop myself.

He brought his face back to mine, letting go of my ponytail. "You know exactly what your misbehaving and coming here makes me want to do."

Unable to stop myself, I arched my pelvis forward. My eyes closed as he brought his arm behind my back, and I drew myself tighter against him and rotated my hips at his hard length. Was I turned on by him torturing someone? No. But by being his bad girl? Apparently.

"Don't give me an invitation on a night like this. I'll take it." At the feel of his warm breath near my lips, I opened my eyes to see his mouth hovering close to mine. "I'll toss whatever's left of that moral compass of mine out the window just to know what it's like to be inside you." His Italian accent took front and center when he talked this time. God help me, it was hot.

Scooching back a touch so my ass was now officially parked on his desk, I quietly studied him, unsure who'd blink first, but I had a feeling it'd be me.

If I was crazy for being aroused, then so be it. The aching need between my legs could only be relieved in one way: by him. At this point, there was no turning back. I wouldn't leave even if the man got on his knees and begged.

Making up my mind, I parted my knees, and his hands flew to my thighs to stop them from opening any more. "You'll regret this." From the looks of it, this was his last-ditch effort to stop me from giving myself over to him, to a man who had blood on his forearm.

"Lesser of two evils," I whispered, hating myself for using that term again, but it fit like the final puzzle piece clicking into place. "If the choice is between one night with you or never at all, I choose this. Here and now."

"Calliope," he gritted out, but some of that darkness was slipping from his eyes, and I needed that man back. The sweet guy wouldn't screw me on his desk without a second thought, like I wanted him to.

Tonight, I needed the villain he was afraid to be with me.

"Be the asshole, not the teddy bear. For one night," I murmured, forgetting he hadn't been clued in on my rambling thoughts or the conversation with Izzy.

"The mask?" One dark brow lifted in question as he brushed his hand over my cheek, keeping his cock at a distance, much to my displeasure. "You want it back on? Would that make this feel less real for you? Is that what you're asking for?"

"No." *I mean . . . no?*

His brows tightened. "I don't know what you mean." Then he blinked as if putting it together without me having to spell it out for him. "I understand." A decisive nod followed, and he surprised me by reaching around to my back, leaning into me as he deftly unhooked my bra. "You're really lucky you wore a bra and didn't let the security team see your nipples poking through this thin shirt."

"Not that you'd spank me for being bad, would you?" I challenged, knowing damn well I was taunting him, and all it did was turn me on even more.

He let go of the clasp and brought his face back into my line of sight. "For you, Calliope, I just might." His tanned throat bobbed from a hard swallow as he lowered his eyes to my T-shirt for a moment. "I'm good at two things. You saw one of them in the basement." He paused, giving me a chance to be afraid, waiting to see if it'd happen. When I didn't budge or blink, he went on, "You sure you want me to show you the other?" He yanked my hair free from the ponytail and threaded a hand through my locks while dropping his mouth over my ear as if someone might hear us. "This will only be fucking for me. This is just something I'm good at. I won't care tomorrow. You understand that, don't you?" Eyes meeting mine in a dare, he rasped, "Is that asshole enough for you, or do you need more from me?"

I could give the attitude right back; didn't he know that by now? "If you don't screw me, I'll go find someone who will."

His hand went straight to my throat.

New kink unlocked. Hand necklace?

He didn't grip hard. No actual choking. Just a light hold of possession as he brought his face closer. "Go ahead. I told you, with the mood I'm in . . ." He angled his head, studying me with cold eyes. The beast was back. *Good.* "Want to suck Hudson's cock in front of me? Have him take you over my desk instead of me?"

"Would he give a damn tomorrow, unlike you? Would he want seconds?" I shot back, curious to see how far he'd take his desire to act like an asshole.

He sneered at me. "He'd be dead for touching my wife. So no, no seconds."

"Jealous?" I asked, unable to stop the provocation, getting off on whatever the hell was going on between us right now too much. No longer caring there had to be something seriously wrong.

"Do you want me, or someone else?" he asked instead, then moved the hand at my throat down, dragging his knuckles across my collarbone.

"You know the answer to that," I whispered, my voice catching. "I want my husband." This time, the sass was gone. Only the truth lay between us. "I want you."

He cocked his head and slid his hand up my neck before making a pass of his thumb along the line of my lips. "Good. So no one needs to die tonight just because my wife loves to provoke and push me over the edge."

There was something in how he'd said *my wife* that had me believing I really was his.

Mesmerized by the moment and the man before me, forgetting all about why I'd come there in the first place, I finally gave him a little agreeable nod.

He stepped back, eyes narrowing as he stared at me, then gritted out, "Fuck it. Fuck it all," before snatching my face between his palms and kissing me.

The kiss at the wedding had been intense but still sweet.

This one, though . . . This one had me grabbing hold of him, hooking my ankles around his back to draw him closer, clutching him as if my life depended on it. Every part of me woke up, even the parts I'd thought were dead.

He groaned and urged me back a bit, as if he might lay me out on his desk. His tongue didn't duel with mine. It took over. Commanded every movement. Told me what to do and how to do it.

When he broke the kiss, I fisted his shirt, begging him to come back. "I hate you," I whispered, our frenzied breaths intertwining as he peered at me.

"Liar," he remarked in an almost lazy tone before he dropped his mouth over mine again. Owning it, my body, and every emotion. They were his and his only.

His hand went to my thigh, and he squeezed before his palm found my center. I was so wet that my arousal had gone through both my panties and gray leggings, and he was about to discover exactly what he did to me.

"My naughty girl," he said against my lips, then killed me by backing away again. Eyes never leaving mine, he worked free the buttons of his shirt but didn't remove it. His attention flicked to his forearm, and a quick frown came and went before he rolled down his sleeves, hiding the dried blood there. "I need you naked and spread out on my desk." He palmed his belt buckle, then snapped the belt off in one fast movement, a crackle lost to the air.

I stood, surprised my legs weren't totally rubber already and could hold my weight. My shirt went off first, the already unclasped bra next. I hooked my thumbs at my waistband, and he quietly coiled the belt, studying each of my movements.

"You have any idea what you've done to me all week?"

"We barely saw each other." I shoved down my leggings, allowing the panties to go with them. "Unless you're the one who's been watching me on camera."

"I better be the only fucking one." The belt unraveled from his hand and fell to the ground, and he grabbed hold of me and dropped me back onto the desk.

"Stalker tendencies, huh?"

"*Checked* in on you," he said before falling to his knees. He knelt before the desk and removed my shoes, socks, and the rest of my clothes still there, being sweet, not an asshole, at the moment. "I've thought about this since the night we met."

"What?" I looked down and met his eyes.

Still on his knees, he ran his fingers up my legs, tickling the insides of my thighs in the process, sending pulsing need to my center. "Eating you out," he said before sliding a finger along my seam, feeling how wet he made me. He closed his eyes for a moment. "I want to see how you've been touching yourself all week first," he added in a husky tone, eyes opening. Then he snatched my hand resting at my side and placed it between my legs.

"So bossy."

"And you like it." He looked up at me with a cocky grin. "Your pussy sure as hell does."

He had me there. I obeyed and ran my fingers over my clit, a slight touch of embarrassment hitting me as I fingered myself.

He sat back on his heels, the hard walls of his chest lifting and falling from deep breaths as he watched me. "My turn," he said an agonizing minute later, and thank God, because it was his mouth on me I craved, not my hand. He grabbed his discarded belt and pushed back up to his knees.

Holding the loose tail end of the belt, he folded it back on top of itself, making a flat loop. Next thing I knew, he had my wrists in one hand, creating makeshift cuffs from his belt. I didn't stop him.

"Much better." He stood, a hand going into his back pocket while staring at me naked on display before him.

He snatched a condom from his wallet and chucked the billfold before ripping the edge of the wrapper with his teeth.

Without removing the rubber from the foil packet, he set the package on the desk, then finally dropped his pants and briefs. He gripped his shaft, sliding his hand from root to crown.

Holy hell. Definitely not overcompensating with the car. Thick, big, and engorged. Ready to explode inside me.

"Open your legs," he commanded huskily, and I peeked down to see my knees pinned together. Clearly, my body was worried about the fit.

Aside from his shirt, he unburdened himself of everything else he wore.

The man couldn't remain the bad guy, could he? He didn't want me seeing the blood on his arms while we made love . . . No wait, not *love*. What we were going to do would be just sex.

His powerful legs drew my eyes as he came back at me while he stroked his cock. "You've had me getting off in the shower morning and night."

"You too, hmm?"

He let go of himself and spread open my legs even farther. "Of course you were." Falling back to his knees, he hooked my legs with his big hands, drawing my pussy straight to his mouth, and I couldn't stifle the cry that left my lips.

He kissed me there softly. Actual kisses. When he guided my legs over his shoulders to better bury his face between my thighs, I lifted my bound wrists and fisted his thick hair.

His tongue slid up my seam, and the moans coming from him, as if he enjoyed this as much as I did, nearly sent me over the edge way too soon.

He added two fingers, pushing them inside my tight walls while devouring me. I couldn't take much more. The pleasure was almost pain. I began shimmying against him, his facial hair tickling my sensitive skin, spurring me on even more as I chased the end even though I didn't want it to come yet.

"Attagirl, fuck my face." His smooth, dark words had me spiraling. And then he spoke to me in Italian, turning me on even more. "Come for me, Calliope." The order vibrated against my skin, and I kept hold of his hair and did exactly as he said. My back went off the desk like I was possessed, and I cried out his name on repeat so loud it'd be clear to everyone what happened.

Before I had a chance to get my bearings, he had me on my feet, wrists still bound, and he bent me over the desk, so my tits smashed into the wood and my hands were over my head. "Tell me what you want." He skated his hand over my ass cheek, then slid a finger from that angle between my legs, and I flinched from being so sensitive from the orgasm.

"Your handprint on my ass." I said what he was waiting to hear.

He gripped hold of my hips now, letting me feel his cock at my back. "You sure?"

"Or the sting of the belt?"

"No," he said without hesitation. "I could never . . . no."

There was my sweet guy. Damn, the sweet guy would destroy me, though. And I needed the darkness right now. The darkness was safe. For the first time in my life, it was comforting. Because tomorrow in the light, when I was a schoolteacher—not a mafia princess—again, I knew I'd fall to pieces and never be the same, knowing this man wasn't mine.

"Your hand, then," I pleaded.

He freed my hips and smoothed his hand there before I felt the heavy weight of his palm slap my ass. No time to process, his lips covered whatever mark he'd left.

"Be an asshole." My voice broke as I reminded him it was better for him to be a jerk than a teddy bear.

"Yes, ma'am." He secured the condom from the desk, and my fingers went into my palms with anticipation of what was to come.

I'd expected him to take me from that angle, but he guided me onto my back, unshackled my wrists, then hooked my ankles around his hips before setting a hand alongside my body.

My hand went to his chest, feeling his heart hammering wildly as he stared at me. His crown was near my center, but he didn't push inside me.

He quietly removed my hand from his chest and set his palm on my stomach before sliding it up between my breasts.

I gave him a nod, an okay to fill me, and he slammed into me in one fast movement, as if preferring to rip off the Band-Aid of pain with how tight he'd assumed I'd be.

"You okay?" He went still, and I blinked back tears.

"Asshole," I mouthed, preferring him to assume the gloss of my eyes was from how thick he was and not from the emotions destroying me with our bodies connected.

His eyes narrowed in question, but then he began moving again. Thrusting slowly to help my body accept his size.

Doing my best to distract myself from the overwhelming sensations, I grabbed hold of his good arm, feeling the rock-solid muscle there as he held his weight over me.

"I'm already close." His jaw strained as he squeezed his eyes shut as if angry at that fact. "I'm trying to hold back until you come. But you're so fucking tight and just . . ."

"Just what?" I practically breathed out, my body aching, the bundle of nerves between my legs on fire with the need to release. I'd never had two back-to-back orgasms, though, normally too sensitive to be so much as touched again after the first one. But this man, well . . .

His eyes flashed open as he stared at me. "I can't answer that." Brows tight, he added, "You don't want me to."

Oh.

Ohhh.

"You still want me to be an—"

"Yes," I forced out, even though it was no longer true. I wanted him to be whoever he chose to be in this moment, but I was too scared to say that. Too scared of the consequences for the both of us.

"I can't look at you while I do this then," he said, his tone almost sad as he eased out, and I felt his loss in so many ways.

He had me on my stomach, bent over, his hand pinning down my back as he pushed back inside me, and I gasped. His free hand shifted around to my sex, and his thumb moved there in perfect rhythm as he thrust in and out.

I tensed up, shocked I might come a second time as he touched my swollen clit while fucking me hard.

"Yes, yes, oh, God, yes." I finally remembered I could move, too; I'd been a bent-over statue before. When that happened, I found my release and his happened just after.

He came in silence, well, aside from a few light grunts and groans and a breathy *fuck*, but no calls to God like me.

He pulled free a moment later and helped me back upright.

I looked down at the semen-filled condom, realizing he could've easily impregnated me, and it was a cold slap of reality as to why we were there: Armani wanted a grandchild.

Alessandro reached for my face, startling me, and he palmed my cheek. "Nashville," he shocked me by saying. "You want it that badly?"

I gulped and met his eyes and nodded.

His shoulders collapsed as he removed his hand from my face. "I'll send some men ahead of time to check out the club and ensure it can be secured. If so, we stay at a hotel, not your house, tomorrow night, then we come back here Saturday. Understood?" He peeled off the condom and set it inside the wastebasket, and my eyes were glued to the marks on his back—fresh little scars all because of me.

"Wait, what?" What'd he just say?

He grabbed his pants from the floor and faced me. "I'm giving you what you want."

"Why?" I should've cut and run before he could change his mind. But I was standing there, naked, emotionally and physically spent, and unable to budge.

He frowned. "My apology for what happened here tonight. For what you saw downstairs. And for losing my control."

"I wanted you to lose control."

"I know . . . but you'll wish I hadn't tomorrow."

"How do you know?" My arms crisscrossed over my chest, smashing down my breasts, an uneasiness working into my throat despite him not pushing back on Nashville.

"Because what we did tonight wasn't the lesser of two evils," he said in a heartbreaking tone, "and I think you know that."

CHAPTER
TWENTY-NINE

Alessandro

Whoever said new days were for fresh starts and new beginnings could go fuck themselves, because all I felt this morning was the desire to go back into the past and relive it. I'd *Groundhog Day* the shit out of last night—relive those thirty minutes with Calliope in my office over and over again. I'd also keep changing how the night ended, hoping for a new outcome, one that didn't make me feel so damn miserable, like I did now.

"Excuse me, I need to . . ." *Just not be here.* I stood from the table inside the meeting at our family's office building, ignoring the looks from the buttoned-up suits surrounding me, and snatched my phone. My father's protests and concerns became background noise on my way out of the conference room.

I didn't stop walking until I'd closed myself in my office and gone to the private bathroom. After splashing water on my face, I looked up and beyond the rivulets rolling down my face to my tired eyes.

Memories from being with Calliope in my other office last night blasted through my mind, and it was like I'd been punched in the gut, thinking about the devastated look in her eyes when I'd made her leave without me, dismissing her as if she were nothing to me.

When what scared me to death was she felt like the opposite—like she was everything. That wasn't supposed to happen. Hell, tomorrow was only two weeks since we'd first spoken, and there I was, losing my mind over her.

I shut off the water and dried my face, then grabbed my phone from the counter, needing the only person who'd kept me sane all week. Well, hunting assholes alongside Hudson had filled in the gaps when Enzo hadn't been on the phone with me. Enzo had become my new shrink since my regular one couldn't know the truth of my situation.

Me: You busy?

Enzo never made me wait, minus one exception—making love to his wife.

Enzo: Going over some new recipes with the staff. You okay?

I set my back to the wall, unable to look at the mirror again, hating my reflection. I'd slept at the security office last night, then showered and changed there before heading to my regular job of helping Dad run our family's empire.

Me: I slept in your old bedroom.

Enzo had kept his bedroom at the office for when he visited, including a bed for his daughter alongside it. For some reason, I'd found myself staring at the crib all night, unable to sleep, wondering for the first time since I'd been in the army what it'd be like to have a kid of my own—something I'd chosen to never think about after my ex left me.

Enzo: I get the feeling you're not telling me that because you plan to complain it's uncomfortable and I need a new one. You two get in a fight? I thought you were avoiding her. What happened?

Me: My control snapped. (In my office)

Enzo: Ohhh. So, the opposite of a fight. Why'd you sleep in my old room then?

Me: Because it shouldn't have happened. It was a mistake. But sharing a room with her after that—couldn't do it.

Enzo: Because you'd want her again, and that scares you?

Me: I'm not answering that.

Enzo: You just did.

Enzo: You're racking up quite the therapy bill with me, brother. Drinks for life on you.

Enzo: But in all seriousness, are you needing someone to tell you that what happened is okay? I get she's part of the job, but who's to say something can't come of your relationship afterward?

Me: I'm killing her father the night she turns 30. She's messed up about that, too. She slipped last week and showed her cards about how she really feels. She tries to act tough, but she's all angel.

Except when she mouthed off to get a rise out of me. And when she was turned on and gave in to her desires. But I kept that to myself.

Me: I convinced her it's okay to kill him, but I still know what that will do to her.

Enzo: So, basically what you're saying is, you're afraid SHE'S going to walk away from YOU. And you don't want to get hurt.

Enzo: And before you say you can't change—she's already changed you. Well, more like she's bringing you back to life.

The knock at my bathroom door stopped me from giving him my *Hell no* response.

"You throwing up or something? You good?" Izzy. Of course she'd worry. Now that she worked at our family business, too, she played the role of Mom there. For everyone, in fact. Not just within our family.

"Be right out."

Me: I have to go. Thanks for the mindfuck chat.

Enzo: Anytime. Later.

I pocketed my phone and went into my office to see *both* Constantine and Izzy waiting for me. It was only shocking that my old man hadn't joined them in their quest to ensure I was still working with a full deck and hadn't completely lost it.

"What?" I barked out, misplacing my anger as I loosened my tie and dropped down behind my desk.

Izzy took a seat on the couch. She crossed her legs, and her one black heel dangled from her foot. The nervous little look she shot me had me even more on edge.

Constantine perched his hip on my desk, resting his forearm on his leg as he looked at me. "Hudson texted me during the meeting. I was about to excuse the three of us had you not made a run for it first."

"So he told you?" I'd figured everyone in our office last night had heard, including half the Upper East Side, because Calliope's moans had been less than quiet, but I'd never thought Hudson would call an emergency meeting over me having sex with my wife.

"Told me what?" Constantine's brows shot up as he waited for me to continue.

"That I'm going to Nashville today," I said on the fly.

Izzy secured her heel and stood. "Why?"

"First, tell me what Hudson said." Clearly, his call hadn't been about my sex life or my trip.

"It's about Gabriel," Izzy said softly.

I couldn't handle much else today, and I was torn whether I wanted to stand or keep my ass seated in preparation for the bad news I felt coming my way. "Go on," I rasped, my heart beating faster.

"He possibly found something," Constantine said while standing, and he slipped his hand into his pocket. I was waiting for the "I told you so" look from him, but he didn't give it to me. "Hudson discovered an anomaly in some CCTV footage from three weeks ago in Rome while retracing Gabriel's movements over the last few months."

"Someone hid the fact Gabriel was in Rome. Went so far as looping footage at the terminal the day of his arrival, and the next day when he departed," Izzy added. "Hudson wanted to get to the bottom of it before he shared it with us."

"And?" I swallowed, my nerves unable to handle the wait.

"The hacker who altered the footage was too good, so he reached out to an old SEAL contact of his, and they connected him with a former CIA officer who could help. She's here in New York. She and her husband met up with him this morning, and she successfully unfucked the footage to its original state."

"Skip the boring details and the suspense and get to the point. What'd Gabriel do?" On my feet now, I lost my patience at Constantine's lack of response. "You didn't see him do anything, did you?"

"He wanted to hide the fact he was in Rome. What if he met with Esposito?" Constantine proposed, and I knew he didn't like the guy, and with good reason given the man's boss, but now my brother was grasping at straws. "Gabriel was in Rome the week *before* he called you to go to Nashville, and it's possible—"

"He sold out Calliope to Esposito," Izzy finished for him. "It was someone from Gabriel's team who questioned the guard in Nashville and got the name Esposito in the first place. Gabriel could've been working with the guard and had him silenced so he couldn't turn on him."

I bowed my head, trying to process their accusation. "Other people live in Rome, you know. He could've been there for Armani, and Armani hid Gabriel's tracks for a reason." *Am I really defending a criminal?*

"I know you don't want to hear this, but we need to consider the possibility Gabriel set everything in motion from the get-go. He chose Esposito to frame, knowing what Armani would do when he found out," Constantine went on, not considering my pathetic efforts to clear Gabriel's name.

"Maybe Gabriel somehow made *Marcello* think bringing Rocco into the picture was his idea—because with Rocco in this mess, he knew it'd guarantee our involvement, as well as The League's," Izzy said, keeping the Gabriel-being-guilty train rolling, and I was ready to pump the brakes.

"Now you're just reaching, dammit." I stood tall and shrugged off my jacket; it was too damn hot in there.

Izzy met my eyes, a request to, at least, listen to the theory. But that's all it still was—and a stretch at that. "Those men in the park only came after her when you were with them, and Gabriel knew you could handle them and protect her. This whole thing could be Gabriel's power-grab moment. He admitted as much to you on night one. He just left out the fact he put everything in motion to ensure he takes over and has The League's protection, too."

"The favor I owed him is a four-year-old one. He couldn't have planned things out this perfectly." *I don't think.*

"The man's patient," Constantine said, "and you know that. When the opportunity presented itself with Calliope's existence being discovered, he more than likely began setting everything in motion the day of her mother's funeral."

"I have to talk to him. He can clear this up." I went to grab my phone, but Constantine got to it first, stopping me.

"Even if Gabriel set everything in motion," Izzy started, "at the end of the day, isn't he still the—"

"Don't. Don't say it," I begged her. "*If* he's behind this, he could've gotten Calliope killed in the park that day. And then we killed people he framed. So no, *if* this is true, he's not the lesser of two anything. He's just as fucking bad." I turned to Constantine, my shoulders falling. "You suspected this theory from the beginning, didn't you? It's why you pushed Hudson to dig deeper."

His quiet, signature apologetic look was all he gave me for an answer.

"What do we do now, then?" Izzy asked, and I looked over at her, feeling torn apart, and I'd already been in bad shape before this news.

"We keep an eye on Gabriel now, too, not just Rocco," Constantine said steadily. "And we still go through with the plan for the party. Only we might just need to kill a few more people than we originally planned."

CHAPTER THIRTY

Alessandro

"Sir, the jet is ready. We're set to fly out." My head of security, Javier, stood in the doorway of my office, only two hours after I'd learned the theory about Gabriel. I still wasn't ready to bite. Innocent until proven guilty in my eyes.

"If you're here, that means so is my wife." He had instructions to never let her out of his sight.

"Yes, sir. But she insisted on coming up instead of waiting in the car. She ran into your father by the elevators. He's with her now."

Shit. On my feet, I circled my desk and made a quick exit to save her from whatever nightmare of a conversation my old man might put her through.

When I spotted the two of them talking, what I hadn't expected was to see my dad laughing, and she was still talking, speaking quickly with her hands. Also, what in God's name was she wearing?

I went still, and Javier slammed into me at my abrupt stop. "Sorry, sir."

Looking back over my shoulder, I reminded him, "How many times have I told you to drop the sir? You're older. Did two more tours of duty than I did, had a higher rank, plus have a Purple Heart. I should be sir-ing you."

Javier smirked, then came up next to me. I planned to hang back and continue watching the scene unfold between Calliope and my father, since they'd yet to realize they had eyes on them. "Can I speak candidly?"

"When have you not?"

"I'm glad you're taking her on this trip. The whole team has been listening to her practicing for the last week, and she has a voice that should be shared, heard by more than just us. And you have my word I won't let anything happen to her."

I'm not a fan of sharing, even her voice, but I guess . . . "She's not mine to keep," I said under my breath.

"I don't understand."

"Ignore me." I looked over at him and nodded. "And thank you; I know you'll keep her safe."

"Oh, there he is. The man we've been talking about," my father called out, and I looked over to see Calliope hanging back behind him, like he was her shield.

Yeah, someone needed to protect her from me, especially in that outfit, but I never thought it'd be my dad.

"Who you've been laughing about, you mean," I corrected him, then stalked their way, feeling the ridiculous need to snatch her hand and drag her back to my office and lay into her about . . . well, something.

"Never." Dad winked at her. "The laugh was about a story she was telling me involving a cow, chicken, and what was the third animal? Right, a coyote."

"I grew up on a farm," she tossed out, reading my puzzled look.

I blinked, oddly hurt she'd never told me that before, which was ridiculous. Almost as absurd as whatever story she'd told my father. "And how'd that pop up in conversation?"

"Not really sure," she said, and I hated that the quick look toward my father and their smile at one another had my pulse flying the way it did.

This was why I didn't want her near Mom or Izzy. It was too damn easy to get attached to this woman. She could capture the hearts of millions with a smile alone. But a laugh? Fuck, she could end wars. *A siren, all right.* "I need a word with my wife before we leave." I faced Javier. "We'll be downstairs in a minute."

"Roger that," Javier answered with a nod.

"Well, Calliope, have a wonderful show tonight." Dad held her forearm, then leaned in and pecked her on the cheek. Then my old man shoulder-checked me while walking by, and I felt his message loud and clear: *Don't break her heart.*

"Come on." I tipped my head, motioning for her to follow me to my office, and it took us a good ten minutes to walk fifty steps because the woman kept talking to everyone she met on the way.

"Sit," I hissed once we were alone, her shoulders startling when I palmed the door shut with too much intensity.

She glared at me, shooting me daggers instead of offering the same taste of sweetness she'd given my father and the five other people she'd talked to in passing on our way there. "You didn't come home last night."

The potential Gabriel problem was now a distant memory with *this* problem standing before me in that light-yellow sundress—*that better not be see-through when the light hits it*—and cowgirl boots. Her wavy blonde locks covered her breasts and hid her ears, but I'd bet a million dollars she had those little music-note studs on she loved to wear.

"You going to talk or keep staring at me like you hate me?" she asked, enough sassy energy in her voice to power half of New York.

"Ever going to do as I asked and sit?"

She whipped her arms in defiance across her chest and lifted her chin, not budging. "Maybe my ass hurts too much to do that."

"Thin ice, dammit," I warned, angry for giving in and spanking her, because what if I had hurt her? Of course, from the feel of her pussy, that part of her, at least, had enjoyed it.

"The ice broke last night, or have you forgotten?" she hissed back.

I bowed my head and gripped my temples. I couldn't face off with Little Miss Tennessee Whiskey right now, not in that dress and wearing those boots, with my handprint on her ass cheek, and that tone of voice of hers that had me wanting to christen this desk, too. Yesterday had been a mistake, but I'd hoped I'd at least get her out of my system. Instead, I was pretty sure I wanted her now more than I had before. *What is wrong with me?*

"Why didn't you come home?" She tamed her tone that time. The sound of her boots clicking across my floors had me looking up to see her finally sitting, and she didn't appear to be uncomfortable.

But hell, I was now. Bad idea to have her sit. I wanted to drop to the floor before her, spread her legs open, and taste her again.

"You just dismissed me like I was a prostitute and you were done with me."

The break in her voice would've done me in just fine, but those words? Fuck me, they were bullets to the chest.

"What?" I swallowed the fist-size lump down my throat, and against my better judgment, walked over to the couch to look her in the eyes.

Her hands were on her lap, and she fidgeted with the rings, not giving me her attention. "I know you think last night was a mistake, and you're probably now over whatever, uh, desire you had for me. The thrill of the chase is gone. And I—"

"Stop." Because really, I couldn't handle any more. Not another word based on the direction she was heading. "Please," I tacked on, doing my best to deploy a little more kindness in my voice that time.

Kindness got me her eyes and her biting her lip.

Now I had to turn away. "I couldn't sleep in the same room with you because I'd wind up in your bed," I admitted, *also* against my better judgment. But I didn't need her feeling cheap, used, or unwanted. Furthest thing from the truth.

"Wait, you still want me after what happened?"

I swiveled back around, unsure what to say, but then her gaze fell to her answer. I looked down to see my traitorous dick tenting my dress pants. "Safe to say that'd be a yes." Why lie now? My cock had betrayed whatever BS I'd planned to say next. "You do realize it's not just me suffering," I began in some pathetic attempt to cover up my real feelings, ones I wasn't supposed to be having. "You're going to make every man you pass hard as a fucking rock when you walk by them today."

She stood and set her hands on her hips like she was about to school me with that sassy tongue of hers.

"You planning on wearing that for your show tonight?" I asked, the words punching out hard and fast before I could stop them.

"No. Probably something sexy."

If she didn't define what she had on now as sexy, I was fucked.

She lifted a brow, waiting for me to snap. Too late. Already had. "Maybe you should consider changing, too. It'd be nice if you could blend in, so you don't stand out in your ten-thousand-dollar suit." She came closer, and I caught a whiff of whatever delicious scent she wore, making me a little dizzy. "And if you plan to tell me not to wear—"

"No, I don't," I said, not letting her finish. "My personal assistant hates doing my laundry when I get blood on white clothes, so I need to make sure I wear something dark."

"Why would you get blood on your clothes tonight?" She stared at me as if genuinely confused.

Makes two of us, given my reaction to you. "Because when some asshole tries to lift your dress, I'll be breaking his nose." *And a few other body parts.*

Her nose wrinkled. "I'd prefer you not break anything at my show." But then her shoulders collapsed as if realizing the very possible reality of that happening, which told me there'd been assholes in the past who had set their hands on her without her consent. "I'll wear something a little less sexy, then."

I should've said, *Good.* Instead, I lost my mind again. "No. You'll wear whatever you feel like. You shouldn't have to change how you dress because someone can't keep their mouth shut or their hands to themselves." Breathing hard at the very idea of someone bothering her,

I added, "You have me now to teach them that lesson if needed." I went over to my desk, dropped my palms to it, and bowed my head, trying to pull myself together.

The click of her boots warned me she was on approach, and my body tensed in anticipation of what she might say or do next. It was a coin toss with her how she'd react when it came to these moments between us.

Her hand on my back had me squeezing my eyes closed, and I'd never been so grateful for a knock on my door as I was now.

"It's Izzy," my sister called out.

"One second," I told her, needing that second to compose myself before my sister read me like a book.

Calliope removed her hand from my back. "I thought she'd spend time with me while I was here, but she's not even called."

"I told everyone to stay away from you. My dad decided to ignore the memo today," I admitted while pushing away from the desk. "Also, how come I didn't know you grew up on a farm? It wasn't in my research."

"I'm not a celebrity." She rolled her eyes. "No play-by-play of every detail of my life online. And why would there be?"

"But you didn't tell me." Why'd this bother me so much? Sensing what was coming next, I lifted a hand and added in an asshole tone, "Roll your eyes one more time at me, and—" I cut myself off when she peered at my desk, and her cheeks pinked, as if remembering the spanking from last night. *Makes two of us now.* "Come in, Izzy," I said instead.

Izzy opened up but remained in the doorway, looking at us and sensing the tension.

Yeah, well, she was one to know about tension. It'd been that way this past week whenever she was in the same room with Hudson, but I'd kept my mouth shut about her weekend staycation at his place, where he claimed nothing happened. I was also certain Hudson hadn't told my sister about all the "hunting" we'd been doing to channel our frustrations elsewhere and away from the women in our lives.

"You going to say anything?" I prompted when Izzy only stared at us, as if she'd caught two animals going at it in the wild and was too stunned to make a comment.

"Grump," Izzy shot back, earning a smile from Calliope.

"Wonder why, after what you told me." Shit, I hadn't planned to tell Calliope about Gabriel. Not until I knew if there was anything even to tell, but I'd forgotten myself with how wound up the woman made me.

"What are you talking about?" Calliope reached for my forearm, and I dropped my focus to her touch, and that was all it took for my thoughts to vault back to last night.

"We should tell her." Izzy came in and shut the door behind her. "It's why I caught you before you left. She shouldn't be left in the dark."

"It's still a theory at best," I said gruffly, but gestured for her to go ahead anyway, since Calliope would never let me slam the door shut on that conversation now.

Izzy did the talking while I closed my laptop and tucked it into my travel bag in preparation of heading out.

How would I survive the night in Nashville with this woman?

After Izzy finished her recap of the new problem involving Gabriel, Calliope shared, "I forgot to tell you this last night because I was distracted"—a blush worked up the column of her throat—"but Leo is onto us. Think he works with Gabriel, though."

I frowned. "What do you mean?"

"He knows we haven't—*hadn't*, er, um . . ." I hated how much I wanted to seal my mouth over hers and catch her nerves with my tongue as she worked through what she was trying to say. "He knows," she said with an emphatic nod, as if those two words were sufficient enough to understand.

Not wanting to force her to spell out what she was saying with Izzy present, I went ahead and said, "Not surprised Gabriel would ensure at least one of your guards was on his side." Pinning Izzy with a hard stare, letting her know I was still on the fence about Gabriel, I added,

"But we'll keep an eye on Leo in light of this *possible* Gabriel-setting-this-all-up-from-the-get-go theory."

"What if Marcello's behind this?" Calliope asked. "Is it possible he's trying to frame Gabriel?"

My gut reaction was no, but I wouldn't rule anything out. "If Marcello wanted you dead, he could've done it long before we met, never giving us a chance to save you in the first place." I grabbed my bag, then gestured toward the door. "And if he had any dirt on Gabriel, he would've shared it with Armani by now."

"Does this change the plans for the party?" Calliope looked between Izzy and me.

"We may need to modify it a bit if Gabriel's been screwing with us, but the party is still our timeline to end this. We'll continue keeping Gabriel in the dark about it as well." Izzy managed to sound more confident than I could've. "At least Armani and Marcello will be there, and with any luck, Rocco will decide to crash the party."

Placing Calliope in that sadistic bastard's line of sight was *not* what I wanted to think about right now.

"Is there a special place in hell for someone who helps have their father killed?" Calliope whispered, letting go of me. And were we back to that again? Guilt over that madman? "Shit, I hate when I refer to him as my dad." She closed her eyes and visibly trembled like a chill had rocked through her, and I had to resist the urge to warm her with my body heat and calm her down.

"There's definitely a reservation in hell for Armani and Marcello. Not you," Izzy said before I could. "Jury's still out about Gabriel." She gave me her big, sad brown eyes at the last part.

Clearing my throat, my emotions mixed the fuck up about everything, I rushed out, "If you plan to rehearse tonight, then we need to go." I wasn't in the mood to think about Gabriel or Rocco without my mood turning south again.

Calliope opened her eyes and nodded.

"Good luck tonight." Izzy hugged her when I wished it had been me instead. "If only I could be there, too." She elbowed me. "Maybe record a song or two?"

"Sure," I grumbled, then directed them both to leave the office, because I could barely breathe in there anymore.

We made it maybe five steps before my admin, Patrick, stopped us. "I couldn't let you leave without getting to meet you." I thought he was offering his hand to shake hers, but instead, it was to look at her wedding ring. "Looks perfect on you."

Calliope gave him a little nod and smiled. "You have great taste, thank you."

"Me?" Patrick slapped a hand to his chest and smirked. "Your husband dragged me and the store manager there after hours and had him teach him everything there is to know about diamonds. Took him forever to pick out the right one."

Not what I needed her to hear or know.

Calliope's green eyes flashed my way in surprise, and I wasn't sure how to dig myself out of this hole.

"We have to go." I snatched her palm with my free hand and nodded my goodbyes to everyone lingering around us. "Later." We fast-walked to the elevators, and I dodged everyone else trying to stop my mission to extract this woman from the building without another word being said.

Once we were alone in the elevator and the doors closed, I dropped my workbag, and my wife took me by surprise when she pushed me against the wall, fisted my shirt, and kissed me.

CHAPTER
THIRTY-ONE

Calliope

Nashville

"It's fine. I'm fine. I can do this and be totally—"

"Fine?"

At the realization I wasn't alone while spiraling in the women's bathroom of the hotel, I looked up at the mirror and gasped. "Nala! Imani!"

I spun around, and the three of us hugged, and tears were going to test my waterproof mascara. I swiped the backs of my hands across my cheeks, trying to hide them before my tears ruined my blush, too. "What are you doing here?"

"You told us you were coming in the group chat, but your husband's assistant reached out on his behalf. Well, on yours, I guess." Nala swapped a quick look with Imani. "He invited us to the hotel tonight on his dime."

Before I could digest the news that Alessandro had arranged a surprise visit with my friends, which also meant he'd perused my contacts and messages to determine *who* I'd want to see when visiting, Imani added, "His hot-as-sin guard, Javier, picked us up and brought us here. He showed us the suite where the three of us are going to have dinner and get ready for your show. It's been decorated like we're having a slumber party and are thirteen, but it's kind of cute."

"What?" I shook my head, still in shock.

"Surprise," Nala said while opening her arms wide. "He's a keeper. Sorry for giving you a hard time about him. Most guys wouldn't give up their new bride so she could spend time with her friends."

And now it clicked. The piece of the puzzle locked securely in place.

Alessandro wanted to avoid sharing a hotel suite with me. He didn't trust himself, and he'd pretty much admitted that was why he hadn't come back with me to the penthouse after the wild night at his office. But what did that mean? It wasn't like he was falling for me; I knew better. But the fact he still wanted to have sex with me when he was apparently supposed to be a one-and-done kind of guy must've been messing with his head.

"You're married, girl. I still can't believe it." Nala played with the gold bangles on her wrist. A fidgeter, like me.

"Neither can I." My stomach protested the sad reality that I couldn't tell the truth about why I was married, but they'd freak and worry. The less they knew, the better.

But I'd give anything to have someone to talk to about what had happened last night, as well as the moment I'd lost my mind and kissed him in the elevator a few hours ago.

Alessandro had kissed me back, too. Hooked my leg to his side and leaned into me, dragging his fingers over my heated skin as he pinned me to him.

And then the elevator dinged, signaling the doors were about to open, and he'd freed my leg and backed away, panting. He'd also killed me by swiping his hand across his mouth, as if hating himself for allowing his lips to touch mine. He'd said something in Italian, shaken his head, then motioned for me to leave the elevator.

He hadn't brought up the kiss on the ride to the airport or on the plane. Definitely hadn't mentioned it when we arrived at the hotel. Nor when he'd shocked me by letting me know he had one of the smaller ballrooms rented out for my use for rehearsal, with my equipment there waiting for me.

"I have to make some calls. Don't let her out of your sight," Alessandro had barked out shortly after our arrival to his team of five guys, which also included my DiMaggio "chaperones." Then he and Javier had left us alone in the rehearsal room.

Braden wasn't due for another twenty minutes or so, but I had a feeling Alessandro would make an appearance before then, given his weird, jealous-like reactions when it came to him.

"Penny for your thoughts?" Imani waved her hand in front of my face, snapping me back to the bathroom. "You're in Alessandro la-la land from the looks of it. Thinking about your hunk of a man, huh?"

Yeah, something like that.

"Why were you in here giving yourself a pep talk in the first place?" Nala nudged my side with her hip. "You shouldn't be nervous about tonight. You've been looking forward to this moment for years."

"That Italian Stallion, Frankie, said you up and walked out of the ballroom like you were going to be sick." Imani met my eyes in the mirror, and I tried not to visibly cringe at her referring to Frankie in any positive manner.

If you knew the truth . . . but you can't. "To be honest, I'm nervous for when Braden gets here. Alessandro's not his greatest fan, and I haven't even told him about the Britt situation."

I'd already vented to Imani and Nala over our group chat about Braden reaching out to Britt for backup if I didn't show, and they'd been pissed on my behalf.

"Does your husband not know your ex cheated with your best friend?" Nala asked, frowning.

"She was a fake best friend." My shoulders fell. "And no, I never told him about that, and why would he want to know? He's a bit . . ."

growly when it comes to other men in my life." *Even if this is temporary, and I'm his assignment, he still is.* When I thought about last night and his dare for me to go off with Hudson, which I never in a million years would've done, nor wanted to do, I was still shocked at how beet red his face had been at the idea of another man touching me. Also, he'd threatened murder, something I knew he was capable of, so there was that.

"So what you're saying is we might get two shows this weekend?" Imani grabbed her purse from where she'd set it on the counter, then motioned for the door. "Onstage and off."

"I hope not. I don't need fists thrown on my behalf." *Men have already died because of me.*

"I'd like to give Braden a piece of my mind for the shit he pulled with reaching out to Britt." Nala squeezed my arm, offering her support. "But come on, let's get you back in the room to rehearse so we have time to eat and get ready before the show. And then we'll stay up all night celebrating after your performance."

I gave Nala a hesitant nod, and we left the bathroom. I hadn't expected my husband to be out there, waiting.

"You okay?" Alessandro had changed into jeans and a gray short-sleeve shirt that had his biceps and triceps looking, well, perfect. He was so focused on me, I wasn't sure whether he realized we weren't alone.

Not that we were alone-alone, because when I looked beyond his shoulder, I spotted Javier and the "Italian Stallion" there, too.

Before I could get my mouth to work, Imani introduced herself to Alessandro. Nala next.

He was gracious and polite to my friends, which I'd expected from a man of his stature, I supposed. But the second his eyes cut back to me, the dark look returned.

"I need a word with my husband." I reached for his forearm.

"Sure; we'll wait for you two in the rehearsal room." Imani gave me a knowing smile, as if assuming I wanted a make-out session with Alessandro as a thank-you-for-the-friends surprise.

Hardly. "Oh, and Nala, would you mind hopping on the keyboard to practice with me? I've been working on a new arrangement for a Stapleton cover song I want to test out."

"Tell me it's not 'Tennessee Whiskey,'" Alessandro remarked in a low voice, and if looks could kill . . .

I about rolled my eyes, but then remembered his reaction back in his office, and we weren't alone, so maybe that'd be a bad idea for my friends and guards to see my husband go off the deep end.

"Not a Stapleton fan?" Nala smirked but didn't wait for him to answer, and instead gestured to Imani to give us privacy.

"Go with them. We're fine out here," Alessandro said, eyes on Frankie and Javier.

"Why do you need so much security, anyway?" Imani asked, not moving when Nala had motioned for her to. "Because you really are a mafia princess?"

"Real funny," I responded a bit too quickly, letting go of Alessandro's arm once it was only us out there. We were on the meeting-room floor of the hotel, and there weren't any other events going on, so I could speak freely without being overheard. "How'd you pull this off?" I spun my finger in the air. "Not the hotel or ballroom part. The whole coming here and not even sharing a room with me without Frankie running his mouth to Armani?" I swallowed, waiting for some of that ice in his look to melt. "Also, you went through my phone again."

He let go of a gruff breath. That was his frustrated one. He had a few different types of breathy breaths, and I was learning how to decode them. "I gave Armani the heads-up personally this morning about the trip and the plan to surprise you with a visit with your friends. I told him you'd been mopey and stressed, which is bad for trying to get pregnant."

"And he went for that?"

He nodded. "I can be convincing when I want to be." Gray eyes flew to my mouth, and was he remembering our elevator kiss?

No, just me?

"And the second suite? The going through my phone?" I folded my arms, and the man had the nerve to lean in and set his hand to the wall, trapping me there.

"You wish I hadn't?" Why'd that question come across so hot? So . . . seductive?

My body was already coiled tight with tension, and being in this position wasn't doing wonders to change that. "I'd much rather spend the evening with them than you," I lied. "Just shocked you're okay with not sharing a room with me. You can be overprotective. And side note, *you* just rolled your eyes at me."

He scoffed. "I did not."

"You did, too." Maybe I did need my suite decorated and prepped as if I were thirteen going on thirty. *What is wrong with me?* At him doing it again, I stabbed his chest. "That makes twice."

"Liar," he said, but his tone was borderline playful instead of rough. "My suite is next to yours. Guards will be in the hall. Javier has access to the hotel security cameras. You'll be good. Plus, you should sleep better without me in the room, and I know my back could use a real bed."

"How'd you sleep last night?"

"Like a baby." His grays narrowed. "Can't wait until I have my bed back to myself."

"Or to share it with someone else." Shit, there went my mouth.

He angled his head, and with his free hand, he ran his knuckles over my cheek. The gentle touch was such a contrast to the fire raging between us. "What happened last night, and in the elevator today, can't happen again." Was he trying to convince himself of that, or me?

"Who's to say I want it to?" I wet my lips, hating how good they'd felt against his. "And I don't, just so we're clear."

He lowered his hand to his side and pushed away from the wall, freeing me from the cage. "Liar," he said again, this time much raspier than lighthearted. "Javier will call me when Braden arrives. I'll be in the coffee shop downstairs working until then."

"You really don't want to share a room with me as much as possible, huh? But you'll make an exception for Braden's arrival," I murmured, hoping he didn't hear the pathetic break in my tone.

"The man wants to fuck my wife. So yeah, I'll make an exception."

I set my hand to my chest at the ache blooming there. "Am I yours, though?"

His grays thinned as he tipped his head, as if unsure how to answer that.

"Just don't fight," I said, giving him an out from answering my question. His gaze softened a touch, probably from relief I'd changed the subject. "Or start a war. I'm nervous enough, and I need to spend the next few hours practicing. Please give me the teddy bear right now, not the asshole. I need sweet."

That deep breath was another one I recognized. It was the breath he took right before giving in to me. "I'll do my best to be cordial with him."

"*Cordial* was what we were supposed to be, and look what happened," I reminded him, chills flying up my dress at the memory of "what happened" last night on his desk. His handprint really was still on my ass cheek. The sight of it had turned me on this morning when I saw it, post shower. "And you just rolled your eyes at me again. Third time's the charm, though."

"I don't roll my eyes."

"Sure, just like you'll behave when Braden arrives," I countered with the appropriate amount of sarcasm of a thirteen-year-old.

He shook his head and pulled his arm back. "You're that concerned about the two of us in the same room, are you? Maybe you don't want him seeing me with you. You have feelings for him." Before I could kill that idea, he added after a frustrated sigh, "Fine. I'll keep my distance until you're ready to go to the venue tonight. I won't watch you rehearse. Now, go practice before I change my mind." Pivoting away, he made it three steps before asking, "What Stapleton song?"

When he faced me and our eyes met, a little tremble rocked through my body as I shared the title. "'Think I'm in Love With You.'"

CHAPTER THIRTY-TWO

Calliope

"You sure this is the right look?" Inside the en suite bathroom open to the bedroom, I studied my reflection in the mirror, feeling underdressed for the show.

"You're giving total Carrie Underwood vibes." Imani smiled. "It's perfect. Simple up top is needed with those sexy-as-sin, fringy boots that go to your knees."

"Maybe some bracelets and earrings, though." Nala busied herself with fishing jewelry from her bag. Among the three of us, her sense of style was far more on point.

While waiting for her to finish the ensemble by adding jewelry, I focused back on the mirror. I had on short, frayed jean shorts, a big brown belt, and a cream-colored tank top—simple but also sexy, especially with the espresso-brown eye shadow and winged eyeliner that matched the color of the boots.

Nala slid the bracelets on my arm next, then I swept my long hair up so she could add the dangly earrings.

"Alessandro is gonna lose his mind. Your legs are fire." Imani drummed her fingers against her lips. "Braden couldn't take his eyes off you during rehearsal, either. Not sure how he'll handle being onstage without—"

"Alessandro wanting to deck him?" Nala beat me to it, because yeah, Braden had not only lectured me about my marriage earlier—thankfully at a safe distance away from Leo and Frankie—but also stared at me like he was in love with me while we'd played together.

The second Alessandro shared a room with him, he'd notice, and now I wasn't sure how I'd missed the fact Braden had had feelings for me. Then again, growing up, I'd always found it easier to have a guy friend who was secretly crushing on me than girl friends who secretly hated me. Britt—case in damn point. Because a true friend wouldn't sleep with your boyfriend.

"Her fancy-pants husband isn't going to hit some guy for checking out his woman. Guys like him don't do that."

Oh, Imani. How very wrong you are . . . at least about this particular "fancy-pants."

Nala chuckled, then grabbed some shimmery powder and a brush and dusted it across my chest. "Rich boy or not, he's got some fight in him. I could see it in his eyes earlier."

At the knock on the bedroom door, I assumed it was Javier or one of Armani's men in the living room of the suite beckoning us, but it was Alessandro who called out, "You ready?"

"Oh, she's ready, all right." Nala set down the bronzer and brush. "Let's give them a minute alone before we leave."

I was grateful we'd be meeting Braden on Broadway in the "beating heart of Nashville" instead of riding together.

Imani swung open the bedroom door, and what I didn't expect was to see Alessandro standing there looking like a man who belonged in Nashville and not Mr. Fancy-Pants.

"Well, damn," Nala said, shooting a quick look back at me from over her shoulder.

Damn is right. I swallowed at the sight of my husband's outfit that would "blend in" with our setting tonight, as I'd joked earlier in his office.

Once he'd moved out of the way to let Nala and Imani leave, he filled the doorway again, eyes flying over my outfit, and I stood there studying him right back.

Well-worn jeans. A denim button-down shirt with sleeves rolled up to his elbows. A black cowboy hat and dark-brown boots.

"Tecovas?" I murmured in surprise while going to him. I knelt and lifted a jean leg to confirm whether I was right. "You're wearing my favorite brand of cowboy boots." I looked up at him while letting the leg of his jeans fall, and he was staring down at me with narrowed eyes.

That deep breath . . . Oh yeah, that was his "control is about to snap" one. I focused on his crotch and realized why it'd been *that* breath of all breaths. After a little awkward throat-clear from me, he offered his hand and helped me stand.

"I may have checked the label on the ones you wear all the time," he said casually once I was back on my feet. "You told me to blend in."

"Apparently, you'll still be standing out," I whispered, unable to digest how he'd gone from businessman to cowboy in the blink of an eye.

"You look . . ." He let go of my hand. "You'll be standing out, too."

"I would hope so since I'll be onstage," I teased. "Thank you for letting me come here. Keeping me safe so I can feel a little normal for the first time in a while." I went ahead and shared what had been on my mind all day, but I'd yet to say because I was stubborn.

He frowned. "Keeping you safe is my job."

"Right." *And buying the Dolly guitar and handpicking my ring was what?* But I didn't dare rock the boat and say those words aloud.

"Javier went ahead of us with two of his guys. Your equipment is there, waiting for you," he said as I grabbed my brown suede purse, which had fringe that matched my boots.

"Oh, okay. Great." I spun back around, and he was no longer in the doorway but right in my face. My free hand went to his chest.

Lowering his eyes to my hand, he asked in a husky tone, "Am I allowed to say good luck? Or is this a break-a-leg thing?"

I waited for him to look at my face again before smiling. "You can say whatever you want."

"Can I? Anything?" He arched a brow, and why'd that feel like he was suggesting there was a lot more he wanted to share?

"As long as it's cordial," I said, opting to be a coward instead of pleading with him to tell me what I really wanted to hear: that I was more than just a job, a debt owed, and a chance at revenge for him.

"You don't need luck. You'll do great." He took my standoffish cue and went with friendly, and I forced a polite nod of thanks and removed my hand from his chest.

We didn't speak another word during the limo ride there. Imani and Nala, thankfully, filled the awkward silence by chatting. Pumping me up for the performance.

When the limo rolled to a stop at our destination, my heart landed in my throat, and my nerves took over—especially seeing Braden on the sidewalk, waiting with Britt.

Nala's hand flew to the door handle. "Why's she here?"

"Who is she?" Alessandro spoke for the first time, searching my face for an answer.

"An *ex*-friend." My shoulders slumped, and at the sight of Javier now on the street with two of his men, Alessandro gave us the go-ahead to exit.

Outside, Alessandro stood alongside me and set his hand at my back as I confronted Braden and Britt.

"Hi." Britt combed her fingers through her hair, her once-brown locks now the same shade as mine. "I came to support you. To make peace."

"Give her a chance. Hear her out." Had Braden lost it? Was he really ambushing me for some reunion twenty minutes before we were set to perform?

"You must be Braden," Alessandro piped up in a clipped voice as Nala and Imani came to stand at my other side, having my back as well in this unexpected showdown.

"*You* must be the husband." Braden did a quick inventory of Alessandro, right down to his boots, then flicked his attention back to me, letting both of us know he had as much interest in playing nice as Alessandro did with him.

"I don't want you here," I told Britt, scooching even closer to Alessandro. Right now, I needed my protector.

"Please." Britt reached for me, but Nala outstretched her arm, motioning her to back off.

"You shouldn't have let her come," Nala said to Braden. "This is bullshit."

"It's a free country, and she was here when I showed up. I had no clue, but—"

"No," I cut Braden off. "I'm not making peace now, or after. I'm going inside to play, and then I'm leaving." I stepped forward, and Alessandro took that step right along with me, letting me handle myself, but I knew he'd intervene if needed. "You pissed away our friendship when you slept with my boyfriend. You hurt me a thousand times more than Dylan did, and I'll never forgive you." I pointed my focus on Braden next. "You want to forgive her, that's your choice. But don't ever corner me like this again, or you can kiss what's left of our friendship goodbye, too." With tears in my eyes about to test my waterproof mascara for the second time today, I sidestepped them both and started for the bar, following Javier in with Alessandro behind me.

Once inside, seeing my guitar and keyboard on the stage, I maneuvered around people talking and milling about to get there.

I went to brush away a tear, but Alessandro snatched my wrist and pulled me over to the side of the stage. "You okay?" he asked, still holding me. The lighting was moody and dim, but I could make out the concern in his eyes.

"Not even a little bit, but I will be."

I knew he had questions about what he'd heard out there, but he wouldn't probe. He let go of my wrist and cupped my cheek and swept his thumb there. "You've got this." He gave me the convincing nod I needed.

"You did good, by the way. Thanks for not getting blood on your shirt when I know you probably wanted to." I forced out a nervous laugh, needing to ease the tension.

His lips twitched into a surprisingly sweet smile. "Not hitting him will probably go down as one of the greatest challenges of my life." When his eyes landed on my mouth, he murmured, "But the night's still young."

I was pretty sure he wasn't talking about Braden, but about the challenge of not taking me in his arms later.

CHAPTER THIRTY-THREE

Calliope

An hour into the set, everything was going smoothly so far. Thankfully, Britt hadn't followed us in. One less problem to deal with, but Braden's required presence seemed to make Alessandro crazy. Braden had no idea he was playing with fire every time he sent me longing looks of love during our performance.

I located my husband on a barstool alongside Javier, quietly watching me instead of sitting with Nala and Imani up front.

I sure as hell didn't want to peer into Braden's eyes for the next song we were about to perform, "Think I'm in Love With You." So I stared at Alessandro, unable to break eye contact when it was my turn to sing.

I'm in lust, not love. I beat the words into my head during the song.

Because no, it couldn't be more than that. It was too soon for love. Yeah, I was a hopeless romantic, but to fall for this man would just make me plain hopeless since he'd never be able to return my feelings. Not to mention the fact I was a teacher from a small town who wanted a forever partner and lots of babies, and Alessandro was a billionaire who played vigilante at night. We were worlds apart in who we were and where we came from.

When Braden and I transitioned smoothly to the next song, "Heart Like A Truck" by Lainey Wilson, I tore my attention away from Alessandro to look around at the audience, my eyes landing last on my two friends. They were bopping their heads enthusiastically, singing along with me.

I nearly stumbled over my next words when I spied Alessandro standing. He discarded his hat on the bar top and was on the move fast, leaving the bar without so much as a parting glance my way.

What the hell?

The second the song ended, I mouthed to Braden, "I need five."

Not waiting for him to say okay, I set aside the guitar, ignoring a man trying to make a pass at me on my way down the steps.

"You good?" Nala asked, on her feet, shooing away the creep for me since I was focused on the door, needing to chase down my husband, worried something was wrong.

"Yeah; be right back," I murmured on the move.

Once on the crowded sidewalk, I looked around for him, finally locating him down the street talking to a woman.

Alessandro must've felt my presence, because he turned to the side, and even from fifty feet away, with only the street and bar lights to illuminate the area, it was obvious he was upset.

He slipped his hand into his back pocket, then handed the mystery woman something. After a quick about-face, he started my way. I'd remained glued in place. Well, mostly. I kept getting knocked into by people trying to get around me.

"You're supposed to be onstage." Alessandro stopped before me, frowning. Then he looked over my shoulder, and I had to assume my shadows were there. "Give us a second." He reached for my arm and guided me into a narrow alley between two bars.

Cold from nerves and not the weather, I folded my arms, and the man didn't miss anything, did he? He brought his hands to my biceps and slid his warm palms up and down a few times. "That was a tabloid reporter threatening to post a story about you and Braden, suggesting you're having an affair. She sent the story and images to my assistant with a message to meet her out here. She had photos of you somehow, and—"

"What?" I gasped, ungluing my hands from just below where he kept rubbing my arms. "What photos? What does she want? I don't understand."

"She wants money. A lot of fucking money not to run the story. I gave her all the cash I had on me now until I can wire the rest later to kill the article." He grimaced and let go of me, shooting a look toward the main street, probably to our security hovering there. "But there's someone I'm going to kill."

"What are you saying?"

He reached into his pocket for his phone and showed me a text. Attached to the message were the alleged photos of me that somehow implicated me in cheating with Braden.

"That's not me, I swear." I pushed away his hand as if I could make it all go away. "I'm going to kill her. That has to be Britt in the photos."

I was shaking now; Alessandro freed his hands to hold me instead. He really was taking the whole "be sweet, not an asshole" thing tonight seriously.

"Braden may be secretly seeing her," I finally managed, "but do you think he'd stoop this low to blackmail me with her? I can't believe that. But I also can't deal with this now. I need to find a way to go back in there and finish." I pulled back to get a read on him, and he kept his hands locked around my waist. "How do I go back in there, though?"

"Because this is your dream," he said with grit in his tone, "and you're not letting them win or take this night and what it means from you." His brows slanted as he peered at my mouth. "Also, you took my breath away back in there, and I want to hear you sing more." His unexpected compliment had me wanting to cry. "And I wasn't even a fan of country music before you."

"You just didn't know what you were missing," I whispered as his eyes made their way back to mine, and that sincere look was somehow everything I needed and then some.

"I'm thinking I didn't," he rasped, and we both stared quietly at each other before he added, "You can do this, though. You're one of the strongest women I know."

I attempted to killjoy the moment. "Guess that's saying something since you know a lot of women." At his eye roll, I slid my palm up his chest. "There you go again. But your eye roll is way broodier than mine, and a bit more subtle. I'll have to teach you to do it more dramatically. Like how my students have taught me."

"Work in progress, remember?" A teasing smile played across his full mouth. "Come on, sweetheart, let's get the show back on."

"Pretty sure you added a southern twang to that 'sweetheart,' just to get me to bend to your will and do whatever you want. Almost as effective as when you speak Italian to me."

"If I knew that's all it'd take to get you to bend to my will, I—"

"Forget I said that," I interjected and chuckled, then he freed me from his hold and offered his hand to walk side by side back to the show.

"You good?" Leo asked us once we joined him and Javier on the sidewalk, and Alessandro only quietly nodded.

When we returned to the bar, Alessandro walked me over to the stage, and at the sight of me, Braden snatched his guitar.

"You got this." Alessandro palmed my cheek, then took me by surprise and leaned in and kissed me. It was soft and sweet, and probably for show, but my heart fluttered at the gesture anyway.

I forced open my eyes after the kiss ended, finding his grays focused on me. That was a look I'd never seen him wear before; my writer's block snatched the words from my head as to how to describe it, but I wanted to cement it to memory. It sure as hell looked a lot like love.

He cleared his throat, like he was trying to break free from whatever bubble we both seemed to be locked inside. A little nod of reassurance from him, then I climbed the short steps to the stage.

"What was that all about?" Braden asked on my way to the keyboard in preparation for the next song.

"I'll tell you after," was all I could get out. The only way I'd survive the show was to keep my eyes on Alessandro.

That plan worked. He somehow grounded me by his very presence, helping me survive the rest of the evening.

When our time was up, Braden set down his guitar and came right for me. He scooped me into his arms without warning and bear-hugged me.

Oh, shit. I went still, my arms outstretched, not wanting to return the embrace, and from the corner of my eye, I noticed Alessandro on his way over. "Let me go."

"Shit. Sorry." Braden quickly unhanded me.

"Did you know?" I whispered, catching sight of Nala and Imani near the stage, anxious to talk to me.

"Know what?" Braden stared at me, confused.

"Britt sold photos to a reporter claiming they were of me and you. She told the reporter I cheated on my husband with you. During the show, the woman asked for money, and—"

"Are you serious?" He tore a hand through his hair, stumbling back, nearly tripping over the guitar stand.

"What?" Imani blurted in shock, clearly overhearing me. I discovered Alessandro now at the steps, waiting for me alongside her.

His restraint tonight was impressive, because mine was being tested at every turn. "Tell me you had nothing to do with that," I said to Braden, needing to finish this conversation before my husband did it for me.

"Of course I didn't," Braden answered, adding a shake of his head.

With the next band coming up to prep, we'd need to go and talk outside.

Not wasting time, I headed down the steps and nodded my thanks to one of the guards on Javier's team swapping places with me to pack up my equipment.

Nala hugged me. Imani next.

"You okay?" Nala asked as Alessandro reached for my hand.

"I just need to get out of here," I said, eyes on him, and he didn't hesitate. He walked us out of there before Braden or anyone else could object.

Thankfully, the limo was waiting for us outside, but I had other plans for where I wanted to go and what I wanted to do. I spun around to see Braden there, looking as uncomfortable as I felt.

"Tell me why that reporter has photos of you and Britt together and she's under the assumption it's me in the pictures instead," I demanded in as steady a voice as possible, ignoring the limo door being opened for me by Javier.

"I was upset about you marrying this guy"—Braden motioned toward Alessandro holding me at his side—"and I ran into Britt and told her I didn't know if you'd even make it to the show. I was drunk, and it . . . it was a mistake. I never would've slept with her had I been in the right state of mind, and you have to know that. I had no fucking clue she had a camera set up."

"Lower. Your. Voice," Alessandro hissed, each word slicing through the air. I realized he'd saved Braden's life when he probably wanted to end it, because Frankie was on his way toward us, and if he learned what happened and told Armani, Armani wouldn't hesitate to take Braden out.

"The thing is that I, uh, think I'm in love with you," Braden said, his voice breaking, drawing my focus back his way. "I've been a mess about your marriage. I was stressed and drunk. I'm sorry."

Alessandro erased the space between himself and Braden, but instead of snapping his neck, he shocked me by saying, "If you really loved her, no amount of alcohol or stress would have you screwing someone else." He stabbed at the air without laying a hand on him.

"You wouldn't notice other women anymore. They'd cease to exist," he went on, his tone low and deep. "And maybe she drives you crazy, and she's either headstrong with a sassy mouth or a nervous fidgeter, but—" He cut himself off, and, well, I would've loved to know where he'd planned to go with that.

Instead of asking for him to continue, I told him, "I want to go home."

"Javier," Alessandro said without losing hold of my eyes, "call the pilot. Tell him to meet us at the airport." Still staring at me, not blinking or moving, he added, "Have her equipment and our stuff from the hotel sent over. And escort her friends wherever they want to go."

"Thank you, Javier." I looked toward Nala and Imani, opting to ignore Braden still not taking the cue to leave. "I'm sorry to bail on our girls' night."

"Don't be sorry." They both reached for me in a group hug. "Go be with your man at home. We'll deal with this problem here for you," Nala said, and I was so freaking grateful for her and Imani.

We said our goodbyes, and Alessandro helped me into the limo. Without a word or blows delivered, he slid in next to me and tossed the cowboy hat on the seat across from us.

"I'm not sure if Braden and I can be friends after tonight," I said as the limo pulled away from the curb. "And how could Britt do that to me?" The tears I'd kept at bay flew down my cheeks.

He hooked his arm behind me, pinning me to his side, and my cheek met his chest. The beats of his heart hammered into my ear. "Because she's jealous of you, that's why."

I wasn't sure if I believed that, but his words triggered a memory of something Nala had said to me before I'd found out Britt had slept with Dylan last year: *She's the kind of friend that points out your crown is slipping, not quietly helps fix it.*

After a few quiet minutes had passed, I fisted his shirt and looked up at him in the dim lighting. "No blood on it."

"Shocking, I know. But some things can be way more painful than getting struck."

I released his shirt. "Like what?"

"Like losing a woman like you." He closed his eyes and tipped his head back, letting me know he needed time to calm down. I'd give it to him, because I knew how hard it'd been for him to rein in his anger and not hurt Braden.

We both remained quiet for the rest of the ride. Heck, neither of us uttered a word to each other until we were at cruising altitude in the jet, when he stood and offered his hand with a simple "Come with me" request. "You should lie down," he added as I followed him into the bedroom. Once the door was shut, he urged me to sit and began removing my boots for me.

"Lie down *with* you?"

"Yes, *with* me," he said once he was standing before me. "You asked me to be sweet, didn't you?" He pointed to the bed. "This is me keeping my promise."

Ohhh. I climbed farther onto the bed, tensing when he joined me. My back met his chest, and he wrapped me in his arms, holding me in place.

It didn't take me long to loosen up. To feel at home in his arms. And that scared me. Because he still wasn't mine to keep. So I attempted to killjoy the moment with a joke. "*A* for effort on being sweet."

Not missing a beat, he responded, "Grading me, huh? Very teacher-y of you."

"Don't act like you hate that," I found myself saying, and he lightly groaned and held me tighter. And yeah, I could feel just how much he definitely didn't hate it with his cock at my ass.

"Sleep," he commanded.

"Yes, sir," I murmured.

"You love to torture me, don't you?" His hand at my waist slid down to my bare outer thigh below the jean shorts, and a flash of warmth and heat traveled between my thighs.

"Only as much as you do me," I admitted. "We're both masochists, apparently." Resisting the impulse to join the Mile High Club—because now was not the time or place to test our control—I reached for his hand and moved it back to a safer place. "Thank you for tonight. For everything. And for your restraint with Braden." I closed my eyes. "And most of all, thank you for this."

CHAPTER THIRTY-FOUR

Alessandro

One Week Later

"The story will never see the light of day," Javier said over the line. "You have my word."

"Thanks for following up." I sat back in the desk chair at my security firm, uneasy with the next question I needed to ask. "And did you confirm the other thing?"

"Yeah, Britt set up Braden for the money. He didn't know about the camera or her plan."

Didn't mean I'd now like the guy, but I supposed I didn't need to unleash Armani's helldogs on him anytime soon. "Maybe we need to vet her friends from now on." How'd she ever trusted a woman like Britt in the first place? My stomach launched deep into some bottomless pit at the memory that Calliope wouldn't be my wife for much longer. Who'd protect her then? Fend off the Britts, Bradens, and other assholes of the world? "Scratch that thought," I said before Javier responded, already on my feet in need of a stiff drink.

"I'm heading back to the house now. Will you be in late again?"

"Same time as always, yeah." *Sometime after midnight.*

"Anything else, sir?"

"Just for you to stop calling me that." Balancing the phone to my ear with my shoulder, I filled my glass with a twenty-five-year-old Macallan.

"Roger that."

Ending the call, I returned to my desk, set aside my phone, and smoothed my palm over the Italian wood, remembering when I'd had my wife sprawled out before me eight days ago.

My plan after Nashville had been to bury myself in work and barely see or talk to her until the birthday party.

I'd successfully bailed every morning before Calliope woke up, but it didn't take long after my Houdini routine to find myself at her mercy every day. Always at lunchtime. She'd park that cute ass of hers at the kitchen island in something sexy, right in front of the security camera where she knew I could see her. So I had lunch delivered wherever I was at, security app opened, and we'd eat "together."

And every night when I went home, I'd wind up crawling into bed with her. Wrapping her up in my arms. And with our limbs entangled, I'd pass out and sleep like a baby.

If that wasn't enough to blow my plan to hell to keep my distance, it was the texts that started up on Monday that did me in.

The messages began as check-in texts. Simple *how are yous?* that somehow morphed into more. I'd found myself sending her paragraphs in response to her essays.

I now knew about the farm her aunt had raised her on, as well as the story that had made my old man laugh, along with a dozen others. I had pretty much committed to memory the names she'd given to every farm animal, whether I wanted to or not.

I also knew about the only ex she'd ever lived with, the one who'd slept with Britt, and I'd had to go to the range and unload my anger after that because I wanted to kill the man for breaking her heart. Not to mention the fact he'd shared a bed with her.

Pretty sure I had more insight into this woman than anyone else in the last two decades, and it'd mostly been because of texts. Not that I'd revealed too much to her about my past—like why I'd become so fucked in the head when I lost my heart in the first place—but I still managed to share with her more than I had with anyone outside my family (or therapist).

About to open the security app to check in on her—according to her last text, she was going to try writing music again—I looked up to see Hudson tapping with the back of his hand at the open door.

"You have news?" I asked him, assuming that was why I wasn't alone at the office at night.

"You feel like hunting later?" Hudson walked in. "The mood I'm in . . ."

I took a guess and asked, "Izzy bothering you?"

"Always, but no." He shook his head, as if freeing a thought he didn't want to have. I knew the feeling. Had around fifty an hour about my wife. "I spoke with Sebastian earlier. He thinks the Barones are still hanging tight at the compound in Romania because of a job, based on the people they've clocked coming and going."

"Define *job*. And what kind of people?" Did I really want to know this? Probably not, which was why Hudson had held back on telling me until now.

"The conflict-starting kind." He grimaced. "The League's guess is the Barones are planning to stir up trouble in Afghanistan to draw the US and other nations back into the region."

"Oh, for fuck's sake." I applied pressure to my temples, pain cutting through at the possibility of what he was suggesting.

"Does that mean you believe Rocco won't crash the birthday party next weekend?" Our plan would work whether he made an appearance or not, but it would've been helpful to have him on-site when he "murdered" Armani and Marcello. It'd be easier to pin their deaths on him if he was actually stateside.

"I don't know. We haven't picked up any chatter about the Barones even so much as whispering your name. It's been radio-fucking-silent from them about you and Calliope."

"Which is why you're on edge and want to go hunting as well."

"That, too, yes. And it bothers me we've yet to figure out why Gabriel was really in Rome, if not to meet with Esposito."

"Maybe that's because there's nothing there to find?" I didn't want to find anything on him. Calliope must've been turning me into an optimist, because she had me wanting to believe Gabriel could become a good guy again. If he could be saved, that meant there was hope for me.

"We're missing something. We have to be. And time's running out."

"Don't remind me. I know time is . . ." I dropped my hands to my desk, prepared to stand, but for some reason I remained glued to my seat, feeling like I was on the verge of losing my mind at the idea I'd soon be completing my assignment as Calliope's husband.

"You don't have to walk away from her after this; you do realize that, right?"

Mind reader, huh? "She doesn't need someone like me with my issues in her life forever."

Hudson's dark eyes narrowed. "And did she tell you that?"

"It's a fact. You know my track record."

"It is what it is because you were burned. You don't need to touch fire more than once to know not to do it again." He stood and finished the job of ridding himself of the tie and began wrapping it around his hand. "Well, until you're certain it's safe to."

"It's never safe to play with fire." *Love only gets you hurt.*

"I'm guessing that's a no to hunting tonight, then?"

"Not in the mood, even after the Barone news." That was also worrisome, because I'd been addicted to the hunt for so long it was the only thing that truly got my adrenaline going. And I hadn't done it all week.

"Maybe that's because you don't need it anymore?" His eyes fell to my wedding band, and I hadn't realized I'd been fidgeting with it. "Go home to her. I'll stay here. Maybe save Izzy from the date she's on with some Wall Street guy and have her help me do another deep dive to look over everything again."

"Weird for her to date while we're in the middle of an op."

"Well, she said he's a friend, but no guy hangs out with a woman like Izzy on a Friday night and doesn't want—" He cut himself off, probably realizing how jealous he sounded.

And damn, he was jealous, wasn't he?

"So that's really why you want to hunt. Maybe accidentally hit Izzy's not-a-date date as your target?"

He laughed. "Not a bad idea, but no." His dismissive shrug was hardly believable. "Why would I care if she's not-dating dating? I just hate her choice in men."

"Mmm-hmm." I smirked.

"Back to you. Like I said, go home early tonight. Be with Calliope."

"I can't be around her." *I want to be is why I shouldn't be.* Hell, I'd been sleeping with her every night without even needing sex. It was . . . "Confusing." I stood. "*I'm* confused, I mean."

"What you are is a man falling for someone you think you can't or shouldn't have. And like I said, maybe it's time you take a chance again."

"I'm screwed up in the head, you know that. If I get what I want, who's to say I'll still want . . ." I let my words hang in the air, because I couldn't refer to Calliope as an "it" when she was the most incredible woman I'd met in my life. And God help me when she sang. Or smiled. Or laughed. Or peered at me with those big eyes of hers. Or ran her sassy southern mouth. Rolled her eyes. Gave me hell for rolling mine. Or just . . . well, existed. Collapsing back onto my seat, I admitted, "Fuck, I have it bad."

"Finally saying what we all know," he said in a light voice, and I tugged at my tie and looked up to see him smiling.

"Yeah, well, you going to do the same and confess you feel something for Izzy?" Shit, where'd that come from?

His smile vanished. "I don't feel that way for her. Just told you that."

"Yeah, okay. Denial is your best friend, like it's mine." I still wasn't sure how I felt about him with my sister, but I had my own problems to deal with at the moment.

"On that note, I'm going." He mock-saluted me. "I'll be in touch if I learn anything new."

"Or if you accidentally shoot the Wall Street guy and need help burying a body?"

He stopped in the doorway and looked back at me. "If I need a shovel and help digging, I'll call Constantine. Just go be with your wife." And with that, he left.

My wife. Could I really go be with her, knowing our marriage already had an expiration date?

I grabbed my phone, needing to at least put eyes on Little Miss Tennessee Whiskey. But when I opened the security app, I about fell out of my chair at who was with her. Had Javier been already at my house, he would've given me the heads-up about the guests.

Without wasting time, I called my mom, and she had the nerve to look up at my kitchen security camera while sending me to voicemail. *Oh, hell no.* Since Izzy was in the room with my wife, too, I tried her next. Straight to voicemail.

At least Calliope answered. But it was a nervous "Heyyy."

"I can see them there. But why are they there?" I cut straight to it.

"Your sister wants to talk to you. One second," she said in a distant tone, and that had me even more worried.

Izzy popped on a moment later, disappearing from the view of the camera. "Shit, you need to get here now. Mom basically kidnapped me with a crate of wine, took my phone, and brought me here," she said in a muffled voice, sounding as though she had her hand cupped over her mouth while talking. "She wants Callie's input about the birthday party plans."

"Fuck. I'm on my way." Already on my feet, I snatched the keys to my Lamborghini and started for the door.

"It gets worse," Izzy shared on my way out the door. "Mom had too much wine, and she slipped and mentioned why you're hell-bent on being single forever." That pause killed me almost as much as her next words. "She told her about Nicole."

CHAPTER THIRTY-FIVE

Alessandro

"Please, just don't. Don't say anything." I handed Mom her purse and opened the front door. "You knew not to come, and you—"

"I'm sorry. You're keeping her from me. From us. And I want to get to know my daughter-in-law," Mom said, looking toward Izzy for an assist. "She can't even tell her aunt, the woman who raised her, what's going on, so I thought she could use family around her with you doing your best to keep away."

Izzy must've told Mom all that, dammit. "She's *not* my wife. Not really," I shot out like a knee-jerk reaction, but I wanted the words to curl up and die. I hated them. Hated that truth. "In a few weeks, we're getting our marriage annulled, and she's going back to her life, and I'm going back to mine." Maybe I was angry and pissed, but more than that, I was scared that what I'd said would actually come true. I knew in my gut losing Calliope would kill me, and I wanted to save my family that pain.

Mom looked over my shoulder, and I twisted to the side to see Calliope there. Shit, had she heard me?

Not that it was a secret. That'd been the plan all along. But . . .

Facing my mother, I pleaded, "Please, just go."

Izzy reached for Mom's arm, encouraging her along. The sad look in Mom's eyes was going to destroy me.

They needed to leave before I snapped, but the guilt had me whispering, "I'm sorry."

Mom peeked in the direction where I knew Calliope was probably still standing, not too far behind me, gave her a little nod goodbye, shot me a dagger or two, then left with Izzy.

I shut the door and set my palms to it, bowing my head as I tried to corral my thoughts and calm down.

"I had no clue they were coming over to talk about the party." Calliope's apologetic tone had me forcing myself around.

There was flour on her cheek because of course, Mom would have her cooking with her, too. She lowered her eyes to the marble floors as I ate up the space between us.

I wasn't sure where Frankie, Leo, or the others were, but this wasn't a conversation I wanted to have in earshot of anyone. "Can we talk in private?"

Without looking at me, she nodded, then we started for the back stairs to get to the bedroom. I quietly let her lead the way, my mind racing.

Once in the bedroom, I flicked on the overhead lights and locked the door. I pushed my hands into my suit pants pockets so I wouldn't reach for her and hold her against me with no plans to ever let go.

She went to the dresser and studied her reflection, and like a lost puppy, I followed her over. She swiped at the flour on her cheek before meeting my eyes in the mirror.

"What are we doing?" She set down her hands, hanging her head. "Are we still only playing pretend? And if it's fake, why is it that when no one's watching us, it feels the most real? You're all I think about, and your climbing into bed at night is what I look forward to every day." She met my eyes in the mirror. "I don't know how I'm going to survive you walking away from me, which is crazy because tomorrow is only three weeks since we met." A single tear slipped down her cheek as she obliterated my thoughts with what she'd confessed. "But what you said out there . . . You'll break my heart, won't you? You warned me, and I tried to listen. I tried to fight it. But then you did what I asked by being sweet in Nashville, and you've been sweet ever since." Her lower lip quivered as a few more tears fell. "Is Nicole really why you're this way? Unwilling to commit? To fall?"

I sank into the dark feeling that overtook me at her words, feeling a little dizzy. "Yes and no." I all but breathed out the confusing response.

I turned away and freed myself of my suit jacket and tie, then undid a few buttons of my gray shirt.

It was now or never. Either I opened up and tried to touch the fire—risk my heart—or I let it shrivel and die in my chest for good.

When I chanced looking at this stunning woman again, I knew the answer. She'd always been worth the risk.

"Not sure what my mom spilled to you already, but Nicole was my high school girlfriend. We were together for five years." She'd been my first relationship and my last. Well, until Calliope. "Right after I got my Ranger tab, I proposed."

Calliope's mouth rounded, and her eyes shot to the ring on her finger.

So Mom didn't tell you I was engaged? "Nicole said yes, and I was deployed shortly afterward to Afghanistan. There was a daylight mission two weeks later—those always sucked even more—but it had to be done. The op went sideways, and my best friend was killed right in front of me. I couldn't save him, and knowing that and having to watch it happen . . ." I went over to the bed and dropped down, head in my hands.

"You don't have to do this if you don't want to," she whispered, sliding her hand up and down my back in soothing motions.

"I think maybe I need to." I looked up at her, finding her glossy eyes on me. Her nod had me choosing to go on. "I was pretty screwed up about his death. Instead of helping me get through the pain, she broke up with me, saying she couldn't deal with me being the next to die. Five years together, and she walked away when I needed her the most." My hands fell to my lap, and Calliope quietly threaded our fingers together. "Then Bianca died, which fucked me up way more. Nicole had the nerve to show up to the funeral with a husband. The real kick to the nuts—he was a Team guy. Military. So she was willing to risk getting her heart broken, just not by me."

There. That's my story. Maybe it was a bullshit excuse to turn my back on love for good, but it had made sense to me at the time, and it had kept making sense until this woman had come into my life.

"I'm so sorry." She slowly pulled her hand from mine and stood, then folded her arms over her chest as if chasing away a chill. "But I'm also . . ." More tears appeared, and she licked one free from her lips. "I'm a horrible person, though."

I joined her on my feet, unsure I'd heard her right. "How are *you* a bad person?"

"Because." Fuck, that sad look and wobbly lip gutted me.

"What is it?" I tipped my head, a hell of a lot more nervous now.

"Because I never would've met you if she hadn't . . . well, screwed you up. And what kind of person does that make me?"

At her confession, I hauled her against me. "It makes you just like me. If Armani hadn't dragged you into this mess, then you wouldn't be in my life now, and I've felt guilty for being . . . thankful you're here with me."

Staying in my arms, she looked up and pointed those gorgeous greens at me. "I kind of love that you feel that way."

"And I kind of love you're glad I was an asshole for eighteen years so I could meet you," I shared in return. *More than kind of.* Maybe we really were masochists, but we belonged together, didn't we? "Hunting criminals and risking my life became what I craved over the years. It became an addiction." I could barely stand to look at her without totally losing it, so I closed my eyes. "And now I'm addicted to you."

Fuck, even after what Hudson had told me about the Barones' war-starting plans earlier, all I could think about was this woman.

Calliope worked her arm between our bodies and set her palm to my cheek, and I forced my eyes back open. "What are you saying?"

I tensed at the only truth I knew that'd been burrowing its way inside me every day since the moment we met. "I'm falling for my wife." Knowing my voice would probably break when I spoke again, I went ahead and revealed, "I don't want to say goodbye to you when the time comes." I paused, giving her a second to absorb my confession. "Or ever . . . I don't want to say goodbye ever."

Her downturned mouth had me worried. "And that terrifies you?"

I brought my lips near hers, prepared to kiss away those nerves. "Not nearly as much as losing you does."

My concerns disappeared when she pushed up and kissed me first. It was the kind of kiss that could heal whatever was still broken inside me.

When her lips left mine, it took me a second to open my eyes.

"Make love to me?" Her fingers began working down the length of my shirt before I had a chance to answer. After waiting eighteen years for this woman to come into my life, I wasn't about to wait another eighteen seconds to be with her, but . . .

I captured her hand, stopping her from finishing the job of removing my shirt.

There was something about this moment, with us laying our cards on the table and having nothing in between us now, that had me nervous. Fuck, was I ever. I needed to remind myself for a second I was nearly forty and not a fumbling twentysomething with no clue how to pleasure a woman.

But make love? How the hell do I do that?

"What's wrong?" With her free hand, she brought her palm to my face and ran it along my clenched jaw.

"How do we . . . ?" I choked out, feeling ridiculous, but I wanted this to be what she wanted and needed, and I'd spent almost two decades removing emotions from the equation.

She slid her palm down the column of my throat and to my bare chest, drawing her hand beneath my open shirt. "The only difference is you use your heart this time." Her light-green gaze flew to my face as she added, "You look me in the eyes like you wanted to last time."

I let go of her wrist and dragged my hands along her silhouette and around to her ass before lifting her up to carry her to the bed.

"Pretty sure my heart was in it back at the office, too." Climbing over her, I held the brunt of my weight on my forearms, staring down at her.

"Mine, too." She reached between us, searching for my belt. I'd forgotten we were both still dressed.

Tonight, I took my time removing our clothes. I stretched out every moment of every single second, because tomorrow wasn't promised.

Once we were both naked and back on my bed, I worked my mouth from the inside of her ankle up her thigh, slowly swiping the pad of my thumb along her other leg. I skipped over her pussy, which had her clawing at my hair with an adorable groan of frustration.

Mouth over her belly button next. Then up to her breasts. Her taut nipples.

"I'll know every inch of your body before the night is over. Every freckle. Every spot that makes you laugh," I promised before working my way back to her face, prepared to take her mouth again.

She anchored her arm behind the back of my neck, urging me closer as she arched into me.

"What if we make love first, then foreplay second? Then sex again?" She bit her lip, staring at me with those seductive eyes of hers. "Then repeat in a different order. And throw a little naughty and dirty in there for good measure, too."

My stiff cock pressed against her center, lined up in the perfect spot, begging to give my little siren what she wanted and then some.

"You don't want my mouth on you first? You're sure?"

She bucked against me at my words, my lips hovering over hers so close I could nearly taste her already. "I need you inside me." Tears pricked the corners of her eyes. "But I want to feel you . . . you know?"

My arms tensed, going as rock hard as my dick at what she was asking. "Bare?"

"That breath you just took . . . Is that your about-to-lose-control one or your panicked one? They're close. I can't tell right now because I'm so nervous." She kept moving her hips in tempting little circles, and the invitation to feel this woman was too much.

But she wasn't just anyone. *Fuck, you're my wife.* We'd said vows before God. Signed the paperwork. *It's not pretend. It's real.* The idea of her having my child didn't scare me. But her giving Armani an heir sure as hell did.

I hated to break the moment, to destroy it with that reminder, but it needed to be done.

Not that I had a chance to do it, because she beat me to it. "I know what you're thinking." She gave me a little nod as if that would settle things. It didn't. "What if you pull out just before?"

A low laugh rumbled free. Was she kidding?

Her other hand went to my chest, and she parked it there. She'd see how much my heart really was in this right now. "I know what's at stake. It'd be crazy; I get that." I lost sight of her eyes as she sealed them shut, but she didn't stop moving her hips. Didn't stop grinding against my cock. Didn't stop killing me.

"But it'd also be very us," I admitted, and that earned me her eyes again. "Three weeks tomorrow since we met . . . are you sure you want to risk it?" And yet, I could see us together, not in a penthouse but on a farm. Lots of land. Animals. Our children running around. *Holy fuck, what's happening to me?*

"Three weeks. Three years. Three decades." A soft breathy sigh left her mouth, and I knew her breaths and looks, too. That was my determined, strong woman peering at me. "If you know, you know."

Her brows slanted. "The question is, do you know, too? And do you want it?"

I bit down on my back teeth, resisting the urge to push inside her as my answer. "I'll pull out, but if . . ." I let the warning hang in the air for a beat. "You sure you want my kid inside of you if it were to happen?"

"Give my child *you* as a father?" She nodded, emotion catching in her voice when she added, "Yeah, you could say I'd be good with that."

Me, a father? Leaning in even closer, I kissed away the tear at the edge of her eye, then reached between us to position my cock at her center. She gave me a firm nod of permission, and I pushed inside her. The connection freed whatever had been caged inside my chest for so long. No longer trapped there for what felt like an eternity.

I gave this woman my soul just then, knowing she'd redeem it.

And I'd give it to her again and again, no matter what.

Die for her. Sacrifice the world for her.

Do anything for her if she asked.

She cried out my name and moved with me, lifting her ass from the bed, allowing me to bury myself even deeper inside her.

When I flipped us around, she straddled me. A devilish smirk that was the sexiest smile I'd seen in my life cut across her mouth as she sat tall, hands on my chest, riding me. I needed her to fall to pieces all over my cock.

She slid up and down a few times before rubbing her clit against me, chasing her orgasm. Her fingers curled on my chest as she climbed closer to release, and I felt her tightening around me. It took all my strength and energy not to come inside her as her yeses became louder and breathier.

When she collapsed on top of me from coming, I flipped her back around and moved slowly in and out of her, helping her orgasm last a bit longer.

"When you're ready, come on my stomach," she said in a hazy, orgasm-drunk tone.

"Fuuuck," I hissed, two seconds away from coming inside her instead, and I pulled out and did as she asked, grunting as I exploded all over her soft stomach.

"That's . . . a lot," she said with a laugh while looking down at her stomach as I rolled off to her side.

"Yeah, well—your fault. You make me crazy." I gave her a quick kiss before standing so I could grab a cloth to clean her up.

When I returned with a warm, wet towel, I sat next to her, and she snatched my wrist and lifted her brows a few playful times. "Or we could move to the shower. You know, foreplay time. Maybe get you hard again with my mouth."

"No 'maybe' about that." Dipping in, I captured her lower lip between my teeth and gently tugged. "I loved making love to you," I whispered. "But I'm also going to enjoy fucking you up against my shower wall." Mouth to her ear now, I let my breath tease the sensitive part of her lobe. "Arms up. Tits smashed to the tile. My cock against your perfect ass while I fill your pussy."

She turned her cheek to find my lips. "I'm getting wet again already, and all you've done is talk dirty."

"I'm just getting started, sweetheart. You asked for all night, and my wife gets what she wants."

CHAPTER THIRTY-SIX

Calliope

Facing me in bed that next morning, my sexy husband smoothed my nipple between his finger and thumb, eyes quietly locked with mine.

We'd barely slept last night. He really had kept his promise to deliver over and over again.

And I'd been a little giddy about how fast I'd had my *former* playboy husband coming from getting down on my knees to suck him off.

But the shower sex.

Damn.

For such a clean place, it'd been . . . *well*, dirty (in the best possible way).

He'd taken me against the wall, all right. And nearly took my virgin ass, too, but he'd decided to save that for another night.

Seems the both of us operated at two speeds: zero or sixty. And last night had been pedal-to-the-metal fast, and it was everything and more.

He'd even mentioned something about us living on a farm with kids and animals one day, but that was probably delirious post-orgasm talk.

"You sore?" he asked, changing the conversation in my head from farming to fucking.

Now that'd be quite the song title. Number one on Apple or Spotify for sure.

I did the little nose-crinkling smile I knew he loved and reached for his hand on my tit and brought it between my legs. "Which part? I'm achy all over."

He returned my smirk and thumbed my sensitive clit. "But a good achy, right?"

I arched into his hand, and what was wrong with me? How was I ready to go again? "I mean, you took excellent care to ensure I felt all kinds of good last night, so most definitely a wonderful achy."

With his free hand, he tossed the covers back and zeroed in on me. "You're a little pinker than normal and swollen."

His concerned brows had me reassuring him. "That's what happens when you've both made love and been properly fucked, I suppose."

Clocking my chills, because the man didn't miss a thing, he covered me, then groaned at his phone ringing. Must've still been in his pants pocket on the floor.

"Who'd call you at seven in the morning on a Saturday? Maybe you should answer," I said when it appeared he had no plans to budge from our comfortable place.

"They can wait. I'm not ready to get up."

"Just get off?" I teased.

"So fucking naughty." He grabbed hold of me beneath the covers and tangled us up in a warm embrace. "And I'm here for it." He kissed me, our tongues battling, and I knew where this would go.

But three more calls had me on edge, and him, too, because he stopped kissing me. "Give me a second. And don't move. I want morning sex with my wife."

Morning sex with my wife. Music to my ears. The view of my muscular, handsome husband walking naked to grab his phone was more than a pleasant way to start the day.

I not so shamelessly stared at those rock-hard glutes as he bent over to retrieve his phone and began touching myself. Yup, already soaking wet.

When he faced me with his phone now ringing from a fourth call, the worried look in his eyes killed the happy feelings swelling inside me. "It's Hudson," he remarked before bringing the phone to his ear.

I sat, back to the headboard, holding the comforter tight at the uneasiness crossing his face while he listened to whatever Hudson told him.

"I'll be right there," was all he said before ending the call.

"What's wrong?"

He cupped his jaw, pointing his eyes toward the ceiling.

My nerves got the best of me and had me crying out, "What is it?"

"Hudson's man watching your aunt didn't check in at zero six hundred our time like he normally does every day. Hudson reached out to Gabriel—he couldn't get ahold of their guy watching her, either."

"What are you saying?" But I already knew what he was suggesting. Someone got the drop on my overprotective and cautious aunt. We'd corresponded via email two days ago, and she'd been fine and even bought my lies that everything was fine on my end as well.

"Hudson checked the footage from the cruise ship. She never reboarded from the port at the stop in Copenhagen yesterday, and neither did his guy or Armani's." He slowly dropped his eyes to meet mine. "He thinks Rocco sent his men to take her. I'm not sure how they found her, but he's running facial recognition on every one of Rocco's known associates at the local airport in Denmark."

I pushed away the covers and stood, too stunned to truly process what he was telling me.

"I've been distracted. Hudson and The League suspected something was off because the Barones have been *too* quiet about us." He chucked his phone on the bed and tore his hands through his hair. "I'm so sorry. It's my fault she was taken. I should've predicted this. Rocco is always three steps ahead of us somehow. He even knew Constantine was coming for his father four years ago and . . . *shit*."

"What is it?" I reached for his arm.

"He must have someone on the inside." His scowl intensified, as if putting something together in his mind. "Of course he would. War is a disgustingly profitable business and—"

"What? Inside of where?"

"Gabriel was in Rome last month, and someone with advanced cyber skills hid the fact he was there." Without further explaining, he eased free from my grip and grabbed his phone, making a call. "We need to talk on a secure line," he rushed out a moment later. "And yeah, I know you have one."

"Is that Gabriel?" I asked, terror still holding my normal voice hostage.

He nodded, barely waiting for the full ring on his cell to answer. "Who do you work for? What government agency? Because someone you're working with is dirty. They just set us up, and they're probably also looking to cash in on a new conflict in the Middle East."

My hands trembled on my lap as Alessandro tore down the road in his Lamborghini. Javier and the others were doing their best to keep up with his pace, following behind us. If we didn't get pulled over, it'd be a miracle.

He reached for my hand and gave it a quick squeeze before reaching for the gear-shift thing (or whatever it was called) to have us flying off an exit for Oyster Bay in Long Island—apparently, his parents' other home in New York.

He'd called for his family to be assembled there like they were part of the Justice League, and he'd barely spoken two words to me since he'd ended his call with Gabriel in the bedroom.

"I don't want to distract you while you're driving this fast, but, um, if it's safe to talk . . . ?" I peeked at him, catching his eyes before he focused back on the exit we were taking.

"You can always talk to me." He slammed on the brakes when a Honda made an abrupt stop before us.

"You're upset, and I'm shocked and confused. I guess I don't even know where to begin," I admitted before my stomach turned as he maneuvered around the next car going too slow for him. "So Gabriel has been working for Italian Intelligence undercover, and so is Leo." I snagged the other details from memory I'd overheard from their call, wondering if I said it all aloud, it'd somehow make more sense. "Gabriel and Leo have been undercover for years, and that's how Gabriel knew Constantine had been taken by Rocco four years ago. Someone at the agency is leaking intel to Rocco. It has to be someone at Italian Intelligence who's unaware Gabriel and Leo are assets."

I understood why he was driving so fast. My aunt's life was on the line. Time was of the essence. But I grabbed hold of the oh-shit handle when he took a sharp turn around another bend. One thing was for sure, the man could drive.

"My contact at the CIA was able to corroborate Gabriel's story," he finally said, confirming he'd heard me. "The Agenzia Informazioni e Sicurezza Esterna—AISE—recruited Gabriel and Leo. Well, gave them no choice but to turn or face multiple life sentences in prison."

"But the goal wasn't to take down the DiMaggios? I'm so confused." *And nauseous from driving so fast.*

"No, the mafia's not who the AISE cares about. Their focus is on foreign problems. Given how many international business deals the DiMaggios are involved in, AISE wanted insiders in the DiMaggio organization to help take down bigger sharks."

"Like Rocco?" I whispered, connecting the dots.

"Exactly. And it was Gabriel's case officer in Rome that he met with three weeks ago, not Esposito." There was relief in Alessandro's tone that

Gabriel hadn't been the reason why those men had come for me in the park in Nashville.

And yeah, same. I didn't want Gabriel to be evil. I just never suspected he'd been secretly working for Team Good Guy. "His case officer can't be the mole at the agency leaking info to Rocco, because Rocco would've given up Gabriel's name to Armani and Marcello."

"Right, to protect an asset in the field, very few people will know their identity," Alessandro quickly answered, and when we finally slowed down, I realized it was because we were in suburbia and passing houses. "Which means someone who is part of the task force to take down the Barones, both now and back then, is an insider for the Barones. But that person doesn't know Gabriel and Leo are assets in the field."

"You think whoever that person is also told Rocco you were coming for his father four years ago, and that's how Rocco managed to get ahold of Constantine?"

He swung his focus my way, his jaw locked tight, and nodded. "Thankfully, Gabriel doesn't know The League is monitoring the compound."

"Which means the insider doesn't know you're aware of Rocco's real location in Romania. But you don't think Rocco will have his men bring my aunt there?"

"No." He turned down another road and further reduced our speed. "He won't expose his current compound, especially with his father on the verge of starting a new conflict in the Middle East."

"So how will you track my aunt's location and ID the inside traitor?"

"Because whoever at AISE miraculously gets intel on her whereabouts is the traitor, and instead of letting them know we're onto them, we'll send a team to that location while simultaneously hitting the compound in Romania."

He stopped outside a gate, punched in a code, and then we began down a long driveway. A gorgeous home was at the end, and other cars were already parked out front.

"And you think Rocco won't have her killed, not just because she's bait but . . . ?" I couldn't finish my words, too queasy from the thought and the drive to get it out.

"You really want me to answer that?"

Unbuckling, I closed my eyes and shook my head. *Torture.* The sadistic son of a bitch liked to torture people first. "But if he's not the one who has her, because he's in Romania, then what?"

At the feel of him squeezing both my hands, I opened my eyes to see him peering at me. "I'll get her back alive. I promise you. The jet is being prepared as we speak. I'm leaving today."

"I can't ask you to risk your life to save her," I sputtered, tears finally catching up with me as reality grabbed hold of me.

"I'm getting her back. Killing Rocco. And then my family will deal with the other problem." He let go of one hand to palm my cheek.

The other problem . . . killing Armani and freeing me from the prison of my bloodline. Right.

"My job isn't done yet."

"Your job?" I frowned.

"You know what I mean. I'm still in the habit of—"

"Trying to push me away?" My shoulders fell. "Well, just so you know, I don't ever want you to be done with your *job*," I whispered, and he caught a tear with the pad of his thumb. "I thought I made that clear last night."

His throat bobbed from a hard swallow. "I know," he began, his voice catching, "but maybe I needed to hear you say it one more time."

CHAPTER THIRTY-SEVEN

Calliope

"The League sent someone from their location in Oslo and confirmed the intelligence," Hudson shared the second we joined everyone inside a large office decorated with warm wood and dark colors.

"That was fast. Rocco must be anxious for us to hurry up and get there," Alessandro said as his mother pulled me in for a hug and murmured apologies as if she were to blame for my nightmare.

I peeked over her shoulder, catching Alessandro peering my way as if the sight of his mother holding on to me for dear life physically pained him.

"So my aunt is being held in Norway?" I asked once she freed me from her grip. "Do they know if she's still okay?" I swiped away tears, sending an acknowledging hello to Mr. Costa when he joined the room.

Hudson handed an iPad to Alessandro, and he gestured for me to join in to view the screen. Did I really want to see that? No, but did I look? Of course. "She's tied to a chair. No visible injuries and alive. This is in real-time."

I'd done my best not to involve Tia in my mess, but what if I'd told her in the first place? Maybe she'd be okay. *This is my fault.*

"Clearly, Rocco was expecting we'd take the bait and send someone to confirm she's there. He wants us to see her," Izzy said, sitting behind the desk in front of a laptop, Constantine off to her side.

"Since you received a location, does that mean you figured out who's the insider at Italian Intelligence?" I directed my question to Hudson as Alessandro handed him back the iPad.

"Yeah. Gabriel let his case officer know the insider is working with the Barones," Hudson shared. "They can't arrest him until after the Barones are taken down, or they'll figure out we're onto them."

"Guess it's a good thing we didn't trust Gabriel." Izzy looked up from her screen.

Because then anything you told him would've wound up back at Rocco.

"But you were right about him." Constantine looked at Alessandro, and was that an apologetic nod from him?

"What are we telling Armani?" I asked them, knowing Leo wouldn't reach out to Armani. But Frankie had to know something was wrong since we'd hightailed it from the penthouse, and Javier was keeping him outside the house right now.

"The truth." Mr. Costa joined in on the conversation. "A version of it, at least."

"That Rocco's family is coming after us for revenge," Alessandro clarified, hooking his arm around my waist, drawing me to his side. When his mother noticed the comforting gesture, a little look of hope reached her eyes despite everything going on right now. "Gabriel will tell him. And I think we should have Gabriel go with the team on the rescue op in Norway, let the insider truly believe we took the bait."

I turned into him, hands flying to his hard chest. "But it's going to be an ambush, right? What if he gets killed and my aunt dies in the cross fire?"

"I'll go with him," Hudson offered. "We need someone from our side to make it more believable. Plus, we'll have League support."

Izzy abruptly stood, her brown eyes shooting his way. Concern etched between her brows. "What, so you can be the one to die in the ambush?"

"No one's dying," Hudson rasped, turning his attention on her as if insulted she'd think he'd go down that easily. I had a feeling there was more going on in that heated look being exchanged than any of us were privy to.

"Clearly, you have the memory of a goldfish," she said, breaking the silent staring contest. "I may have been in the dark about what happened to Constantine four years ago while it was going on, but he was taken for weeks, and . . ." She let her words to Hudson hang in the air while catching Constantine's eyes as her next target.

"It's different this time," Constantine said after an awkward minute ticked by. "We have the advantage."

"But do we?" If Izzy was this on edge, how was I supposed to feel? Would the shell shock wear off and I'd become hysterical with worry? "What if Rocco has an exfil plan? An emergency way off the compound we're unaware of?"

"We have no choice but to go," Constantine said, his tone steady and reassuring. "And The League has been prepping for the infil into the compound for weeks. We're doing a HAHO jump, and once inside, The League will breach from the Black Sea. This needs to end with the Barones, and now."

"Hey-ho?" I looked up at my husband. "What does that mean?"

"High altitude, high opening jump," Alessandro explained, as if that'd make perfect sense to me. "We have to jump from high up so no one can hear or see the plane. Then we glide into the landing zone at a horizontal distance for quite some time."

When you put it like that . . . "You make it sound like it's no big deal. Are there risks from jumping from high-high up?"

"Hypoxia. Not opening the chute in time." At Hudson's words, Izzy grabbed a pen from the desk and launched it across the room. He snatched it before it hit his face. "We'll be fine." He mumbled under his breath and asked her, "That better?"

"Then what happens?" I knew Alessandro didn't want to share details that'd make me worry, but I needed reassurances he'd be fine and that the mysterious League group really did have it all covered.

"The League will enter from the sea as we drop in from above." Constantine repeated what he'd already said but with smaller words this time. "They have overwatch—guys on snipers with a view into the compound—set up as well. Not to mention a drone overhead to keep a watch out. There are four towers we'll hit first so we can safely move in without drawing fire."

"I think that's all she needs to know," Alessandro said, as if worried I was heading into fight-or-flight mode.

Probably already there.

"Ignorance can be bliss," my mother-in-law said. How in the world had she handled her sons all operating over the years? "Wine. Lots of wine," she added, reading the worried look on my face and somehow hearing the question in my head.

"What about Armani? If you kill Rocco, don't you lose your scapegoat for his death?" my father-in-law asked, raising an important issue.

"We'll find someone else to pin Armani's death on," Constantine replied, almost like a brush-off, and I wasn't sure how to interpret that.

"Unless you bring him and Marcello on the op. It's obvious now they're not in on this with the Barones and definitely not with the insider at AISE," Izzy suggested. "We could ask them for their help, and ensure they die in the cross fire on the mission."

"I don't trust Marcello not to shoot me in the back while there. I can't look over my shoulder the whole time," Alessandro said, quickly shutting down the idea. "We'll deal with them when we get home."

"We should get a move on to the airport," Constantine said with a curt nod, letting Izzy and, well, probably everyone know the conversation was now over. He motioned toward the door, and his parents quietly followed him.

"I guess I don't understand why our government can't handle this?" I asked once it was only the four of us there. "Is that such a wild idea?" *I mean, is it?*

Izzy peered at Hudson, her eyes narrowing on him as if she might chuck her laptop at him next for placing himself in danger. "Aside from concerns someone could wind up leaking the fact we're hitting Rocco's real location to the insider, there's another issue." Redirecting her attention on me, she shared, "There's no guarantee our government, or the Italians, will get the Romanians to allow for a mission on their soil. And even if they agree to coordinate a joint op, your aunt doesn't have time to wait for the ink to dry on the paperwork."

"Bureaucracy and red tape slow missions down," Hudson drawled, clearly knowing a thing or two about that as a SEAL.

"What about Enzo? Is he going with you?" I asked them. "And are you heading out with them, Izzy?"

"She's staying here," Hudson said before Alessandro could. "Enzo will be on the next flight here. He's staying with you. Plus, Javier and his team will be here. Frankie and Leo."

Alessandro pointed at the floor. "There's a safe room here. I need to know you'll be okay no matter what happens."

"*Me* okay?" I stabbed at my chest, feeling frantic. "I'm not the one risking my life because of a side gig, and I can't lose you because I . . ." Tears fast-tracked down my cheeks as my stomach turned.

Yeah, I was officially off the deep end.

And Alessandro noticed. He snatched my hand and had me on the move within seconds. Once inside a bedroom, he closed the door, and my back went to it. He caged me there, hands over my shoulders.

"If you say something about you sacrificing yourself for the greater good being the lesser of two evils, I'll snap. For real." I fisted his black tee, looking up at him. "Fuck the greater good. And if feeling that way means I'm joining the dark side like Armani said would happen, well so be it. Because without you, the world's not even worth fighting for, and—"

His lips crashed over mine, cutting off my hysteria. For those few seconds he kissed me, I forgot every last problem.

It wasn't until our mouths broke that the heavy weight of the world came back. God, I wished it'd go away again.

"Tell me you're going to be fine," I begged when he'd yet to talk. He bowed his head to mine, cupping my face. "It's what I need to hear you say."

"I can't promise you that," he whispered.

"But you promised you'd get my aunt back alive. Why can't you say the same about yourself?" Pulling away, I searched for his eyes, needing him to look at me. He hesitantly lifted his head.

That's when I realized what was going on in his mind. Nicole had fucked him up eighteen years ago by running out of fear something would happen to him, and there I was . . . *Dammit.* "I'm not her. I'm not going to bail because of what may happen." At the sight of his eyes going glossy, I continued, "I'll wait for you." I let go of his shirt to position my hand over his heart. "I'm a fighter. Stubborn. Not going anywhere." I sniffled. "I thought you weren't mine to keep, and here you are, becoming all I want."

At the sight of a single tear rolling down his cheek, I had to do my best not to let that sign of emotion from such a tough guy paralyze me with fear.

"Okay." He covered my hand with his own. "I promise I'll make it back to you. To my *wife.*"

Chills scattered across my skin, and I about sobbed in his arms. But I had to keep it together for him. For us. For my aunt. Hell, for the world. "Good."

"You're much bossier than me, by the way." His lighter tone eased free a half cry, half laugh from my chest.

"Bossy is to keep you safe. You'll need to deal with it," I said, tossing his own words to me from weeks ago back at him.

He leaned in, smiling against my lips. "Mmm. I could get used to always having a reason to make it home alive."

"You have a lot of reasons." My heart broke a little at his confession, despite the smile from him. I moved our hands to my stomach. "And who knows, maybe one day you'll have more than just me to come home to."

CHAPTER
THIRTY-EIGHT

Alessandro

Constanţa, Romania

We were twenty mikes—a.k.a. *minutes*—from the Barone compound that was sandwiched between a forest and the Black Sea.

It was 0400 hours now, and The League had confirmed with their eyes in the sky both Rocco and Claudio were currently on-site and more than likely awake, anticipating the ambush to happen in Oslo.

Hudson, Gabriel, and the other team members we'd assembled at the last second were also a few mikes from their target. I wouldn't be able to hear the good news Calliope's aunt was safe, because I'd already be falling from the sky to infil the compound at the south side when they infiltrated the home in Norway.

Sebastian Renaud, Sean McGregor, and Sean's cousin, Cole McGregor, were heading up a team of ten other League members and were in place on a yacht off the coast, waiting for our go-ahead to move in by sea.

When Constantine and I had arrived in Romania, the six former SF guys we'd asked for help, who were now in private security and stationed abroad, had been at the airport in Bucharest, waiting for us with Sebastian.

Sebastian's words of encouragement had gone something like, *"No one dies tonight. My wife is pregnant with our second kid. Cole's wife—my sister—just had a kid. You already know the drill with Emilia."* He'd stabbed at the air, looking at us all like he'd kill us himself if we fucked up and placed him or his men in danger. *"We clear? No one goes home in a body bag."*

"Roger that," I'd said, not a fan of taking orders from someone who'd never served, but from what I knew, Sebastian had killed a hell of a lot more bad guys than I had, so I supposed that counted for something. I'd tip my hat to him and be an obedient soldier tonight if it'd help get the job done, because as long as it was mission success and I made it home to Calliope, I didn't give a damn who was calling the shots.

It'd been a few years since I'd done a HAHO jump, and I wasn't afraid of heights, but the idea of not making it home sure as hell scared me now. I'd never dealt with the weird butterfly sensation in my stomach pre-op before. Normally, I was pumped up and charged, ready to go. But now? The afterlife be damned.

I took a knee and went through my things, doing another weapons check. I had my Ruger Precision rifle, which was my preferred long-range shooter. I was also equipped with a Sig Sauer P320-M18, which was the civilian version of the military's M18. Then there was the seven-inch blade sheathed at my side. Plenty of ammo. Night vision goggles attached to my helmet. The same body armor I'd worn as a Ranger, but much improved since then. So yeah, I was good to go.

Standing now, I snatched my phone from my pocket and started toward Constantine, who was talking to our pilot. I read Calliope's last message, my mind wandering back to our kiss goodbye at my parents' house yesterday.

My Wife: Be careful. Come home soon. X

My Wife: And don't forget the research I sent you. I know The League did their own, but just in case . . .

I'd changed her contact name in my phone yet again on the flight over.

Me: Hopefully no tunnels here, but I let the team know to be on the lookout. Thank you 😊

Me: And define 'X' 😏

My Wife: Love

My lips twitched into a full-on grin at the sight of the word instead of the standard "kiss" for an *X*.

Me: Well, then 😊 X squared.

My Wife: Define X squared.

Me: Love. You. More.

I backspaced the words before I sent the message, because fuck, I couldn't confess my love over text before I was about to infil a compound and kill people. It'd look like an "If I die" text and not genuine.

Me: You know exactly what it means.

My Wife: Mmm-hmm. Tell me when you get home.

Me: Roger that 😊

Me: And don't be nervous. Everything will be okay. Your aunt is minutes away from being safe, and I'm about two hours away from being on a plane to head home to you.

I powered off my phone before I could read her response, feeling a bit torn up about making a promise like that without being prophetic and knowing the final outcome. I tossed my phone to the pilot to hold on to, then turned my attention to my brother as he checked his MK 13 sniper rifle.

"When we get in there, don't forget that The League wants Claudio taken out alive if possible." I didn't need the reminder from him, but I had a feeling what was coming next. "And Rocco—"

"Is yours?" I finished for him, then looked over at the SF guys who'd be having our six as Foxtrot Team tonight, grateful for their assist.

Constantine set aside his rifle and wrapped his hand over my shoulder. "I don't care who gets him. I just want him dead so he can't hurt anyone anymore." Well, I hadn't expected that. "So if you have the shot, take it. Fucking take his head right off."

After we'd HAHO'd in, the four towers were simultaneously taken out by our SF guys, giving us fire superiority with Foxtrot Team on overwatch.

We left three guys to handle suppressive fire while Constantine and I moved on the target, passing through enemy territory.

"Shift fire," Constantine mouthed to me just before we split ways as planned to flow in, letting the tangos believe we were still striking the main area of the compound, when in reality, we were about to infil our target locations.

I set my back flat to the brick wall on the south side, holding my Ruger while waiting for a clear path.

"This is Foxtrot One," the team leader for our SF backup said over my tactical earpiece. "Alpha Two, you have two tangos on your nine o'clock, coming in hot," he let me know.

I pushed the small button on the headset at my neck to respond, "That's a good copy." Taking a knee, I knocked my night vision back in place. I shifted around the wall and took out the two marks on my dirty side—a.k.a. the area where shots were being fired. "Tangos down."

"This is Foxtrot Two, you're clear to move, Alpha One and Two."

"Roger," my brother and I responded in unison.

Keeping my head low, still under NODs, I started for my target location.

"This is Alpha One. Three more tangos down. Entering the Rabbit Hole," my brother shared.

I held back on the *be careful* warning to my brother with two other teams on the line.

"This is Delta One," Sebastian announced a minute later. "My team, breachers up. It's a go."

"Roger," we all answered before a battery of gunfire sounded from somewhere on the property, and it wasn't coming from my point of entry, or from the March Hare's House, which was the building I was about to breach.

The League had gone with *Alice in Wonderland* as our mission theme. It somehow felt fitting, but hopefully my wife was wrong and we wouldn't be falling down any actual holes. Or in this case, tunnels.

"Alpha One, you good?"

"Four tangos down. But I have eyes on the Mad Hatter," Constantine alerted back, letting us know he had Rocco Barone in his sights. I'd prefer he have my six right now.

"Keep him alive until we get the White Rabbit. He may need to lead us to him," Sebastian popped over the line after their breaching charges went off in the distance. "This is Delta One," he continued once they successfully breached the property. "Do you copy, Alpha One?"

No response from Constantine. "Alpha One, do you copy?" I asked this time at the sound of more gunfire in the distance—*not* from Constantine's direction, at least. But the fact he was unresponsive had me barking out, "Foxtrot Three, take the March Hare's House instead. I need to head to the Rabbit Hole." Already on the move, not waiting for confirmation, I ditched my current path, needing to get to Constantine and determine why he was radio silent.

"Foxtrot Three. On it," I barely heard in my earpiece as I took down two more tangos, nearly getting clipped in the same arm that Esposito's wife shot me as I rounded a thick bank of shrubs.

"This is Foxtrot Two," overwatch began. "Alpha Two, hold position. You have a sniper waiting for you to take that next corner."

I halted and slammed my back to one of the walls of shrubs and waited for Foxtrot to handle the asshole on the long gun.

"This is Delta Two," Sean piped up over comms. "White Rabbit is on the move. Looks like he's heading to an exfil spot outside the compound. He's heavily guarded. I need backup."

"This is Delta Three. On it," Cole McGregor said.

"Alpha Two, come in. This is Foxtrot Three, you're clear to move to the Rabbit Hole. I repeat, you're clear to move."

"That's a good copy." Not wasting any more time, I flowed to the target location. "Anyone have eyes on Alpha One? On the Mad Hatter?" I asked, forgetting my call sign, but so help me, if anything happened to Constantine . . .

"Nothing," someone said from some-fucking-where over comms. I was starting to lose focus, worried I was already too late to get to Constantine.

"Entering the Rabbit Hole." No call sign again. I needed to pull it together. I knocked my NODs up when I entered the lit-up building and swapped my rifle for my Sig and knife. "Clearing the property now. No sign of Alpha One or the Mad Hatter," I said as I began clearing rooms, finding the four dead tangos my brother had mentioned, which meant I was going in the right direction.

"This is Delta One, overwatch has eyes on the White Rabbit and his men. Engaging now." Sebastian let us know he had Claudio Barone in his sights. "Still no sign of Alpha One. Delta Four and Six, move into positions."

"This is Delta Two. Alpha Team, be advised, he . . ."

I stopped listening to the chatter on comms the moment I rounded the corner and saw Rocco. And not just him. He was crouched alongside Constantine, a knife beneath my brother's throat. Constantine was slumped against the wall, head hung forward and eyes shut.

"Move and he dies," Rocco warned.

"He looks dead already." I did my best not to lose it at my words and empty an entire magazine into the bastard.

"I drugged him. He's out cold. *But* alive," Rocco sneered, not removing his eyes from me. "You know I like to play with my food first before I kill it."

I lunged forward on impulse but stopped the second he nicked my brother's neck with the blade. Standing six feet away from him, I kept my Sig trained on Rocco, unsure what the hell to do right now.

"You're not supposed to be here," Rocco said, his tone eerily calm.

"You weren't ahead of us this time. Your inside source at AISE screwed up." I tapped at my neck and shared over comms, "I have the Mad Hatter. Has the White Rabbit been neutralized?"

"Not the worst code name for me." Rocco shrugged. The sick prick. "Better than Cinderella like those asshole AISE officers called me on their op five years ago before I flipped an agent."

"The one you flipped is about to get strung up on charges and hung right along with you." *Not that I plan to let you make it out alive.*

At the slight twitch of Constantine's foot, I about choked out a breath of relief Rocco hadn't been lying about him being alive.

"This is Delta One." Sebastian finally came over the line. "The White Rabbit is down. Pulse is faint. Everyone needs to exfil now. We just got word there's a drone locked in overhead and missile capable. It's not one of ours or the Romanians'. Someone may be looking to destroy evidence."

At the news, I hissed to Rocco, "Who hired you to start another conflict in Afghanistan? Get them on the phone and tell them to stand down. They're about to kill you with a drone strike."

"And kill you and your brother. I guess we all go down." The look in his eyes betrayed his casual tone. He didn't want to die.

"Russian oligarch," he grunted out, his chest heaving from a deep sigh of all fucking things right now. "He's not going to back down if I call." He looked toward the hallway behind me, as if contemplating a way out that wouldn't involve capture or death.

"Alpha One, Alpha Two: you're the last ones in there. Evac immediately," Sebastian rushed out that time. "We have incoming. Sixty seconds out. Do you copy?"

I could shoot Rocco and hope to kill him before he slit my brother's throat, but I'd never be able to drag Constantine out in time with a missile already locked on to us.

"Such a fucking dilemma," Rocco said, pushing the knife closer to Constantine's jugular. "You either ask for my help to get you two out or leave your brother here to die so you can make a run for it."

"Forty seconds," Sebastian said into my ear, and I shook my head and lowered my Sig to my side. I'd never clear the compound with Constantine in time.

"Working on a way out," I told Sebastian, not taking the time to announce myself first. "What's your backup exit plan?" I asked Rocco, unsure if I could believe him, but at this point, I had no choice but to take my chances.

"Not sure if we'll find our way out of the maze, but it's better than getting blown to fucking pieces, right?"

"Tunnels," I said under my breath. But if his old man hadn't gone to them for an escape plan, that meant they weren't exactly user friendly and hadn't been operated by anyone on-site in recent years—something my wife had mentioned. "Help me with him." It took every part of me to ask that. Even if Rocco removed the knife from beneath Constantine's throat, I wouldn't be able to shoot him until I knew where the alleged tunnel entrance was, and he'd anticipate that move.

"Weapons down. Same time. All of them," he ordered. "You can fight me once we're underground, don't worry."

I set aside the Sig and knife, then quickly went for the rifle sling and removed the Ruger. "We're out of time. We need to go."

A flash of hesitation crossed his face, but he tossed the knife.

I hurried to Constantine, kicked away his rifle resting near his limp body that Rocco had opted not to take for whatever reason, then tossed my brother's sidearm, too.

"Let's go," I directed to Rocco now that we were *all* weaponless, and we hoisted Constantine from under his armpits to drag him to safety with us.

Well, I sure as hell hoped to safety.

I met Rocco's eyes, both of us sweating and breathing hard, and we began down the hall. I let the motherfucker who once tortured

Constantine lead the way, uncertain if he was leading us all to our deaths.

"There," Rocco remarked, lifting his chin to point the direction we had to go—through a narrow and dark passageway.

I quickly knocked my NODs back in place so I could use my night vision to see in the dark, then grabbed hold of my brother with both hands and crouched even lower to fit through the snug entrance.

The fact Rocco hadn't taken off on his own for his freedom once I was weaponless meant he had plans that involved keeping us alive.

"Ten seconds, why don't I see you two yet?" Sebastian rasped over comms, not identifying himself.

I didn't have time to think through what would happen next, or to answer Sebastian and tell him the plan, because the ground rumbled, and the regret I never told Calliope I loved her was the last thing on my mind before everything went dark.

CHAPTER THIRTY-NINE

Calliope

Oyster Bay, Long Island

My aunt was safe. Hudson and his team were fine. And the corrupt AISE agent had been arrested.

But nothing from my husband.

Not a word.

Holding my phone while waiting for him to call, I continued to pace the living room alone, unsure where everyone else was, but I knew no one was asleep. It was after midnight here but daylight now in Romania.

"Come on." I checked my phone again. His last message to me had been three hours ago. Three freaking hours. He'd said he'd be on a plane within two.

When I looked up, catching sight of Izzy and her mother standing at the edge of the room with tears in their eyes and pale faces, my phone slipped from my hand.

"What happened?" I asked as Enzo and his father joined us.

"We finally spoke to The League," Enzo said, his voice strained, and when he came farther into the room, his bloodshot eyes had me taking two steps back.

"What?" The word rattled free between my clenched teeth, and my hands knotted at my sides.

"Constantine and Alessandro were still inside the compound when a missile took out . . . took out the . . ." Enzo slammed his hand over his mouth, unable to finish, and I couldn't connect the dots that were left hanging in the air.

"No." I whipped my hands up and pushed the words away instead. Jedi'd them right to hell.

When my mother-in-law turned to Izzy and began sobbing, Izzy hugged her, and that officially destroyed me. Cut my legs from under me, and I fell to my knees, then to all fours. Searching for air. For life. For a reason to want to keep breathing.

"We don't know anything for certain," Mr. Costa snapped out.

I lifted my chin to see Enzo's long jeaned legs before me. "What do we know?"

"Sebastian and his people are searching for them, even though it's still . . . Well, the fires aren't all out yet. Before the missile struck, Alessandro had said he was working on finding a way out, but Sebastian doesn't think he found one." Enzo crouched closer to eye level. "He believes whoever hired the Barones to start up a new conflict in the Middle East was alerted to the compound breach, and they had eyes on the place and a contingency plan: take out the compound to destroy the evidence." I had no clue how he was remaining so steady. So focused on my eyes without crying himself as he got through answering me.

"But maybe he did make it out but couldn't tell him?" I blinked back tears of denial.

Enzo reached for my shoulder and bowed his head, and his chest broke forward with movement as if he were about to lose it. He brought his other fist over his mouth while closing his eyes. "They were definitely inside. Their teammates had eyes on the property just before the missile strike. They didn't make it out. At least not aboveground." At that, he let go of me and pushed upright.

I forced myself to sit, falling back on my heels. My eyes fell to the rings on my finger. "Alessandro said the Barones were always ahead of . . ." Where was I going with this? I looked up at their father, who was still standing like a statue of shock. "The Barones would have an escape plan, wouldn't they? Somehow The League must not have known about it." My hand went to my stomach, and now wasn't the time to throw up, dammit.

"I want to think that," Enzo said, facing me again while thumbing away tears. He looked over at his mom and sister still crying. "It's the one time I want to believe they were one step ahead of us . . . but why hasn't anyone reached out?"

"Unless the research I sent them was right? What if . . . ?" I thought back to my research. "Constanţa is one of their oldest seaports, and, um, during the Romanian War of Independence, to break from the Ottomans, there were elaborate tunnels built all over the city, leading to the sea to help bring troops and supplies."

Mr. Costa finally budged from his fixed position, coming over to offer his hand. I allowed him to help me rise. I wasn't sure if Alessandro had filled them in on my research, or just his team back in Romania—but considering how Enzo was looking at me like I'd lost it, I doubted they knew.

"During World War One, the tunnels were used again," I continued, refusing to believe I was grasping at straws. No, Alessandro and his brother had made it out; there had to be tunnels. No other option was acceptable. "What if the Barones chose that location for a reason?"

"The League had the architectural blueprints. Nothing listed there about tunnels in any of their research. They had eyes on them the whole time. If that were the case, Claudio Barone would've gone underground instead of risking heading toward the sea, where a team was waiting to intercept him," Enzo said, *nearly* shooting down my hope.

"But it's possible," I whispered.

Enzo frowned, but then looked at his father for direction on what to say. To do.

"Alessandro's stubborn. So is Constantine." Mr. Costa turned his attention on me. "No way will some missile strike be what takes them out."

"Dad," Izzy began, her tone somber, as if worried he was getting ahead of himself, "they're not indestructible. I know you like to think that, but—"

"They are," he hissed back at her, and that one tear gliding down his cheek had me falling to the floor again.

◆ ◆ ◆

Six Hours Later

Constantine's face filled the iPad screen his mother held, and he demanded, "Where's Alessandro?"

Constantine was okay, but . . .

Chills scattered across my skin as Constantine tugged at the wires connected to his body, trying to remove the IV. Two nurses rushed to his side, speaking in another language—presumably Romanian—begging him to stop.

"Where. Is. He?" he hissed, one eye swollen shut. His head was wrapped as if he'd taken a blow there. One arm bandaged up, too.

"You were in surgery, sir. You need to calm down," the nurse said, switching to English.

Enzo was already gone. The second he'd learned Alessandro was missing, he took off for the airport.

"Just tell me where my brother is," Constantine barked out, setting his focus once again on the screen. When he visibly relaxed, I had to assume someone had upped his morphine drip to calm him down. His head rolled back, hitting the pillow. "Where is he?" he asked, groggily that time. "I was fighting Rocco . . . and then the fucker jabbed something in my neck. Next thing I know, I'm here. So what the hell happened after that?" He didn't peer around the room for answers, only looked at us over the screen, so I had to assume none of his other teammates were there.

No, they'd be trying to track down Alessandro.

"We think Rocco has him," Izzy whispered, the first to break the quiet on our side. "Sebastian found you, unconscious, just inside an entrance to an old underground tunnel network."

"There was a missile strike," Mr. Costa added, his throat thick with emotion. "The League believes the Russians—well, an oligarch—hired the Barones to start the war, and they had an armed drone on standby in case of . . ." He let Constantine fill in the blanks.

At this point, I'd cried so much, I was dehydrated and was pretty sure I'd temporarily lost the ability to produce tears.

"Alessandro was with you before you were drugged," Mr. Costa continued, clearly doing his best to keep it together. One of us had to, I supposed.

"What do you mean?" Constantine sputtered. "Callie's research was right?"

Yeah, it was. But from the looks of it, the tunnels aren't exactly usable anymore. Probably not used in a hundred years. I couldn't get those words out, though. Because I couldn't tell him what he wanted to hear—what I needed to hear, too. That Alessandro was safe.

"The League said the tunnels are a mess. Parts appear to have collapsed and caved in decades ago," Izzy shared in a timid tone. "They could still be down there, though. There's a search underway."

Constantine's red eyes became glossy as he put it together, and his free hand curled into a fist atop his chest. "What you're saying is you have no clue where Alessandro is?"

"There were signs a body was dragged away from where Sebastian found you." Izzy revealed more details that Sebastian had shared with us. "The trail stopped after about a hundred feet. But they're looking. They won't give up. They'll find him."

"That means . . ." Constantine closed his eyes. "Rocco has my brother. He took him instead of me. Must've drugged him, too, and you know how Alessandro reacts to drugs." A few tears slid down his cheeks.

"I'm relieved you're okay," Izzy said, her voice hitching, "but that surprised me, too, given your history together."

"He did it to torture me. Because losing my brother hurts more than whatever physical pain he could put me through." Constantine opened his eyes. "I'm sorry, Callie." He searched me out on screen. "I couldn't protect him. I failed . . . again."

"Don't say that," Mrs. Costa cried, setting her hand on the screen as if she could physically comfort her son. "You didn't fail, and we'll find him."

"If Rocco gets him out of that tunnel, he'll go off the grid," Constantine rasped. "Tell me they kept someone alive from the compound to torture for information. Claudio?"

"Claudio didn't survive. Died being medevaced to the hospital." Izzy gave him the bad news. "And only one man from his team made it, and he's a foot soldier. Doesn't know anything."

"What about the op in Oslo? Successful?" Constantine asked, a touch of optimism there. "Anyone there know where Rocco may try and take Alessandro?"

"Mission success, but Rocco's men died. No one there to help us," Izzy told him.

"I need to get out of this bed. Help search for him. I know how that fucker thinks." Constantine tried once again to detach himself from wires, but it didn't take much effort for the nurses to pin him back down.

"Son, every intelligence agency on that side of the hemisphere has Rocco on their radar now. The second they make it out of the tunnel, if they haven't already, and Rocco shows his face on any CCTV footage, they'll lock on to him and follow the trail," Mr. Costa said, and I wanted to immerse myself in the same kind of optimism, but . . . "Keeping Alessandro alive is Rocco's insurance policy. He's his hostage."

"They'll find him." Izzy's turn to be the confident one. "Enzo's already on a plane, heading there to help."

"Tell Enzo to pick me up the second he arrives." Constantine lifted his hands and pushed at the air. "Don't argue with me. I can walk out of here now. I'm fine."

"But The League—"

"Doesn't know Rocco like I do," Constantine cut off Izzy. "I'm not losing more family. Are we clear?"

I stepped back from the screen, hating how helpless I felt. I'd begged Enzo to take me with him, but I'd been shot down. Same for Izzy.

Constantine shifted his attention to his father. "There's something else you're not telling me. What is it?"

I exchanged a look with Izzy, and she focused back on the screen and told him, "Armani heard Alessandro is missing and possibly"—Izzy paused—"dead or in Rocco's custody. He's already en route to New York with Marcello. He's coming for Callie to take her home."

"We're not letting him take her," Mr. Costa said before Constantine could object. "Gabriel wanted to help search for Alessandro, but at this news, he's escorting Callie's aunt to New York, and so he can deal with the Armani situation."

I'd spoken to my aunt briefly, murmured a few apologies, but I'd been too much of a mess to carry on any real conversation. Until Alessandro was okay, I couldn't think about anything else. "I'm not your problem. All I care about is that you find Alessandro." Unsure if I could handle staying in the room any longer without another breakdown, I started for the hall, but Mr. Costa blocked the door.

"You're family. My daughter." He reached for my arm. "My son's wife. That means I'll protect you with my own life."

"Listen to him," Constantine said. I jolted at his deep voice and slowly turned toward the room. He'd sounded just like Alessandro then. "If Armani tries to take her, kill him, Dad. Fuck the plan to pin his death on someone else."

My eyes went wide at his order. "No, his people will come after you for revenge. And you don't need that, especially not now. Please, don't do this. Not for me." Before I could plead some more not to make any sacrifices for me, my phone chimed from a new message.

I grabbed it from the pocket of my sweatpants, prepared to ignore whoever it was.

Unknown number: *Video*

"What is it?" my father-in-law asked, and I supposed it was okay to think of him as Dad, because I refused to believe Alessandro was gone. He'd be back. *So yeah, Dad it is.* "Open it," he prompted.

The blood drained from my face at the image visible behind the play button of the video.

No talking. No sound at all in the clip. Only Alessandro on the ground—*but* he was alive. *Out* of the tunnel, because he was on a bed of leaves, surrounded by trees. Still in his military clothes, but his face . . . he was lying there, banged up. Wrists and ankles bound. Mouth gagged.

He had to have given Rocco my number, but I knew he wouldn't want me to see him like this, so the asshole must've forced him to do it.

"What is it?" Constantine asked.

"A video of Alessandro tied up, but he's alive and they're not in the tunnel anymore," I said, surprised my voice worked. When I looked at my father-in-law, he appeared to be . . . Well, this broke him. *This* was what broke him.

"He's doing this to fuck with me," Constantine hissed. "Screw with us all. Let us know Alessandro's alive but that *he's* in control."

"Call Sebastian," their dad ordered, probably to Izzy. "Tell him they're out and in the forest."

I shivered, my eyes shooting back to my phone. I was about to replay the short clip, but my father-in-law took the phone from my hand.

"Location and timestamp are turned off on the video details, but we'll try and trace this anyway," he said a moment later.

"I want to see him again." I held open my palm. He nodded and handed back the phone, and I pressed play.

All I could focus on were Alessandro's eyes.

"Is he signaling something to us?" my father-in-law asked.

I zoomed in to see Alessandro subtly lifting his bound wrists near his heart, and with his finger he was tracing something there.

"I think so," I whispered as I put it together. Then choked out, "X squared."

CHAPTER FORTY

Calliope

"Still nothing from The League about Alessandro?" Gabriel asked as he entered the Costas' front living room, where Izzy and I had been waiting for him. All it felt like I'd been doing since we'd lost contact with Alessandro fourteen hours ago was wait. Now there we were, waiting for the reason we were in this mess to arrive and for Armani to try and whisk me away.

"Unfortunately nothing new," Izzy told him.

I admired her and how she managed to package her emotions up inside and hide them so neatly when necessary. Or maybe that was a survival mechanism, because before Alessandro took down my walls, I'd been that girl, too. I had known how to conceal my thoughts and feelings behind well-placed smiles and perfectly timed laughs.

"How's my aunt? She doing okay?" On my feet, I joined Izzy in the face-off she was in with Gabriel.

She blamed him for bringing Armani into their lives, but I knew she wouldn't say it out loud because my marriage was the by-product of his decision, and she was happy about that part.

"She wanted to come here, as you predicted, but she's at your place in the city with two of Javier's men." He checked his gold watch.

"Armani and Marcello will be here within fifteen minutes, so we need to figure out next steps."

"You're kidding me, right? You didn't think of next steps on your flight from Oslo?" Izzy fixed her arms across her chest, whereas mine remained like useless rubbery limbs dangling at my sides. "Your intelligence buddies didn't come up with a plan to keep DiMaggio off our backs?" The bite to her tone was like a gravitational pull, drawing my gaze her way.

"They were a little tied up taking down the Russian who'd been trying to start a war." He matched her posture and her guarded stance. "You know, the same one who dropped a missile on your brother."

"So they found the man responsible?" That'd be one less thing to worry about, if so, but until Alessandro was safe, nothing else truly mattered.

Gabriel gave me his eyes for a split second and nodded before returning to the staring contest my sister-in-law was having with him.

"AISE wants to try and turn Armani instead of killing him," Gabriel revealed. "I don't think that's a good idea, though."

I agreed with him on that. "He's dying. He'll never betray his organization."

"We need to find a way to kill him," Gabriel said, like a declaration of war. "Since we can't blame Rocco for his death, we have to pin it on Marcello."

"How would we do that?" Izzy asked.

My rag-doll arms decided to become rigid in that moment and lock across my chest. Now we were all in defensive positions, like we were enemies instead of on the same side.

"Calliope, is how. We bait Marcello into going after her, and I think Armani will try and save her." Gabriel acted as though the "her" in question wasn't in the room, dammit, but I was right freaking there. "If we do this right, Armani gets killed in the cross fire."

"You're kidding, right? My brother would put his hands around your throat for even suggesting something like that if he were here."

Izzy unfolded her arms, set her palms on his chest, and pushed, but he didn't budge.

"But he's not here." Gabriel's words were both the silver bullet and the stake to the heart that'd turn me to dust.

I whirled away from them both, panic mode setting in as I dove my hands through my tangled hair.

"This plan can work, I know it," Gabriel went on, despite my borderline meltdown on the way. "Armani will sacrifice himself to save his bloodline."

I bent forward and dropped my hands to my thighs, trying to remember how to breathe properly so I didn't faint.

"And if Marcello winds up killing Calliope?" Izzy cut over to me and began rubbing her palm in small circles on my back.

"Hidden armor beneath a hoodie. It'll hurt if she's shot, but she won't die," Gabriel said casually, and I had a feeling this wasn't him talking. These were his marching orders from Italian Intelligence. "The choice is yours, Calliope."

Forcing myself to stand upright, my hand went to the column of my throat, unsure if I could get a *yes* to come out.

"What's it going to be?" The kindness in his eyes remained despite what he was asking of me. "Are you helping us take out your father, or not?"

"I know, and I'm sorry." I raced my hand along the spines of the books in the library, stopping at the sight of *The Odyssey* there as I talked on the phone to my aunt.

The story of Scylla and Charybdis popped back into my head, and I cringed and closed my eyes.

"Keeping everything a secret was the lesser of two evils." That was a phrase I wanted to erase from memory. "I thought so, at least. But because of me, you were placed in harm's way."

"You think I care about myself?" Aunt Tia said in an exasperated tone. "I could have helped you."

"You mean have your friends from Kentucky take us away, and we'd have to hide forever? Not what either of us wanted." I opened my eyes, backing away from the wall of books. "You're only fifty-five, by the way. You have your whole life ahead of you, too. Maybe everything happens for a reason, though. I can only say that now since you're okay and, well, because I know in my heart Alessandro will be, too." *He has to be.*

"They'll get him back. But right now, you need to focus on what's coming with Armani."

"I know." Not that she knew exactly what was coming—that I'd be placing myself in danger in the hope that Marcello snapped and Armani chose to protect me. But my husband's life was on the line because of me, so I'd do what was necessary to protect his family now. It was my turn to step up.

Before she could summon whatever it was she'd planned to say next, I spied my father-in-law in the doorway. I quickly wrapped up the call and tried not to show my nerves when I choked out an *I love you* before hanging up.

"You know," my father-in-law began once I'd set aside my phone, "this was my daughter's bedroom. My wife converted it to a library since Bianca loved to read and write."

I wanted to offer my condolences a hundred times over for his loss, and to promise he wouldn't lose another child, but when he closed *and* locked the door, my lips sealed together, trapping the words behind them.

"I'd never let my daughter do what you offered to do." The deep frown lines were only a hint at the true pain beneath the surface. "And my son would never forgive me for it."

"What are you saying?" I whispered, struggling to turn up the volume while talking.

"Gabriel's been *mafioso* too long. He may work for AISE now, but he's not one of us. If he was, he'd never suggest you place yourself in danger. Or for you to help kill your own father."

He reached behind his back, and at the sight of a 9mm, my nerves bested me and corrupted my ability to think clearly.

Danger gleamed wickedly in his hand, a sharp contrast to his calming tone as he said, "Your father would win if you helped take his life. That light of yours is bright. It'll be extinguished if you personally help kill Armani. And it'd destroy my son to see that happen." Erasing the space between us, he rested a hand on my shoulder. "We'll get my son back, but I will not tell him I let you risk your life to murder your father."

"What choice do we have?" I was choking back a sob, though, because he was right. Risk taking a bullet to keep Alessandro and his family from danger? Yes. But I didn't have it in me to help kill someone, especially not someone who shared my blood, even if I hated the man. "You can't kill him. I know Constantine said—"

"No one is dying today." His hand slipped free from my shoulder, and he quietly reached into his pocket for his phone. "Well, hopefully not."

"How, then?"

Facing the wall of books, he asked me in a somber tone, "Did my son tell you what happened after his sister died?"

I swallowed. "Yes."

He kept his eyes on the bookshelves. "I did everything in my power to save my sons so they didn't wind up behind bars or dead. Although I know your father doesn't know you well, I do believe Gabriel's right in that he'll do what it takes to protect you, not just for the sake of his bloodline."

"Because it's what you'd do?"

"It's what any father who gives a damn would do." His shoulders dropped as if the weight were too much to bear. "I've been working on a plan. I was waiting to get confirmation it was a go, so Gabriel was unaware I'd set the wheels in motion before his arrival here."

"What, um, wheels?"

He faced me, and I knew he was every bit as emotional as I was, but like Izzy, he hid it well. "I called in a favor to the CIA director, urging him to call in a favor to AISE." He checked the time on his phone. "An FBI SWAT team will arrest your father and his men when they get here."

My body shuddered. "Wait. How's that an option now, and it wasn't before?"

"I need you to trust me, okay?" His eyes narrowed as he waited for confirmation, so I nodded. "We don't need to risk your life for Armani to sacrifice his, but he can still *think* he's saving you."

Attempting to chase away my chills, I rubbed my arms.

"You'll be arrested today, too." He let his words sink in before continuing. "And then AISE will offer him a deal. Your freedom and immunity in exchange for him to talk. He knows he's dying. He'll accept the offer to keep you out of jail in the hope that you can run the organization in his absence."

"Oh." The chills journeyed from my arms straight down my torso to my legs.

He swiped at his phone screen, opening an app. "You're going to hear and see a lot out there in a minute. Just go with it. I don't have time to explain it now, but it's all part of the plan, I promise." He shared the screen with me, revealing exterior security footage of the property.

Two unmarked vehicles were driving toward the front of the house. As the first one neared, I recognized Frankie behind the wheel, which meant Armani was most likely inside with him.

"My wife and Izzy are waiting in a secure location inside the home. Unfortunately, I do need to keep you upstairs for Armani to witness our arrests as well."

"To make it less suspicious that we're framing him?"

He nodded, then motioned toward the door with his gun. "But I'm keeping you back here until the Feds have Armani and Marcello pinned down and unarmed. I don't want to risk you getting caught in the cross fire if they return fire. I don't think they will, but I'd rather not take chances."

Yeah, same.

"Next, the Feds will come for us as planned and walk us out cuffed, too." He lifted his free hand, an apology in his eyes as he added, "I'm so sorry to do that to you, but it'll keep you safe."

I looked back at the app, seeing Frankie opening the door for Armani. "Why are you being arrested, too?"

"Because for the sake of appearances, when you married my son, we became in league with the DiMaggios. Armani can't have any doubts who was behind his arrest. He can't think it was our doing."

I reached for his forearm. "I don't want you having to do this."

"You're my son's wife. That makes you family. And we stick together, got it?" He peered at me, a sad look in his eyes. "But don't worry, my family will be cleared of any wrongdoing."

Tears gathered in my eyes, and I let him go to try and get rid of them.

"It's time," he said.

I looked at the security app as multiple vehicles made their approach, a blur of red and blue flashing lights, converging on Armani's parked SUVs.

Uncertain what Armani would do, I waited with a hand over my mouth. "He's not resisting arrest." At that realization, relief swelled in my chest, and my palm slipped back to my side.

I thought Marcello would be a question mark and fight back, but I could read the command on Armani's lips to back off.

"Was that too easy?" I whispered.

"This isn't their first time being arrested. He's used to this," he shared calmly. "But it'll be his first time not being released, like normal." At the sound of steps in the hallway growing closer, he quietly pocketed his phone and unlocked the door. Two men in uniform, along with a man in a suit, were there waiting for us.

The suit gave my father-in-law a subtle nod as he accepted his 9mm. "Cuff them," he ordered the uniformed officers.

Here we go. Never in a million years had I envisioned a moment like this in my life, that I'd be handcuffed.

My heart thundered in my chest as we were walked to the front of the house. The moment the door swung open and Armani saw me, he attempted to stand from where he'd been kneeling by the SWAT vehicle.

"Let her go," Armani snarled, and two SWAT team members swooped in and shoved him back down. "She's innocent." I wasn't sure if he genuinely gave a damn about me, but it didn't matter. He wasn't a good guy, and I'd never forget that.

The man in the suit removed what looked like a thumb drive from his pocket as we neared where Armani, Marcello, and now Gabriel were on their knees on the driveway. Leo and Frankie, along with two of Armani's other men, were cuffed as well.

"Take them all in for questioning. See if the Costas are working with this asshole or not," the Suit said, directing us closer to the squad cars and swarm of officers. "But you," he went on, eyes on Armani, "are going to prison for the rest of your life once you're back in Italy." He waved the thumb drive near Armani's face, then looked over at Marcello as if sending Armani a message, letting him know who betrayed him.

"It wasn't me. He's lying," Marcello hissed, eyes going wide with alarm.

We stopped walking, but the uniformed officer kept hold of me at his side as we watched the scene unfold, and I had to remind myself this was all part of the plan.

"Marcello is right in a way. He didn't give AISE the evidence on this drive," the Suit said. "But your right-hand man has been feeding intel to the Barone family for years, and he was plotting to have your daughter marry into that family. He had a backdoor deal with them to run your company once Rocco married your daughter. But things went sideways, didn't they?" He shook his head. "Rocco sold you out, Marcello. A last-ditch effort to try and save himself after his father was killed."

That was definitely a lie. Aside from the one video Rocco sent, no one had heard from him since. As long as Armani believed it, though, that was all that mattered.

"Because of your deal with Rocco, you wound up betraying yourself and your boss." The Suit pocketed the thumb drive. "Take them away. All of them."

"You lying son of a bitch." Marcello attempted to stand, then his eyes shot to me. "This is your fault. You fucking bitch. You were sup-posed to die in the park that day, then none of this would've happened."

Armani twisted around, struggling with the uniforms holding him back, peering at the traitor. "You're dead, you hear me. You're dead. You won't survive a day behind bars," he barked out to Marcello.

A rush of adrenaline shot through me as I watched the two try to go at each other only to be pulled farther apart.

"I'll get you out of this," were Armani's last words to me before he was nudged inside a different vehicle than Marcello.

I gave him a little nod as if I truly gave a shit about what he'd said, then he nodded back and disappeared behind the door.

Once I was inside the back of a different SUV alongside my father-in-law, the Suit joined us in the front seat, then twisted around to look at us. "We'll get you uncuffed the second you're out of your father's sight at the office. I'm sorry about the cuffs."

"What was really on that thumb drive?" my father-in-law asked him.

The Suit smirked. "The first ten chapters of a book I've been writing." He faced forward as I spied Gabriel being pushed inside another SUV.

"Are you sure this will all work out?" I closed my eyes, my mind racing. I did my best to keep myself together, knowing this wasn't truly over yet, not until Alessandro was safe and Rocco was behind bars or dead.

But this piece of my life—this disaster—was it finally over?

The Suit looked at me again. "Let's just say you're lucky to have a family like the Costas in your corner."

"And we'll get your husband back," my father-in-law said in a low voice. "I'm not losing another child, that much I can promise you."

CHAPTER
FORTY-ONE

Calliope

Six Days Later

I stared in a daze at the "30" on the vanilla-frosted cake. "Cake?" *Cake? Really?* My eyes sealed shut as I revisited the last six days since I'd been paraded through the FBI's New York field office for the purpose of Armani and the others believing I was in danger of being detained for life.

My father-in-law and I were discreetly let go after Armani was processed, and negotiations between Armani and AISE were underway now that Armani was back in Italy.

The Costas had been cleared of any involvement, of course. Gabriel and Leo were still behind bars for the sake of appearances for the time being. And Marcello never made it to Italy, or even to the next morning.

All that mattered to me right now, though, was that my husband was still missing. Seven days without him. And day by day, I was slowly losing it.

"Callie." My aunt murmured my name, and I opened my eyes. She swapped a sad look with my mother-in-law. I was seconds away from taking the cake from the counter and throwing it against the bay window in the kitchen, hating the sun shining down over the water, making it sparkle. Hating everything because my husband was gone. So screw cake and sunshine.

My aunt rounded the kitchen island, reading me well enough to know I was having another breakdown. I'd lost count of how many times I'd broken down that week.

Javier had brought my aunt to stay with us only after Armani and his main guys were no longer in the US and were with Italian police.

Izzy and her father had spent all week focusing on the search for Alessandro, contacting everyone they knew for help in locating him. My only contribution had been to find a Romanian history expert who knew all about the old tunnels, and he'd offered up possible exit points as to where Rocco and Alessandro may have escaped.

With the historian's help, The League managed to track the exact location where the video had been taken in the woods near one of the tunnels' exits. Professional K9 trackers were brought in and sniffed out the spot, finding Alessandro's blood there.

My aunt hugged me, but my arms remained limp at my sides as she whispered, "I'm so sorry. I thought you could use a distraction after all you went through this week. It's your birthday, after all."

It had been nice having her there, but between her and my mother-in-law channeling their fears and nervous energy by cooking nonstop—and force-feeding Javier and his men—I was just done, ready to tap out.

"I probably smell," was the unrelated brilliance that came from my mouth as I tried to unglue myself from her hold. "I've showered maybe twice this week." Spent most days in the same pair of singing cherries PJs Javier's men had packed for me. "It's Alessandro's birthday, too." That was what bothered me most about the cake. "A four should be here instead." I pointed at the candles on the cake. "He's forty today."

My mother-in-law quietly opened a drawer, took something out, then came back over. She placed a "4" and "0" next to the "30." "For when he's back. We'll wait."

"I'm so sorry," I apologized to her. "The hell you're going through and yet staying so strong somehow, and I'm a mess and can't keep it together. I just need a minute alone." I hurried for the hallway before anyone could stop me. The second I was in Alessandro's old room, I shut the door, threw myself on his bed, brought my nose to his pillow, and inhaled.

I'd found cologne on the dresser, so I'd sprayed it on the pillows, my pathetic attempt at pretending he was with me when I slept. I'd never heard of the brand Creed before this week. It was a different cologne than the one he kept on the vanity counter at the penthouse. There was a guy riding a horse next to the name Aventus on the label; it somehow felt perfect for Alessandro, and I'd latch on to anything "him" I could get right now.

"Mrs. Costa?" someone called out before I'd even had a chance to wedge a pillow between my legs and curl into the fetal position.

"Wrong room," I called back, recognizing Javier's voice, tightening my hold on the pillow.

"*Callie* Costa," he corrected. "Can I talk to you?"

"Do you know where my husband is?"

"No, but I'd like to see you anyway."

"Yeah, okay." I couldn't be a jerk to the guy, who'd been kind to me for four weeks. He'd also helped distract my aunt by allowing her to feed him a "taste of the South," as she'd called it. They were both single and in their fifties; if my world didn't feel like it was ending right now, I'd be the one playing matchmaker between them.

The door cracked open, and it wasn't until I abandoned the pillow and sat upright that he came in.

At the sight of the familiar guitar case in his hand, I sputtered, "Why do you have that?"

He set it on the bed. "Alessandro said that if he didn't make it back, to give you this on your birthday."

"No," I shot back, staring at The Legend's guitar my husband had said he'd give away our first night in New York. Clearly, he hadn't listened. "He's coming home."

"Of course he is, but it's your birthday, and an order is an order. So here it is."

"I hate him for doing this," I whispered, crying as I went to my knees and opened the case. Inside was a handwritten note from him, too.

Calliope,

"Storms make trees take deeper roots."—I had to look that one up. Dolly Parton's a wise woman. I see why you like her and her music.

And I promise you, we'll get through this storm together. Even if I'm not there with you . . . I'm there with you, you know?

Love, your husband—a royal pain in your ass, just like you're a pain in mine.

Alessandro

P.S.—You don't really hate me, and you know it.

The note fell from my hand when Izzy flew into the room and yelled, "They found him! Well, they found Rocco, at least."

"Where is he?" I stood, trembling with shock, and Javier hooked his arm with mine for support.

"They caught Rocco on CCTV footage in Slobozia earlier today. Looks like they're still in Romania. Crazy enough, they ID'd him while walking by a car from the reflection in the passenger-side mirror. Once they had the location, they were able to track him to an abandoned-looking home outside the city. There are civilians in the area, so they have to be extra cautious when they move in. Plus make sure they're not being—"

"Set up," I finished, my nerves getting to me again.

"My brothers and Hudson are moving into position. A quiet approach from the front and back. There's a basement there, so they think that's where Alessandro's being kept." She gestured for me to get a move on. "We're heading to the airport now. Enzo had our other jet sent back the other day in case we needed it."

"Wait, we're going? Finally?" I went for the buttons on my PJs, anxious to change.

"Assuming my brother needs to go to the hospital after, we should—"

"Of course," I blurted, then stopped the job of finishing unbuttoning at the realization of what I was doing in front of others. "But Javier, will you stay here and watch my aunt? I know the government said we're no longer in danger, but just in case?"

He nodded, then reached for the note from the bed and set it in my palm before curling my fingers over it. "Go get your husband back."

CHAPTER FORTY-TWO

Alessandro

Unknown Location

I lifted my chin, flashing Rocco a dark smile, but it took all my energy to do so.

My brothers and I had been trained by the best of the best years ago to withstand torture and interrogation without giving up intel. Rocco couldn't break Constantine, and he wouldn't break me when he tried now.

It was my first time seeing him since he'd drugged and dragged me out of the tunnels. He'd had his men watching over me while he was off doing whatever the fuck it was, and I sure as hell hadn't missed the bastard. But I was starting to lose track of time. Had it been five days or seven since he'd had his men tie me up in an empty basement somewhere?

"Go fuck yourself," I finally said in response to the question he'd asked me three times and I'd yet to answer.

"How about I fuck you instead?" Rocco crouched in front of me and set a hand on my knee. "Too bad your wife is my type." He patted my thigh. "Bet my cock would feel great in both her pussy and ass. Mmm, in her mouth, too."

I kept quiet, knowing that'd irritate him even more. He wanted me to lash out, but there wasn't a chance I'd let him near Calliope, which meant she'd be safe from this asshole.

"I suppose if you want something done right, you have to do it yourself." He yelled out in Russian instead of his native Italian tongue, and one of the four men who'd been trying to wear me down appeared at the bottom of the staircase.

They exchanged a few heated words. Reprimands, from the sounds of it, since his guys had been unsuccessful in beating me down to the point of submission for Rocco.

Starvation. Hosed. Waterboarding. Nothing I couldn't handle that those fuckers had brought to the table.

But Rocco? He was on another level of fuck-around-and-find-out when it came to torture, and I hated to admit I was so worn out I could barely hold up my head.

Rocco knew people were hunting him, so whatever money and other assets he'd presumably been securing while gone that week would get him only so far. Keeping me alive was his insurance policy.

Rocco snickered at something the Russian said, but I'd roughly translated that last directive to him, and it goddamn terrified me.

Drugs. He'd ordered him to grab the drugs. My weakness. My fucking kryptonite. It was how he'd gotten Calliope's new cell number from me after he'd taken a video. I barely remembered being carted away and tossed into the bed of a truck before waking in this basement.

Rocco removed his jacket and began working up his sleeves, revealing snake tattoos on both arms.

The Russian returned a moment later with a syringe, and I offered the man a chance to switch sides again, same as I'd been doing all week. "Stick with him, and he'll get you killed. Ransom me for millions and pocket the cash instead," I proposed, but same as before, he rejected me. So even as tired as I was, I couldn't give up, and I switched targets to Rocco. "Your dad is locked up or dead. And all you were to him was a soldier. Not the brains behind any op. Just a killer. You won't be able to survive without him."

Rocco traced his fingertip down my chest, and if I'd had food in me, I would've puked on him for setting a hand on me.

"I'm your only leverage. Your ticket to freedom," I added, doing my best to suck it up and keep going.

"You're worth more to me alive than dead. But you know I don't want you for money. When the time comes, you'll be useful to me. For now, I'll do what these men couldn't and break you." His hand went to my forearm, and he rested the tip of the needle there.

"My brothers won't stop looking for me."

"I'm going to screw your wife right in front of you," he said with a sadistic smile, then pushed the tip of the needle down against the vein inside my arm, breaking the skin. He held off on emptying the fuckery into my bloodstream, though. "Spread her cunt open with my tongue. Lick her from asshole to slit. Shove my cock in her mouth. And you're going to get off watching me fuck every one of her holes. You won't be able to help it."

My hands were bound together behind the chair, and on reflex, I tried to break free—forgetting this was part of his game, letting him win.

Then my eyes rolled up and my head lolled forward, body feeling like deadweight, and gravity pulled me down.

All I could see were his shoes where he stood before me while chucking the needle on the concrete floor.

"So as I was asking—" He stopped talking for some reason.

Maybe I just stopped listening.

But there was sound coming from somewhere.

What was that?

Russian being yelled now. Well, maybe.

I could've been hallucinating.

Then came the gunfire—a welcome sound right now, even if I'd lost my mind and was imagining everything.

I forced open my eyes and looked up, not realizing they'd even closed at some point. The drugs were too strong, defeating me from the inside out.

"Seems your brothers want to play, too," was all I heard Rocco say before my eyes closed again, and my head lolled forward, too heavy to keep up.

I wasn't sure how much time had passed between the shots being fired and the grunts and movements that seemed to echo all around me before I heard, "Alessandro, it's us."

My hands . . . are they being untied? My eyes closed. Opened. Closed again. *Fuck this drug.*

"Take this." Was that Hudson?

A Glock now rested on my palm as someone started to help me up. I looked over to see two men tumbling down the stairs. One of them . . . was that Constantine? The other—Rocco fucking Barone.

Hudson let go of me to go to my brother, and I fell to my knees, dropping the Glock.

Get up. Get the fuck up. I shook my head, trying to override the drugs flooding my system.

I slowly lifted my head, trying to make sense of my surroundings and that Constantine was in the middle of a fistfight with Rocco while Hudson killed one of the Russians who'd waterboarded me all week.

Groggy, I snatched the Glock where it rested near my hand and shifted back to a seated position on the concrete, sitting on my ankles.

At the sound of more steps from somewhere, I discovered Enzo with us.

This isn't a dream. It's real, isn't it?

"He's been drugged," Hudson told him. "Is the rest of the house secure?"

"All tangos down aside from Barone, but Constantine wants to finish him," Enzo confirmed, kneeling alongside me to hook his arm around mine. "Keep an eye on them while I get my brother up."

Hudson focused on me, then back at the brawl happening before me.

Constantine was getting his revenge against the man who'd tortured him all those years ago, and he was most likely assuming the prick had done the same to me this week. But no, I'd been spared that fate.

Somehow, Enzo managed to get me back on the chair, and he removed the Glock I weakly clutched. "Is Calliope okay?" I whispered, hating how fucked up I was.

"She's fine," Enzo reassured me, wrapping a hand over my shoulder as the three of us waited for Constantine to finish the job so we could exfil.

And I was ready to do exactly that. Ready to get the hell out of there and to my wife.

"Knife," Hudson warned a moment later, and I witnessed my brother narrowly dodging the blade from Rocco only to take it from him.

"Go to hell, where you fucking belong," Constantine rasped, just before sliding the blade across Rocco's throat.

At that, my eyes fell closed again. The drugs were too powerful, and I welcomed the rush of warmth flowing through my body, allowing thoughts of my gorgeous wife to besiege me, hoping this was all real and that I'd see her soon.

CHAPTER FORTY-THREE

Alessandro

Bucharest, Romania—*Nine and a Half Hours Later*

"He's awake. What the fuck did that asshole give him?"

"You know how he is with legal drugs. Forget it when it comes to the illegal shit."

"Why didn't the meds they gave him here counteract what Rocco gave him?"

There were people talking somewhere. Familiar voices. None a match to Rocco. *I don't think.*

"You know him. He's weird like that." A pause. Then from what I could tell, the same person kept talking. "But he's alive; that's all that matters."

"Just some bruises and cuts. Starved, from what the doc said."

"No sign he was . . . violated, either. Thank fuck for that."

I blinked, trying to get used to the lights. Where was I? My head rolled to the side, and I saw a hand resting on my forearm near an IV. "Constantine?" Narrowing my eyes, I tried to make out the blurry faces. "You made it. You're alive." My eyes closed. "Where's Rocco?"

"I slit his throat and shot him." That was definitely Constantine.

So that was real. He'd had his revenge. Fucking finally, and he deserved it. Not that I remembered everything that had gone down, especially not the gunshot after the blade to Rocco's throat, but it was done. Thank God.

"I'm so sorry I let him take you," my brother apologized, and I forced my eyes open to confirm my mind wasn't playing tricks on me.

"I'm okay. Rocco only just showed up. He'd been away most of the time." Fuck, I was still too out of it to focus and remember everything.

"Thank God for that," Enzo said, and I looked around the room to see two more people there. Hudson and Sebastian Renaud.

"Mom, Dad, Izzy, and your wife will be here any second. They boarded the jet as we hit the house." Enzo gave me the good news, reaching for my hand, and shit, was he crying? "Everyone's okay. Armani's even in prison, too. And Marcello is dead."

What?

"You know, your wife helped find you, in a matter of speaking, too," Hudson said, skipping right over the what-the-fuck information that'd been casually tossed my way as he circled the other side of the bed. "Calliope located a historian to help us find the tunnel exits, and we were able to confirm the location of where he shot that video to help narrow our search area."

Of course she did. Smart girl. "Rocco had us wait it out somewhere in the woods after he dragged me out of the tunnel, and once he got a signal, he called in some people he had on standby, I guess, for help." The drugs had messed up my perception of time and reality, so I wasn't 100 percent on the details after that; I only knew I'd woken up in a basement somewhere and had the good fortune not to have to look at Rocco's face that week.

"Good to see you're okay," Sebastian commented, his tone casual.

"Thank you for sticking around." And I was damn grateful for his help.

"Mission wasn't over until you were found." Sebastian's gaze shot to the hallway, and there was a slight smile there, and it didn't take long for me to figure out why.

My parents and Izzy came into the room. And just behind them, nervously hanging in the doorway . . . was my wife.

I lost sight of her as my mom rushed to my bedside and flung her weight down, hugging me.

"Easy, Ma," Enzo said as she squeezed me, and Izzy came up alongside Hudson to get to me from the other side of the bed.

I looked over at my dad, and he quietly nodded. But the tears in his eyes . . . *fuck*.

"Calliope," I whispered, still unable to see her around Mom blocking the doorway.

"I'm here." Her voice sounded so small.

Izzy and Mom let me go and stepped to the side. Drugged or not, I'd get myself upright for my girl. I opened my hand, and she took small steps my way, tears spilling over her cheeks.

"Get over here," I begged, my voice breaking as Constantine gestured for everyone to step out so we had privacy.

As soon as she was close enough, I snatched her wrist and hooked my other arm behind her back, hauling her to me before setting my forehead to hers.

"Hey, you," I said, hating how drunk I sounded. "Little Miss Tennessee Whiskey."

Tears rolled down her cheeks, but she was smiling. Giving it her best effort to, at least.

"Tell me those are happy tears, sweetheart," I rasped, just now realizing I'd called her by a nickname she'd never heard me use before. She probably thought I was drugged out of my mind.

"Very happy." She gently kissed me, and it was ecstasy having her mouth on mine. "You had us worried, though."

"What day is it?" I asked.

"The twenty-second."

"Your birthday . . ." *Dammit.*

"I never went to bed last night, so it's still kind of yesterday, and if you dismiss the time change, then really it's practically still our birthday," she rambled, and it was the best sound, the best fucking everything I'd heard in a long damn time.

"Happy birthday." I nearly sighed out the words. "I'll make it up to you, I promise."

"The best birthday gift is that you're okay." The tears and wobbling of her bottom lip started up. "But I did get your gift and note."

"Do you kind of hate me for not giving it away like I promised?"

She caught a tear on her lip with her tongue. "More like kind of love you."

I rolled my eyes. And yeah, on purpose that time.

"What's that for?" She cry-laughed while gently shoving at my chest.

"Only 'kind of' love me, huh?" I arched a brow. "I don't kind of anything." I stared into her eyes and said, "I love you." My free hand slipped over my chest.

"X squared." Eyes flashing to mine, she translated, "Love you more."

"Like how much more?" I caught her bottom lip between my teeth, doing my best not to actually bite, but given my current state, no promise it wouldn't happen.

"Way, way more," she murmured once I freed her lip and she had me forgetting we were in Romania. Forgetting everything that had happened in the last week.

"Not possible." I kissed her back harder this time. "You'll never love me more than I love you. Don't argue with me on this. It's a fight you won't win."

She wedged her hand between our bodies and clasped mine resting over my heart. "So, so bossy."

"You know you like it."

"I do," she returned in a soft voice. "Now tell me about this name . . . Little Miss Tennessee Whiskey."

CHAPTER
FORTY-FOUR

Alessandro

Oyster Bay, Long Island—*Three Days Later*

"Yes, yesss—"

I cupped her mouth, silencing her cries as she climbed closer to orgasm, and the little devil stuck her tongue out, swiping at my palm.

"My parents are going to hear we're being bad and breaking the doctor's orders." I continued thrusting in her without losing momentum. "Be a good girl and give me a second before you moan again, okay?"

She nodded, and I kept moving so she didn't lose the high she was chasing, making sure my pelvic bone rubbed against her sensitive spot every time I slammed into her. Spying the belt atop my jeans on the floor next to us, I grabbed it. I barely remembered how or when we'd wound up going from the bed to the hardwood.

"You've been looking for a reason to put that in my mouth, and you know it." A wicked gleam flashed across her face before I offered her the leather to bite down on.

"Maybe." I smirked, waiting for her to follow orders and clamp down on the belt. "That's my girl."

Both hands on each side of her again, I bucked and moved harder, taking her all the way to the peak. When she arched off the floor while coming, I shifted my weight to one forearm and pinned her back down beneath me, fucking her with everything I had in me.

The belt slipped free from her mouth, and she stared at me with drunk-looking, sated eyes.

"Come inside me." She whispered the reminder . . . not that I needed one. How could I forget her asking me to do that?

"Yes, ma'am," I said before grunting, zero hesitation as I spilled inside my wife.

A few seconds later, I collapsed alongside her on the blanket beneath us.

"We had sex in your parents' house." She rolled to the side and propped her head up with her hand and elbow. My cum had to be dripping everywhere, but she didn't seem to notice. "And we broke the doctor's orders."

"There was no reason to hold back. I'm fine. Nothing broken. Not even a sprain. Wasn't shot or cut. Could've been much worse."

She cringed. "Every time I think about you and . . ." Her eyes closed, and a shaky exhalation fell from her barely parted lips.

"I'm fine." Nothing compared with what Constantine had endured.

"If you're so fine," she said while peeling open her eyes and I shifted to my side to face her, "then why didn't we make love last night?"

"You mistook my groan while kissing as pain because my bottom lip's still a bit busted." Not totally a lie. But the pain had been silenced by the pleasure of her mouth on mine. Same as it had been the other days since I'd been rescued by my brothers.

"Mmm. Your mouth seemed just fine between my legs not too long ago," she murmured, her tone part worry, part fuck me again.

Or maybe that was my imagination. I couldn't get enough of her. Screw the remnants of pain.

"But really, you sure you're good? Like good-good?"

I considered what to say, knowing lying wouldn't be the best way to handle things if I wanted to be a better man than I was before we met. "*Maybe* Rocco got into my head once or twice." In truth, the asshole had hijacked my thoughts when I'd been making out with my wife last night. His words about what he'd wanted to do with her didn't break me when he'd been alive, but they'd managed to throw me off now that he was gone. *Go figure.*

She reached for my arm and slid her hand along the ridges of muscles. "I know you haven't been home long, but you can see someone and talk about what happened. Post-traumatic stress is nothing to be ashamed about."

My shoulders relented from their tensed position. "I've been seeing a therapist for years. I guess I never told you that."

Her mouth rounded into a little surprised O, like an invitation for my tongue to slide in, but I refrained from kissing her, assuming she wanted to hear more.

"I've been seeing a shrink because of my addiction to the hunt," I admitted. "Well, my former addiction." My attention fell to her breasts. "I have a new addiction. A much healthier one. Never want to be cured of it." Trying to pull off a charming look but probably failing since my face was still a bit rough, I added, "I think I told you about my obsession with you."

"Mmm, you may have mentioned it," she murmured before sighing. "Do you think you'll keep seeing your therapist?"

"Probably, but you should see someone, too. You've been through quite a lot."

"Maybeeee, but first, I need to figure out our next steps."

"Well, next we get you cleaned up. So we take some steps to my bathroom. Then sneak the blanket into the wash without my mom catching us. Third step, we make love again, but maybe on the bed, and—" I let go of my words at the knock on the door, and my wife's startled eyes had me nearly laughing.

"You decent?" Constantine called out.

"Hardly," I answered, not yet ready to move. "What's up?"

"Surprise guest visitor. Gabriel's here and talking to Dad."

That had me getting up quickly. I helped Calliope to her feet, unable to miss my cum now sliding down the inside of her thigh. "Give us five minutes, and we'll be down."

"Take ten and wash up. Mom will lecture you about not keeping your dick in your pants after the doctor told you to."

"Thanks," I grumbled, watching Calliope's cheeks pink from embarrassment. I balled up the blanket on the floor and felt like I was fifteen when I shoved it under my bed to hide it. "Let's take a quick shower."

"Good idea." She led the way to the en suite bathroom, and I reminded myself I'd need to keep my hands to myself while we washed up.

But once beneath the water, as she did her best not to get her hair wet, not touching her proved too hard to do. Those perfect tits and the water rivulets sliding down her skin had me reaching for her. I cupped her breasts with one hand and her ass cheek with the other.

"Gabriel's downstairs." She stared at me with wet lashes and her fuck-me eyes.

"This ass, Little Miss"—that was now my abbreviated nickname for her—"needs to be taken and soon."

"Maybe not in your parents' house with Gabriel downstairs." She smiled but leaned forward and kissed me. "They're going to let us go to our place soon, right? How long will your mom keep us here?"

"Surprised she's even letting us share a bedroom, considering she wants us to follow the doc's orders." I pushed a finger around between her ass cheeks, just testing the waters a little, and she still didn't budge. *That's my girl.*

"Gabriel," she sputtered, but closed her eyes when I dropped my mouth over hers and kissed her, pushing the tip of my finger into her puckered hole. Her soft sounds of pleasure dropped into my mouth as we made out.

As I tested another inch inside her, my hand at her breast went to the column of her throat, and I lightly gripped. "You're fuck-tight, sweetheart," I said against her mouth. "Yeah, you're right, this can't happen here. You're going to scream—in a good way—when I fuck you there."

"Guess I'll need the belt again." She lifted her brows, and we were seemingly both oblivious to time, space, and life outside of right now.

I removed my finger from my woman's tight hole, and I could feel her ass cheeks unclench.

"We need to get free of Mom's house arrest and fast." I grabbed the loofah and squirted soap on it before lathering her up.

Nothing better than making her dirty, only to clean her up myself after. I couldn't wait to spend my entire life doing exactly this.

CHAPTER
FORTY-FIVE

Alessandro

"I know you've been looking for a reason to hit me for a long time, so go ahead. Do it."

Not the words I'd expected to hear from Gabriel as Calliope and I rounded the corner into the living room. Seeing Gabriel shoved against the wall, Constantine's hand on his chest, pinning him there, had me letting go of my wife.

"What in the hell is going on?" I hurried by my father, who was wordlessly observing the scene alongside Izzy without trying to intervene. "Constantine, let him go." Wrapping my hand over my brother's shoulder, I urged him to back off, but he didn't budge.

"Tell him what you just told me." My brother didn't usually become unhinged so easily, so what in God's name had Gabriel said? He lifted his hand from Gabriel's chest, so I let go of his shoulder, then he faced Dad and Izzy. "Why didn't you tell us what happened?"

Gabriel shot me his signature look—it was his *I fucked up* one.

"Someone needs to tell me what's going on." I turned to the side, hands settling on my hips just over the hem of my clean T-shirt I'd thrown on after the shower. Izzy motioned my wife over to her, and damn it all to hell, I also knew that look in Calliope's eyes, too. "What is it?"

"There's nothing to worry about, and it was something I didn't feel you needed to know unless your wife wanted to tell you." Dad took the reins and also took me to the edge of frustration at being in the dark about something related to Calliope. "You've been through a lot. I wanted to focus on having my boys back. And Gabriel's here to share good news. Not sure why in God's name he decided to share with Constantine his original plan."

"The original plan for what?" Patience was no longer a virtue or a fucking anything right now.

"Armani dying," Calliope whispered. "I was going to help kill him while you were . . . well, gone." I clocked the nervous movement in her throat. The hard swallow. Replayed her words to ensure I'd heard them correctly. Couldn't be possible, though.

I left Gabriel to get to my wife. And yeah, no one was going to save her from me right now. I was about to toss her over my shoulder, then take her over my knee, dammit. What had she been thinking?

"Come again?" was all I could get from my mouth that didn't involve swear words.

Calliope turned her attention to Gabriel, who was hanging back by the wall, then reached for my wrist. She'd feel my pulse flying if she held me a bit tighter. "While you were missing, Armani and Marcello decided to fly to the US to take me back to Italy." She lightly shook her head. "Sorry, you know that."

And I knew both my wife and father had been arrested for the sake of appearances while I'd been detained.

Then there was the fact Armani ensured Marcello never again saw the light of day and was shanked by someone that first night in custody.

Considering Marcello had been working with the crooked guard and the Espositos to send those men to kill her in the park in Nashville that day, I'd been more than happy the man was gone. I was only upset it hadn't been by my hand.

I was also very familiar with the surprising bit of truth that once Armani was back in Italy, he not only sacrificed himself for Calliope but also for Gabriel. Armani exchanged Gabriel's freedom for whatever additional intel he could offer to help bring down the rest of the Barone organization. Leo had been freed, too, not that Armani knew that part.

Dad's plan had worked, though. Perfectly, in fact. I owed him so damn much. But right now what I wanted to know was the one thing I apparently had been in the dark about.

"It's not her fault," Gabriel said, stealing my focus. "I asked Calliope to piss off Marcello in the hope that we could get him to try and kill her. Then with any luck, Armani would take the bullet for her. We could pin Armani's death on Marcello." He lifted his palms in surrender. "It sounds insane now that I say it. I had AISE on my ass, and I never should've suggested something that crazy. Had your father told me he had a plan already in motion, I never would've made the suggestion. Of course, your father would've shut down my idea anyway."

I looked at my wife's hold of my wrist, trying to wrap my head around what the hell Gabriel just said. Place my wife in danger and also make her complicit in murdering her own father? Did he really . . . ?

I understood why Constantine had snapped, because I was going to do a lot more than kill Gabriel.

I freed myself of her touch and cut across the room to my target. I fisted Gabriel's shirt and pinned him to the wall. He didn't resist or react. He knew it was coming. And it was like he wanted it.

"I'm sorry." He closed his eyes, and the break in his voice managed to halt me from losing control. "I had to tell you because I keep making mistakes, and that had to be one of my worst ones."

"What's going on?" Now my mom had joined the party. Perfect.

I was teetering just on the edge of sanity as I replayed the plan again. I owed my father beers for life for intervening.

"I was the one who agreed," Calliope said. "Be mad at me, too. I-I just wanted to help somehow. Make myself useful because you were gone, and maybe I . . . was scared you weren't going to come home, so why not risk my life? And I'd rather it be my life than your family taking more chances, and—"

"Stop." I let go of Gabriel at her words and spun around to see her crying. Crushing her against me, I held her tight, resting my chin on top of her head. "You're never allowed to risk your life, you hear me?" I shifted my mouth closer to her ear and whispered, "And I'm not mad at you. I never could be." Okay, maybe that was a lie, because I was pissed. The fact she was willing to possibly take a bullet . . . fuck that. Fuck it to hell and back and then again. "Never ever do anything that places your life in danger. You got it?" I stroked her back, then met my father's eyes and gave him a nod of thanks.

He nodded back, then gestured for my mom, Izzy, and Constantine to clear out.

Right, I still needed to confront Gabriel about why else he was here. But first I had to get my heart to calm down from wild to normal.

"I'm sorry," she said into my chest.

"Don't." I swallowed. "Don't apologize. You're okay, that's all that matters." I untangled our bodies and turned to look at Gabriel.

"I shouldn't have listened to my case officer," Gabriel said once Calliope was at my side. "I'm sorry, Callie. But I'm here for more than an apology."

Keeping my distance, still kind of wanting to throttle him, I hooked my arm behind her back and waited for him to continue.

Gabriel stepped away from the wall. "First, I'm glad you're okay. I wanted to reach out sooner after they found you, but I was tied up in jail until Armani accepted the offer. I had to wrap up things with AISE after that."

Armani was why we'd all begun working together in the first place, and if not for him, the Barones wouldn't be dead, a new conflict may not have been averted, a Russian oligarch wouldn't be arrested, and I wouldn't be . . . well, *married*.

"As you know, AISE had enough evidence to lock Armani up for three lifetimes regardless," he went on when I remained quiet. "But since the DiMaggios weren't their targets, they held off on doing anything with it. Clearly, AISE has no choice now but to convict him."

"Get to your point," I urged, still a bit unhinged.

"The plan was always for Calliope to pass the power over to me, so I could continue to help AISE catch more dangerous criminals, and then eventually we'd dismantle the DiMaggio organization from the inside, once Armani died." Gabriel said what I already knew. "They were concerned that arresting Armani would jeopardize that opportunity, but he gave us the new plan on a silver fucking platter, just as your father predicted he would."

Calliope took an eager step forward, so I went with her. I was never letting this woman from my sight again, dammit.

"I visited Armani with his lawyer yesterday, and he told me why he arranged for my release. He hoped I could help Calliope prevent the collapse of the organization. Transition her into the role of taking over one day. But to remove some heat from his daughter, he wants me to run things until you two have an heir. By then, he thinks it'll be safer for Calliope to step in." He opened his palms. "Of course, he'll be dead and never know you won't be taking over anything. But this keeps you safe from anyone connected to the DiMaggio crime family ever coming after you." He gave me a subtle nod as if hoping for my approval, but I wasn't ready to give it quite yet. "Then when the time comes, I'll help end the organization for good as planned, and Calliope can keep living her life how she wants without worry."

Calliope shocked me, and probably Gabriel, by reaching out and hugging him. "Thank you."

How could I kill him now? "If anything changes, you'll let us know," I said once she was back at my side.

"Of course." Gabriel tipped his head toward my wife. "Rosa sends her love. And so does . . . Armani."

"I would've regretted personally killing him, but that doesn't change the fact I want nothing to do with that man," she said. "So he can take his love and shove it up his ass."

And there was my Little Miss. God, I loved this woman so much. Gabriel eyed me next. "Too soon for a handshake or something?"

"Too soon. But keep doing the right thing, and maybe one day we'll have a drink together." That was a big *maybe*.

His smile made it hard to hate the fucker. Damn him. Then he quietly left the room, and once I was alone with my wife, I pulled her back into my arms.

"I still can't believe you agreed to his plan," I said into her ear in case my family happened to be hovering out in the hall. "The idea makes me want to—"

"Swat my ass?" Her hands slid to my chest, and I dropped my chin to catch her eyes.

"We really need to get back to our place." As I dipped in, preparing to kiss her, she closed her eyes, but first there was something I wanted to ask. "Unless you want our home to be in Nashville?"

Her eyes flashed open, and she quietly stared at me before whispering, "I want to be around family. Your family. And now they're my family. If you'll have me, I want to stay in New York."

"You're sure?" My heart had been racing earlier, during the confrontation with Gabriel, but now it flew.

"I'm more than sure," she said before my mouth crashed down over hers.

We both abruptly startled and stopped kissing at an excited "Yes!" coming from the hall.

"Mommmm," I teasingly hollered out, but then my wife began laughing, and yeah, her laugh could really stop wars and save the world.

She for sure saved mine.

CHAPTER FORTY-SIX

Calliope

A Few Weeks Later

"Your mom really knows how to throw a party." I closed my notebook and looked around the crowded yard at the Costas' house in Long Island, where we'd spent a lot of time recently.

"And she's managed to get us all back under her roof again when we only just escaped last week." Alessandro took a knee, unfurled the throw blanket to make room for himself, and dropped down beside me.

Holding the neck of his beer, he rested it on his thigh, eyes on the yacht docked not far away. Izzy, Hudson, and a few others were prepping it to take it out.

"You think they'll wind up together?" I wasn't sure why I'd asked that, or whether he'd know who I was referring to, but when I peeked at him, he had a goofy grin on his face. That smile was good news for Hudson. No plans to kill him for wanting his little sister.

"Bianca would love them together." His tone wasn't sad. More hopeful. And there was nothing I loved more than when he showed his teddy bear side.

Of course, I didn't exactly hate the other side, especially in the bedroom. Or, well, whatever room at the penthouse we wound up making love in.

"Would Constantine love it?"

He tossed a look over his shoulder at the man in question. "I don't know, to be honest." Twisting back around, he stretched one leg out and sighed. "Maybe he'd be okay."

"After you two did the brother routine on him?" I laughed. "Izzy told me about her exes and how you guys all—"

"Took out the trash." He playfully nudged me in the side, turning his attention to the grill station, where Enzo had all but kicked to the curb the chef hired for the party. Maria was at his side, one hand over her pregnant belly and the other stroking her husband's back. "I'm glad Maria was cleared to travel. And that Enzo actually let her."

"She's pretty incredible. So is her daughter." Maybe one day we'd have kids. I'd had my period last week, so no luck yet, but I didn't think it'd take too long at the rate we were going lately. The man couldn't keep his hands off me, and I loved it.

"Three daughters." He took a healthy gulp of his beer, shaking his head while laughing at his father chasing after Chiara not far away, acting as though she were ten times faster than him. "God help my brother when they all start dating."

"More like help their dates." Speaking of dating, my aunt was now seeing Javier on the regular. So much so she'd yet to go back to Tennessee since she'd come home from being rescued. She deserved to finally meet a great guy and be happy. To stop worrying about me, and thank God, there was no longer any need to do so.

"I've been meaning to ask you something." At Alessandro's slightly somber tone, I focused back on him, and he locked eyes with me. "I haven't brought this up because I was waiting to make sure the whole Armani-being-in-prison thing stuck. And no fallout from all the other stuff . . ."

Wait, were we doing this now? Out here? Finally having the conversation I'd been waiting for him to broach since coming back from Romania. And here I was in jean shorts and only a red bikini top for it.

He finished whatever was left of his beer, then set aside the bottle. I drummed my fingers on the notepad on my lap as I waited for him to get the words out. And as for words, I'd finally been able to write again.

I'd opted to go separate ways with Braden after his awkward declaration of love last month, though. I didn't need a guy in my life who had a crush on me.

I did, however, manage to convince Nala to perform with me if I were to land any future gigs. We wouldn't be teaching at the high school together anymore since I'd resigned and would be focusing on my music—Alessandro was encouraging me to follow my dreams—but at least Nala and I might get to work together down the road in another way.

"Okay, Mr. Mysterious, you're making me nervous." What if he wasn't planning to discuss the thing I'd been waiting for him to talk about for weeks now?

He fingered the collar of his cream-colored linen shirt before smoothing his palm over his trimmed beard. A touch of silver was sprinkled in here and there with the brown. I blamed all the stress he'd endured.

"Alessandro," I prompted when he'd yet to speak.

"I was waiting for you to finish your internal monologue." He shot me a devilish smirk that had me in a puddle. "I know that look of yours." He pointed to my notebook. "You finish the song you've been working on? Ready to show me yet?"

"Maybeee. But first, what do you want to talk about?" I poked him in the ribs.

He poked me right back, and then his finger skirted beneath the little red material, catching the underside of my breast. "I may have a belated birthday gift. It's sort of for the both of us."

"Oh." Not what I'd been hoping for. We'd spent the last few weeks "dating" to truly get to know each other, since we'd done things backward, thanks to Armani. And the man had dated the fuck out of me. Boy, had he ever, but didn't he know by now I didn't care about gifts? He was all I wanted. "Why are you smiling like that?"

"Because you're pouting, and it's cute."

"You like me pouting, huh?" I caught my lip between my teeth, and he dragged his finger down to my belly button almost hidden by my high-waisted shorts.

"You make it as sexy as I make the eye-roll thing broody," he teased. "But I think you'll like the gift. Well, I hope you will. I was going to wait until we were back at our place tomorrow, but now feels like the time. And I'm not patient, as my therapist keeps reminding me."

He'd been seeing his therapist once a week again, and although I didn't feel the need to see anyone myself, because I felt better than ever, I knew I had the option and the support from Alessandro if I ever wanted to.

"Okayyy, well, what is it?" I playfully lifted my brows a few times. "Lay it on me."

"Close your eyes, and I'll give it to you." His tone was the perfect amount of husky and commanding he always managed to pull off. Like sin sweeping under your skin but without the guilt and only the pleasure.

"Yes, sir."

"Open your palms," he ordered once I complied.

I did as he asked, and he set something nearly weightless on my palm before curling my fingers inward. "Okay."

I opened my eyes, but when I went to unfurl my fingers, he stopped me, covering my hand. And I only just now realized he wasn't wearing his wedding band.

"The rings at the ceremony were from Armani. The wedding was— well, everything was because of him." I met his eyes, my heart pounding hard at the realization my pout had been truly unnecessary. "I was hoping you'd marry me again and make everything ours. Marry me because *we* want to."

I couldn't see clearly anymore. My glossy eyes unleashed the tears momentarily trapped there.

"In your hand are our new bands that I picked out in the hope that you'd say yes."

I blinked away more tears as he opened my hand and took both rings from my grasp. He shifted it to show the inside of the plain band, bringing it closer for me to see an inscription.

"X squared," I whispered, and a little laugh-cry fell from my mouth as emotion choked me up. "You . . ." I basically grunted the word. When I looked at the inside of his band, I shook my head at only an *X* engraved there. "I see what you did there, and I'm going to—"

"But I love you more. Always." He leaned in and brought his mouth to mine.

"Not a chance." I kissed him back, allowing him to take over, like he was so damn good at, nearly forgetting we weren't alone out there, but no one bothered us. We were in our little bubble. "When do you want to remarry?" I asked once his expert tongue left my mouth, and I dropped my eyes back to the rings.

"August is next month. It was our deadline for divorce. How about we make it our month to get married instead? Maybe have it in English, too, so you know what you're really getting yourself into by marrying me."

I brushed the pad of my thumb across one of *his* tears. My teddy bear. A total softie with me. But still the man who hunted bad guys as a side gig. And maybe it was no longer an addiction for him—which was good—but he was who he was, and I wouldn't change him. Because I fell in love with this man. And screw Armani; there could be light without dark, and our love was proof of that.

"I love the idea," I finally answered. "But what am I supposed to get a man who has—"

"Everything?" His smile met his eyes that time. "I do have everything, but"—he peered at my notebook—"I'd love to hear you sing one of your own songs. That'd be the best belated birthday and pre-wedding gift I could think of . . . and, well, maybe to let me sink my mouth between your thighs later and eat you out. That'd be great, too."

I laughed and melted at the same time. "I guess I could handle that." But first, the song. I handed him the rings so I could open the notebook to my messy handwriting. "The song *was* going to be called 'Not Mine to Keep.'" I let go of a shaky, slightly nervous breath. The word *not* was now scratched out at the top. "I only came up with the title weeks ago while still dealing with writer's block."

"And now?" He touched my forearm, urging me to look at him.

"Writer's block is gone, and the song is now 'Mine to Keep.'"

"I love it." His brows drew tight. "Sing it for me?"

"Out here?" I looked around, aware again of our surroundings and all the people there.

"Hmm. Maybe I don't want to share it with others for the first time." He stood and offered me his hand and helped me to my feet. "Let's go inside."

"We'll wind up making love in your parents' house again."

He leaned in and dropped his mouth just over mine without kissing me. "Not getting caught will be our mission, then."

"That's one mission I think I'd like to join you on." I blinked back more tears, then looked around the yard and grinned from ear to ear. I really was happy. And this man really was mine to keep.

Forever.

EPILOGUE

Calliope

One Month Later
Franklin, Tennessee

"I still can't believe you did this." The wedding reception was in full swing, and it was a clear and sunny day. Everything was perfect, but I was still in shock at how it'd all been pulled together so fast and *where* it happened. "At this point, I shouldn't be surprised by anything you do. But you helped plan our wedding and kept half the details a secret from me."

Alessandro quietly took my hand, guiding me off the outdoor dance floor setup near a stage where a local band performed.

At the sight of Nala and one of Javier's guards kissing, I about tripped over the train of my beautiful wedding gown. Ella McAdams from Birmingham had designed it at the last minute for me, and as a thank-you, I'd begged her to come to the wedding.

She was on the dance floor with her husband and cute son, Remi.

One day, I couldn't wait to have my own little Remi. Or Chiara. Or all the kids. A whole bunch of them.

"Love is in the air, huh?" I said with a smile as I walked by my aunt and Javier dancing. "Where are you taking me now?"

"The front porch." Keeping hold of my hand, he walked me farther away from the party and to the two-person swing at the front of the gorgeous farmhouse.

Once seated, he knelt before me and removed my shoes, and if I didn't already love the man, I could love him that much more for saving my aching soles and giving my feet a quick rub.

"You're my hero." I sighed when he sat next to me. "You keep outdoing yourself. I don't know what to do with you." I reached for his hand resting on my lap and squeezed it.

"I plan to make you happy for the rest of our lives, so get used to it."

"You bought us this house. A farm. Was it really just to have the wedding here? I mean, you know you could've asked the owners to only rent it out." I leaned into him, resting my head on his shoulder, feeling at peace there, surrounded by not just family but also nature. My heart was with Alessandro, but I could feel it there in Nashville, too.

"The idea of a farm with kids and chickens and all that . . ." I felt him shrug against me. "We can have both. The home near family in New York. A home here, too. We can have it all if you'll let me give it to you."

My head shot up at his words. "You're going to milk cows? Take care of chickens?" Was he serious?

He closed one eye and smiled. "There are people who can do that for us, right?"

"You're looking at *people* now." I let the laugh bubbling in my chest free, unable to contain it. "But if you're busy saving the world, and I'm singing, I suppose we could get some help."

"Sooo, you're considering it?" A triumphant smirk graced his lips. "Or are you worried about me not fitting in down here?" He held up his free hand as if saying, *Scout's honor.* "I swear, I can blend in."

Speaking of blending in . . . "The truck purchase was another shocker." He'd picked me up out front of the hotel in the shiny black Ford F-150 last night for our dress rehearsal dinner, and I'd been stunned to see him behind the wheel of that beast. "It was almost as shocking as the fact you invited Mr. Crabby to the wedding." I looked toward the dance floor, where Imani was being Imani—kind and sweet—dancing with the old-timer, making his night. "Our honeymoon is tonight, and I even have a gig tomorrow on Broadway. And I get to sing my own songs, and I just . . ." Now I was going to ruin my makeup, but screw it. Happy tears were worth it.

"I'm happy where you are, Little Miss. Here or in New York. I don't care. I can work from anywhere. When our kids are in school, I'd like them to grow up here, and we can spend holidays and summers in New York. My family will visit more than we want them to, trust me." He smirked. "Plus, didn't you say Nashville and country music go together?" When I'd yet to give him a firm yes or say anything at all, he went on, "I know you said you wanted to live up there, but this"—he lifted his open palm toward the party—"is who you are. I want our kids to have this life, too. And in your heart, I think that's what you want. Little cowgirl boots for our daughter. Or cowboy boots for our son." He closed his eyes as if imagining the idea, and now it was grabbing hold of me as well.

I mean, how could it not? What a gorgeous picture he painted. "I love you so, so much." I wasn't sure if my heart might max out at some point from how big it kept getting because of this man. "And you're right. I want it, too."

"Good." He opened his eyes, beaming. "One more surprise, though."

"No." I shook my head. "You've done enough. Please."

He grinned, looking so handsome in his tux, and he ignored me and reached into his pocket.

"You brought your phone to our reception?" I joked as he began texting someone.

"I needed it to let Izzy know when it was go time." He pocketed his phone a moment later. I looked around in search of her, unsure what in the world this man had planned next.

And then my jaw fell wide open. "You're kidding me." I slapped a hand over my mouth, searching for the breath in my lungs. To not faint. "Alessandro. How? I mean . . . Are you serious?" My hand plummeted to my lap. "Is this happening?"

"Are you up for playing at our wedding? Consider it the rehearsal for your gig tomorrow." He stood, kicked aside my heels as if to say *screw them*, and held out his hand, and I stared at him, locked in a state of shock.

"You want me to play with him?" I finally managed to ask. "*The* man himself? Not a cover song, but with . . ." I couldn't even finish that line of thought, it was so wild.

"His music is why you hit on me in the first place."

"I did not hit on you," I said with a laugh, and his big-ass smile sent me over the edge to admit, "Okay, okay. *Maybe* I did."

"Oh, you definitely did." His grin was ridiculously sexy. "It'd only make sense for you to sing with him tonight. I mean, if you want to?"

I looked out at my music idol and whispered, "You just might get lucky tonight."

He wrapped a hand around my hip, drawing me against him, then crooked his finger beneath my chin, commanding my attention. "Ohhh, I'm sure as hell counting on that, Little Miss Tennessee Whiskey."

AUTHOR'S NOTE

Ready for more? Hudson and Izzy's story is next in the series.

Haven't yet read Enzo and Maria's book, *Let Me Love You*? It's now available and is a spin-off from Maria's sister's book, *Until You Can't*.

Curious about The League? Sebastian, Emilia, and the McGregors are from the Dublin Nights series. Sebastian's book is *The Real Deal*.

Each book in the series may be read as a stand-alone, but for best enjoyment, I recommend starting with Book 1, *On the Edge*.

WHERE ELSE CAN YOU FIND BRITTNEY?

I love interacting with readers in my Facebook groups, as well as on my Instagram page. Join me over there as we talk characters, books, and more! 😊

FB Reader Groups:

Brittney's Book Babes
Stealth Ops Spoiler Room

Facebook
Instagram
TikTok

www.brittneysahin.com

ABOUT THE AUTHOR

Brittney Sahin is the *Wall Street Journal* bestselling author of *Let Me Love You* in the Costa Family series, *Until You Can't,* and many other novels of romantic suspense. She began writing at an early age with the dream to be a published author before the age of eighteen. Although academic pursuits (and later a teaching career) interrupted her aspirations, she never stopped writing—never stopped imagining. It wasn't until her students encouraged her to follow her dreams that Brittney said goodbye to Upstate New York in order to start a new adventure in the place she was raised: Charlotte, North Carolina. Here, she decided to take her students' advice and begin to write again. When she's not working on upcoming novels, she spends time with her family. She is a proud mother of two boys, and a lover of suspense novels, coffee, and the outdoors. For more information, visit www.brittneysahin.com.